MY MOTHER'S SECRET

A NOVEL OF THE
JEWISH AUTONOMOUS REGION

ALINA
ADAMS

ISBNs: 978-1-7364990-3-0 (pb);
978-1-7364990-2-3 (hc);
978-1-7364990-4-7 (eBook)

Book Cover Design: The Book Cover Whisperer, OpenBookDesign.biz
Interior Book Design: Vyrdolak, By Light Unseen Media

Library of Congress Control Number: 2022931549
First Printing: 2022

Printed in the United States of America

Publisher's Cataloging-In-Publication Data
(Prepared by The Donohue Group, Inc.)
Names: Adams, Alina, author.
Title: My mother's secret : a novel of the Jewish Autonomous Region / by New York Times bestselling author, Alina Adams.
Description: [Roseville, Minnesota] : [History Through Fiction], [2022]
Identifiers: ISBN 9781736499030 (pb) | ISBN 9781736499023 (hc) | ISBN 9781736499047 (eBook)
Subjects: LCSH: Jewish women--Soviet Union--History--20th century--Fiction. | Birobidzhan (Russia)--History--20th century--Fiction. | Soviet Union--History--German occupation, 1941-1944. | Man-woman relationships--Fiction. | Family secrets--Fiction. | LCGFT: Historical fiction.
Classification: LCC PS3601.D367 M9 2022 (print) | LCC PS3601.D367 (ebook) | DDC 813/.6--dc23

Also by Alina Adams

The Nesting Dolls
The Man From Oakdale
Jonathan's Story (with Julia London)
Oakdale Confidential
Skate Crime: A Figure Skating Mystery
Death Drop: A Figure Skating Mystery
Axel of Evil: A Figure Skating Mystery
On Thin Ice: A Figure Skating Mystery
Murder on Ice: A Figure Skating Mystery
Sarah Hughes: Skating to the Stars
Inside Figure Skating
When a Man Loves a Woman
Annie's Wild Ride
Thieves at Heart
The Fictitious Marquis

Dedication

**For my parents, Nelly and Genrikh Sivorinovsky,
who brought me to America.**

Prologue: San Francisco

1988

Lena Mirapolsky's father was dying.

Her husband was trying to get a discount on it.

"What is this?" Vadik thrust his finger at the itemized bill he'd demanded Lena's mother show him. His bellowing voice echoed off the hospital's sterile walls.

"Dad's new medicine."

Vadik turned to Mama, "They're playing you for a fool, Regina Solomonovna," he said, using her patronymic to drive home how respectful he was being. "It's not the money. We can afford the fees, no question. It's the principle. They think we're fresh off the boat, easy marks. We'll do what they say because Soviet immigrants are supposed to be afraid of authority. This is a scam. We must be realistic. They're feeding you false hope to line their own pockets."

Lena winced, hoping Dad couldn't hear Vadik's fatalistic take on his condition. Mama must have felt the same, because she stepped forward to plant her body between Vadik and Dad's bed, as if that might deflect Vadik's negativity.

Her father's nurse, previously darting between the three of them, head lowered to appear as unobtrusive as possible while adjusting Dad's IV, began to hum; first under his breath, then progressively louder. Lena recognized the popular Russian song, *Nadezhda*, its lyric: "Hope, my earthly compass/ It's luck, it's a trophy for bravery."

Vadik lost his power of speech. Lena could only stare. Mama smiled. It was the first smile Lena had seen from her since Dad had been admitted to the hospital, all of them knowing he'd never be discharged.

Unfazed by their astonishment, the nurse, nametag: *Sergei*, clarified in Russian, "Hope is like salt to food. It is not on its own, it is in addition to all else."

Lena had noticed Sergei before. Of all Dad's nurses, he was the only one Mama didn't track like a hawk as he went about his duties. When he ambled in, Mama would even step away from Dad's bed. With Sergei on Dad watch, Mama might sit, rub her eyes, and sip from the Styrofoam cup of lukewarm black tea Lena delivered every morning. She might even take the risk of stepping out of the room for a bathroom break. Twice now, Lena had arrived to find Mama and Sergei with their heads together, whispering. At the sight of her, they'd sprung apart. Though Lena felt certain their conversation was continuing behind her back, via raised eyebrows. She was dying to hear what they were discussing, but Lena didn't dare ask. If Mama wanted Lena to know, she'd tell her. And Mama rarely wanted Lena to know anything. Lena also didn't want to put Sergei on the spot. She felt grateful to him for providing comfort to Mama, whatever he may have been saying. God knows it was more than Lena had managed.

"Who cares what the nurse thinks?" Having gotten past his initial shock at being refuted—in song, no less—Vadik exploded. "What kind of profession is nursing for a man? Listen to his accent, he sounds like he got off the tarmac at SFO last week. I bet his medical credential isn't even real. Everyone knows you can buy a diploma on any corner along Geary Street!"

Vadik wasn't wrong. So many Soviet immigrants had settled in the area it had acquired the nickname *Gearybasovskaya,* after the boulevard Deribasovskaya in Odessa. It was the place to go for help with adjusting documented reality. A med school diploma was certainly one of the items on offer, along with paperwork testifying to government benefits qualifying disability and poverty.

"Vadik!" Lena cried out, mortified. She snuck a peak at Sergei to gauge his reaction. He had none. Her father's nurse had melted back into unobtrusiveness. He made a note on the chart at the foot of Dad's bed, and, with a smile and wave in Mama's direction, took his leave.

Still humming the song about hope.

For a moment, the three of them simply stood there, stupefied and staring in his wake.

"I am looking out for you, Lenachka." Her husband sounded hurt. Lena had no doubt he was. Vadik was always looking out for her. Seventeen years ago, it was one of the things that had made her fall in love with him. Lena couldn't pinpoint the moment when his regard began to feel like mistrust, when his concern turned into suffocation.

It wasn't his fault. Vadik had stayed the same.

Lena was the one who'd changed.

"CALL DOCTOR." AFTER Vadik left, Mama was fussing over Dad, fluffing his pillow, rearranging his blanket, brushing stray hair from his face. She still shaved him—a task she didn't trust even Sergei to handle. "He doesn't like looking unkempt." Mama pronounced the word carefully. Lena heard Dad's intonation—Mama learned her English from him. One minute, everything was calm, the next, she was shouting at Lena, "Now!"

"Why?" Lena startled at her urgency. She couldn't see anything different.

Mama pointed at Dad's hands, twitching against his thighs, trying to burrow through his blankets to pinch the flesh. "When they to do this, is end. They are trying to escape body."

It was the most poetic thing Lena had ever heard her mother say. It also made no sense.

"They're muscle spasms, they don't mean anything." She referenced the monitors on the other side of the bed, their green lights as steady as ever. "He's fine."

"Get doctor!"

Before Lena could decide whether to follow her mother's directive, Dad's eyes popped open. Another muscle spasm. Except he also swiveled his head from side to side, searching.

"I am here," Mama cooed, tones Lena couldn't remember hearing before. "I am holding your hand. Look." Mama grabbed his palm and pulled it up so Dad could see their clasped fingers. "I am here with you. You are not alone."

Dad opened his mouth. The sound that came out proved part croak, part creak. His jaw appeared paralyzed. His voice sounded like he was drowning in bile running down the back of his throat. He focused on his and Mama's hands, then painstakingly followed with his eyes from her wrist, to her elbow, up her arm to her shoulder, until he settled on her face. "Like you promised."

"Like I promised," Mama confirmed.

"I tried." Dad turned first red, then white from his exertion. "Tell him I tried."

Lena expected Mama to urge Dad to hush, save his strength, not talk, he didn't need to. Instead, Mama swore, "Yes, yes, you did it. You did everything for us. Yes, I will tell."

"Dad!" Lena cried out, interrupting this moment she didn't understand like some needy toddler, squeezing between her hugging Mommy and Daddy, begging for attention.

Her father heard Lena and, with more difficulty than he'd had homing in on Mama's face, swiveled so he was looking at Lena. The red then white of his flesh dissolved into a sickly blue around his lips. Yet, Dad still found the strength to ask, "You couldn't tell, could you?"

She didn't know what he meant. Mama glaring over Dad's head made it clear Lena had better agree with anything he said, nonetheless.

"No," Lena swore, "I couldn't tell."

Dad's body went slack, head jerking backwards as the hand Mama held swung to the side, hitting Mama in the chest. He still didn't let go.

Or maybe it was Mama who didn't.

LENA CALLED VADIK as soon as Dad's doctors pronounced him deceased and a pair of attendants materialized to wheel out the body. He was no longer Dad. He was "the body." They covered his face with a sheet and looped a tag around his toe. Lena glanced at Mama to observe how she was taking the impersonal treatment. Mama was watching as keenly as she had when Dad was alive. She expected him to be treated with respect. She followed the gurney on its journey to the morgue like an honor guard.

Meanwhile, Lena's husband sprang into action. He announced he was on his way to the hospital, he would take care of everything. And Lena relaxed. With Vadik on the job, there was no danger of a detail being overlooked. Or of Lena doing the wrong thing.

"Done," Vadik reported upon entering Dad's empty room. "Paperwork signed." He gave Mama, whom he'd dragged back with him, a laudatory nod. "I contacted the funeral home. It's arranged. We have a date and time for the service."

"Oh," Lena said, unable to summon up the energy for any action beyond, which included leaving Dad's room. She'd just sat here, waiting for Vadik, waiting for Mama, waiting to be told what to do—and how to feel. "Thank you for taking care of it, Vadik."

"Better than one of you making a mess of things, me needing to clean it up after."

Had that ever actually happened? Lena couldn't remember. Vadik was always warning that it could happen. She did remember that.

"We can go home now." He swept both hands towards the door, in case Lena or Mama forgot how leaving worked. "Angela misses you." Vadik invoked their twelve-year-old daughter like a trump card. If it was for Angela, Lena had no choice but jumping right to it.

When she still failed to budge, Vadik let out an exasperated sigh. "What are you waiting for?" His good humor crackled at the edges, like burning paper.

"Sergei, Dad's nurse…" The words tumbled from her lips without Lena realizing she meant them. "He wasn't here when Dad died. I want to wait for him to come back on duty. So we can tell him good-bye. And thank you."

"You can write him a card. Send him chocolates or a bottle of wine. This isn't the USSR." Vadik used the Russian term, *v'Soyuze,* which literally meant *in the Union.* "You don't have to bribe nurses to get adequate care here. Besides..." he trailed off, realizing finishing his sentence would be gauche. A bribe was useless at this point. Dad was already dead.

"I want to wait," Lena insisted.

"*Bozhe moy!*" The hands that had shown Lena the exit now swung up past Vadik's shoulders, as her husband did what he always did when things weren't going his way. He left Lena and her mother, and stomped around the corridor's corner.

"Here he is," Vadik announced, sweeping a dazed Sergei into the room a few moments later—moments during which Lena and her mother found they had nothing to say to each other.

"How did you—" Lena began.

"I had him paged." Vadik didn't understand why Lena hadn't already done so.

She turned apologetically to Sergei. "Were you performing another patient's procedure?"

"Yes," Vadik answered, "and he needs to get back to it. So say what you need to say."

"I wanted to say..." You'd think, as a lawyer, Lena would be better at on the spot oratory. "I wanted to say... Thank you. For everything you did. For my dad." She wanted to say much more, but the words weren't coming. Neither was anything else.

"It's his job," Vadik reminded.

"Yes," Sergei confirmed, "this is my job. This is also my pleasure." He turned to Mama and told her, in Russian, "May the ground be as feathers for him."

"*Spasibo,*" Mama said. Though Lena couldn't help feeling like she meant a great deal more.

VADIK SWUNG BY Mama's house to drop her off. She crept out of his car, the weeks of sitting, eating and sleeping in a stiff chair finally catching up with her. Lena climbed out the front and held the back door open, extending a hand to help Mama keep her balance. Mama took it. That was new. Lena almost let it slip in surprise. Mama stood in the driveway of the Sunset District two-story home she'd moved into upon arriving in America. Whenever Dad suggested they could relocate someplace bigger, newer, Mama declined. "I have moved around enough."

Dad's dental practice was on the ground level, behind the garage. Entering their house required a climb up a dozen stairs to the second floor. The inappropriateness of Mama needing to make all that effort to get into her own home now seemed insurmountable to Lena.

She asked, timidly, "Do you want me to help you up? Go in with you? We could—we could sort through Dad's things, start packing them up?"

"Don't be ridiculous, Lena." Vadik ducked his head so he could peer at her from behind the steering wheel. "Your mother needs rest. You do, too. What's the point of both of you ending up exhausted in the hospital, this time in side-by-side beds?"

Lena could see Vadik's point. Lena could always see Vadik's point. Vadik was reasonable. He knew what was best. She'd loved that about him. How he could make decisions. How he saved Lena from self-doubt by advising her on a best course of action. His confidence gave Lena confidence. So what if, to prove he was right, Vadik had to demonstrate that she was wrong? Vadik was pointing out the flaws in Lena's reasoning before she got herself into trouble. Wasn't it better he did so before she embarked on some disastrous course? What good would his advice do her after? It wasn't that Lena was stupid and couldn't decide for herself. It was that Vadik was better equipped to root out potential pitfalls. That's what Lena got for growing up all American. That *gosh, golly, you can do anything* mentality. Believing the world was your oyster, looking on the bright side; it was a recipe for disaster. Vadik, who'd lived *v'Soyuze*, understood that everyone was out to screw you. Vadik saw everything that could go wrong. And he was happy to share his wisdom. For Lena's—for their family's!—good. She couldn't begrudge Vadik for looking out for his family. Especially when, she admitted, he was usually right.

"MAYBE WE SHOULD take a break," Lena suggested.

Much to her surprise, the moment they'd entered the house after

Lena told Vadik to go home and check on Angela—she'd call him when she was ready to be picked up—Mama had embraced Lena's plan of action. She proceeded straight to her and Dad's bedroom, where she began pulling his suits off hooks in the walk-in closet, folding them and stacking them on the bed. She shuffled between the closet and bed with eyes locked straight ahead. Lena yearned to help. But she was terrified of getting in Mama's way. Instead, Lena went into the kitchen, grabbing a fistful of garbage bags from beneath the sink. As Mama discarded Dad's clothes, Lena slid them into the bags. The fact that Mama didn't bark at her to stop, Lena took as acquiescence.

Once she'd finished with the suits, Mama moved onto Dad's drawers. Undershirts and T-shirts, socks and boxers. Intimate items that used to embarrass Lena to touch when she did the laundry as a child. Their existence had forced Lena to imagine her parents without their outer clothes, her parents getting naked, her parents getting naked with each other. Merely touching garments that had touched their skin raised goosebumps on Lena's arms. Now, however, it all went into a separate garbage bag, the third one piled by the door.

They were done within the hour.

How could such a full life shrivel down to so little? Not that a million overstuffed bags of mere things could ever summarize Dad. Things couldn't evoke how he insisted that he didn't mind waking up early to drive Lena to debating tournaments, or lumbering out in the middle of the night to pick her up from slumber parties gone wrong. Things offered no recall of how Dad would sing duets with her from *The King & I*, *Oliver*, and, of course, *Fiddler on the Roof*, when Lena was in grade school so she'd deign to take grudging bites of her dinner when it was his turn to vocalize. That was their deal. If Dad sang, Lena would eat. Mama fumed, disgusted at what she dubbed his American indulgence. But after Dad reminded, "I can't stand seeing anyone go hungry. Not if I can help it," Mama never brought the objection up again.

Lena's mother froze, deprived of tasks, stymied about what she could do next. Her eyes darted side to side, hoping to spy an errant item she'd missed. It reminded Lena of how Dad had looked in his final moments.

"Mama?" Lena tries not to startle her, like a sleepwalker.

Mama startled, nonetheless. Yet another of Lena's good intentions gone wrong.

"What did Dad—what do you think Dad meant? At the end? When he told you to tell him he did his best? Tell whom? Tell him what?"

Mama's eyes narrowed. Lena feared she would claim to remember Dad saying no such thing. Often, in Lena's childhood, Lena remembered an incident, only for Mama to claim it hadn't happened that way. Mama said Lena's versions were more melodramatic.

"And what did he mean when he asked me if I could tell? You gestured for me to tell him I couldn't." Mama wouldn't deny that aspect of the exchange. "What couldn't I tell?"

They remained in standoff, Mama glaring at Lena, willing her to back down, Lena glaring back, willing herself not to. Mama crumpled first. This was new. One minute, she was standing, formidable as always, head up, back straight, hands by her sides, fingers curled into fists. The next, it was like pulling the strings of a marionette. Her chin sagged, her shoulders slumped, hands slipping open. Lena was afraid Mama would collapse. She rushed to her side, grabbing her around the waist, maneuvering her onto the bed.

"He is dead," Mama mumbled. Lena couldn't be sure if Mama was speaking to Lena or herself. "Who knows what a man so close to death means? Who knows what he is thinking, what he is remembering? He wants me to say I will promise, I will promise. He wants you to say you could not tell, you say you could not tell. What difference does it make? It is last moments. Last moments should be happy, peaceful. No worries, no regrets. What if, in his last moments, he's thinking regrets?"

"Regrets about what?"

Mama refused to answer.

LENA COULDN'T SIT still. Lying down and keeping calm long enough to go to sleep in her old bedroom was out of the question. Lena couldn't read, she couldn't watch TV, no matter how hard *Dynasty's* Alexis Carrington was strutting to keep her attention. Lena needed to do something. It didn't have to be productive, though that would make it easier to justify.

What about Dad's office? The thought rose—unbidden, she swore—in Lena's mind as she wandered past the door leading to the garage. Dad had retired from private practice over a decade earlier, but he still sometimes went down there. Lena would be helping Mama, getting a head start on the files and bills. Most of it should be shredded, a few records saved in case of an audit. If Lena had any trouble telling what was what, she could call Vadik. He took care of such details for them.

Lena flipped on the light switch and tread downstairs. Dad's office looked the same. He kept his medical equipment in one room, his desk and filing cabinet in another. Lena assumed any records that needed to be transferred to the patients' new providers already had been. All that should be left were inactive files and billing information. She could begin shredding before Mama woke up. It would make Lena feel she had contributed something.

The top cabinet drawer was what Lena expected. Patient histories with a sticker reading *deceased* or *forwarded*. Lena fed each mindlessly into the automated blades, sweeping up the remnant strips into yet another garbage bag. She anticipated more of the same from the drawer underneath. But it wasn't records Lena discovered; it was three bulging files of letters. One had copies of missives Dad had written, the other, replies, the third, newspaper clippings. The letters were addressed to congresspeople, senators, diplomats. Each covered the same topic: The fates of Soviet World War II veterans in general, and one veteran in particular.

For the past forty years, Lena's father had been trying to ascertain the whereabouts of a Soviet vet named Aaron Kramer. He'd provided Kramer's last known whereabouts, his military branch, his rank, his unit, the town where he'd enlisted. Anything that should have made tracking a missing man down easier. In return, Dad received an unprecedented amount of stonewalling.

Yet he'd pressed on. Who was this man, and what had made him so important that her father had devoted forty years of his life to search for him? The irony of Dad passing away just as the USSR had promised more openness and transparency wasn't lost on Lena.

Ever since Mikhail Gorbachev had become General Secretary of the Communist Party of the Soviet Union in 1985 and declared his policy of *perestroika*, the world—no one more than those who'd fled his Party over the past seventy years—wondered where it would lead. So far, articles had come out in *Pravda* criticizing the rule of Josef Stalin and supporting Gorbachev's more open policies, which included market reforms granting state enterprises greater control over the goods they produced based on demand, rather than top-down planning. Perestroika also allowed, for the first time since Vladimir Illych Lenin's New Economic Policy in the 1920s, private business ownership and foreign investment. Of course, it also came with higher taxes and employment restrictions. Most recently, the USSR had held its inaugural Soviet beauty pageant. Something was changing. The ten-thousand-ruble question was, changing into what?

"It's late." Mama appeared in the doorway, still wearing the clothes Lena had left her in, dissolving her hope that Mama had been able to snatch some rest in the hours passed.

"I'm alright," Lena said, aware Mama hadn't asked. Mama never asked. Lena's mother never inquired how she was feeling or what she was thinking. Unlike other mothers, Lena's also never told her what to do or offered her advice. Lena's friends envied how her mother never butted into her life. Only Lena knew it was because Mama didn't care enough to bother.

She waited for her mother to chastise Lena for snooping where she wasn't wanted, or to order her up to bed. To tell her, like Vadik had, that she should be resting. Lena would settle for any kind of interaction. Any interaction was better than the prolonged, leaden silence.

"Who is Aaron Kramer?" Lena blurted out. She hadn't meant to. She'd meant to introduce the subject gradually. For all she knew, Mama hadn't been aware of Dad's search.

Mama was looking at Lena, at the bag of shredded files, at the ink-stained letters in her hands. She wasn't saying anything. So Lena felt she had to say something. She should know better, as a lawyer. Never speak to fill the silence. That was how you got in trouble. That was how you lost control of your situation.

Part One: 1935 – 1940

Chapter One

===

She had her ticket. All that was necessary now was to get on the train.

Regina glanced over her shoulder. Yaroslavsky Railway Station was as bustling as ever. Men in grey suits and ties, patched jackets, and caps with brims that flopped over their eyes jostled women wearing wool coats trimmed with rabbit fur, some with kerchiefs over their heads, others sporting more fashionable berets. All rushed to board trains for Vladivostok, Kirov, Tomsk, and a host of other eastern destinations. No one had any reason to pay attention to an eighteen-year-old girl struggling to drag a scuffed leather bag she'd thrown together a few hours earlier, blindly tossing in random items in Regina's haste to be gone before the black-booted *militsioners* returned for her. They might only want to ask her questions about people she knew, people who'd already been arrested. They might arrest and then release her… if she provided them with the answers they were seeking. Or they might put her on trial. The kind of trial where an innocent verdict wasn't an option. If Regina were braver, she might have stuck around to find out. If Regina were braver, she might have stuck around to defend her friends, who she knew had done nothing wrong, same as her. If Regina were braver, she wouldn't currently be at the train station, glancing furtively over her shoulder.

She had her ticket. What she didn't have was permission to leave. Or settle elsewhere. Soviet citizens were the freest in the world. Maintaining this freedom necessitated their leaders knowing where each was at all times. This led to stability, the seedbed of liberty. There were over two dozen scheduled stops between Moscow and Regina's destination in the Far East. At any of them, the conductor could demand to review her *propiska*. If she failed to provide one, he had every right to yank her off his train and deposit Regina in the care of local authorities. Who would promptly, likely under armed guard, return her to Moscow—where Regina's attempt to run would bury her into deeper trouble. The proper course of action for those who wished to relocate to Birobidzhan, the newly formed Jewish Autonomous Region (JAR) between the Bira and Bidzhan rivers of the Russian-Chinese border, was to register a request with KOMZET, the Committee for the Settlement of Jewish Toilers on the Land. KOMZET would authorize the appropriate travel documents. They might also bring her name to the attention of the authorities. She couldn't risk that. Not until everything blew over. Which it would have to, sooner or later. Regina hadn't done anything wrong. It wasn't her fault she'd failed to realize until it was too late that those around her might have.

If only she could make it to Birobidzhan. Comrade Kaminsky, head of the village Soviet, would surely vouch for her loyalty to the state. They'd always had a good rapport whenever he'd visited Moscow. Regina had listened, enthralled, to his tales of Birobidzhan, its rich farmland, its plump livestock, the trees full of fruit and the rivers full of fish. As Comrade Stalin had pronounced one month earlier, "For the first time in the history of the Jewish people, its burning desire for a homeland, for the achievement of its own national statehood, has been fulfilled." It was one of the many reasons why all Soviet children dressed in school uniforms of brown dresses with black pinafores for every day, white ones for special occasions for girls, or brown pants with white shirts for boys and crimson scarves for all, began their day by reciting, "Thank you, Great Comrade Stalin, for my joyous childhood."

KOMZET flourished under the oversight of Lazar Kaganovitch, Secretary of the Central Committee, Commissar of Communications, the most powerful Jew in the Soviet Union. "The nationality of the Jew is the nationality of the merchant," he quoted Karl Marx when establishing the JAR. "Emancipation from huckstering and money will be the self-emancipation of our time."

Regina had always intended to go there. She'd always intended to be part of the pioneer movement to build an independent, thriving, Jewish, socialist state, where Yiddish literature was taught in schools, Yiddish plays were performed in theaters, Yiddish newspapers educated the public, and Yiddish speakers could walk streets marked with Yiddish signs, safe from violent attacks. Regina may not have spoken Yiddish herself, but she was enthralled with the notion of a place where others could. At the close of the Great October Revolution, Jews, like all worthy Soviet citizens, had been accorded their own plots of land to work. Unfortunately, the previous owners—kulaks Comrade Stalin needed to show the error of their ways a decade earlier—weren't happy with the redistribution. Thus it was determined that, in the interest of keeping antisemitic violence to acceptable levels, the optimal course of action was to convince Jews living in the USSR and its surrounding territories to relocate to the furthest eastern point on the Trans-Siberian railroad, where they would be safe, out of the way, and no longer annoying their neighbors.

Regina had always intended to go there. She didn't need the posters paid for by ICOR, the American Association for Jewish Colonization in the Soviet Union; black and white lithographs promoting spending fifty kopeks on a lottery ticket to help "build a socialist Jewish Autonomous Region," or garishly colored illustrations of workers with bulging muscles carrying sacks urging, "Let us give millions to settle poor Jews on the land and to attract them to industry."

Regina had always intended to go there. She simply hadn't intended to go this soon. Or this hurriedly. She'd intended to finish University first. Regina was studying agriculture, horticulture, animal husbandry, and medicine, human and veterinary, so that she could be of the most use once she arrived in her new home.

She never intended to be sneaking out of town, feeling, though it was the middle of the day, like a thief in the night, a scarf tossed over her head, chin pressed nearly into her chest, not making eye contact with anyone. Regina attempted to take as little space as possible, to shuffle her feet along the concrete station floor lest the clack of her high-heels attract attention.

She only looked up when it came time to hand her ticket to the conductor. She peered into his face, eyes open wide, lashes quivering, and offered her most dazzling smile—as well as a peek down her blouse. It was a maneuver she'd evolved during her early teens. It worked on male teachers wavering between a higher and lower grade on an exam. It worked on butchers to double-check if there was truly not a scrap of meat left for sale. It worked on boys who felt inspired to buy you a slice of Napoleon cake. Regina could hope it worked on train conductors.

It did. He barely glanced at Regina's ticket. He was too busy leering at her. And he never got around to asking for her travel documents.

THE TRIP FROM Moscow to Birobidzhan took eight days. Regina passed every one sitting upright atop her barely cushioned seat, staring out the window, gritting her teeth to keep from clicking her fingernails, tapping her feet, or performing any other nervous tick which might betray her anxiety. Except whenever the conductor came by. Then, Regina lay on her side, face turned towards the seatback, knees tucked under, pretending to be asleep. It was the most stomach-churning portion of the journey. She could hear the conductor's footsteps growing closer. Would this be the day he decided the hell with good manners and shook Regina awake to demand her travel documents? There was the moment he would pause above her, his breathing as audible as if he were puffing into her ear. Her impulse was to squinch her eyes tighter. She worried that wouldn't look natural. Truly sleeping people weren't tensed up. Truly sleeping people were blissfully relaxed. Regina attempted to imitate that state while her throat cramped, her lungs shriveled, and her intestines pinched each other mercilessly. For eight days the conductor paused right above her. Then he moved on.

That wasn't the worst part of pretending to be asleep, though. The worst part was how, the second Regina closed her eyes, her eyelids turned into a blank screen for the projection of her otherwise repressed panic. There were flickering images of her future, where she arrived in Birobidzhan to be judged wanting and unwanted. And there were images of her past. The nights of arguments and outbursts. The joking, the singing, the drinking, the planning. Comrade Berger. Comrade Kaminsky. Cecilia. They'd seemed so heroic, so united. So unaware of what was lurking on the outskirts of their grand dreams. Or maybe she'd been the one unaware. She'd been the fool. Mama and Papa had implied as much from the moment Regina first got herself entangled. They stopped implying, moving on to flat out saying it when Regina stood before them, begging for help. She'd trusted the wrong people. She'd listened to the wrong voices. She'd heeded the wrong advice. Regina vowed to never make such a mistake again.

If she ever got the chance.

REGINA'S TRAIN PULLED into Birobidzhan's solitary station, Tikhonkaya, after one in the morning, the darkest possible hour. Regina suspected it would have appeared so even without the rain whipping her window. She was the only passenger disembarking. She felt like tiptoeing, as you would into a library. Or a funeral home.

One more sweep past the conductor, one more smile, one more loosened button, and she would be home free. None of her efforts proved necessary. At one in the morning, the conductor wasn't faking sleep like Regina had for over a week. He was deeply in it.

While in Moscow Regina had curled into herself, trying to appear insignificant. Here, she strove to make a robust first impression. To appear confident, strong, the sort of woman who'd be welcomed to join in building a socialist Jewish state, not deported home in disgrace, trailed by disparaging laughter like a foul stench.

So Regina forced herself to stride down the train steps and onto the platform. A woman who had nothing to fear. A woman who had nothing to hide.

Her attempt to appear confident—and guileless—proved super-
fluous. There was no one there to see it. Rain poured down in tor-
rents, soaking Regina the instant she left the cover of her train. She
couldn't make out an awning or a station door to duck through. No
attendant manned the ticket office. She'd disembarked on the left
side of a wooden platform between two tracks. There was a second
train across from her. Not a passenger one, but freight. A flash of
lightning corrected Regina's perception. Each car was bursting with
people. Men? Women? Regina couldn't tell. They were pressed against
the walls, faces peering out the few barred windows. They reminded
Regina of Uzbekh, Kazakh, and Kyrgyz people who'd been coming to
Moscow to work and study ever since their republics became members of the USSR.

The idling train's engine sputtered in preparation for pulling out.
Which was when Regina caught sight of a second figure on the platform. A man was running alongside the departing train, holding a
sack, reaching into it, pulling out a handful of something Regina
couldn't identify, and shoving it into the outstretched hands of those
who'd managed to squeeze their arms through the windows' slats. As
the train sped up, so did he, running so quickly he tripped at Regina's feet, dropping his sack. She bent to help him retrieve the loaves
of bread he'd fumbled. Not the kind she knew from Moscow—machine baked, uniform and soft—but misshapen lumps, coarse, heavy,
soaked. He scrambled up, frantically continuing distribution as waiting hands whipped by at swifter and swifter speeds. Regina imitated
his actions, lifting a grimy trio of loaves, standing on tip-toe to reach.
The bread was ripped from her grip with such force that it knocked
Regina down, back, and over her bag.

She thrust out her hands behind her, hoping to break her fall,
feeling the splinters of the wooden railway floor dig into her palms
as her teeth scraped against each other, ringing in her ears. She rolled
onto her stomach and pushed herself up, first to her knees, then to
her feet. Regina dabbed at the front of her dress, as if a few swipes
with dirty, bloodied hands would do any good against the streaks of
mud, wondering why she was bothering, no one would see her.

By the time she looked up again, the man with the sack was gone.

REGINA STOOD, SOAKED, on an abandoned railway platform. She'd expected the town of Amurzet to be there, the way all of Moscow's nine stations were within city limits. You stepped off the platform, and there you were. Regina stepped off the platform in Birobidzhan, and she was ankle deep in a swampy, unplowed field, surrounded by mountains in the distance, and the outline of a dirt road that led into more darkness. Tree branches whipped in the wind. Waist-high grasses bent and curled. The road, Regina reasoned, had to lead... somewhere. If she followed it, she would eventually emerge... somewhere. If it wasn't the settlement she was looking for, it would likely be some other, where she could solicit directions to her desired destination. Regina started walking. No, Regina started dragging; her feet through the mud, her face through the sheets of rain, her bag behind her, bumping into every rock, slipping into every cavity.

Her clothes clung to her skin, her feet slid in her shoes. Regina's hair fell into her eyes and, after a half-dozen futile attempts, she quit trying to prevent it. She peered out into the world through a slit in her dripping bangs, which scratched her eyes like bugs crawling on her pupils. Regina stared ahead, willing herself to think only of her destination, ordering herself to ignore the voice in her head, the one reminding Regina she could turn around, retrace her sloshing steps, and catch the next train back to Moscow. What was waiting for her there might be worse, but at least it wasn't the unknown. She was concentrating so hard on ignoring that voice, telling herself the danger in Moscow couldn't possibly be less than the danger of a stroll in a light mist, that it took several moments for her to comprehend the voice she was hearing—a male one—was coming not from inside her head, but from the side of the road.

Regina craned her neck, raising an arm to rub the back of her wrist across her face to clear her vision. Through the torrent, she caught sight of a horse, its hooves digging a parallel gulley of mud Regina's way. Presuming it wasn't the animal she'd heard addressing her, Regina squinted, following the horse's reins to the accompanying wagon, where legs, wrists, and a head peeked out from beneath a loose muslin covering to beckon Regina.

The man from the station had come back for her.

Chapter Two

===

"Come!" She more read his lips than heard his invitation.

Regina had no idea where he was going. He could be headed in the exact opposite direction of where she needed to be. Then again, he clearly knew where he was going better than she did.

Regina lifted her skirt—a pointless exercise, she was soaked, mud weighing down her hem like it was lined with ball bearings—and sloshed to the wagon. A hand reached to lift her onto the seat, then darted out again to grab her suitcase and toss it into the back. Only once she was settled did Regina get a clear look at her champion. Her first instinct was to recoil. Because her first, unbidden thought was: Cossack.

She'd been prepared. She knew that, before KOMZET, this had been a Cossack territory called Alexandrovka. The establishment of Amurzet was the first historical instance of a Jewish settlement subsuming a Cossack one. The transition hadn't exactly gone smoothly. Vindictive Cossacks were rumored to be lurking everywhere. And Regina had climbed into one of their wagons alone, in the middle of the night, on a stretch of abandoned road.

What had she promised herself about never again trusting the wrong people?

She was half-turning back to scramble out of his wagon and take off running into any direction where he couldn't follow, when the broad-shouldered, blond-haired, blue-eyed, dimples in his cheeks—a deeper one in his chin—young man opened his mouth, and out came flawless, unaccented Yiddish, asking her where she was headed. Yiddish much better than Regina's. Her parents had been against her learning.

She was so stunned, she blurted out, "*Yid?*"

"*Ja.*" Then, presumably hearing her own accent, he helpfully translated, unable to hide a twitch of a smile at her confusion, "*Da.*"

His Russian was as good, though provincial. Regina had been raised to believe anything less than a Moscow accent was provincial. Pretenders in Leningrad liked to claim otherwise.

"I'm sorry," Regina stammered, wondering how she'd managed to get herself into trouble again so quickly after explicitly vowing to watch everything she did or said to avoid a repeat of what was snapping at her heels from Moscow. "I didn't mean to offend you."

"You're cold." He fumbled under his seat, unearthing a blanket only half soaked through. He switched the reins to his left hand and, while navigating the mud-drenched road with his right, attempted to wrap Regina's shoulders in the least damp edges. The back of his hand brushed Regina's cheek. She'd expected it to feel cold, muddy, viscid. The warmth struck her out of the blue when it plunged straight through her. Even Regina's toes startled at the sensation.

"Are you lost?" he asked.

He had no idea how much.

She ached to tell him. It would be such a relief to share a tiny fraction of her burden, to quit stuffing everything down like choking on stones. His smile seemed so concerned, so kind. As did the arm he was withdrawing from around her shoulders, handing Regina the ends of his blanket to hold together like a makeshift cape. She remembered all the other snap judgements she'd made. All the other times when a warm smile and a kind word had convinced her their owners were trustworthy. That they wouldn't betray her. That her association with them wouldn't send her fleeing to the ends of the Earth.

She ached to tell him everything. Which was why Regina knew it would be wrong. As of the past week, she felt certain any instinct of hers was doomed to be wrong.

Regina's inclination was to lean forward, drawing as close as possible to the comfort emanating from him like the heat of a blazing stove on a frigid day. So she forced herself to lean backwards, even if that meant moving further from beneath the canopy and growing wetter. He cocked his head, confused by the counterintuitive action, but made no move to pull her back or verbally redress her decision. He took it for granted Regina knew what she was doing. If he only knew how wrong he was. No. Better if he never knew.

"Could you please take me to the home of Comrade Kaminsky," she requested. "If it isn't too far out of your way."

"He's gone."

"Gone?" Regina repeated dumbly. Then felt foolishly compelled to clarify, in case there were more than one of them, "Comrade Julian Kaminsky. The village Soviet head. Is he away?" Regina grasped at straws, recalling how often he traveled.

"Comrade Kaminsky was removed last month. Accused of participating in a murderous, Bundist, Fascist, Nazi conspiracy to maliciously undermine the Soviet state." He recited the charges by rote, the warm smile of a moment before fading to one of bitterness he didn't quite manage to conceal. Regina suspected he wasn't trying to.

"That's impossible." She wasn't arguing with him. She was arguing with the desperate expectation that had driven Regina this far east, convinced she'd be able to find sanctuary and absolution. All of it hinged on Comrade Kaminsky coming to her defense. "He's an important man. Comrade Kagonovitch visited him several months ago. There was a banquet." Regina grasped at the fact that had seemed most humanizing when she'd heard the story. "He ate gefilte fish. Made by Mrs. Kaminsky. He said it was the best he'd ever tasted."

"Kamisnky's wife was arrested, too. For plotting to poison Kagonovitch." There went that flash of bitterness again. "With gefilte fish."

If she weren't so shocked and terrified by what it signified for her, Regina might well have laughed at the ridiculousness of the charge. "No! It's a mistake! Comrade Kaminsky is a patriot! And—and he's an American! They can't keep an American against his will!"

"He surrendered his passport. He's a Soviet citizen. Same as the rest of us."

A reminder of where she was, and who she was. And what she was wanted for.

Was it only a month ago Regina had walked confident, believing she and her friends were on the right side of history, and nothing could hurt them? Of course they'd heard about the assassination of Sergei Kirov at Communist Party headquarters in Leningrad's Smolny Institute. The killer, Leonid Nikolayev, was arrested, tried, and sentenced to death, as were his mother, sisters, brother, and cousin. At his trial, the traitor revealed a vast network of disgruntled, jealous, power-hungry Bolsheviks and Trotskyites out to undermine Comrade Stalin. His confession allowed The People's Commissariat for Internal Affairs, NKVD, to round up thousands of turncoats, most of whom were masquerading as loyal citizens. It was those same quislings who spread rumors that Kirov's death had been an assassination ordered by Comrade Stalin himself via NKVD Commissar Genrikh Yagoda after Kirov countermanded Stalin's order to replace the head of Leningrad NKVD with a more trusted ally. Kirov's bodyguard, Borisov, might have been able to dismiss those fairy-tales, except he, tragically, fell out of a truck and died the day following Kirov's execution. Borisov's inconsolable wife was committed to a mental institution soon after, grief having driven her to profess all sorts of mad things. "Trouble happens," Cecilia had shrugged upon learning the news, "to those who go looking for it."

Had Cecilia gone looking for it? Had Regina? She certainly hadn't thought so at the time.

But the way this man was peering at her now, did he assume Regina had brought her troubles upon herself? Why else would she be running? Innocent people didn't run!

Cecilia had directed Regina to disregard the whispers and attempts to smear Comrade Stalin's character. He was their benefactor, the one making Birobidzhan possible. As long as they gave him no cause to suspect their loyalty, all of them—Cecilia, Regina, Kaminsky—would remain under his protection. There would be no trials, no trucks, no mental institutions. They were untouchable. Until they weren't.

They'd come for Cecilia. They'd come for Kaminsky. Regina had to be next on their list. Not on Comrade Stalin's list. On the list of those who plotted to undermine him. They were the ones behind the arrests of steadfast citizens like Cecilia and Kaminsky. Once Comrade Stalin was appraised of the situation, they would all be rehabilitated. Well, those still alive. Until then, who knew what those who'd been shipped to Butyrka prison were saying. It was reported to be a hellish waystation for political prisoners of all types. An inferno in the summer, an icebox in the winter. A hundred souls packed into cells built to hold no more than ten during the Czar's days. It was a breeding ground for lice and disease. A desperate man—or woman—would incriminate anyone to secure their own release.

Once, Regina had believed her friends would never point the conspiratorial finger at her to save themselves. Once, she'd never believed they'd need to. Once, she'd felt confident she'd never break, not even under torture from her enemies. Now, she had no interest in finding out whether or not that was true. Because she no longer knew who her enemies were.

It was imperative Regina tread carefully. Her resolve to keep from confessing how lost she was, was proving more practical by the second. Regina figured it was in her interest to learn more about the precarious situation before making any split-second decisions.

"I will take you to Felix Luria. He is head of the Soviet now. Another American."

Or she could let him make her split-second decisions for her. This total stranger with the nice smile couldn't possibly make a bigger mess of it than Regina already had.

"Thank you," Regina said, hoping she didn't sound as awkward as she felt.

He nodded, and tapped the horse on its side, slightly altering its trajectory. Was he going to ask her why she needed to see the Soviet head so desperately? The only way Regina could think of to avert any questions she didn't want to answer was by asking one of her own. Not to mention, she'd been wondering from the start. "What were you doing? At the station? Who were those people on the trains?"

"Koreans."

"From Korea?" Regina had read of Oriental infiltrators sneaking across Soviet lines to commit sabotage. She'd never imagined there would be so many of them. She'd seen women and children on the trains, too. Weren't enemy saboteurs exclusively men? Regina chastised herself for the reactionary thought. Hadn't Cecilia lectured her how the USSR was the only nation to offer full equality to the sexes? Full equality of the sexes meant equal opportunity for women saboteurs. That was Socialist progress. But what about the children...

"They've lived here for generations. Rice farmers, mostly. We don't bother them, they don't bother us. When the NKVD came for Kaminsky and some of the other party leaders, they posted a decree announcing all Koreans had been determined to be spies for Japan. Packed them up on trains, shipping them who knows where."

It was a terrible—albeit familiar—story. Regina thought of the kulaks, Poles, and Finns who'd been deported in recent years. That had been their fault, though. Kulaks were landowners who'd refused to turn their property over for the good of the people. The Finns of the Leningrad region had betrayed the Soviet Union and couldn't be allowed to remain living along the border, so close to their home country. The same applied to Poles who'd settled in Ukraine. They were all enemies of the state, of that there could be no doubt. Which was why the primary image that continued to dominate Regina's memory proved so confusing, "You were feeding them..."

"Long trip, not given time to pack, most won't bring enough."

He'd committed a crime. The definition of going looking for trouble. He'd offered aid to those who sought to destroy the USSR. Regina knew she should recoil, chastise, remind him of everything their homeland had given them, and what they owed it in return. *You have no rights*, Comrade Stalin preached, *only obligations*. Especially people like them. Jews had to work twice as hard to prove their loyalty. Or risk ending up like kulaks, Finns, and Poles. Ending up like her. Unless Regina worked quickly to mitigate the situation, her grand escape might well conclude with her mired in greater danger. She couldn't risk so much as the appearance of the possibility of the suggestion of impropriety. Which was exactly what she'd allowed to happen when she unwittingly helped his unsanctioned attempt to save others. Even though there'd been nobody around to see them, and presumably nobody around to hear them, Regina still recognized that it was imperative she denounce him and his actions. It was the rational thing to do.

Yet, to Regina's surprise, what actually came out of her mouth was not a reproach or a reminder of duty. "That was terribly kind of you," she heard herself say.

He shrugged, refusing to meet her eyes, as if what he'd done hadn't been embarrassing, but acknowledging her complimenting him would be. He mumbled, "Can't stand seeing people go hungry. Not if I can help it."

Once upon a time, Regina would have felt no qualms about echoing, *Me neither.*

She didn't dare risk it now.

Still, she ached to say something. To let him know she truly appreciated his bravery and compassion, even if she couldn't say so for the record.

"Thank you," Regina let her words hang in the air for the appropriate amount of time before rushing to add, "for giving me a ride."

There, that should be alright. Nothing too nefarious could be twisted out of that sentiment. She couldn't be accused of supporting his illegality. But she'd said something nice, nonetheless.

He nodded to indicate he understood. The things she'd said. And the things she'd been too afraid to say.

Was he judging her cowardice? Nothing in his actions suggested it. She was convinced he'd understand why she needed to be cautious if she explained her predicament. He seemed to be that sort of understanding person. But Regina couldn't risk that any more than she could risk openly praising what he'd done for the Koreans. Their coded communication would need to suffice. She hoped the unspoken, somehow mutually agreed upon, yet plausibly deniable cryptic language of the USSR worked here as well as in Moscow.

They jounced on through potholes and over rocks, cosseted in a waterlogged silence that could have been easily dispersed via banalities no one would dare take offense at. Except that would have ruined it, demeaned it.

Each bounce of the wagon tossed the pair of them towards each other. Shoulders, arms, elbows, wrists, thighs, knees, feet bumping, then springing apart just as quickly. Regina resisted the first few knocks, white-knuckling the bench beneath her and attempting to ride out the waves like clutching a rubber inner tube bobbing atop the sea. She gave up after less than a half-dozen tries. The force was too great, the effort too onerous. The alternative too pleasant. The next time centrifugal force tossed Regina in her driver's direction, she went limp, going so far as to allow her head to rest briefly on his shoulder. She couldn't help it, after all.

The time after that, Regina allowed herself to look at him. The time after that, she smiled.

He smiled back. She'd seen his kind smile. She'd seen his embarrassed smile.

This one was dangerous.

To Regina, anyway.

Because it was the kind of smile that took the plans you'd been assembling since leaving Moscow, and made you believe they were unnecessary.

"Here." Without Regina noticing, they'd turned off the dirt trail onto a roadway made of wood planks laid atop the mud. She heard the different sound made by the horse's hooves, less of a squish, more of a clop. Ahead stood a two-story house beneath a slanted roof, a chimney poking out the back. The walk from the whitewashed fence to the door, elevated above a single porch step, was lined with uneven bits of stone. "Village Soviet."

Regina supposed, if pressed, she'd have admitted realizing their ride would need to end. She simply hadn't expected it to come so soon. She struggled to keep the disappointment from her voice as she corroborated, "We're here."

A nod. He sat there. Waiting for her. Waiting for her to do what?

"Thank you," Regina said. "Again."

Another nod. So that wasn't it.

She turned to go. He placed a hand on her arm. Again, that

warmth. How did he manage to run so hot in such a numbing climate? For a moment, Regina imagined the world around them was black and white. It was easy enough, the sky, the trees, the mud, the air quivered in undifferentiated shades of grey. The only spot of color were his cobalt eyes, dotted in a golden fringe of lashes.

"If you came here to hide," he said. "You've come to the wrong place."

This time, the heat that tore through Regina was more an electrical shock, and no longer of the pleasant kind. She recoiled, pulling out of his grasp. Of all of the things she'd expected—even hoped— he'd say, this was the least welcome. It couldn't be true. Not after everything she'd already been through. She couldn't have made yet another terrible decision. At this point, she'd have thought that would be mathematically impossible. The equivalent of stepping out onto a four-way intersection and turning in the wrong direction—all four times. If Birobidzhan couldn't offer her asylum, then Regina was out of options.

And Regina wouldn't allow herself to believe she was out of options.

She shook her head, unable to articulate all the thoughts and emotions wrestling for dominance inside her. She hopped off the wagon and stumbled to the back, grabbing her bag with both hands, yanking it up with such force Regina nearly went sprawling again. She had to get away. Away from her fears. Away from him.

He made no move to stop her.

Regina couldn't leave things like this. No matter how terrified he'd made her about her future, no matter how badly she wanted to believe he was nothing, his portents of doom didn't matter, he didn't know what he was talking about, Regina still felt driven to ask, "What's your name?"

Like in the fairy stories, knowing his name would give Regina some whisper of power over him. Some whisper of power over the way he'd made her feel.

"Kramer." He flicked his reins, turning the horse back to where they'd come from, leaving the remainder of his answer to drown in the remnants of the storm. "Aaron Kramer."

Chapter Three

Regina nearly sprinted up the uneven stone walk leading up to Felix Luria's house. She told herself it was to get away from the pounding rain. She knew it was to get away from Aaron Kramer. His words about Birobidzhan being the wrong place to hide had chilled Regina in spots no mere storm could reach.

She'd lost track of what time it was. She suspected it was still the middle of the night. It would be rude to come busting in. Then again, it might be deadly to wait until morning.

Suppressing the good manners Mama spent eighteen years drilling into her—then again, that had been for a different place and definitely a different time—Regina raised her fist to knock. Tentatively at first, then with more desperation.

The door was opened by a dark-haired woman twice Regina's size, if not in height, then at least in width. She wore a threadbare, olive muslin robe over a nightgown of the same coarse material, her hair pulled back with a kerchief. She expressed no visible surprise at discovering a waterlogged urchin on her front porch.

"F-Felix Luria?" Regina managed to inquire through chattering teeth, hugging herself with one arm for warmth, while holding tight to her bag with the other.

The woman nodded briskly, her face conveying that there was no one else Regina could be here to see, especially at this hour.

Footsteps scurrying down from the second floor produced a fellow closer to Regina's height. His dark curly hair, wide-set brown eyes, and a nose that revealed itself a split second before any other feature, marked him close enough in looks to Regina to fancy him a long-lost cousin. A stark difference from her first impression of Aaron, and a much more comforting sight.

He too wore a robe over pajamas, albeit the former was a vibrant crimson, and the latter cotton rather than muslin. He flicked on the entryway's overhead light, giving Regina her uncountable shock of the day—or was it night? The woman who'd let her in looked exactly like the faces Regina had spied peering through the bars of the deportation train at the station.

Misinterpreting her confusion, Felix explained, "Don't worry, Chunhua isn't *honghutzu*."

As Regina had no idea what that was, she was neither soothed nor worried.

"*Honghutzu*," Felix translated. "Red-bearded ones. Chinese thugs. They wander the countryside, crossing our side of the border, terrorizing locals. Most of those are poppy growers, criminals. We've made it illegal to fraternize with them, but our weaker-willed citizens can't help themselves. Chunhua isn't like the rest. She's civilized, the best of their kind. I wouldn't trust her in my home, otherwise."

"She's not Korean?" Regina asked, seeking clarification, head spinning from realizing how much she still had to learn about the place she hoped would be her safe haven.

"Oh, no." Felix hesitated, the open good nature he'd come bounding down the steps with flickering slightly. "What do you know about our Koreans?"

This was a test. It had to be a test. Not just Regina's intelligence but her allegiance was being tested. Regina was ashamed to confess all she knew about any Koreans—not only the ones who lived, well, once lived, in Birobidzhan—was limited to what Aaron had described to her in the wagon. Had he been telling the truth? Regina had no idea whether he might be trustworthy. Did she dare repeat his words, unchecked, to a man as important as Felix Luria?

"They are Japanese spies," Regina ventured tentatively, ready to backpedal should Felix offer any hint of disagreeing with her assertion.

Fortunately for Regina, Felix's smile broadened at her words. As Chunhua made herself scarce, Felix beckoned Regina deeper into his home, towards a man-sized masonry stove in the far corner of the parlor. In Russian folklore, such a stove could not only be used for cooking and warming a home, but for curing the sick, issuing directions, as a hiding place, and even a form of flying transportation. Regina leaned gratefully towards its warmth, feeling her skin bake and her clothes tighten as both crisped from the heat. She suspected she was turning a less than attractive shade of red. Sweat poured down her forehead and pooled beneath her arms. She no longer cared. After a week on a train without washing, then the dowsing she received after disembarking, it felt too good to stand clean and dry for a change.

Felix allowed Regina her moment to wallow in the sensation. Then, all too quickly, he did what any reasonable man would under the circumstances. He asked Regina her name. And then he asked her business in Birobidzhan.

Regina answered his first question without hesitation. If word of her transgression had beaten Regina East enough for him to already know of her, then nothing Regina said afterwards could possibly matter.

He gave no indication of that being the case.

His second question was a more delicate matter. How much, exactly, was she obliged to divulge to him? How much could she get away with concealing? How much was enough to get him to believe her version of events without further interrogation? What would it take to get him on her side? Or, at least, not against it?

Regina tread carefully, taking the same approach she had earlier with his question about Koreans. She'd release a few words, then hold her breath, gauging his reaction before offering a smidge more, deftly changing course in response to each perceived squint of displeasure or nod of encouragement.

"I am from Moscow," Regina said. "It's where I met Comrade Kaminsky."

The way Felix narrowed his eyes at the name inspired Regina to wonder if she'd already miscalculated. So much for taking it slow and steady. It appeared no matter which speed Regina attempted to speak at, her foot ended up in her mouth just the same.

Perhaps there was still a chance to salvage her situation. Felix wasn't looking ready to lock Regina up and throw away the key quite yet. He presented every indication he was still listening. Which meant she should keep talking.

And she had better start saying the appropriate things. The clock was ticking.

Regina said, "Comrade Kaminsky came to Moscow to tell us about the wonders of Birobidzhan." Surely, Felix couldn't take offense at that.

He didn't.

Emboldened, Regina went on, "He told us how hundreds of families were coming every day, thousands were resettling, working side by side to establish the modern world's first Jewish state, independent and socialist."

Alright, no missteps there. The tide was turning.

"He talked about the agriculture, the crops you were sowing, the livestock, the cows, pigs and goats you were breeding and using for meat and milk, the factories..."

What was that? Did Felix flinch at that last part?

He did! He definitely did! And he raised his arms, crossing them against his chest. Even someone as tone deaf as Regina could recognize a disapproving posture when she saw it.

And then she had it. She knew what she needed to say to prove she had never been a compatriot of Comrade Kaminsky's. That she was a good, loyal Soviet citizen and would be an exemplary addition to the Birobidzhan self-actualization effort.

"Comrade Kaminsky insisted factories were your path to financial independence, that they were critical to convincing those who might grant us independence that we could be self-sufficient." Regina hoped Felix noticed how she'd transitioned to possessive pronouns to make it clear whose side she was on. "He was incensed that despite his American ICOR providing equipment to put three-fourths of his settlement's population to work in factories, the goods they produced remained mediocre—according to him. We would never be able to compete with the rest of the world at this rate, Kaminsky claimed. Even Soviets would begin to demand quality goods eventually. He wanted his factories ready to take advantage."

Regina observed Felix growing angrier and angrier. His face was nearly as red as hers now, and he wasn't standing as close to the stove. Before it looked like his ears might emit the steam of a teakettle, Regina announced, "I disagreed with him."

That brought Felix up short. She could almost see him sucking the steam back inside, as if filling his lungs prior to plunging underwater.

She hurried to put him out of his misery. "Birobidzhan was established to be the Jewish cultural center of the world. Jewish literature, Jewish theater, Jewish political thought. And it was established by the *Committee for the Settlement of Toiling Jews on Land.* The goal was to finally allow Jews to subsist off our own farming labor. It wasn't to enslave us in factories like a modern day Pharaoh. Kaminsky believed because ICOR, as his countrymen say, pays the piper and funds our settlement, they should pick the tune we dance to. He wished to see our collective farms turned into soulless factories, our farmers, our craftsmen, our teachers, our artists become nothing but cogs to fuel his ravenous machine."

Regina watched Felix's grin grow bigger with her every word. By the end, it felt like he could barely contain himself from leaping forward, grabbing Regina in his arms and spinning her around with glee, delighted to have discovered a like-minded thinker.

She felt no compulsion to tell him the majority of her words, well, all of them, had initially been uttered not by Regina, but by a Comrade Berger, who was forever arguing with Comrade Kaminsky whenever both happened to be in Moscow.

Comrade Berger would accuse, 'Comrade Kaminsky, like all Americans, believes everything must be quantified in terms of money.'

Kaminsky would counter, 'Comrade Berger wishes to see the Yiddish press flower in Birobidzhan, with nary a thought to the cost of printing supplies, shipping costs, writer's fees. No, I take that back. Comrade Berger is never late billing for his own writer's fees. He has only visited our settlement of Amurzet once. I reside there year-round. I am chairman of the village Soviet, and responsible for the fate of five hundred families. Comrade Berger writes poetry about Jewish farmers toiling in the fields, singing patriotic folk songs. I'm the one who has to deal with the flooding which wipes out our crops, the mosquitoes which feast on our cattle. My families would be better served working in industry.'

Which was where Comrade Berger's response, which Regina appropriated for herself, came in.

"Absolutely." Felix nodded his head so emphatically Regina feared it might come loose and begin rolling down the road like the children's fable of *kolobok*. "Kaminsky was undermining our settlement from the inside, right under the noses of ICOR. You can imagine how bad it made the rest of us Americans look once he was finally exposed and arrested."

It was time for Regina to tread carefully again. Because if she got this step wrong, getting all the previous ones right wouldn't make a difference.

"In Moscow, Comrade Kaminsky had a friend. Cecilia Melamed. I—She—We lived in the same communalka."

Their communal apartment once belonged exclusively to Regina's family. She could barely comprehend it. What did Mama and Papa mean the two of them used to occupy the entire flat, instead of the single room all three now shared? So much space for two people? It was indecent! A crime! How could they justify hoarding when so many others lacked an equally palatial residence? The way they currently lived made more sense. Mama, Papa, and Regina in the room off the kitchen where someone called a maid previously boarded. (One citizen serving another? How unprogressive!) A family of four, Old Woman, Daughter, Son, and Son's Wife packed into the bigger bedroom, a Husband, Wife and their twin teenage boys in the room that used to be for greeting guests (how wasteful!), and a student allowed to remain in Moscow until he completed his university studies in what had been a closet for storing linens. Who in the world had more than one set of linens that required storing? All twelve of them shared the water closet, their individual toilet seats hanging on pegs outside the door, as well as the kitchen, where cooking food necessitated watching over it. Walking away for so much as a moment risked the condensed milk you put to bake in the oven disappearing, to be replaced by a neighbor's potatoes. After standing in lines for hours, often not knowing what was being sold, terrified the supply would run out before you reached the front of the que, they stashed tins of sardines, loaves of bread, and burlap sacks of onions under the beds and in musty corners of chifforobes, rather than risk them going missing from the kitchen.

When Regina was twelve years old, without warning, Old Woman, Daughter, Son, and Son's Wife unexpectedly moved out. The neighbors told themselves it had to be good news. Son's Wife was pregnant. Perhaps they'd qualified for a bigger residence? In any case, if it wasn't good news, as Comrade Stalin said, the less they knew, the sounder they'd sleep.

The next day, Cecilia Melamed moved in. The room four adults used to occupy, she claimed all for herself. A powerful woman, Regina had thought.

That was her first mistake.

She told Felix, "They thought I was on her side. Hers and Kaminsky's and the rest of them. Just because of where I lived. I never was. Same as here. They thought you supported Kaminsky's ideas because you were both Americans!"

A lie and a wager in one. If Regina hadn't been so terrified, she might have felt impressed with herself. She'd never bluffed like this before. She had no idea if she was doing it right. Most people got their feet wet with easy card games, then moved onto gambling with money. Regina went straight for gambling with her life.

Would it prove to be her worst decision yet in an unbroken streak of rotten ones?

Felix appeared to be swallowing her story. But it was entirely possible he was simply the more experienced card player. He was from

America, after all. Their children sucked up roadmaps for exploiting others with their mother's milk.

He was listening closely, nodding his head in some parts, growing furious in others. And then there was that moment when he'd looked ready to dance a celebratory mazurka. Regina knew that ultimately meant little. Look how long she'd believed what Cecilia told her. You could believe someone was your compatriot—your friend—for years. Then, in the space of a single knock on the door, everything could fall apart.

Felix said, "I understand."

Regina's heart did a flip to match any celebratory mazurka. "You do?"

"I'm in a bit of a similar bind myself. With a fellow by the name of Aaron Kramer."

Her dancing heart froze in place, then proceeded to hammer in double time, ricocheting about her rib-cage, one moment jammed in her throat, the next in her lungs.

This was another test. It had to be. It was too much of a co-incidence otherwise. Or a set-up. Though that was ridiculous. The only way this could be a set-up was if Felix had known Regina was coming. If he'd set it up for her and Aaron to meet at the station. If he'd wanted her to catch Aaron offering illegal aid to their enemies, then waited to see whether she would report him. It was why he was so curious about Regina's knowledge of Koreans earlier. It had to be.

But that would only be true if Felix knew she was coming.

And if he knew she was coming, then all of this had been for nothing.

Chapter Four

"Aaron Kramer," Felix repeated, watching Regina closely, assessing her reaction.

She struggled not to give one away until she could feel certain she knew what it should be. If Aaron and Felix were in on this together, then revealing what she'd seen would benefit Regina and not hurt Aaron in the slightest. If Aaron and Felix weren't working together, then she would greatly benefit herself... but likely doom Aaron. Regina supposed she could claim utter ignorance. If challenged, she could say he'd never given her his name. That was true up until the last moment of their brief acquaintance. If Aaron claimed otherwise, Regina could counter that his answer had been lost in the rain and wind. Would Aaron betray her? There was no reason he shouldn't. They were complete strangers. And yet, he didn't seem like the type. Not that Regina had any faith left in her ability to read people.

"The fellow who dropped you off," Felix clarified, thus cutting off any plans Regina might have harbored to play dumb.

She'd wondered earlier if Felix were a better gambler than her. Now she had no doubts.

The only thing still in doubt was how Regina should react to his call.

It was time for one more, desperate bluff. "He saw me waiting at the train station in the rain. He offered me a lift. I was in no position to refuse."

"You should be more careful. Birobidzhan can be a dangerous place for those who don't have its best interests at heart."

"I don't understand." It was the first truly honest thing Regina had said in weeks.

Felix sighed, sorry to be the bearer of bad news. "I'm afraid a substantial number of new arrivals to our settlement didn't come to build socialism, but out of selfish motives, to better their own lots in life. Uneducated, unskilled, clinging to their ancient superstitions. Longbeards hiding in synagogues, unwilling to do their share of labor. Worse are the comrades who've gone native, taking advice from local savages who haven't evolved their practices in two centuries, instead of those of us bringing scientific advances to help them progress!"

Regina leapt on the opportunity to further ingratiate herself into Felix's good graces. "I studied modern collective agriculture techniques at University. We spent a week on how kulaks rejecting collectivization and hoarding resources for their private-enterprise farms led to the Holodomor. Millions dead in Ukraine because they wouldn't listen to science!"

"Precisely," Felix beamed. "That is precisely what I meant about those like Kramer. He has the audacity to claim the Holodomor, rather than, as you so aptly put it, being caused by resource hoarding on the part of those who refused to surrender their land for the good of others, was, in fact, a man-made famine! A deliberate plot by no less than Comrade Stalin, created to starve malefactors into submission! Why, even Americans, in their *New York Times*, confirmed there was no such famine. American reporters are under orders from their moneybag owners to discredit the USSR by any means necessary, to the point of making up lies about us. So if they said the Holodomor never happened—and won a Pulitzer for that—you know it's the truth!"

"Why would he—why would this Aaron Kramer," Regina

distanced herself from Aaron and his views while, at the same time, focusing her question on him, rather than other troublemakers, "do such a thing?" Aaron must grasp the dangers of espousing unendorsed, downright traitorous opinions. Why would anyone take such a risk? Had word of Butyrka prison not made it this far east?

"I have my suspicions about Kramer," Felix confided. "He says he's from some Jewish village in Ukraine, outside Odessa; next door to a kulak settlement that got deliberately starved out. That's where he gets off making his ridiculous accusations. No one here has ever heard of this alleged Jewish village. And look at him! A Ukrainian peasant if I've ever seen one—and I've seen plenty!"

"You think he's lying about being Jewish?" Regina could not fathom a scenario in which that would be an advantage.

"I think he's a saboteur. Sent here by the same forces that planted Kaminsky and turned the Koreans. They want to see our collective fail. They want to embarrass the Party members who granted us independent status."

After the past two weeks, Regina had presumed herself immune to shocking. Yet Felix's words shocked her. How could any fellow Jew wish to sabotage Birobidzhan? Why? Wasn't this what some Jews had been praying—while others worked—towards for centuries? Their own state? The chance to forge their own destiny? No longer beholden to the whims of statesmen and monarchs who invited them to settle, then capriciously cast them out? Birobidzhan was the fulfilment of a dream, more necessary than ever now that Soviet cities were overrun with Jewish refugees attempting to ply their trades. Cobblers, tailors, milliners, blacksmiths, butchers, milkmen, pharmacists, all competing for customers in areas already overstaffed. Competing, not cooperating! Like greedy capitalists! Worse were those who'd fled their decimated villages with no skills whatsoever. They begged in the streets, giving the erroneous impression the USSR couldn't adequately provide for all their citizens. This couldn't be allowed to continue. It didn't look proper. Jews' hope for survival was to learn how to farm their own land, to feed themselves. Who else but the Union of Soviet Socialist Republics would grant them such a magnanimous gift? When choosing a place to run to, Regina hadn't selected Birobidzhan simply due to its distance from Moscow. She'd chosen it because it was where she'd dreamed of going ever since Cecilia first let Regina know of its existence. The idea that anyone else might not feel the same had never crossed her mind. She'd assumed everyone in Birobidzhan would have come for a common dream.

Yet here Felix stood, claiming there was a plot afoot to undermine their collective goal. "A plot by whom?"

Felix paused, index finger tapping against his lips as he considered how much Regina could be told, how much she could be trusted. Regina attempted to look open-minded, yet discerning. Difficult to squeeze both into a single facial expression that was also guileless, yet politically upstanding. Regina settled for looking pretty. She'd found the latter motivated men to assume all of the former. She agreed with Cecilia that it was a terribly unprogressive way to behave. Cecilia would have to agree with her that it usually worked.

"You've heard of Kirov, of course."

He was giving her the benefit of a doubt Regina was happy to confirm. "Of course."

"He was just the beginning. Those who would go after Comrade Stalin will stop at nothing until we are all living under their Fascist thumbs. Two-faced allies of our great Vladimir Illich Lenin never accepted Comrade Stalin's succession to leadership. Even after Comrade Lenin named him General Secretary of the Party as far back as 1922! They follow that rootless cosmopolitan, Trotsky. They don't believe the USSR can establish socialism on our own. They wish to hand us over to our enemies in the name of internationalism. They'd like to see the Soviet Union cease to exist! Worst of them all, however, are the Zionists. They hate that we have succeeded where they have failed. That we have created the first independent Jewish state in a thousand years. And they hate that Comrade Stalin has granted this to us, earning *him* our loyalty, not their illegal nationalistic movement."

"Aaron Kramer is a Zionist?" The only thing worse than being a Jew in the USSR was being a Zionist. Zionists thought Jews were better than everyone else. They wanted to separate people, while Communists strove to bring all people, even their ungrateful Jews, into one fold.

"He has a brother in Palestine." That was all the proof of guilt Felix needed. "A brother who deserted the USSR, the state which housed, clothed, and educated him. He abandons us to employ the skills we gave him to build a capitalist, ethnocentric nation. You know what Russians say about us: *No matter how much you feed the wolf, he will always look towards the forest.* They think we're disloyal. That we'll always put our co-religionists before the international brotherhood of workers. Those Goddamn Zionists are confirming their assumption, making it harder for the rest of us. It was difficult enough when we were all lumped in with that Judas bastard, Trotsky. He's a Jew, so the rest of us Jews must be on his side. We'd barely cleared ourselves of that blood libel when here come the Zionists, and we're back to where we started. At least Trotskyites claim to be on the side of all workers, Jews and non-Jews. Zionists actively promote the idea of Jews separating themselves, putting themselves on a pedestal. If they could undermine us here in Birobidzhan, ensure our failure, they could commandeer the mantle of global Jewish leadership and redirect the weaker-minded from the inevitable Socialist path."

Felix's voice went up with every accusation, matching the shades of crimson his cheeks were spiraling through. He took a breath, returning to normal tone and pallor to reassure Regina that, "Luckily, Comrade Stalin figured out their conspiracy and arrested those responsible. As soon as the NKVD came for Kaminsky, I saw what had been right in front me! Kaminsky was one of them! A Zionist! The USA is full of them, you know, it's one of the reasons I had to leave. Can you imagine if he had gotten away with it? He would have taken the rest of us Americans down with him! Jews are only loyal to other Jews, Americans are only loyal to other Americans. We fight this slur on a daily basis. They wanted to shut down the foreigners' collective, claimed we couldn't be trusted, that we were more loyal to our home country than to the USSR. I did some quick thinking and some faster talking, let me tell you, convincing them to let us keep working here, to name me the new village Soviet. I promised I'd weed out any remaining subversive elements before they could rise to a position of power like Kaminsky. I was proud to give evidence against him and his wife, proud to be a part of the solution, not the problem."

Weeks ago, his words would have struck terror in Regina. Today, they heartened her. Felix was a man of power. He was a man who saw which way the political winds were blowing and made sure to place himself on the correct side. Felix was everything Regina wasn't. Felix was who Regina desperately needed. Felix was likely the only person capable of saving her life.

Unaware of Regina's relief, Felix went on, "All we need to do is expose Kramer, and Birobidzhan will be safe from the Zionist threat."

What? Regina had honestly stopped listening for a moment, so relieved was she to find herself, at long last, in the right place at the right time. In order to remain there, she realized she needed to continue agreeing with whatever Felix said.

Nonetheless, Regina couldn't help wondering—a habit which had gotten her into plenty of trouble in the past. "Why didn't the NKVD arrest Aaron when they came for Kaminsky?"

It seemed logical, if his nefarious motives were equally well known.

"They were after the big fish. Kramer wasn't important enough for them to bother. And he has so many champions here. Women, mostly. They see that face, they lose their reason. They believe he can do no wrong, they're prepared to swear to it. Uneducated peasants, the whole lot of them. No erudition, no sophistication, no sense. They are nothing like you."

"Oh, no." Regina agreed so quickly, her words practically shoved Felix's to the floor. She had already resolved to agree with anything Felix said sans hesitation. A compliment lobbed her way was particularly effortless to embrace. "I am certainly nothing like them."

"I am wondering," Felix said, and Regina began preemptively nodding. What choice did she have? "If we might not be able to help each other? You provide me with assistance for my delicate situation, and I, in turn, can aid you with yours…"

Chapter Five

"Of course I will help you." Regina's confirmation shot out before Felix completed his request. It gave him less time to change his mind. Agreeing with those who held your future in their hands was a skill all Soviet children should have absorbed with their mothers' milk. In Regina's case, it was better late than never. She hoped.

"Wonderful!" Felix clapped his hands loud enough to startle Regina into jumping. She couldn't feel certain if the smile that came afterwards was due to her agreeing, or because it pleased him to see her flinch. As long as he was pleased with her. "You will spend to-night here. Tomorrow we will register you in the settlers' quarters. Put you to use."

"May I sleep by the stove?" Regina asked. "Unless this is someone else's spot?"

Felix's grin broadened. "You may, of course, if that is your desire. But wouldn't you prefer a bed?" His final word lingered in the air like a puff of garlic.

Cecilia was forever lecturing Regina not to be reactionary. Did she think they were living in the previous century, with their opiate of the masses morality, and their overwrought cosseting of women allegedly for an innocent girl's own good; in reality, as another way to control not just their lives, but also their labor? If Felix was offering Regina a transaction—spend the night in his bed with him in exchange for his arranging her residency—it was up to Regina to decide whether or not to accept. Someone else's outdated notion of what was or wasn't proper behavior had naught to do with it. A good Socialist woman was not only in charge of her own mind, but her own body. Felix was paying Regina a compliment in treating her like a freethinker instead of a bourgeois maiden. To refuse might be a political insult as well as a personal one! Was Regina willing to take either risk? Did she have the option of doing so, under the circumstances?

Like every other question Regina had been faced with that night, this one had one right answer. And no second chances.

"A bed for the night would be lovely." Regina recited what was expected. Her smile matched Felix's own. He wasn't repulsive. Hadn't she felt assuaged by his familiarity? So different from Aaron Kramer's enticing foreignness.

"Take the stairs," Felix advised. "The first room on your left. The bed is made up." And then he added, "My room is right across the hall, should you need anything."

If Aaron's news about Kaminsky slammed Regina's skull as if a branch had broken loose in the wind, Felix's clarification felt like being heaved into a rosebush full of thorns. Competing thoughts and sensations pricked Regina from all sides. He was offering her her own room. With her own bed. Across the hall from his. Was she relieved? Insulted? Confused?

So many questions. And yet the one that made it out of Regina's mouth first was, "You have a spare room?"

It made no sense. Everything Regina ever gathered about why her parents had been ordered to share their pre-Revolutionary apartment with other families was because it was the Communist way. Anything else was hoarding resources. A room going to waste was the same as snatching food from the hands of a starving child.

"It's for guests," Felix explained smoothly. "We can't expect important, visiting dignitaries to bunk down on top of each other, like animals. How would that make Birobidzhan look?"

"I understand," Regina assured. She didn't. Shouldn't the important, visiting dignitaries be the ones leading by example? That's what Regina's parents were told. It was the duty of the privileged classes to show the ignorant masses the correct way to behave. Then again, as had already been repeatedly established, Regina's common sense was not to be trusted. Look how badly she'd misconstrued Felix's generous offer.

"I will see you in the morning," he said. "We have important work waiting."

REGINA AWOKE AT DAWN the next day to the sounds of cocks crowing, cows mooing, and farm machinery cranking up to begin work. After a week of feigned sleep lying down, and brief snatches of unconsciousness sitting up atop a train's threadbare seat cushion, it felt downright decadent to be able to stretch both arms to the sides and still feel nothing but mattress, sheet, and duvet. Regina wondered if she were betraying her Socialist principles, wallowing in such luxury while others lacked. She quickly corrected herself. She was thinking like a capitalist, living in a world where, for her to have more, someone inevitably must have less. That wasn't how things worked in Birobidzhan. It was the reason a Jewish Autonomous Region had been established. Regina recalled the lyrical prose Comrade Berger wrote about their fertile land, majestic mountains, rivers full of fish, fields full of grazing cattle, and clear blue skies. It was all theirs now. Which meant it was all hers. There was no difference between the two.

Impatient to fling herself into her new life, Regina pulled on her still damp clothes from the previous night and hurried downstairs, where, as promised, Felix—he'd told her to call him Felix, no patronymics, they were all equals in the JAR!—was waiting. He directed her to the kitchen. A kettle whistled on the stove. A plate of the same bread, sliced, that Aaron had been so frantically shoving into grasping hands the night before, stood on the table, next to a metal tin of what Felix identified as locally canned gooseberry jam. Involuntarily, Regina thought of the men, women, and children on the train, ripping off chunks of desiccated crusts with their teeth, attempting to force sharp gulps down parched throats without the benefit of tea or jam. Or were the loaves covered in mold, having been soaked in the rain? It made Regina's own stomach churn.

Sensing her hesitation, Felix urged Regina to drink her tea and grab a piece of bread with jam for the road, beckoning her to follow him outside. She did as directed, swallowing quickly, not wishing to appear rude, not wishing to cause any trouble.

On the porch, Regina's initial thought was that it's still raining, so difficult was it to see more than a few centimeters in front of her face. But the air was dry. Drier than dry. It was filled with smoke. Regina coughed, covering her mouth and nose with her hand, squinting her watering eyes. "Is something on fire?"

Felix shook his head, running for the GAZ-A car parked on the other side of his fence. Regina had seen similar models in Moscow. Rumors circulated that its design was based on the Americans' Model A and it was being produced in partnership with the plutocrat Ford Motor Company, using their foreigner-manufactured parts. *Pravda* had recently reassured readers this was nonsense. The USSR was capable of designing and assembling their own automobiles, made of their own parts. If anything, the resemblance was the result of the criminal Henry Ford looting Soviet blueprints. Soviet technology, developed in the spirit of cooperation, was decades ahead of anything devised through competition. How could progress happen when men worked for their own interests rather than the common good?

Felix gestured for Regina to follow him. She darted down the stone walkway. Once they were in the car, doors and windows shut, Felix exhaled and rubbed his eyes. Regina did the same, noting her bread was covered in soot. Felix explained, "It's insects. Mosquitoes, midges, gadflies. Locals have no tolerance for them. They burn anything they can, think the smoke will keep bites at bay. We keep trying to tell them there are more scientific methods. You know how stuck in their ways these primitives can be. It's the same with their farming. If we listened to the Cossacks and Koreans, not to mention the Chinese, we'd be farming like we were still in the seventeenth century. ICOR came to develop modern, collective agricultural techniques, not turn into a bunch of kulaks."

Regina nodded in emphatic agreement. Felix did not require much more.

After they'd driven past a series of makeshift wooden cottages, each noticeably smaller than Felix's home, their pathetic patches of faded greenery like the swirl of an archery target around the shack as center, Felix directed Regina to look out her window. "Over there, by the river. Kaminsky's factory. Look how it mars our beautiful countryside!"

Regina raised a palm to shield her eyes from the sun and the window's reflection. The smoke wasn't as thick here as it had been by Felix's house. It was still difficult to make out what he was pointing at. She spied a three-story metal structure, a chimney belching black into the sky. Behind it, mud-colored mountains loomed. In front, grass sprouted half-burned, seemingly incapable of ever blooming again.

Felix explained, "So many families arrived in the beginning, there was no place to house them. They lived outside until we could erect proper tents. Of course, the families who choose to work in the factories are given housing right on site."

"They live inside the factories?" Regina imagined the noise that must pound their ears night and day, not to mention the stench and grime rising from the machinery.

Felix shrugged. "Comrade Stalin said: *A nation is a historically constituted community of people, formed on the basis of a common language, territory, economic life, and psychological make-up manifested in a common culture. Among the Jews there is no large and stable stratum connected with the land, which would naturally rivet the nation together.* Comrade Stalin gave us the gift of land so we may finally be a worthwhile people. Those who choose to reject his gift and engage in capitalist pursuits—" He waved in the general direction of the factory— "are, of course, free to do so."

Felix pressed the gas pedal, increasing his speed, wishing to put the sacrilege behind them. Soon, they were back in the countryside. Instead of makeshift homes, fences encircled much larger tracts of land, each furrowed in raggedy lines of waist-high bushes, some with firm green, some with drooping brown leaves.

"Soybeans and rye," Felix announced proudly. "You are finally seeing Birobidzhan as it's meant to be! Soon we will grow potatoes, cabbage, onions, apples, corn, anything we need to be completely self-sufficient. You have come at the best time!"

No roads surrounded the crops, so Felix maneuvered his way broadly around before he arrived at a white-washed, two-story barracks, almost as large as one of the hectare-sized fields. He stepped out of the car, gallantly opened Regina's door, then headed for the primary entrance. She followed, discreetly dropping the soot-encrusted bread she hadn't been able to bring herself to eat into the dirt and covering it up with her foot, feeling guilty for the waste. Especially when she thought of the trouble Aaron had gone through to give the families on the train that little.

The building's front door opened into a windowless entryway. An old woman sat, staring grimly ahead. Felix approached her table. Whispered words were exchanged, along with furtive looks Regina's way. Unsure of what impression she was supposed to be making, Regina tried looking serious about socialist labor, as well as non-problematic and pleasant to be around. She wanted her new comrades to like her. Though she knew individualism wasn't the point. It was the exact opposite. She'd need to work on that about herself.

After a few minutes, Felix returned, looking pleased with himself.

"Usually, you're supposed to go through KOMZET, the Committee for the Settlement of Jewish Toilers on the Land, to receive permission to relocate, you know." Regina did know that. She didn't tell Felix she'd been too terrified to stop by the government office in Moscow, lest her name show up on a forbidden-to-emigrate list. "I took care of it," Felix crowed. "You've received consent to stay in Birobidzhan and become a vital agricultural worker. I've arranged for you to board right here, so you needn't go scavenging for a spare room in town."

"How can I ever thank you for all this?" Regina asked Felix.

He smiled and kissed her on the cheek. "It's all arranged."

THE ROOM FELIX arranged for Regina was on the second floor of the barracks, at the far end of a corridor illuminated by intermittent light bulbs. Half were broken or missing. A trio of girls were already in residence, though since the chamber had no windows, Regina could only make out her new roommates in shadow. A pair of bunk beds were hammered into opposing walls, the span between them wide enough to pass through if you turned sideways. A petite redhead with a peeling, sunburned nose introduced herself, in accented Russian, as Marta, from Argentina. She directed Regina to what would be her bed—the top left one under a fist-sized hole in the roof through which spittles of grit drifted in on damp bursts of wind, leaving a permanent smear of black on the faded pillow. Then Marta asked; she couldn't believe it herself, "Can you imagine leaving the sunshine of Buenos Aires for this?"

Regina had never tried to imagine Buenos Aires under any circumstances. What was the point of imagining places you'd never go? The Soviet Union was the best country in the world, so travel was unnecessary. All Regina recalled about Argentina was that Cecilia had written in support of their seamstress' strike. And they were all Fascists there.

Marta pointed to the two other girls. The blonde, she explained, "is Agneska. She's from Poland." The brunette, "Georgetta from Romania." Back to Regina. "Where are you from?"

"Moscow."

"Moscow?" Marta's mouth stayed in the "oh" of the final vowel. "Why in the world would you leave the center of everywhere to come to the middle of nowhere?"

"Maybe because it wasn't sunny Argentina?" Regina offered.

Marta's lips stretched into a grin. "I like you."

Anything to make them accept her; though, again, Regina wasn't here to be liked, she was here to contribute. "So why in the world would you leave the sunshine of Buenos Aires for this?"

"I didn't," Marta defended, less offended than resigned. "My parents did. They had to pay KOMZET for the privilege, too; couple hundred dollars, American."

Regina blanched. Why was it, every time she felt she'd finally gotten a handle on how things worked, it felt like the ground was being ripped out from under her? "I didn't—I didn't know. I don't have..." Would they force her to go home if Regina couldn't pay her residency fee?

"Don't worry about it." Marta appeared sorry to have upset her. "It's for foreigners only. My parents sold everything they had, moved, paid the tariff on themselves, tried to survive a single winter out here, then died. One after the other."

Regina gasped. In the back of her mind she still had faith that, if matters got truly, truly unbearable here, she could run home to her parents, hide behind Mama and Papa, beg them to fix the mess she'd gotten herself into. She knew it was childish and unrealistic, and nothing like the strong, Socialist woman she expected herself to embody. But it was instinctive. Such an option being permanently unavailable to anyone seemed the saddest thing of all.

Yet Marta acted resigned to her tragedy, amused by it. "That was years ago. I got by. What I wouldn't give for a chance to see Moscow, though. For a chance to see anywhere other than this place!"

How ironic, Regina thought, this place was all she'd dreamt of seeing.

A bugle blaring insistently in the distance prompted Agneska and Georgetta to shuffle to their feet and head for the door, facial expressions unchanging, while Marta looked Regina up and down critically.

What had she done wrong now?

"You'll need clothes," Marta said.

Regina glanced down at her mud-soiled skirt, the blouse covered in ash, and indicated the suitcase she was still dragging behind her. "I brought a dress with me. Would that be better?"

"Not for working," Marta laughed. "Come on." She grasped Regina by the hand, dragging her out of the room.

They hurried down the staircase, past walls covered in brightly colored, professionally printed posters inviting residents to a lecture on "The Struggle Against Religion, The Struggle for Socialism," and another on "The Woman in the Front Ranks of Militant Atheists." Both had been pasted over an older spring offering on "The Class Nature of Passover."

Bodies streamed past on either side of Regina and Marta. Young women their own age, young men, older people. Regina had assumed the barracks were temporary boarding for newly arrived agricultural workers. The sight of couples ancient enough to be grandparents disoriented her. Shouldn't the elderly have moved on from fieldwork? Granted, the justification for Birobidzhan was to forge a Jewish connection to the land that never before existed. Hadn't Mikhail Kalinin, when sanctioning the JAR, said: *A large part of the Jewish population must be transformed into an economically stable, agriculturally compact group which should number at least hundreds of thousands?* Working with your hands was the noble profession, as opposed to the greedy shopkeepers and money lenders they'd been in the past. Tilling soil would allow the Jews to become true Soviets, to integrate into global proletariat society in a manner they, with their clannish, isolationist ways, had stubbornly refused to embrace.

Still, the idea of pensioners doing backbreaking work while younger citizens like Felix handled administrative tasks broadcast wrong to Regina. She chastised herself for thinking like the bourgeoisie who believed society owed them veneration due to years lived, rather than collective goals achieved. The old men and women Regina ignorantly pitied likely volunteered for their work as a way of atoning for past sins and glorifying the independent Jewish state, while Regina selfishly focused on abstract personal comfort over a common cause.

"This way." Marta yanked Regina out of the throng, into a side room on the first floor. A young man perched on a chair in front. When he spied Marta, he leapt up, drawing himself to full height at the same time as he tugged down on his shirttail, striving to look neater, handsomer.

Marta flashed him what Regina suspected was her brightest smile. She pointed to Regina. "New girl needs new things. Open up." A gentle hand on his shoulder, "Please, Leon?"

The boy blushed, averted his eyes, then fumbled inside his pants' pocket for a ring of keys. He selected the one in the middle, wriggling it into the door behind him.

"You're a dear." Marta kissed him on the cheek as she and Regina pranced by. Regina couldn't help thinking how much it reminded her of the kiss Felix had given her earlier.

The room Marta led Regina into was crammed with overflowing burlap sacks of clothes, some folded neatly, others wrinkled and tossed on the floor. An attempt had been made to sort by type— pants, shirts, skirts, coats, boots—but not by size or season. Without needing to take stock, Marta headed straight for the far corner. Using both hands, she dragged a dusty sack towards Regina, splitting it open at the top, rifling through. She pulled out a gray garment, held it by the collar and gave it two shakes, tossing it Regina's way. "Try this."

It was a pair of overalls with mismatched buttons, cut for a man, but hemmed at the cuffs, so the legs weren't too long.

"Who," Regina looked around the eclectic inventory, "do all of these belong to?"

"The glorious people," Marta intoned solemnly, then giggled. "The glorious people who snuck off in the middle of the night and didn't want to be weighed down, anyway."

"Why did they need to sneak off?"

"Because deserting is illegal. In the beginning, two-thirds of the migrants who came left within a year. They couldn't handle the cold, living underground in filthy *zemlinkas*, a muddy hole with some sod thrown over it; not that it did any good once the real rains came. My parents might have been some of the ones who turned back, if they hadn't died their first winter. JAR didn't used to stop you from leaving. But so many people did, the village Soviet thought it made us look bad. How could this be the Jewish homeland we'd yearned for, if Jews were fleeing it in droves, right? So nobody's allowed to leave without special permission. The desperate sneak away. Their things get confiscated for redistribution." Marta pointed to Leon standing guard. "There's a committee in charge. Clothing requests are supposed to go through them, make sure everyone only takes what they need. Especially us girls. You know how us girls are, so hungry for pretty things." Marta kicked a long-skirted frock that once might have been green, but now lay dotted with similarly colored mold. "Except the committee takes forever. They spend so long dithering whether you warrant a raincoat for fall storms that winter snows beat them to it. My way is more efficient."

Alina Adams

Seeing Leon anxiously peeking in to check if they were done, Marta blew him a kiss, then whispered to Regina, quoting Marx, "From each according to her ability, to each according to her needs. You need overalls, I have the ability to get them. Hurry up and put them on, they're about to take roll in the field. This, too." She tossed Regina a blouse to go underneath.

Regina did as she was directed, stuffing in first one leg, then the other, nearly tripping over herself as Marta hustled Regina from the room after a quick thank you wink to Leon.

Regina hurried to keep up with Marta, buttoning her overalls along her chest, down to the pasture, where she could see three dozen men and women gathering. Regina asked, genuinely baffled, "If it's so unlivable here, why does anyone stay? Besides the law?"

"Some think it's our last chance for a homeland. Suffering alongside your own people beats suffering among strangers. Or so the logic goes. And what's the alternative? Go back to where we came from and wait for a pogrom to wipe us out? Some of us have nowhere else to go. Besides, there are upsides to Birobidzhan." Marta appeared incapable of remaining down for long. Her eyebrows did a happy dance as she told Regina, "Wait till you get a look at the Adonis in charge of our hectare! Gives a girl something to fantasize about while you're up to your knees in mud and cow shit."

Though he couldn't have heard her—they were still too far away—at Marta's plaudits, said Adonis turned around, frowning their way, taking note of the tardy arrival.

It was—it could only be—Aaron Kramer.

Chapter Six

══════════

She'd been expecting it, of course. Aaron was the reason Felix had arranged for Regina to be assigned to this collective. Surprise wasn't what made her stumble as she ran, needing to grab Marta's hand to keep balance. Marta tittered like she knew exactly how Regina felt.

The night before, Aaron had sat hunched over. Regina hadn't seen him at his full height. Now she did. She could see he was tall. Well, no taller than the width of his shoulders suggested. Last night, she'd been distracted by them. Now she could see them in context. Last night his hair had been plastered to his head. While Regina had noted it was blond, the morning sun demonstrated that it was actually golden. His eyes were blue. Ocean blue, now she was paying closer attention. She'd also previously noticed the two dimples, the cleft chin. She'd seen it all before. And she'd nearly been taken in by all of it. Despite the heat, Regina shivered thinking how close she'd come to making yet another tragically misguided choice.

"You're late again." Aaron addressed Marta, somehow making his words sound less like a reprimand and more like concern. The same way he'd spoken to Regina the night before.

"Showing the new girl around." When Marta flirted with Leon, she did it with a natural ease that made the poor, besotted boy blush and Marta giggle. When she tried the same with Aaron, Marta was the one turning pink, stammering, wiping the sweaty palms on her thighs.

Aaron could have tallied her tardiness on the sheet of paper he was holding. Instead, he stuffed it, unmarked, into his overall's pocket, and turned to Regina. He smiled. Once again, the air around him appeared to shimmer, making everything in her peripheral vision fade away until that smile, those eyes, those damn dimples were all Regina could focus on. "You made it," Aaron said. "Congratulations."

He sounded as sincere as he had with Marta. Which was a good thing, too. Because it reminded Regina of two things. One, what Felix said about the besotted women of Birobidzhan. And two, how close Regina had come to becoming one of them. Last night, she'd been tempted to tell him everything. Because he'd appeared so darn sympathetic. Who knows what he might have done with the information? Used it to turn her in and protect himself? Used it to lure her—whether through charm or blackmail—into his own treasonous activities? Regina best remain on guard at all times. The suggestion of allyship could be used against her when the NKVD inevitably returned for Aaron's arrest. Same as with Cecilia in Moscow. Not again. Never again.

"Yes," Regina answered Aaron as coolly as possible, ignoring her heart as it trilled up and down her ribs like a xylophone. "Felix arranged everything."

Regina's message could not have been any clearer. She was under Felix's protection. Aaron should keep his distance.

She watched with what felt like disappointment yet she insisted on interpreting to herself as satisfaction, as Aaron's smile shrunk into itself, the warmth in his eyes curdling. He definitely received her message.

"Congratulations," Aaron repeated. "I'm glad you found what you were looking for." He glanced away from Regina, towards the assembled workers, clapping his hands over his head three times. "Let's get to work, comrades. There's rye to harvest!"

Each clap felt like a slap.

The men and women split into smaller batches, taking their assigned places along the flowering rows. Regina followed Marta, hoping she didn't look like too much of a newcomer. It necessitated all her self-control not to glance over her shoulder to check if Aaron was watching.

Marta showed Regina where to start picking.

Regina looked around, confused. "Where are the scythes?"

If she were honest, Regina would admit that, when Felix told her she'd be assigned to an agricultural detail, she'd harbored romantic fantasies of sweeping grandly through crops the way Tolstoy described it in his novels and short stories. A tiller of the land, a true worker among men. There may have been some folk-song humming.

"Don't have any," Aaron informed her as he moved among the stalks. If he were put out from Regina putting him in his place, he was hiding it beautifully. She'd morphed into just another worker to him. Regina told herself that fit in perfectly with her and Felix's plan. The less attention Aaron paid her, the less likely he was to notice her keeping tabs on him. Regina not standing out to Aaron in any way was a good thing. No matter what it might feel like. It was a well-established fact Regina's feelings were not to be trusted.

"What do you mean?" Regina realized questioning procedure her first morning on the job was hardly an optimal method for keeping a low profile except, no matter how insecure she felt about her personal decision making skills, she felt utterly confident in what she knew of proper Soviet agricultural practice. "Rye must be harvested with scythes. I learned it at university."

"We don't have any," he repeated, not a hint of frustration, merely amusement that she seemed unable to grasp what he was saying. "We weren't sent any from Moscow."

"Impossible. Narkomzem, the People's Commissariat for Agriculture, provides every collective with the precise tools they require to ensure success."

"They didn't."

Regina blinked, unsure of how to respond. Back at Cecilia's, political debates could go on for hours. Point, counterpoint, example, anecdote, political slogan, Lenin quote, Stalin quote, Marx quote, a parsing of what each word meant and how it could be interpreted to back up this particular claim. Regina found the entire process exhilarating, if also exhausting and, truth be told, rather unproductive. At the end, all that had been exchanged were words, not tangible actions. Listening to Cecilia had prepared Regina to go verbally toe to toe with anyone. Except a man who refused to engage. He'd given Regina nothing concrete to fight against. He obviously meant to have the last word.

Regina couldn't let him have the last word.

"Well, then." She struggled to recall what else she'd learned about harvesting rye during a painfully dull course. It consisted of reviewing how the USSR already had the most progressive farming system in the world and how everything was working exactly as decreed by the latest Five-Year Plan. Except they all weren't working hard enough. It wasn't the plan's fault they were failing to make quota. It was theirs. "What about pruning shears? Those can substitute."

"Weren't sent any of those either."

Facts. Regina was arguing ideas while Aaron insisted on clinging to facts. Was that how he was sabotaging their productivity? By trapping his workers in a dull, mundane, practical reality instead of motivating them with inspirational slogans? As long as they were forced to face what was rather than what could be, they'd never be moved to produce at the quota level required by the state. It was a most insidious form of obstruction. Devastating, yet impossible to prove. This man was more clever than Regina ever dreamed! She puffed up a bit, thinking Felix believed her capable of matching wits with him. She vowed not to let him down. And not merely because her own life depended on it. This was for the good of Birobidzhan!

"What do we have then?" Regina vowed to play his practicality game, while seeking out every opportunity to reverse the tide.

Aaron looked to Marta. She held out her hands. She reached for the stalk in front of her, wringing it like a chicken's neck, until she'd ripped it clean. Aaron handed Marta a sack into which she tossed her hard-won prize.

"One," Marta counted dully.

One? Regina looked up and down the stalks. There were thousands here. Cutting them one at a time posed a Sisyphean task. Was this the best they could do? She could recall neither Comrade Berger nor Kaminsky mentioning how primitive their harvesting methods were. They were supposed to be utilizing the latest scientific advances. They were supposed to be setting an example for the rest of the USSR with their forward thinking ways.

"Need cover?" Aaron turned away from Regina, then turned back, toting a tin bucket filled to the brim with a white, waxy substance the smell of which assaulted Regina's nostrils like the hammering needle of a sewing machine.

"Oh, yes, please!" Marta drew up her sleeves and bared her forearms, cocking her head to the side, neck exposed.

Aaron dipped his hand into the gummy liquid, smearing it generously over all of Marta's accessible flesh. When he got to her neck and face, Regina expected Marta to titter the way she had earlier, but her new friend grimaced and bore it stoically.

"What's that?" Regina wrinkled her nose from the odor.

"Chinese call it *zhangshu*," Aaron explained. "Extracted from the bark of the camphora tree. For keeping mosquitoes away. Want some?"

"Oh, no," Regina took a step back, not from the smell or the way her skin crawled and her stomach churned from looking at the sticky secretion, but because she recalled what Felix said about new arrivals listening to primitives who clung to their antiquated nostrums despite being shown the latest in scientific Soviet advances. And also because the thought of Aaron touching her the way he'd touched Marta was abhorrent. Felix said Aaron used his looks, his charms, and other underhanded methods to escape censure for his disloyal activities. Well, Regina would prove the exception. She wouldn't fall for his tricks. She would remain steadfast and true to the Socialist cause. She wouldn't allow Aaron to hoodwink her. Regina resolved that, whatever Aaron suggested, she would do the opposite. That would show him she wasn't like the others! (She'd figure out how to square her decision with the Soviet disapproval of individualism at another time.) Regina was convinced she could pull it off. As long as she never let him touch her, never permitted the tips of his fingers to graze her skin, not her ear, not her cheek, not the tender hollow at the base of her throat. Nowhere. Never.

"No," Regina repeated, determined Aaron would glean everything she'd just thought from how much passion she placed in the single word. "*Nyet.*"

Aaron moved on to the next worker eager to receive his ministrations.

Regina felt like she'd made her point. Aaron might choose to slow down their productivity by wasting time with his useless concoction. Regina had come to build an autonomous Jewish state. Which meant getting to work without any sham delay tactics. She turned to the looming stalks of rye. Without slicing instruments, Regina was forced to use her hands. She wrapped both around as dense a bundle as would fit, grit her teeth, steadied her spine, and tugged. Her palms burned as they slid upward despite Regina's efforts to keep them steady and not shake loose precious seeds. It took her multiple tries to understand she had two choices: She could go for volume and rip her hands to shreds but get more done, or she could proceed practically one thistle at a time, which hurt less, but yielded hardly any grain. Regina understood it was her duty to harvest as much as possible, regardless of personal comfort. It was those who refused to do their share who caused famine and other shortages. She wouldn't become a shirker. Yet, she'd barely been at work an hour before Regina could no longer prevent her thoughts from drifting towards how she could get out of this. Her palms bubbled with blisters, her eyes watered from the merciless sun, her calves throbbed from the effort of dragging them through gelatinous mud. Insects feasted on her cheeks, the back of her neck, inside her ears. She tried shaking her head to wag them loose. That made her light-headed, and only worked seconds at a time. She tried raising her arm to swipe at her face with the inside of her elbow. That meant loosening her grip on the rye. She tried swaying to make herself a moving target. That looked ridiculous. She felt certain Aaron was laughing at her. Though, when she dared sneak a peek, he wasn't looking anywhere in her direction.

This was all his fault. He was getting back at her, punishing Regina for not swooning at his flirtation the way other women inevitably must. Or maybe it was the first time he'd laid eyes on her, he'd decided Regina wasn't tough enough for this life, she couldn't be a heroic pioneer, not like him. He likely expected her to burst into tears from the pain, faint from the heat, go running back first to the barracks, then all the way back to Moscow, humbled and humiliated.

Regina decided she would never give him the satisfaction of driving—or seeing—her in anything less than a confident state. She would never admit defeat. Because Regina was a patriot committed to building the world's first Communist nation.

And because it would annoy Aaron.

To that end, when he passed her row, asking if Regina wanted a break, without so much as turning around, she blithely dismissed, "Don't need one."

Regina wished she could have seen what she knew had to be disappointment and frustration on his face.

"Need a break?" Aaron repeated, and Regina was about to snap, ready to ask why he hadn't heard her the first time, when Marta piped up, "Thanks, yes!" and stepped away from the crop to collapse a few meters away, gulping water from the dipper attached to a metal bucket. Aaron stepped in to assume her place, snatching up Marta's sack and proceeding to fill it. When Marta returned to her post a few minutes later with a grateful smile, Aaron moved one position down, tapping the next person out for a rest, while he picked up where they'd left off.

It took Regina a full day of watching closely—while pretending to be doing no such thing—to confirm that while everyone else got periodic breathers, Aaron had toiled non-stop.

"HE'S DOING IT to show off, isn't he?" Regina cross-examined Marta as they dragged themselves back uphill towards the barracks. When the workday had finally concluded, Regina didn't expect she'd have the strength to so much as recall her own name, much less make it back to her bunk without resorting to crawling. Yet, somehow, getting out of Aaron's hearing range seemed to have imbued her with a second wind. "To make the rest of us look like we aren't doing our share?" Regina persisted.

She understood she was being un-Soviet, accusing a comrade of having ulterior motives in giving his all for the cause. And she risked Marta reporting her for the infraction. Especially if she was on Aaron's side. But his behavior made no sense. As Head, he wasn't required to do anything beyond ensure the rest of them were working. He wasn't obligated to join in. This had to be part of the larger plot Felix had sent her to suss out.

"If we don't meet our quota for the day," Marta said, "we won't meet it for the week. If we don't meet it for the week, no way will we meet it for the year before the serious rains start. If our yield is short, we all lose food rations for the winter. The only way to stay on course is if Aaron picks, too, then lets us take turns going on break. Otherwise, too many workers get sick and collapse, and then we don't have enough to bring in the quota." Marta made circular motions with her hand to demonstrate how it was a never-ending wheel. "It's why NKVD didn't remove him when they came for Kaminsky and the rest. Aaron is the only one whose group regularly meets quotas."

No, that wasn't right. How could Aaron be undermining the JAR if his cohort was their most productive? Was he somehow obstructing other cohorts? Impairing their progress while making himself appear blameless and irreplaceable? Regina had judged him clever before. Now she believed Aaron downright diabolical. It would be a pleasure to expose him—for the common good, of course. It was the solitary pleasure Regina could imagine in the same breath as Aaron.

Regina, Marta, and the rest had made it back to the barracks. As they ascended to their floor, Marta pointed out various people and whispered in Regina's ear, "He's the senior Party member. Anything he wants you to do, he quotes Lenin, Stalin, or Marx. They love their quotes here! Don't ever correct him—he'll make you read a textbook to prove he was right. And if he wasn't, he'll claim you're the one who got it wrong... Over there, she's who girls go to if they get in trouble. Got potions, sometimes she doesn't need to bring out the needles if you get to her early... That guy works as a cook at the workers' *stolovaya*. He can sneak you extra dinner, as long as you don't mind letting his hands go wherever… Her, you do your best to stay away from. Every *samokritika*, she's first up with a list of any infraction you committed, real or imagined."

Regina stared at the woman Marta hurried them past. She looked utterly unexceptional, wearing the same grey shift dress as the rest, her thinning brown hair tied back with a *kasenka*, hands rough and chapped. She didn't lift her feet when she walked. She shuffled them to keep from stepping out of galoshes several sizes too big. The woman Marta advised Regina to avoid looked no different than the ones who knew where to get extra rations, or contraband medicine, or make-up, or maybe a forbidden book.

Moving down the hall toward their room, Regina caught glimpses through the partially open doors of other accommodations. None of the boxes had windows. All featured wooden roofs and slatted floors. Regina spied carpets, some handwoven after taking apart scarves or hats, others purchased from department stores, remnants of a past life. She saw beds occupied by singles, by couples, and by families, mothers, fathers, children, elderly. She noticed buckets for water, buckets for human waste, and buckets for bringing up coal to feed tiny corner stoves, the walls, floor, and people around them covered in a fine, black dust.

"You either freeze," Marta said once they'd finally made it to their room, "or you cough. I prefer to freeze. We have so many choices here. Shame none of them are good."

THE MEANING OF Marta's words sunk in fully for Regina as she lay on her bunk that night. Her shoulder muscles tightened until they were squeezing her neck. Her eyes and nose dripped from spores still wedged there. The parts of her that had been exposed to the bugs itched. The parts that had been covered by clothing chafed, rubbed raw by sweat-coarsened fabric. If she scratched a mosquito bite, her nails ripped skin, leaving crescent-shaped crimson trails. If she resisted scratching, she squirmed.

Regina refused to accept what Marta had said about there being no good choices. There had to be a solution. If there was one thing Regina had learned from listening to the all-night debates at Cecilia's salon, it was that all questions had answers. All breaks had fixes. Intelligent people were bound to eventually conceive of them, if they thought hard enough.

The next day, Regina attempted to cover more of her flesh, pulling up her collar until it shielded her back, rolling down her shirt sleeves, using a rag she'd ripped from the bottom of the skirt she'd arrived in to obscure most of her face and ears so only Regina's eyes showed.

She overheated before the sun was fully up in the sky. She felt like a horse with blinders on. Her breath came so quickly it was either tear off the mask or hyperventilate.

The day after, Regina went in the opposite direction. She rolled up her overall's legs and her shirt's sleeves, covering her skin in mud, gambling the insects wouldn't be able to penetrate. What she didn't gamble on was the sludge sliding down her arms and shins within minutes of being applied, moistening her fingers until she had trouble clasping the rye, dripping into her shoes, settling around her toes and heels as a turgid mass.

Aaron must think her insane.

Not that Regina cared what Aaron thought.

He still came to ask her if she needed a break. She did. The work was too grueling, the food inadequately nutritive—semolina porridge for breakfast, boiled with water, not milk, getting rid of flavor and protein; coarse bread for dinner in the field, along with salted fish, bones calcified to where they were impossible to pry out of flesh, yet managed to break loose inside mouths; and for supper, a ground vegetable stew tasting of cans the turnips and carrots came in.

Regina took her break in turn with everyone else now, plopping onto the ground, sipping her allocated water, stretching her arms over her head, flexing and unflexing her fingers, rolling her neck, and sending her mind into the future, where Birobidzhan was, at long last, the Eden Comrade Berger had prematurely described. Where the earth was rich and fertile, where they grew all the grain they needed and had enough left over to feed the chicks, cows, ducks, and pigs (there would definitely be pigs; no obsolescent dietary superstitions would be humored in a socialist Jewish state!) that would provide their meat and milk—which they would certainly mix together. Fruit trees would bloom and grant them shade. They'd have the most modern farming equipment. Insects would be exorcised.

The one thing Regina had yet to do was avail herself of the slop Aaron distributed at the start of every workday. She viewed her capitulation to this final thing as her capitulation to all things. If she accepted that the optimal way to protect herself was to coat her skin in smelly wax the color of the dead, then Regina would also have to accept that the Birobidzhan she'd arrived in was not the Birobidzhan she'd been promised. That either Cecilia had been lied to, or she'd lied to Regina. That the fault was not of a single seditious man, like Aaron or Kaminsky, but all of them, for believing they could will their dream into existence. Either way, Regina was a fool.

She was alone on the edge of the world. No parents to turn to. Her only friend, whom Regina was pathetically grateful for, was in a worse state than Regina. Marta couldn't even dream of going home. Her parents had exchanged their Argentinian passports for Birobidzhan residency. Worst of all, Regina hadn't heard from Felix since he'd had registered her for work. Had he already forgotten her? Was she as foolish to count on him as she once had on Cecilia? Was Regina destined to spend her life always betting on the wrong horse?

She was famished. Her hands shook from exhaustion. Her skin blazed, no longer from individual gadfly bites, but as one red, lacerated, throbbing pulse. She could barely move, could barely speak, her cheeks were so inflamed. Which was the moment when, almost a week after she'd first arrived, Aaron stepped in front of her with his salve.

As always, he didn't pressure. He merely paused before Regina and waited for her verdict. Their eyes met. Where she'd been expecting judgement, she saw compassion. And that was what finally broke her. She could have resisted judgement. Judgement might have given her the jolt of ire she needed to dismiss him, the way she'd dismissed him every other day. Compassion, she had no defense for.

When had she last seen compassion? Mama and Papa, when saying goodbye to their only child, had made it clear this was Regina's fault. She would reap what she'd sown. Felix had offered Regina hospitality and affirmation. Marta offered friendship and commiseration. But Aaron was looking at her with the same compassion she'd first spotted when he'd talked about the deported Korean families. It was because of that, not because she was giving up—Regina wasn't ready to go that far yet, this was a small aberration in her behavior—but because of the compassion she saw in his eyes, that Regina cocked her head the way she'd seen others do, and exposed her neck, face, and arms to Aaron's care.

He expressed no surprise or conceit. If he was tempted to smirk, 'I told you so,' he gave no indication of it. He started with Regina's throat. A simple swipe from her chin down into the hollow of her collarbones. It was discreet, restorative, dispassionate.

The first brush instantly cooled Regina's skin.

He made a mirror image pass, then moved onto her face. Forehead first, brushing aside her bangs. Then across her nose. Her left cheek, her right. Her chin.

With a single finger, he traced the line below Regina's lips, then the one above it.

She couldn't imagine what she looked like.

She couldn't understand what she felt like.

Her skin was no longer on fire.

Unfortunately, everything else seemed to be.

Chapter Seven

She closed her eyes. Every fiber, muscle, and tendon in Regina's body yearned to lean in, the way it had that first night in the rain, when she'd assured herself it was merely the warmth he was emanating that drew her. If Regina were honest, she'd admit it was Aaron's compassion which pulled her. She sensed that this was a man you could tell anything, confess your darkest secrets to. He wouldn't judge, and he wouldn't castigate. He would listen. And sympathize. And forgive. It was the most dangerous thought Regina could conceive herself having. Because it was the kind of thought that could lead to her doing all of the above.

Felix told Regina that Aaron was an enemy of the people. Given access to her darkest secrets, he could destroy her life. If he so much as suspected what she was wanted for...

As unexpectedly as she'd yielded to him, Regina jerked away, sliding out of Aaron's ministering grasp, the leftover salve dripping impotently between them, sinking into the earth.

He frowned. "Did I hurt you?"

She shook her head, terrified that cracking open her lips would cause her teeth to chatter. She couldn't let Aaron see. She couldn't let him know what an effect he had on her. He'd take advantage. He'd be a fool not to. She'd be a fool to grant him any opportunity.

"I'm fine," Regina insisted, wrestling with her tongue as well as her timbre. No quiver, no crack, nothing to contradict her words. "Thank you."

Aaron didn't press further, moving on to the next person requiring his aid. Regina wanted to exhale. She found she couldn't breathe.

"Silly girl." Marta sidled up, giggling, covering her mouth with her palm as she whispered, "The objective is to keep his hands on you as long as possible."

Regina ignored her. Maybe, if she ignored Marta, she could also ignore the sensations coursing through her. Maybe if she focused on her outer discomfort, the sticky salve, the insect bites, the heat, she could press down the inner turmoil, like swallowing a hand grenade.

Regina refused to make eye contact with anyone for the remainder of the work day. It was too dangerous. They might see right through her! How could so many conflicting emotions possibly leave her face unmarked? Regina spurned her water breaks, keeping her head down, tugging at the rye as if each stalk she wrenched from the ground was one more brick in the wall she was building around herself.

It wasn't until they were all dragging themselves back to the barracks that Regina felt Marta's hand resting on her shoulder, and turned to hear her say, "It gets easier, honestly. The mosquitoes are much less a bother in the winter. And your muscles get used to the work until it hardly hurts at all. Also, calluses." She turned her hands, palms up.

Regina bobbed her head to make it clear she heard Marta's words, and she appreciated them. If only the tears welling beneath her lashes could have been for the physical discomforts.

They were about to head upstairs, Marta offering, "I can loan you a cloth to wrap around your neck, that helps with the sun and flies," when the elderly woman who monitored everyone's comings and goings rose from her chair and waddled Regina's way.

"Message for you!" Delighted to be the bearer of unprecedented news. Her otherwise sullen demeanor suggested it would take a great deal to make this woman delighted. Marta looked shocked. And concerned. It took a great deal to make Marta concerned, too.

"You are to report," the matron began. Regina's heartbeat plummeted into her galoshes. Had any sentence ever ended well after such a beginning? They'd found her. They'd come for her. Someone had talked. Who? Aaron? Felix? Marta? Regina's head swiveled, looking for an escape and wondering whom to blame. "Report to Felix Davidovitch's home for supper at eighteen hours tonight." The matron surveyed Regina's sweat-stained clothes and balsam encrusted flesh. "You should clean up, first."

REGINA HURRIEDLY SCRUBBED her face, neck, and arms with the tepid water that had been sitting in the bucket at the corner of their room since that morning, collecting soot and ash while they were out, then sifted the surface with her fingers to make an unsoiled spot. She found it restorative to use her nails to scrape off the remnants of the day, and all the sense memories that came with it, leaving the scraps on the floor, using the side of her foot to nudge them through a crack in the wall. The bigger question was what Regina had to put on over her nearly cleansed skin. Not her overalls and work shirt. The other outfit she owned was the skirt and blouse she'd arrived in. They'd been washed by the rain, dried by Felix's stove, and lain folded under her bed ever since. They smelled of sweat and mold, but she didn't have much choice in the matter.

Regina rubbed at the creases with her hands, futilely attempting to smooth them out into invisibility, and unfastened her no cleaner hair from the braid she wound around her head during the work day. She set out on the walk to Felix's home feeling more than seeing the curious eyes watching her go forth. She wondered if Aaron's were among them. He deserved to glimpse her neither waterlogged nor sunbaked. She deserved it.

Regina followed the road Felix had taken when driving her to the fields, recognizing the barracks which became lean-tos, which became permanent housing, the further away she got from the crops and the factory. She knocked on his door, expecting to see Chunhua. Instead, it was Felix himself. He wore a crisp, white shirt, and tan slacks. It had been so long since Regina had seen anyone wearing anything besides laundered grey, she'd forgotten clothes could come in an assortment of colors.

"You're here! Wonderful!" Felix exclaimed. He turned to a couple who'd come up behind him, the woman wearing a purple dress with tiny pearls down the front, the man in dark pants and yet another blindingly white shirt. "Here she is, the young lady I've been raving to you about. Regina, these are James and Barbara Cohen. From Boston. In the United States," he added, "the state of Massachusetts."

Did he think Regina didn't know where Boston, Massachusetts was? Hadn't he called her more educated than the average Birobidzhan immigrant? Regina tried not to take offense as she shook the husband's hand, then the wife's. They purred her greetings in Russian more heavily accented than Felix's. Regina wondered if they were new arrivals. Would they be opting for field or factory work? She had a hard time imagining them participating in either.

Felix slipped his arm through hers and escorted Regina to the dining room table, followed by the Cohens. She spied Chunhua diligently setting out sterling silver forks, knives and spoons. The aroma hit Regina first. It'd been so long since she'd smelled food not produced in bulk, her body responded before her mind. Like Pavlov's dog, Regina gulped to force down the tides of saliva filling her mouth as her stomach clenched, shrinking upon itself to fill the emptiness, then expanding in anticipation of, at long last, being filled. A tureen of steaming soup stood on the table, chicken stuffed kreplach bobbing along the surface in coronas of fat you could skim straight off the top, next to a platter of fried potatoes sprinkled with dill, and a side of meat roasted so thoroughly it crumbled into buttery soft folds. Regina fought her urge to charge the table, grab at the offering with her hands and shove each course indiscriminately into her mouth, not bothering to sit. Her legs shook. Regina grasped the back of a chair to keep from collapsing, and smiled weakly toward Chunhua in a combination of apology for her uncouth impulses and gratitude for the feast she'd wrought. Felix's housekeeper deliberately avoided Regina's eyes, finishing her task and melting back into the kitchen, a sign the guests could take their seats.

Felix gently pried Regina's fingers from the chair and gallantly pulled it out for her. She settled with a nod of thanks, clasping her hands between her knees, lest her compulsions overwhelm her and she follow through with the urge to blindly dive into their meal.

Felix took a seat at the head of the table, with James and Barbara Cohen across from Regina. He said, "I realize my invitation said supper, but I'm afraid old habits die hard for us American expats. We prefer our heaviest meal at the end of the day. I hope you don't mind."

Regina shook her head, afraid if she so much as took her eyes off the table for a second, it would disappear to the same place where all dreams went come sun up.

"We're so proud of you," Barbara cooed. Regina thought she was complimenting her self-control, before Mrs. Cohen went on, as Chunhua materialized in time to ladle out the soup, "You didn't fall for the propaganda about America being the land where streets are paved with gold and made the correct decision to immigrate to Birobidzhan, instead."

"All nonsense," her husband confirmed. "Americans tout their freedom of the press, as if freedom to spread lies is superior to printing only appropriate facts so citizens aren't confused by conflicting opinions. They claim to print the truth about others, yet never print the truth about themselves. They write how all men are created equal! Hypocrites! Not only does that exclude women, you should know how they treat our people in America. Ban us from their clubs, their universities, jobs, neighborhoods."

Regina nodded in sympathy, clutching her spoon and dipping it into her plate at the same rate as everyone else, sipping politely rather than downing the burning liquid in one gulp, ignoring the scalding of her tongue in exchange for letting its warmth radiate down the length of her legs and to the tips of her fingers, surreptitiously eyeing the tureen, wondering if there'd be enough for seconds, attempting to formulate a request that wouldn't sound greedy.

"Tell her about the coloreds," Felix urged, prompting a delighted smile from Barbara.

"It's absolutely terrible," she trilled. "You've heard about slavery, even they couldn't keep a travesty of that level quiet. What they've done to those poor savages since is worse. Locking them up in filthy, crime-ridden ghettos. Our former cleaning woman used to travel over an hour on three buses to come to work! The government won't lift a finger to teach them how to better themselves. Without examples of how to behave properly, what chance do any of them have?"

"And it isn't just our side of the country," James chimed in. "Over on the West Coast, they passed the Chinese Exclusion Act to keep the Orientals from coming and taking jobs from Americans."

"They do lower wages," his wife murmured, stymied by how to reconcile her ire with the compulsion to protect the working class by limiting employment competition.

"The fat cats can afford to pay everyone an equal wage," her husband dismissed. They'd clearly had this argument before. "Look what we accomplished in the USSR. A job for absolutely everyone. Man, woman, Jew, Oriental. All equal."

Chunhua discreetly removed their soup bowls and spoons in anticipation of the second course. Regina wistfully watched the still half-full tureen disappear into the kitchen.

"I wouldn't say we were all equal here," Felix countered, a sly look on his face. When the Cohens turned to him in shock, he burst out laughing, unwilling to continue his cruel joke. "Here, the worker is the most important, most exalted, most honored person."

Barbara and James chortled in relief, followed by cries of, "Of course, of course."

"It's the exact opposite in America," Felix enlightened Regina. "Those who labor are pressed to the bottom of society, worked past the breaking point, then discarded once they are no longer useful to the capitalist machine, while those who produce nothing live it up at the top. Mansions, servants, automobiles."

"We got rid of all those things once we made the commitment to relocate to Birobidzhan," Barbara advised. "Our friends were shocked when we refused to hoard our wealth like they did, pass it all onto our son. Why, we might as well have kept it under our mattress, for all the good it would do to the greater world, there."

"We distributed it equally among our son, our daughter, and our grandchildren," James beamed. "College funds for our boys and our girls. Can you imagine a system where a smart young woman like you is banned from top universities simply due to her gender? That's what it's like in America. Harvard for boys, Radcliffe for girls! Separate but equal, they call it. We couldn't stand living in such an oppressive place for another moment."

"We should have made the move sooner," Barbara sighed. "When we were still young like Felix. When we could have contributed more, the way you are, Regina."

"We are so proud of you," James repeated, "and so grateful. Felix told us about what you're doing to protect this land we all love so much."

Regina paused mid-chew to look questioningly at Felix.

"James and Barbara know about Kramer. They were as shocked as I when the NKVD failed to arrest him alongside Kaminsky and the others. They are equally as terrified as to what that miscreant might do to sabotage our good work here."

Regina wondered if now would be a good time to bring up her question about how, if Aaron was working to undermine them, his collective was the most productive? She opted to fill her mouth with potato, instead. Asking a question risked her bringing up a topic they'd chosen to ignore, either deliberately or accidentally. Keeping quiet, she'd learned too late but was making up for lost time, was always the safest option.

"You must be wondering why we spend so much time talking about America," James ventured, "when it's our past."

"It's because we're worried about the future," Barbara tacked on. "Birobidzhan is at such a delicate, critical juncture. The idea that our hard work could be wiped away due to the actions of a few malcontents, well, it's devastating, as you can imagine."

"It's so different from how it used to be," Felix sighed. "In the beginning, all of us who came to build an independent Jewish homeland, we were dedicated to the same goal, the same cause. But then, when we were required to accept everyone..."

"Of course, a true Jewish state must be open to all Jews."

"Of course, of course." Felix raised his hands to indicate she'd be getting no argument from him. "But if they aren't truly committed to our vision of what it should be…"

"Like the religious ones," James sighed, "they contribute so little, and take so much."

"And the ones who won't listen, won't learn, no matter how hard we struggle to enlighten them. Stubborn superstition, pig-headed prejudice, they simply relocated it from the shtetl to Amurzet. How can we build the new, Socialist man, when who knows how many citizens are still clinging to their old ways? If it was up to them, they'd have us shirking our patriotic duty all Saturday to mumble prayers, and commence each meal by thanking some imaginary Creator instead of the workers who made it possible! Would you believe we have a thriving black market here? We provide them with absolutely everything, and still, for the ungrateful, it's not enough. They steal, they sell, they trade, they speculate! If we lower our guard for a second, they'll turn it into another America. And then all will be for nothing."

Regina put down her fork. Her appetite wasn't exactly lost. But it was dampened.

"Can that happen?" Her voice barely rose above a whisper.

"It's already happening, I'm afraid. Kramer is just the beginning. Every day, he turns more citizens against their homeland."

"A house divided against itself cannot stand." A Marx quote Regina wasn't familiar with.

"It's why we're so happy to have you as our line of defense." Barbara reached across the table to clasp Regina's hand. "You are a godsend."

"Before you," Felix said, "we had no one to keep us apprised of what was being whispered in the fields and barracks. Well, no one we could trust to not put their own interests ahead of what's best for Birobidzhan. We received regular reports, but those were Kaminsky's people. We couldn't trust them to not still be on his side."

Regina blinked in surprise, clarifying, "You asked me to keep an eye on Aaron…"

"And anyone Aaron speaks to. How could we chart his negative influence, otherwise?"

"You want me to watch… everybody?"

"You're the only one we trust to do the job ."

She appreciated the compliment. Self-confidence had been in rather short supply lately, so the boost of faith couldn't have come at a better time.

Sensing her hesitation, Felix added, "We are asking you to report on those who are doing something wrong, not those who are behaving properly."

"Those who are against us."

"Enemies determined to bring Birobidzhan down."

"We can't risk the rise of another America and all the oppression that comes with it."

"We can't risk losing everything we've worked for."

"Where would the people who have no other safe haven go then?"

"People like you," Felix suggested.

Chapter Eight

＝＝＝＝＝

Her roommates were long asleep by the time Regina returned from Felix's, which was a relief. Regina had no doubt Marta would want every detail of the evening, and Regina wasn't yet sure how to express it in words to herself, much less to anyone else. Felix, James and Barbara had been clear: For the good of Birobidzhan, for the good of the Jewish people, for the good of those who'd given up everything, uprooted themselves and took the plunge, settling on the edge of the world to take part in something greater than themselves, and for the good of those tragic souls who had no safe home to return to, it was Regina's duty to help them unearth those who were secretly plotting against it. A massive burden to rest on a pair of already quite exhausted shoulders. And yet, wasn't it exactly what Regina deserved?

For far too long, she'd talked the talk of looking out for the welfare of others—it was all anyone in Cecilia's salons talked about. They told themselves everything they said and wrote was for a higher purpose. Ultimately, that was all they did. Talked. Wrote. Here, Regina was truly contributing to the building of the JAR. And Felix was offering her the opportunity to contribute more. He was offering her the chance to protect future young women from Regina's fate. The fate of listening to the wrong person, of accidentally ending up on the wrong side of orthodoxy, evicted from their lives in order to outrun the consequences. He was offering her the chance to be truly useful. To make up for her past sins. Why was she wavering?

She was wavering because Felix wanted Regina to report on her comrades, on her co-workers, on her friends.

Well, not exactly. Felix wanted Regina to report on those who sought to undermine Birobidzhan. Which meant they weren't her comrades, and they certainly weren't her friends. The people Felix was asking Regina to betray were those who had already betrayed them. Which made her reporting on them not a betrayal at all, but a patriotic duty.

Those who'd done nothing wrong had nothing to fear. Except that's what Regina had thought about herself in Moscow. She shook her head to dismiss the false equivalency. Her experience was irrelevant. That had been an error. A fortunate one, in retrospect. Now Regina knew what it was like to stand falsely accused, she would take greater care to never make a false accusation herself. Another reason why she was the perfect person for this job: If she didn't do it, someone else would. And they might not be as meticulous about it. Not that Regina wished to cast aspersions on a fellow citizen, or suggest she was a cut above. She was simply more aware. It was a matter of sympathy, not any sort of innate, cultural, or ethnic superiority. Not that Regina sympathized with law-breakers. Only those who had been wrongly targeted. Which Regina would never do.

Her head hurt.

Likely too much rich food after a prolonged absence.

She'd better get to sleep. It was critical to know exactly when to stop thinking.

REGINA PEELED HER eyes open the next morning, awakened for the first time in weeks not by the hunger clawing her stomach, but by the bustle of bodies moving about the room, getting dressed. Outside their door, dozens more rushed through the hallway and down the stairs in order to be first in the dining hall. Agneska, Georgetta, and

Marta were ready for work. Regina scrambled to catch up, pulling on her field clothes, cringing anew from how rough they felt compared to the civilian fare she'd donned the night before. The evening had been a brief glimpse at how life used to be. At how—though Regina knew it was morally wrong to think so—it should be. No, she corrected herself, it was a glimpse at how life *could* be, as soon as they got Birobidzhan fully up on its feet, and all citizens could enjoy the fruits of their labors equally. For now, they'd have to keep working. The harder they worked, the sooner that day of true Socialism would arrive for everyone.

Regina opened her mouth to bid good-morning to Marta. She couldn't wait to fill her in on meeting the Cohens. Marta was always eager for any settlement gossip, especially about the exotic Americans. But Marta blew by so quickly, Regina never got the chance to say anything. That was strange. Her friend usually preferred to linger until the very last minute. It's why Aaron regularly chastised her about being late to work—even if he never quite got around to putting her on report. Regina resolved to ask Marta about it once they were harvesting side by side. If there was one thing endless hours of monotonous physical labor were good for, it was chatting.

Yet, when Regina reported to her designated spot in the field, Marta wasn't at her side. Regina assumed she was late again—though she did wonder where Marta went when she left their room early. She glanced around, expecting to see her friend rushing down the hill like always. Instead, she spotted her across the stalks, talking to Aaron. He stood with his head cocked, listening. Marta made a request and, after a moment, Aaron shrugged and gestured for her to go ahead. Marta assumed her new harvesting spot, which was as far as possible from Regina, while still remaining within the same hectare.

How odd. Regina felt lost for a reaction. Her first instinct was not to take it personally. Not everything was about her. The sooner she broke herself of such bourgeois thinking, the better. Then again, how could this not be about her? Marta ignored Regina this morning, then requested to be assigned to work away from her. Who else could this be about? The only other explanation was that Regina had completely misinterpreted her relationship with Marta. What if what she'd taken as overtures of friendship was merely token politeness? It wouldn't be the first time someone Regina considered a friend had turned on her. She thought of Cecilia… she thought of Kaminsky.

Worse, what if what Regina had taken as overtures of friendship was merely Marta feeling Regina out, seeing what usefulness she could get out of her, and, when she realized that answer was: nothing much, losing interest?

Either way, the fault was, once again, Regina's, for making snap judgments which lead to heartbreak. The day before she'd been counting Marta as her only friend in Amurzet, using the knowledge to paper over her loneliness. Now her illusions were shattered. She was more alone than she'd previously feared.

Except for Felix. His name bubbled into Regina's consciousness at the same moment she caught sight of him striding down the field, to the point where she wasn't sure which came first, her seeing him, or her conjuring him up via her thoughts. In any case, he was a welcome manifestation, a reminder that maybe she wasn't as alone as she'd been mourning.

Felix made a beeline for Aaron, barking instructions and waving his arm in the workers' direction. Aaron frowned and attempted to protest. Felix overruled. He pressed the sides of his hands to his mouth and attempted to make some sort of announcement. When no one paid any attention, he glared accusingly at Aaron. Aaron slightly raised his voice and called everybody over. Regina couldn't recall another time when everyone stopped work simultaneously. Hadn't Marta said they needed to pick constantly in order to make their quota?

She told herself Felix knew what he was doing. If he didn't, he would be in the fields with them—or in jail with Kaminsky—instead of the village Soviet. Regina could take a lesson.

She followed her coworkers to surround Felix in a semi-circle, instinctively rooting out a spot next to Marta in the hope… Marta saw Regina coming and took a deliberate step to the side. Regina swallowed and cast her eyes down at the ground, knowing she was at fault even if she didn't know exactly why.

"I have wonderful news," Felix said, attempting to stand on his toes so the missive would appear to come from on high. "Due to Amurzet's unprecedented success in meeting our production quotas, Lazar Kaganovitch, Secretary of the Central Committee, Commissar of Communications, the most powerful Jew in the Soviet Union," Regina wondered if that was the man's official name, "has elevated his support for our cooperative by predicting we shall double our yield next season!"

Predicted? Was that another way of saying required? Was it another way of saying expected? They were working themselves to exhaustion to meet state-mandated requirements now. How in the world could they be required or expected to double it without also doubling their workforce, not to mention their allotment of land?

A pause, then a smattering of applause which quickly grew into an ovation. Being late to commence cheering was a smaller offense than failing to join in. And neither was as bad as being the first to stop.

As if unaware of his transgression, Aaron began speaking. He didn't yell. He wasn't even as loud as he'd been when calling them all over. Nonetheless, it suffocated the cheering, which trailed off as the crowd glanced nervously from side to side, checking whether their neighbors were doing the same before letting their hands drop to their sides.

"Impossible," Aaron said flatly. "We don't have the manpower, or the seed."

"Those will come. Moscow will send us any supplies we need."

"We are still waiting for scythes. Or at least pruning shears." Was it Regina's imagination or did Aaron look her way when he said the words? And all but winked.

"The People's Commissariat for Agriculture assures we have received all the equipment we require."

Aaron felt no need to comment on that. Instead, he proposed, "If Narkomzem," he called the Commissariat by its acronym, "requires us to amend our practices, the prudent thing to do is repurpose half our rye fields to planting corn. We'll improve soil quality, prevent erosion, diversify our food supply."

"Ridiculous!" Felix barely waited for Aaron to complete his pitch. "Can you not do basic math, Kramer? You're talking about cutting our main cash crop in half to roll the dice on a chimera. If your corn withers, we'll end up with starvation rye rations for the winter. And if it poisons our rye along with it, we will be left with nothing at all."

"If you don't rotate your crops, you'll end up with a smaller yield every year."

"Yes," Felix chortled, "and exercising every day leads to poorer health. Practice does not make perfect. My goodness, man, learn some proper science." He indicated the bucket of salve by Aaron's feet. "Your *muzhik* alchemy will be the death of us all."

Aaron was right. Regina knew he was right. They'd studied such scenarios at University. It was imperative to plant different crops in rotation in order to refresh nutrients in the soil and interrupt pest and disease cycles before they took root. If she spoke up and said so, Felix would be furious at her disloyalty. Regina couldn't afford to lose her last remaining ally.

So, instead, Regina did what was expected of her. Quickly, before somebody else had the same idea and stole her thunder, not to mention the political capital that came with it, Regina pushed her way to the front of the watching crowd, took her place next to an intrigued Felix, and, raising a fist in the air, boldly shouted, "Thank you, Lazar Kaganovitch, Secretary of the Central Committee, Commissar of Communications, the most powerful Jew in the Soviet Union," she didn't dare leave out any honorific which might be considered indispensable, "for your support of our cooperative! We shall reward your faith in us and double our yield next season! And thank you, Felix Luria, our glorious village Soviet, for leading and inspiring us to this achievement!"

The applause was instantaneous and pronounced. It commenced before Regina started speaking and built in intensity, followed by cheers and foot-stomping and cries of, "Glory to the Union of Soviet Socialist Republics!" and "Long live Comrade Stalin!" Each worker tried to outdo their neighbor, slapping their palms together louder, raising their voices higher. Felix beamed at Regina, lifting his arm in solidarity and pointing at the horizon in a deliberate echo of the artworks glorifying Vladimir Lenin giving his stirring speeches at the barricades, in lecture halls, and, yes, like them, in the fields among his proudly toiling laborers. Regina noticed Marta was clapping as enthusiastically as everyone else, grinning and looking Regina's way for the first time that day.

Maybe this was all Regina needed. Maybe Marta was angry with her because, last night, Regina had expressed dissatisfaction with her lot here in Birobidzhan. She'd dismissed Marta's kind attempts to bolster her spirits. Regina didn't blame Marta for feeling offended. Regina was behaving like the spoiled, provincial, illiberal reactionary she'd recently been. Regina was acting as if her material comforts were more important than the common good, as if pursuit of Socialist ideals was only worthwhile if it didn't inconvenience Regina! What selfishness! What arrogance! What... what... what individualism! Regina's cheeks burned with shame as her hopes soared that she'd finally unearthed the action that would allow her to fully integrate into the Amurzet fold. That would allow her to be accepted, even, dare she say it, embraced?

Marta was clapping for her. Felix was beaming. Regina's comrades were cheering.

The only one doing none of those things was Aaron.

As those around him scrambled to demonstrate themselves the most enthusiastic, Aaron neither clapped, nor cheered. And he certainly didn't beam. He ignored the mob the same way he ignored Felix. His attention was focused on Regina. Even with his gaze set on her, she couldn't discern his expression. She'd expected disappointment or condemnation. Contempt.

She'd expected to see Aaron thinking she was the worst.

Instead, what Regina couldn't help thinking she saw was his conviction that she could do better.

Chapter Nine

She liked it.

Regina could tell herself she was proud of her collective, proud of her role in inspiring her comrades to greater heights, proud to be building the first autonomous Jewish region, proud to be serving the Union of Soviet Socialist Republics in whatever capacity was asked of her. Truth was, she liked the clapping. She liked the cheering. She liked—Aaron aside—the support and acceptance and, yes, veneration she'd received. After weeks of feeling like a fool, a cuckold, a simpleton, and, worst of all, a criminal, it made for a nice change of pace.

Regina preferred to keep it going.

Felix had given Regina a warm look before bidding them farewell, climbing in his GAZ-A and driving away, shouting a final, motivational, "Each new agricultural cooperative plays its part in guaranteeing the improvement of peasant life!"

More importantly, Marta finished out her work day at her new location, but, when it came time to return to the barracks, she walked alongside Regina, telling her, "You did good today."

Yes. Regina felt she had.

"I expect Comrade Luria will offer you a commendation at tonight's meeting."

Tonight was Amurzet's voluntary convention, where citizens communally evaluated past output, made plans for future production, entertained new proposals, and dealt with infractions. It would be Regina's first such cooperative gathering since arriving over a month ago. Attendance was mandatory.

"There is no need to single out any individual." Regina modestly quoted Comrade Stalin, "*Courage consists in being strong enough to master and overcome oneself and subordinate one's will to the will of the collective higher party body.*"

As Regina was already planning how she would make her mark tonight.

For the common good, of course.

Regina had thought it through carefully. Her key objective was to confirm what a useful, productive and loyal member of the community she was. And if that happened to lead to some spontaneous cheering, so be it. She also needed to prove to Felix she was completely on board with his vision for the future of Amurzet, and she was committed to weeding out any miscreant who felt differently. In addition she would like for Marta to be her friend again.

And then there was Aaron.

Regina had nothing to prove to Aaron. She certainly wasn't on board with his vision for Amurzet—whatever it may be. And she didn't care whether or not he was her friend.

And yet, there was a problem. When it came to next season's planting strategy, Aaron was right, and Felix was wrong.

Regina couldn't come right out and say so. Not if she wanted to achieve her other goals. She did want to help Amerzut in any way she could. She had a plan. She just needed to select the right moment to present it. Based on her decision making record up to this point, that would be easier said—or thought—than done. Yet, Regina was determined to give it a shot. For the common good. What other reason could there be? It wasn't as if she cared what Aaron thought of her…

To that end, she resolved to spend the bulk of the meeting listening to what others had to say. After all, how obnoxious would it be for her to burst into her very first cooperative forum and attempt to take it over? Even if she was particularly proud of her idea for improvement, one that would satisfy multiple parties simultaneously.

Regina followed Marta into the packed hall built specifically for such gatherings. The rest of the time it sat idle. It had been decreed that letting smaller groups meet in such a spacious room while others were shunted off to smaller ones was anti-Soviet. A table stood against the far wall, behind which sat Felix, as head of the village Soviet. To his left were one man and one woman. To his right sat two more women. Regina beamed with pride. She couldn't help thinking how happy Cecilia would have been, seeing such gender equality in action. Regina quickly shut down her pleasure, lest so much as thinking about an enemy of the state might express itself on her face and be taken as a sign of antisocial behavior.

She and Marta took seats to the side of the crowd. There must have been three hundred people in the room, and the smell of so many unwashed bodies packed shoulder to shoulder in the heat of late summer made being within breathing distance of an open window a premium.

Regina didn't look around for Aaron. She was simply surveying the crowd, searching for familiar faces to nod hello to. She spotted Aaron at the back of the hall. He wasn't even sitting. He was leaning against a wall, arms crossed along his chest. She expected him to attempt to stare Felix down. Instead, Aaron lowered his chin, studying the floor; the effort of pretending to engage was beneath him.

Regina should have been feeling morally superior. Look at that disrespectful show of blatant individualism! He was a disgrace, an embarrassment to the entire JAR! But what she primarily felt was instinctive fear. Did Aaron not understand what kind of danger he was putting himself in by flaunting such outlaw behavior?

Her staring at him—no, not at him, in his direction; what did he expect, standing so close to the hall's entrance?—prompted Aaron to glance up and catch Regina's eye. She expected to see anger, contempt, defiance, smug superiority. What she got was a repeat of the same look Aaron had offered her earlier in the fields.

She could do better than this.

Felix called the meeting to order. Marta tugged on Regina's sleeve, urging her to turn and take her seat. She caught sight of where Regina had been looking. Last time, she'd giggled. This time, she frowned. Regina wasn't sure how to interpret the shift. She sat down, still confused.

Felix cleared his throat. The room quieted down immediately. Regina was impressed. In Cecilia's salon, getting even one person to stop speaking long enough to lend an ear could be an extended affair. "You know what they say, two Jews, three opinions," Comrade Berger had joked. That didn't seem to be the case, here. Here, everyone was already in agreement. Regina could see how that would make governing much easier, not to mention daily life a great deal more peaceful. Marx had been right in this, as in much else. Separating Jews from their money-hungry habits and resettling them to work the land could break them of their very worst ethnic characteristics.

The first order of business was last season's agricultural quotas. Everyone agreed, with a democratic show of hands, that they had been met.

The next order of business was next season's agricultural quotas. Everyone agreed, with a democratic show of hands, that there would be no trouble meeting them.

Each vote was followed by a raucous round of applause.

With that settled, Felix announced it was time to move on to *samokritika*. If it was possible for an already quiet room to grow quieter, then that's what happened. Not so much as a cough, not so much as a sigh, not so much as the scrape of a chair or a creak of a latch. Even the furniture had gone silent. Regina feared moving her head to look around and see how other people were reacting, lest a squeak of her neck be interpreted as a desire to speak up.

Felix did not appear perturbed by the lack of response. He leaned back in his chair, fingers linked and resting on his chest, patiently waiting, confident no one would rise to leave before he gave them permission, and thus having all the time in the world.

A minute ticked by. Five minutes. Ten. By fifteen, the stench in the room had gone up considerably, palatable anxiety adding to the sweat of heat and toil. Still, no one spoke. No one moved. Three hundred pairs of eyes studied their nails, their palms, the floor. The tension kept building. Felix kept waiting. It felt like the ceiling was slowly being lowered, brushing the tips of their heads, pressing them to slouch, crushing their chests into their knees. Regina had fled to Birobidzhan vowing to protect her secrets at all costs. Yet, under such circumstances, the urge to confess was nearly unbearable.

A man sprung from his seat. Regina recognized him from her cohort, and her heart clenched. Was he rising to admit to infractions of his own—or to accuse someone else? Others must have thought the same, because a gasp of air went up—and refused to exhale, especially among those he worked or lived with.

"Kaminsky," he said.

A slight murmur. Was he about to accuse a man already judged guilty? It was one way to contribute without implicating anybody else.

"Kaminsky and I, we passed many an evening together, playing chess." That, as far as Regina could see, wasn't a crime. "And talking." That, definitely could be. Regina expected Felix to ask the man what they'd talked about. The village Soviet continued reclining in his chair, encouraging the silence to be filled by not rushing to do so himself. The man cleared his throat. He took off his cap, then reconsidered and put it back on again. He said, "Once in a while, Comrade Kaminsky would say he did not believe Amerzut was capable of meeting the production quotes we'd been set."

Regina expected cries of objection, hisses of derision, at least a vexed murmur or two. The room remained as silent as ever. Everyone was waiting to see what the person next to them did first. And the person next to them was waiting for Felix.

Still no word from their leader. Just the endless, empty silence.

"And I... I... I did not..."

Felix leaned forward, newly interested. Everyone in the room grew equally interested.

"I did not... challenge him. I did not correct him. And I did not report him."

A sharp intake of collective breath. That last one was the true offense.

"You knew you were in the wrong, Comrade." It wasn't a question.

"Yes, of course. Of course, I knew."

"So why did you not report him?"

"Because… I thought… he was the village Soviet. He knew best."

"Better than the Central Committee which set our quotas?"

"Yes… no." The speaker looked around desperately, seeking guidance as to what the correct answer might be. Not a single soul dared glance in his direction. And not a single soul dared look away, lest they be accused of indifference to such an important topic. Not caring about the correct opinion was even worse than voicing an opposing one.

"Better than the Birobidzhan Council which determines which cooperative settlement will be responsible for which appropriation?"

"No," he said, more firmly this time, having made up his mind.

"So you thought you knew better than those appointed to their positions?"

"No!"

Felix nodded. His fellow executive committee members followed suit. So did the majority of those listening. Regina felt her head moving up and down of its own accord.

"You were correct to confess."

"I confessed," the man repeated. "I stepped forward of my own volition."

"Duly noted." Felix stood, and the assembly promptly straightened up in their chairs. "All decisions in the Soviet Union, in Birobidzhan, in Amerzut are made democratically. I would like to see a unanimous vote. All those in favor of overlooking our Comrade's unfortunate lapse in judgement in light of his coming to confess voluntarily, raise your hand. Remember, it cannot be true Socialism unless we are all in agreement on the issue."

Regina moved to lift hers, when Marta grabbed her by the wrist and pinned it to Regina's thigh. She gave an almost imperceptible shake of the head, and mouthed, "Not yet."

No one else had raised theirs. No one else had so much as moved.

Not until Felix lifted his. Followed by the other four members of the Soviet. Followed, near instantaneously, by everyone else. Some knocked down the hands of the person next to them to make it seem like they'd been quicker to approve.

The man under discussion nearly burst into tears. He collapsed in his chair, shaking, whimpering, "Thank you. Thank you, Comrades, for your generosity. I swear, I will never falter again. Never again. Thank you. Thank you."

Felix sat back down. He folded his hands in front of him on the table. In a tone utterly ignorant of the tension which had filled not only the hall but the chest of everyone in it, he asked, "Any further business?"

Regina's hand flew up, as Marta recoiled. Regina had been waiting for this moment since Felix had called the meeting to order. She'd been planning it for even longer.

"Yes, Comrade?" Felix looked surprised, also intrigued.

Regina stood up awkwardly, not sure how to address Felix and the audience. Mama had taught her never to turn her back on anyone while speaking. She'd said it was common and rude. Cecilia, on the other hand, had teased Regina about her middle class affectations. Where you looked when you spoke didn't matter. Only what you had to say.

Regina raised her voice, projecting in the confident way she'd learned from Cecilia. She had to pretend to be her. If she remained herself, she'd barely get a syllable out. "This afternoon, Comrade Luria paid us the great compliment of increasing our rye production quotas for next year. We are honored by the confidence the Central Committee has invested in us. To prove their faith was not misplaced, I propose we not only raise our yields of rye for next season, but take advantage of our steadfast workforce by planting a winter crop." Regina paused to see how Felix was responding to her submission. He'd raised his linked fingers so they were underneath his chin. He was listening. And didn't seem upset. Emboldened, Regina went on, "If we plant rye in the fall and harvest it in the summer, then we will have manpower to plant potatoes and beets in the spring and harvest them in the winter. This will greatly increase our food supply without needing to add more workers. We could plant this new crop in the fields adjacent to our current output." While it wasn't as good as rotating crops, it was still helpful when it came to the issues Aaron had brought up earlier.

Regina didn't say that part out loud. She hoped Aaron heard it, nonetheless. She didn't dare turn her head to seek out his reaction.

"A brilliant suggestion," Felix exclaimed. Which was good. Only his reaction mattered.

This was instantly followed by a round of applause.

Regina expected he'd like it. Her suggestion allowed Felix to make Amerzut the most productive settlement in Birobidzhan, without needing to depend on Aaron, or follow his advice.

"No."

The denial shot over the clapping, halting it cold. Aaron said, "Harvesting potatoes and beets in winter is possible, but their yield isn't worth the labor required. If you want to plant root vegetables, you pause the rye for a year, and plant in its place."

"Again with this nonsense!" Felix had remained calm through the previous proceedings, but Aaron worked his last nerve. "Was I not clear with you before? I will not risk this settlement starving. Our comrade has come up with a brilliant plan which will benefit every citizen. Yet, you cannot let go of your stubborn, foolish, *individualistic* pride to admit she has succeeded where you've failed!"

Unlike Felix, who was turning a shade of crimson akin to the flag they all rallied under, Aaron appeared unperturbed. He was still where Regina had last seen him, leaning against the wall by the door. The difference was he was no longer studying the floor. Then again, he wasn't looking at Felix, either. Aaron was ignoring the village Soviet entirely as he addressed the people they were there to serve.

"Comrade Luria is asking you to spend not only your spring, summer, and autumn in the fields, but your winter, too. All so you might harvest enough to barely feed those assembled here tonight. That's assuming we'd be allowed to keep what we grew, instead of sending it to Moscow for redistribution."

Regina couldn't believe what she was hearing. Did he not understand all the effort she'd put into coming up with a plan that gave him and Felix what they wanted? Felix would get to take credit for their becoming the highest producing settlement, without needing to ask for extra labor or supplies. And Aaron would get the rotating crops he advocated for. It wouldn't be exactly what he'd recommended, but it would be closer—and better—than doing nothing.

Felix said, "All in favor of putting in a winter potato and beet crop, raise your hands."

Every palm dutifully went up, Regina's first and foremost.

"We need the vote to be unanimous," Felix reminded.

Regina raised her arm higher, lest it had gone uncounted. Others did the same.

They weren't the problem. Aaron was the problem. He stood as he was, arms still crossed, his facial expression not exactly defiant, more resigned.

"A true dictatorship of the people," Felix reminded, "requires everyone to be in complete agreement. Anything else is individualism."

Multiple heads turned Aaron's way, Regina's among them. She knew she wasn't the only one looking at him. So why did it feel like she was the only one he was looking back at?

What was wrong with the man? Did he not understand that what she suggested was for the good of Birobidzhan? For the good of all of them? Did he not understand what she was trying to do... for him?

The thought came to Regina, unbidden. She knew it was the wrong thought. She was putting one person ahead of the collective. And not just any one person. The one she'd been warned about. Regina was trying to help Aaron when she should be helping herself. She needed this proposal to pass. She needed to stay in Felix's good graces. She'd been a fool to include a provision for Aaron in her plan. She had no idea what possessed her to do so! He might be the one to sink it all!

Her arm grew sore from remaining in the air. Many of her fellow citizens were old enough to be Regina's grandparents. She saw them using their opposing palms to prop up their elbows and keep their hands up. Yet no one dared lower them.

"We shall stay here," Felix declared, "until the yes vote of everybody in the hall has made it unanimous."

"Please," Regina mouthed in Aaron's direction. She thought she was begging him for his sake, for the sake of everyone, for her sake. Why then, did it feel like so much more?

Alina Adams

He saw her plea.

He did not raise his hand.

Instead, arms still languid by his sides, Aaron pushed himself off the wall with his foot, and passed through the door, pausing on the stoop to turn and grant Felix, "It's unanimous."

Chapter Ten

———

"The gall of that man, the unmitigated gall!" Adjourning the meeting, Felix stomped out of the hall, triggering an exodus from the rest. He waited outside, grabbing Regina by the hand as she was leaving with Marta. Her friend immediately drew back and faded into the shadows.

"Do you see?" Felix demanded when he and Regina were alone. "Do you see what I mean? Son of a bitch won't rest until he has destroyed everything we are working to build!"

Regina bit her lip to keep from responding. That wasn't precisely what she'd seen. What she'd seen was a man giving his sincere opinion about what would be best for their collective. Then, when he was dismissed, he withdrew from the vote so the rest of them wouldn't be forced to perch for who knew how long, afraid to lower their arms no matter how badly they might begin cramping, until the tally was unanimous. It seemed to Regina he'd done the proper thing.

Good she knew what her opinion was worth.

"You saw what he was doing? You saw how he was trying to turn the people against me? If we are to have true socialism, we must have complete agreement on all issues. Otherwise, it's bedlam, like in America. Everyone doing what is best for them, instead of what is best for the group. This is how it starts, believe me, I've seen it. Even among socialists in America, there is dissent. Which is why revolution utterly failed there. All energy is spent on fighting each other, instead of on fighting the actual, capitalist enemy. It's why free speech is the first amendment in their constitution, you know. The plutocrats who wrote it, they understood its power. They knew the minute you allow any rabble with the ability to lift a pen or utter a sound to have their say, that's when a revolutionary movement falls apart. It was deviously clever of them. We won't fall for it here. We are an authentic democracy. We proceed with one hundred percent cooperation. No tyranny of the majority in the USSR! All speak as one. Which is why men like Kramer need to be silenced. Today he is the single opposition, tomorrow there will be more of them. And then what? Then nothing will get done. We will be paralyzed, incapacitated. We'll lose our settlement, we'll starve, be thrown on the mercy of the Cossacks who have slaughtered us for decades. It's what he wants. It's what all who refuse to cooperate want. Our utter and complete destruction."

"I KNOW WHAT you did," Aaron said.

Regina froze. No more frightening words could ever be uttered in the Soviet Union. Once someone knew what you did, they had two options. They could report you, or they could use the threat of it to make you work for them. Regina wasn't sure which she feared more. Especially considering who the words were coming from.

Once again, Marta had hurried off to work without Regina. She'd thought they were on good terms again. Apparently not. Regina vowed to get to the bottom of what was going on with her friend sooner rather than later. For now, Marta's early departure meant Regina was left to make her way to the fields alone—until Aaron joined her.

He matched Regina step for step, walking an arm's length beside her, hands in his pockets, shoulders low, the picture of nonchalance. Regina, conversely, had tensed up to the point of rounding her shoulders until they nearly brushed her ears, hugging herself, a palm on each elbow, as she attempted to speed up without making it appear she was rushing ahead of him. She told herself it was because of what Aaron had said, instead of his mere proximity.

"You tried to help me." In another place, at another time, that might have been a compliment. Here, now, Regina heard a threat. "I've tried it before. Compromising. Luria isn't that sort of man. If it's not his idea, it can't be correct."

"He wants what's best for Amerzut." Regina said what she needed to.

"He doesn't know anything about farming. He learned from books."

"I studied agriculture at University! Our USSR has developed the most progressive techniques in order to produce maximum yields!"

"Then why isn't it working?"

"It is! Our rye quota for next year has been doubled, that proves it!"

Aaron said, "The soil here can't take it. And the weather isn't optimal for root vegetables, like you suggested. There's a reason the Chinese and Koreans prefer to grow soybeans."

"There's a reason they're gone," Regina snapped back. "And, for the record, I did not try to help you. I made a proposal of what would be best for us all."

Aaron nodded, as if he agreed with her. How could he possibly agree with her? She stood for everything he was against. Didn't she? Regina felt so confused she no longer knew what she truly believed versus what she was supposed to believe versus what she had no right to believe. All she knew was agreeing with Felix would protect her. Agreeing with Aaron would expose her. In more ways than one.

He said, "You did the right thing. That took a lot of bravery."

Which left Regina more confused than ever.

"ARE YOU ANGRY with me?" Regina had to wait until they were back in their room before asking Marta, Agneska, and Georgetta, too. The others may not have been as friendly as Marta from the start, but they'd also recently become more distant.

"No," Agneska said.

"Of course not," Georgetta echoed.

"Why would you say that?" Marta wondered.

The answers tripped one over the other in their swiftness.

Regina hadn't expected such an onslaught of denial, leaving her to stutter, "I thought, maybe, because of what I said at the meeting…"

"Everyone liked what you said," Agneska insisted.

"Your motion was approved unanimously," Georgetta reminded.

Marta, Regina noticed, didn't say anything.

So Regina addressed her when she prodded, "It'll mean we'll have to work more, and in the winter, outdoors." She was arguing Aaron's points.

"It will be wonderful to have more food. Not be afraid of going hungry. We are not angry with you," Marta said, "we are grateful for your proposal."

Agneska and Georgetta nodded with great enthusiasm.

Their agreement was also unanimous.

"SO TELL ME, what are they whispering about in the fields?"

Regina and Felix were sitting in two chairs drawn close to the stove for warmth. He'd invited her to dinner once again, this time to meet Comrade Klara, Felix's Number Two in the village Soviet, the woman who sat to his right during all meetings. Klara, Felix explained, had been delighted with Regina's participation the other night. Coming from Germany, she'd been disappointed by the quality of immigrants Birobidzhan was attracting. Instead of intellectuals capable of building up the artistic and cultural output of the JAR, they were being inundated with illiterate, Yiddish speaking peasants. Regina was such a pleasant change!

After Klara left, Regina felt compelled to defend her comrades to Felix. "They are very enthusiastic about my proposal to plant winter root vegetables. So happy there will be more food to eat."

"All of them are enthusiastic?" Felix wondered. "Even Comrade Kramer?" When Regina didn't answer immediately, he advised, "You were seen speaking privately with him."

With all the confidence she could muster, Regina replied, "He was attempting to lure me to his side." At least, that's what Regina assumed he'd been doing. Why else be so kind to her? "I thought it best to play along. See what I could learn about what he was planning."

"And what did you learn?"

An excellent question. Nothing Felix didn't already know. And that obviously wasn't yet enough to have Aaron arrested and banished from Birobidzhan permanently. A development Regina told herself she was most looking forward to.

"He disparaged Soviet science. He said Koreans and Chinese understood how to work this land better than those who learned about agriculture from books. Like me," Regina added, to keep Felix from figuring out that Aaron had actually been talking about him.

"Thank you," Felix said. This time, when he walked Regina to the door, instead of kissing her on the cheek, he offered a quick peck on the lips, and a smile. "You've been very helpful."

AT THE NEXT monthly gathering, Regina vowed to remain silent. She'd caused enough trouble at the previous one. Regina didn't want to come off as monopolizing the discussion, especially since she was still relatively new to the JAR. Despite her roommates insisting they were not angry with her in the slightest, Regina couldn't help feeling like they were keeping their distance from her. And everyone else in the village was following suit.

Regina told herself not to be so sensitive, not to mention self-absorbed. The citizens of Amerzut had a great deal more on their minds than her feeling welcome. She should spend less time thinking about her individual feelings being hurt, and more on how she could better fit in with the collective. That onus was on her. Which was why, this time, Regina resolved to merely sit quietly and listen. She obviously still had a great deal to learn about how things worked here.

Felix, once again, called the meeting to order. From his side, Klara flashed Regina a warm smile. Regina smiled back, then quickly stifled it. She didn't want anyone thinking she was receiving any sort of special treatment.

They went quickly through the production reports, each field supervisor boasting about how they'd exceeded quotas this month, and expected to do better the next. When it was Aaron's turn, he merely provided the numbers. No embellishments, no grandiose praise of either his workers—or the wonderful leaders who'd inspired them to such heights. He also added, "The rainy season is coming. We won't be able to continue at this rate much longer."

Felix ignored the comment. It did make Regina wonder, though. If Aaron, who even Felix admitted had the highest producing hectare in Amerzut, didn't think he'd be able to stay on track once the rains came, how could the other field supervisors promise differently? Surely, it didn't only rain on Aaron? Regina knew Felix, like every village Soviet across the USSR, sent his predicted yield numbers to Moscow, so they could plan redistribution to all for the coming year. *From each according to his ability, to each according to his needs.* But if the field supervisors' numbers were inflated, then Felix's numbers were inflated. If that was happening across the country, in hundreds and thousands of collectives like theirs, how could the Central Committee assemble an accurate picture of how much food would ultimately be available so they could ensure precise allocation?

Felix ignored Aaron's warning. Instead, he moved aside the sheet of paper he'd been taking notes on and announced it was time for new business. The *samokritika* session would begin. Did anyone have anything they wished to confess?

Silence again. Not so much as a throat clearing or a foot shuffling, lest that be seen as an admission of guilt. A minute ticked by on the clock. Two. Three.

At five, Felix announced, "It has been brought to my attention that some members of our community don't believe we offer them enough food."

Regina's head jerked up. Surely, Felix wasn't referring to her telling him Georgetta, Agneska, and Marta approved of her proposal to plant more because that would mean more to eat? She'd meant it as an example of how complimentary they were. Why was Felix twisting their words into a criticism?

"Would those members care to stand up and identify themselves?"

There wasn't a mad rush to do so. Regina felt her cheeks turning a brighter and brighter scarlet. Anyone looking her way would be able to tell this was her doing. They'd never believe she hadn't meant it to happen. Regina didn't dare look at her roommates. Not if it meant seeing the inevitable betrayal in their eyes.

"It was me." The voice that spoke up didn't belong to Marta, Agneska, or Georgetta. It was a voice Regina had never heard before. "I did it." An elderly woman, her cheeks so sunk in Regina could see the missing teeth along her lower gums, rose with great difficulty.

"You're dissatisfied with what the state provides for you?" Felix asked, almost politely.

"We're hungry," the woman blurted out.

"So why do you not work harder?" He sounded so reasonable, so helpful.

"My husband went to his grave, digging in your fields. How much harder can we work?"

"My fields?" Now, confusion was the order of the day. "These are our fields. The effort we put in is the crop we take out. Are you suggesting the workers of Amerzut are slacking? Are you accusing us of deliberately starving you?"

"There's never enough to eat," she insisted stubbornly.

"Because of you!" Felix's voice unexpectedly jumped twenty decibels, and Regina's heart along with it. He'd gone from calm to irate in the blink of an eye. "You are faulting us for your own failure. You are saying we don't provide for the people, when it is the people's job to provide. Any lack can be traced back to those who complain of it. If you saw, why did you not step in to fix it? And if you did not step in to fix it, then you are the one who caused it!"

Felix's turning the accusation back on the person who'd cited it, unleashed a floodgate of pent up emotion from his audience. A half dozen more people leaped from their seats, shouting they'd witnessed the woman deliberately hoarding food for her own use, they'd seen her husband doing the same; he hadn't died, as she claimed, working in the fields, but sneaking out of town to sell his stolen wares. The chorus of voices was quickly joined by others, pointing their fingers at a new crop of wrongdoers. *He* was deliberately slowing down work, claiming back pain! *She* complained about being asked to haul water from the well, using pregnancy, a natural and healthy condition expected of all loyal women, as an excuse! *Those* children failed a history exam, willfully rejecting the education of the state!

As the voices grew louder and louder, Regina attempted to shrink herself smaller and smaller. She could barely understand what was happening. She only understood that the blame lay with her.

EVERYONE HATED HER. The day following the *samokritika* session, Regina believed it was true. No amount of reminders that such self-pity was self-centered, self-absorbed and not the Soviet way could dissuade her. Every time she turned around, Regina was saying or doing something to cause a communal disruption. If she'd been a long-term resident of Amerzut, she'd hate the newly arrived trouble-maker, too. She wouldn't blame them if they voted to expel her from Birobidzhan. Felix wouldn't be able to deny the will of the people. That is, if Felix didn't hate her too. Last month, she'd been the cause of him almost not being able to get a unanimous vote. What an embarrassment that would have been! This month, her innocent comment had led him to believe there were dissenters in his midst, when Regina meant no such thing. How was Felix supposed to curate accurate intelligence on what was happening in his settlement if Regina couldn't convey information properly?

She couldn't risk losing Felix's favor. She couldn't risk being deported back to Moscow. She would need to change the hearts and minds of those who begrudged her presence.

And Regina could think of only one way to do that.

Chapter Eleven

Regina needed to convince her detractors she was not a source of disruption, but a productive and useful member of the collective. As Comrade Marx wrote: *It will be the workers, with their courage, resolution and self-sacrifice, who will be responsible for achieving victory.*

Felix presented her with a golden opportunity when he opened their subsequent meeting with the words, "We all want Birobidzhan to be better. The way to make Birobidzhan better is to make ourselves better. The purpose of *samokritika* is to confess what is keeping us back from becoming the ideal citizens the Union of Soviet Socialist Republic demands. Our words not only purge ourselves, they are an inspiration for others. The success of Birobidzhan depends on all citizens speaking with one voice, thinking with one mind, living with one purpose. We cannot reach the same destination, if we embark on different paths. Opposition is obstruction. Dissent is disruption. Individuality is insurgency."

He wasn't yelling. Felix spoke in a low, soothing voice. Regina already agreed with all he had to say. Even if she hadn't, this speech would have convinced her. A boat could never move forward if all on board were rowing in different directions. If one bad apple ruined the bunch, then what sort of damage could one dissenter do in a community? They lived on such a fine margin, if just one comrade slowed down their work and didn't pull their weight, it could plunge them all into starvation. Didn't the collective deserve to know who among them might be harboring plans to hinder the harvest? Of course, they had to know about it ahead of time. What good did it do to learn about the undermining after the fact? Innocent until proven guilty may have been fine for Americans, who already starved their workers and hoarded the spoils of production. They could fight it out, dog eat dog style, among the elite. In the USSR, where everyone was entitled to their fair share of resources, it was up to citizens to make sure everyone contributed equally, and to punish those who shirked their duties.

The words were barely out of Felix's mouth before a young man popped up from his seat to declare, "This is my second season in Amerzut and, as the weather grows rainier, I have found myself questioning the wisdom of establishing a Jewish Autonomous Region in such inhospitable weather conditions. Please forgive me."

He was followed immediately by a girl Regina's age, admitting, "I am jealous that some live in houses while others are relegated to sharing barracks, when I should be grateful for the JAR providing me with a roof over my head and food to eat."

Others quickly followed suit:

"I complained about no days off during the planting season, when I know the earth takes no days off, why should we?"

"I failed to keep a comrade from abandoning the JAR."

"I was accidentally served a second helping of soup and did not draw attention to the error, taking more than my share."

"My daughter was friendly with a Korean boy, and I did not report it."

"My mother says we were better off before we came here!"

The *samokritika* went on and on, one admission triggering another until it became a contest of who could abnegate themselves more. Regina wanted to join. She wasn't perfect. She could stand to confess her crimes against the state and become a better person for it. And yet, despite the hysteria whipping around her, she held back.

The reason for it was the same as Regina's would-be disclosure: She wanted people to like her.

It was a terrible, individualistic, non-Socialist, selfish objective. Still, Regina wanted Felix to like her. She wanted her roommates to like her. She wanted her comrades to like her. And she wanted Aaron to like her.

That last was the most galling. And the most embarrassing. Regina told herself what she meant was she wanted to obtain Aaron's trust and respect so she could best understand his intentions and convey any troubling ones to Felix. The truth, when she dared admit it to herself, was she simply wanted Aaron to like her. Especially after she'd gone out of her way to try and implement his agriculture proposal. Without making it look like that's what she was doing. She hadn't expected gratitude. Though gratitude would have been nice. So would acknowledgement. But she'd expected some kind of response. Beyond shooting her down. She knew her proposal wasn't as good as his. But it wasn't as bad as Felix's. Shouldn't that count for something?

Her next suggestion, Regina decided, would do the trick. It would prove to everyone how invested she was in Birobidzhan's successful future. And it would impress Aaron, too.

Regina waited for Felix to open the floor to new business before she raised her hand and stood up, conscious of being the center of attention, aware she was enjoying it though she knew she shouldn't. She said, "When I was at University in Moscow," she put that in to make herself sound important, though she knew she shouldn't, "we studied the work of Trofim Lysenko. With Comrade Stalin, they have modernized Soviet agriculture along the principles of Marxism. As a Socialist environment shapes a man, it shapes animals and plants. Comrade Lysenko advises we put seeds into freezing water. In this manner, they grow accustomed to the cold and can be planted at any time of the year. Furthermore, seeds produced from that first, cold-resistant crop, retain the memory of their forebears, and don't need to be treated again in order to continue the successful pattern. Following his philosophies, Comrade Lysenko promises we will soon be able to group any crop anywhere, even oranges in Siberia!"

"Nonsense." A voice boomed from the back. Regina didn't need to turn to know who it was. "Such logic is the equivalent of saying stabbing a woman in the eye causes her to give birth to a blind child."

"Comrade Kramer." Felix smiled at the interruption. "You are an expert in genetics? You purport to know more than the USSR's top agronomist?"

"I know what happened when his theories were implemented in the Ukraine."

The Holodomor, again. Regina remembered what Felix told her months ago about Aaron using lies regarding how that famine came about to discredit any policy he disagreed with.

"So you, like the American scientist, Hermann Mueller, believe our lives are run by utter random, natural selection? You deny the Marxist-Leninist principle of revolutionary biologic development? Mr. Mueller and his fruit flies were graciously invited to defend themselves at the Leningrad Institute of Genetics. He was sent packing in disgrace after Comrade Lysenko proved his Darwinism to be capitalist, imperialist fascism. The West deliberately pushes their false theory of gradual change to keep the USSR from out-producing them and demonstrating the superiority of our Soviet system. We know evolution can be manipulated to create a superior result. We can do it with man, we can do it with animal, we can certainly do it with seed."

You can't do it with Aaron, Regina thought. She believed in science. She believed in Comrade Lysenko. She believed in Felix. She believed in Marxism. She believed you could make summer crops grow in the winter, even oranges in Siberia, and she believed they were in the process of creating the ideal Socialist man. But she did not believe Aaron Kramer could be turned into anything he didn't want to be.

It was an absolutely terrifying thought. What if there were more Aaron Kramers out there? The Soviet Union couldn't achieve its Socialist goals without every citizen agreeing to them—like they couldn't pass any measure unless the vote was unanimous, it would be undemocratic. Unbending men like Aaron Kramer would be the death of the USSR.

And yet, through her terror, Regina couldn't help thinking that unbending men like Aaron Kramer would also be the ones to save them.

Which made no sense at all.

"Let's take a vote!" Felix announced like his exchange with Aaron had never happened.

Something else which made no sense at all: Aaron's hand was the first one up.

"Why would he do that?" Regina asked later as she helped Felix and Klara finalize the list of those who had spoken at the *samokritika*, so that they might be disciplined.

"Because he knew he was beaten," Felix proclaimed.

Regina would have liked to believe that was true. It would have made everything simple. Except she knew their situation was anything but.

"WHAT ARE YOU doing?" Regina hissed, whispering though she and Aaron were the only ones in the storehouse this late at night. They were to begin planting their scientifically treated seeds the following morning. After the unanimous vote to go forward with her proposal, Felix appointed Regina to lead the effort. She'd demurred, asking if maybe this wasn't a job for an agricultural expert, not someone who'd had less than a year of schooling. Felix explained that so-called experts were stuck in the reactionary past. A revolutionary land needed revolutionary thinkers, whose minds were untethered to the teachings of bourgeois scholars like Mendel and his peas. As if the glorious worker could be reduced to the banality of a pea! It was the greatest responsibility Regina had been given! Save for the responsibility of keeping Felix appraised of brewing inappropriate sentiments at the barracks. The latter was everyone's job. Supervising the winter planting was solely Regina's. She was eager to make good. Not for her own sake. For the good of Birobidzhan. Unable to sleep for worrying, Regina had climbed out of bed, careful not to wake the girls, wrapped herself in every piece of clothing she owned to fend off December's arctic wind, and let herself into the storehouse where the precious bags of seeds sat.

Except she wasn't the sole late night visitor. Aaron had beaten her to it.

If it were anyone else, Regina would have known exactly what he was up to. He'd come to siphon off a portion of the community seedlings to either plant on his own, or sell to someone else. It was a disturbingly recurrent problem in the JAR. Felix was right. Some had emigrated not to build together, but to enrich themselves. Regina could imagine Aaron committing a variety of crimes. She'd seen him commit a variety of crimes. Except this one.

He straightened up, those translucent azure eyes glittering in the darkness like a cat's. The sound of his steady breathing filled the cavernous space, surrounding Regina like a small, personal tornado. She found her breaths synching with his. She'd opened her mouth to speak, to confront him. What came out was a faint puff of white, visible air.

"I'm mixing the cold treated seed with the untreated. If we fill one entire field with your scientific nonsense we'll lose the entire crop. Spread across multiple hectares, we'll have a fighting chance not to starve."

He was as wrong as Darwin, as wrong as Mendel. As wrong as Comrade Lysenko's mentor, who'd lost his mind, jealous of his prize pupil's success, until deporting him to a labor camp became the only way to prevent him from disparaging the latest progress.

But Regina knew Aaron wasn't wrong about this.

She should have argued with him, quoted facts, figures, studies. She should have run to Felix to report him. She should have, at the very least, banned him from her stock and fixed what he'd attempted to ruin.

Instead, Regina stepped forward, reaching for the nearest sack. "I'll help you," she said.

THEY LABORED ALL through that winter without a single day of rest. If the fields weren't being flooded, they were freezing over. If they weren't freezing over, they were dissolving into sludge, their painstakingly spaced seeds sliding and clumping. Regina finally understood why, before she'd gone and opened her mouth, no one in the JAR

thought to plant during the coldest months. If she'd found it difficult
to work when set upon by flies and coated in a sticky paste, that was
nothing compared to the agony of attempting to force frost-bitten
fingers into grasping miniscule, precious seedlings without spilling
the lot. If she'd thought tepid mud overflowing and filling her galoshes was uncomfortable, that was nothing compared to icy dirt mixed
with snow. If she'd found the work tedious when you could exchange
snatches of conversation with the folks next to you, that was nothing
compared to spending endless hours in silence because the skin of
your face had been wind-chilled immobile.

Regina took a lesson from Aaron. He never took a break when
supervising his hectare, and so Regina resolved to work tirelessly, to
lead by example. She was the first one to arrive in the fields and
the last to leave. She volunteered for the dirtiest jobs, the ones that
wedged dirt not just beneath her nails, but in her ears, eyes, and
mouth. She felt her shoulders freeze in the hunched position. No
amount of heat would ever wrench them free. As February turned
into March turned into April with no change in weather conditions,
it was difficult to imagine that they would ever be warm again. As
Regina quickly learned entering her second year in Birobidzhan, they
actually wouldn't be. Here, the weather transformed from freezing
cold to scorching hot in an instant. There were no temperate, nice
days in the JAR.

Equally as consistent were Regina's ongoing visits to Felix's. There
were still occasional group suppers with the Cohens or Klara, where
Regina could be paraded as a typical citizen of Amerzut to passing
through dignitaries. But, more and more, Regina was meeting with
Felix in private. In addition to listening to her reports, he now asked
personal questions. How did Regina feel about the progress they
were making here? What should leadership do to better inspire the
populace? Did they need a committee dedicated to young people?
What was Regina's favorite thing about living in Birobidzhan? Which
of Felix's initiatives did she believe most successful? Maybe it was
Regina's imagination, but it felt like, with every query, Felix drew a
little closer in his chair, his knee touching her knee, his arm brushing
against hers, his hand patting her on the shoulder, on her breastbone.
In a less than pure Comrade-like fashion.

She cringed beneath the spotlight of his interest. Such individuality, the suggestion that her opinions might carry more weight than any other worker's, went against Regina's socialist principles. Also, it felt more like an interrogation than a conversation, especially when she knew he was seeking one particular answer, and any divergence would not hold her in good stead. Mostly, though, it was Regina's sensation that, with each word, Felix was poking through her mind, her soul, her heart. Every question raised goosebumps on Regina's flesh, no matter what the weather. She wanted to shudder and pull away, yet knew that wouldn't be in her interest, either. Proof that even Regina's baser instincts didn't know what was good for her. Regina should be relishing Felix's attention, she should be encouraging it. Instead, she couldn't help wishing he'd turn his endearment toward someone else. Which, in practical terms, would be the worst thing that could possibly happen to her. Especially now.

The seeds they planted in the winter required harvesting in the fall. The final crop total came to about half of what they'd been planning on.

Felix pronounced it a triumph, announcing they were fifty percent more successful than last year, thanks to their implementation of the latest in Soviet scientific methodology. Aaron merely looked over Felix's head at Regina, and winked.

The wink shot through Regina like an arrow to the chest that instantaneously spread its tentacles throughout her body. It was like the goose pimples Regina got from talking to Felix. Except the exact opposite.

WITH THE NEW crop, their harvesting season was year round. They'd barely finished the root vegetables before it was time to move on to fruit. They barely completed picking and canning the fruit before it was rye time again. Regina's days became an endless interchangeable wheel. She lay in bed at night and felt her fingers vibrating, muscles unable to settle down. She closed her eyes and saw shadows; bending, tugging, bagging figures, their routine imprinted on her retinas. The clothes she'd come in turned to rags. No great loss, they were all too large for her now, anyway. Felix said they'd produced twice as much food this year. So why did everyone appear half the person they'd been when Regina arrived?

The only thing that remained the same was the distance everyone still kept from her. She'd first attributed it to being new. Then to her not yet having proven her loyalty. Now she didn't know what to think.

It wasn't as if anyone were outright rude to her. Everyone was polite. Too polite. Eerily polite. Everyone said good morning to her. And good evening. Not much in between. Even her roommates, who slept so close to her Regina could reach out and touch all three without fully extending her elbow, who ate beside her in the communal dining room, who sat beside her at every *samokritika*, all stopped talking when Regina entered the barracks. No. They didn't stop talking. They stopped giggling. Regina would have given anything for a good giggle.

Instead, as yet another placid summer evening passed with Agneska, Georgetta and Marta scurrying off without so much as saying where they were going, much less asking if Regina might like to come, Regina found herself wandering to the rye field. She'd been doing it more often lately, needing a reminder that her time in the JAR hadn't been a total waste. She might feel just as lonely, desperate and friendless as she had when she stepped off the train and into a blinding storm, but, at least she'd done some good. Their latest harvest may have come in half of what they'd planted, but if Regina hadn't helped Aaron distribute the seed, they could have ended up with nothing. It was a confusing reality to ponder. She'd made a decision she still knew was wrong. Yet it had turned out right. As she knew it would. It was all too much. The physical exhaustion, the mental gymnastics. The knowing what needed to be done and knowing why it couldn't be done while knowing it should be done as she realized she shouldn't. Regina wanted to stomp her foot and scream. Regina wanted to throw up her hands and cry. So she did both.

Why not?

There was nobody around to see her.

Of course, Aaron was around to see her.

Who else could it have possibly been?

He appeared out of the shadows the same way he had at the station. Who knew he also had a penchant for visiting half-reaped rye fields in the dead of night?

Regina's instinct was to wipe her shirt sleeve across her face, obscure the evidence of her disgrace. It was shameful to weep. Not because it demonstrated weakness, but because it suggested unhappiness with one's station in life. Which was the same as being unhappy with those who'd granted it to her.

But this was Aaron. Aaron had demonstrated his unhappiness in such a wide variety of ways Regina couldn't imagine him being impressed with any of hers. Or feeling inclined to report her for it.

Besides, she was exhausted from putting on a brave face twenty-four hours a day, seven days a week, going on seven hundred days now. In the beginning, she'd been afraid of deportation. Afraid a hint of frustration would brand her antisocial and ungrateful. Next, Regina had wanted desperately to fit in, to be accepted and befriended. No one chose to pal around with a perpetually complaining sourpuss. So she'd acted cheerful. With Regina's promotion to head of scientific planting, she was perennially on guard against skepticism and doubt. She'd gotten so good at playing the part of a true adherer that, sometimes, Regina found herself accepting Felix's math that they'd increased their yield by half, rather than decreased it, and that Comrade Lysenko's frozen seeds had successfully sprouted, though she'd been the one to help Aaron with the deception that salvaged at least a portion of their crop.

Regina was thoroughly spent from the effort. She had no more strength left to give, she had no more strength left to fight. And no more interest in doing so.

The tears streamed down her cheeks.

She didn't care who saw.

She didn't care if Aaron saw.

Of course, Aaron saw.

If he'd been anyone else, he would've known there were two responses. Discreetly fade away, pretend he didn't see her distress. That would have been the gentlemanly thing to do. The reactionary thing. The progressive thing would have been to loudly—in case anyone was nearby listening—urge Regina to buck up, remind her of how fortunate she was to be living in this time, in this place, perhaps quote Comrade Marx: *If we have chosen the position in life in which we can most of all work for mankind, no burdens can bow us down, because they are sacrifices for the benefit of all; then we shall experience no petty, limited, selfish joy, but our happiness will belong to millions, our deeds will live on quietly but perpetually at work, and over our ashes will be shed the hot tears of noble people.*

Leave it to Aaron to do none of those things.

Instead of turning his back or reciting slogans, he stepped forward, cupping Regina's chin in his hand and using his thumb to brush the tears from her cheek. It had been almost two years since the first—and last—time he'd touched her. It felt exactly the same, only more. He didn't say anything. Yet it felt like he understood everything.

"Why?" Regina blurted out in frustration, the confusion, rage and resentment she'd been keeping bottled up in the name of blending in, retching out of her like the mudslides they'd been battling all winter. "Why do they all keep treating me like I'm a pariah? Why don't they trust me? Why don't they like me? Why doesn't anyone want to be friends with me?"

She understood she sounded like a petulant schoolgirl. Which was fine. She felt like a petulant schoolgirl. A petulant schoolgirl is what she'd still be if she'd stayed in Moscow like a normal, sensible individual, instead of the fugitive she'd inadvertently become.

She feared Aaron would laugh at her. It wasn't yet too late to whip out a bit of Marx.

He dropped his arm, so he was no longer touching Regina—a loss she experienced like a blow—and said, "It's because you're Felix's girl."

What? No!

"No!" Regina echoed the denial thundering through her head. "He—I—We're not—I'm not—" She rejected memories of Felix's chair inching closer, him touching her thigh, her arm, saying how different Regina was from other women. She told herself those actions couldn't be genuine. Because they didn't make her feel the way she felt when Aaron did much less. It was suddenly imperative to Regina that Aaron understood that. "He and I are not... like that."

An expression Regina couldn't identify flickered across Aaron's face. Didn't he believe her? It was suddenly imperative to Regina that Aaron believe her.

He didn't argue her point. "You're Felix's girl. You report to him. Everyone knows it."

Oh.

"I..." Regina began, with no idea of how she intended to finish her sentence, "We—It's for the good of Birobidzhan."

Aaron didn't bother correcting her. All he said was, "They can't trust you. The risk is too great. You have to choose which side you're on."

Chapter Twelve

─────

Aaron was wrong.

He had to be.

Regina shouldn't have to choose between friendship and serving her community. In a socialist society, there should be no difference between the two. The challenge was proving to Marta, Agneska, and Georgetta that rooming with "Felix's girl" wasn't a hazard. It was an advantage. Regina got her chance the next time it rained. The hole in the ceiling that covered her pillow in grit her first night in Biro-bidzhan had grown larger. They'd tried stuffing it with grass from the fields, with the rag remains of their clothes and burlap sacks too ripped to be of harvesting use. The night the four of them resorted to tearing pages from an old textbook of Agneska's—they'd been issued new editions to correct ideological mistakes from earlier printings—and layering them, one on top of the other against the rotting boards in an attempt to keep out the worst of the damp, gave Regina an idea.

At her meeting with Felix, as his hand wandered upward, twisting a bit of her hair around his fingers, expressing concern she might have caught a chill getting caught in a downpour on her way over, Regina took advantage of Felix bringing up the weather to tell him about their dilemma. The following day, a carpenter was on their roof, nailing down a sheet of wood to make sure there'd be no more leaks.

"Thanks to Comrade Luria," Regina told her roommates, hoping they'd understand the message behind their good fortune.

"Thanks to Comrade Luria," the three of them echoed.

"I'M AFRAID TO report we've been selfish," Felix announced at *samokritika*. The hall grew silent. Heads swiveled, wondering who was being accused, as eyes hit the ceiling, the floor, the backs of one's hands. "We've been so focused on exercising the subversive guilt in ourselves, we have shirked our responsibility to serve others. It's our duty as citizens to help those who do not yet realize the danger they pose to our collective's cohesiveness, whether through deed, speech, or thought, to recognize the error of their ways and be granted an equal chance to make amends. Tonight, let's not be selfish. Let us turn the spotlight onto those who could benefit from enlightenment. Has a neighbor of yours shirked their work duty? Expressed dissatisfaction with an aspect of their lives? Have they said something another might interpret as being against Marxist-Leninist teachings? Against Comrade Stalin? It doesn't matter what they meant. All that matters is how someone else may have taken their words. The speaker must be made aware of the jeopardy they pose to the collective. As must anyone who heard but didn't fulfill their obligation to report it. Erroneous ideas are like a virus. The worst spreaders are those who don't recognize they are infected themselves. It's up to us to identify and neutralize them, before the whole of Birobidzhan is at death's door. *Samokritika* means the criticism of oneself. But we are also obligated to look outward towards our fellow man, and help them reach the consciousness we already possess. Anything less would be selfish and anti-Soviet."

Regina didn't know how Felix managed it. How did he take an idea that seemed utterly clear, turn it into something utterly confounding, then bring it around so that not doing what you were not supposed to do became the only thing you could do?

Was she the only one confused? Around Regina, heads bobbed

up and down in sync with Felix's directives. Though no one had yet to take advantage of his invitation.

After several moments of no volunteers, Felix continued, in the same cadence, as if that had been the plan all along, "For instance, it has come to my attention that Comrade Agneska." He swept his arm in her roommate's direction and Regina's heart dropped into her lap. She knew what he was about to say. "Comrade Agneska has desecrated the sayings of our great Vladimir Ilych Lenin by tearing up the textbooks she was so generously issued, at great expense, if I may add, by our Education Committee. The USSR went to an immense amount of trouble to translate Comrades Lenin, Marx, and Stalin's wisdom into multiple languages, including Yiddish for stubborn Jews unwilling to make the effort to learn our noble mother tongue."

Here, Felix paused, so all could remember the poster hanging in every Soviet classroom depicting an otherwise uneducated African, smiling with his great white teeth and proclaiming, "I would learn Russian because Lenin spoke it." Nonetheless, there were Jews, some right here in Birobidzhan, who didn't have half the sense and gratitude of that wise African. The Soviet Union did not hold their ignorance against them. Instead, it chose to educate them via the same books loyal citizens got, in Yiddish.

"The Soviet Union offers even the undeserving equity and access." Felix went on once he felt confident the appropriate image was lodged in everyone's mind. "Yet, Comrade Agneska thinks so little of the percipience which built our union that she crumpled up venerated pages to patch a hole in her roof. A hole that, as soon as appropriate authorities were made aware of it, was instantly fixed, no less!"

That wasn't true. The hole had been there—and repeatedly reported to the appropriate authorities—since before Regina moved in. It was why she'd turned to Felix. She knew a word from him would get something done.

"That's not true!" Agneska leapt out of her seat, glaring at Regina on her way up, aware of who'd put her in this position. Regina shriveled in response. Why, why, why was it whenever she tried to do the right thing, it all inevitably blew up in her face? "The book we used," Marta and Georgetta flinched at her choice of pronouns, "was an old copy. The words in it were no longer the correct ones. It was as you said, Comrade Luria, I feared the book might fall into the hands of someone less enlightened, and they might draw the wrong lesson from it. I was heeding your example," Agneska swore despite her actions having preceded Felix's instruction by multiple days. She must have known it wasn't a strong enough defense because, before Felix had the chance to respond, Agneska continued, "I did my duty! It's her," a finger jab at Marta sitting on the other side of Regina, "and him," the same jab in Leon's direction, sitting three rows behind them, "they are the ones who should be confessing!"

Regina expected Marta to look shocked. The expression on her face was more one of resignation. She'd always known the axe would eventually swing at her neck. The goal had been to push the inevitable back, one day at a time.

"Marta and Leon," Agneska raged on, fully aware the way to keep the spotlight off herself was to keep shoving it at someone else, "have been stealing from the communal clothing room for years. Leon lets her in, she picks the very best on offer, then sells it on the black market."

That wasn't true, as far as Regina knew. Then again, as had well been established time after time, what did Regina know?

Still, she found it hard to believe. Marta never dressed better than the rest of them. Marta never had more than the rest of them. If she were truly enriching herself at others' expense, wouldn't there be evidence of it?

"What do you have to say for yourselves?" Felix gestured for the accused to rise.

Marta needed to grab the back of her chair to forcefully complete the action, her knees were shaking so badly. Regina reached out a hand to steady her, at least to catch her if she fell. Marta ignored it. Regina didn't know whether to feel grateful or offended. Was Marta protecting Regina from an accusation of collaboration, or did she not trust Regina's sincerity in offering support?

Leon, on the other hand, leapt to his feet, babbling. "Forgive me, forgive us. We have betrayed Birobidzhan, we have betrayed the

collective. We have been selfish and individualistic. We have per-
verted the ideology of Marx, of Lenin. We have let down Comrade
Stalin."

"You've done no such thing!" The words shot from Regina's lips,
but she heard them for the first time along with everyone else. They'd
bypassed her brain and her sense. She couldn't take it anymore.
Couldn't keep looking at Marta's stricken face as Leon buried them
deeper. Regina's friend, her spirited, funny, generous friend, had been
drained of blood, of energy, of fight. This wasn't Marta. This wasn't
right. And if she was too terror-stricken to defend herself, the obligation fell to Regina. Even if she had no idea what she was about to
do or say. Some would note that Regina risked making the situation
worse. So what else was new?

Regina's initial comment had been to Leon. Now she turned
to Felix, Klara, and the rest of the council. All decisions required a
unanimous vote from those present, but, in the end, the council's
was the only opinion which mattered. "Did our Comrade Lenin not
tell us: *Exchange, fair or unfair, always presupposes and includes the
rule of the bourgeoisie?* Did he not say: *The feminine section of the
proletarian army is of particularly great significance. The success of a
revolution depends on the extent to which women take part?*" Regina
was spewing slogans, no matter how tangentially related, knowing
anything prefaced as a quote from the great Lenin, Stalin, or Marx
would be carefully parsed before being contradicted. "Women like
Comrade Marta are at the forefront of our revolt against the petty
grievances of the bourgeoisie! What she did, she did in the name of
the revolution! Comrade Lenin also instructed us: *Measures must be
taken to substitute for the specific methods of official administration by
state officials.* Which was precisely her intention! *We shall rely on our
experience as workers, we shall establish strict, iron discipline supported
by the state power of the armed workers, we shall reduce the role of the
state officials to that of simply carrying out our instructions. This is our
proletarian task, this is what we can and must start with in carrying out
the proletarian revolution!*" Regina's voice kept rising. She replaced
sense with volume, logic with conviction, and, most importantly,
reason with ideology. Who could say no to Comrade Lenin? Who
could say no to her?

Felix definitely appeared to be considering it. His face remained grim, even in light of Regina's passion. Her voice nearly cracked on the final exultation, but Regina didn't dare cough or display weakness. Her own knees were shaking as much as Marta's. The only thing keeping her upright was utter and complete panic. Every muscle was so tense, she expected to shatter no matter what Felix's final verdict.

"Thank you, Comrade," he said. "Most enlightening."

Never had a single word carried so much double meaning. What was Felix trying to say? Had he accepted Regina's argument, or was he thanking her for enlightening him regarding her true, disloyal nature. Has she saved Marta or doomed herself?

It was time to find out.

"A vote," Felix directed. "All those in favor of forgiving our comrades their trespasses?" Was he including Regina in that group? His expression gave no indication one way or the other. Which is why, despite an audible shifting in the seats, not a single hand had yet to go up.

"Comrade Kramer," Felix called out. "Are we keeping you from pressing business?"

Regina's head swiveled in Aaron's direction.

Aaron had moved from his traditional place by the exit towards a window to the left of it. He was peering into the night through the glass. Following Aaron's gaze, those sitting closest to the back cried out in alarm, "There's somebody in the field!"

That shouldn't be. This voluntary gathering was compulsory. Every able bodied adult should be present and accounted for.

Displeased by the breach in protocol, Felix strode down the aisle, the rest of the council rushing to keep up. He shouldered Aaron aside.

"Cossacks," Felix seethed.

It may have taken their votes a few minutes to become unanimous but, in that moment, every citizen inhaled on a single count. Wherever they hailed from, everyone had either firsthand or anecdotal experience with the Czar's *soslovive*, his military class. Some may have recalled the Cossack's assigned role in stopping mobs from rampaging through Jewish villages. Equally as many recalled their enthusiastic participation in identical pogroms, complete with setting fire to homes and crops, raping any women they could get their hands on, and beating men, some to unconsciousness, some to death. Thankfully, The Great October Revolution put a stop to that. The Cossacks had formed the backbone of the White Army, fighting brutally against our Bolsheviks. As with other elitist groups, their homelands were seized, their noble status stripped upon defeat. They'd been completely disbanded, as far as Regina knew.

"Cossacks?" she blurted out. "Here?"

Felix graciously illuminated, "A batch escaped to China. A local warlord offered them sanctuary and employed them as mercenaries against a Muslim Turk uprising. Our Red Army was forward thinking enough to strike a deal with that same warlord afterwards. He allowed the NKVD to enter Chinese territory and purge the remaining Cossack threat."

"Along with anyone else the Chinese felt needed purging," Aaron added. "The NKVD practiced on Turkish Muslims before turning on the ones inside their own borders."

"You would prefer our Army stand by and do nothing while enemy combatants make incursions onto our lands?"

"Enemy combatants? Incursions?" Aaron snorted, gesturing towards what Regina discerned were a dozen shadowy figures scrounging through their fields, digging in soil long since stripped clean in desperate hope of an overlooked scrap. "They're starving old men!"

"Where is your loyalty, Kramer? Where is your patriotism? Where is your kinship? You claim you're from the Pale of Settlement. You claim to have personally witnessed the so-called Holodomor, despite authorities across the globe exposing it as a vast capitalist lie to discredit the USSR. Yet when it comes to indisputable truths, that they," Felix jammed his finger out the window, "are the ones who've slaughtered our people by the thousands, suddenly they're merely starving old men?"

"We should kill them all!"

Regina was stunned to hear the bloodthirsty suggestion spurt from the mouth of none other than shy, blushing Leon. Then again, what better way to distract from the accusations against Leon and Marta which still lingered along the edges?

A chorus of voices chimed in with enthusiastic agreement. Marta, Regina noticed, wasn't one of them. Yet she didn't dissent, either. While Leon's cheeks were, for a change, crimson due to uncharacteristic bloodlust, Marta's remained abnormally pale from the charge she still couldn't feel certain she'd ducked.

"Kill them before they kill us!"

"It's payback!"

"For the motherland!"

"For Birobidzhan!"

"For what they did to us!"

"How?" Aaron didn't raise his voice, yet it managed to carry over the growing frenzy of the crowd. "Are you going to go out there and charge them?" He turned to Felix. "Will you lead the way, Comrade?"

Felix's audible contempt for Aaron grew stronger with every word Felix deigned utter. "Do you have a better idea, Comrade?"

Was Regina the only one who noticed Felix didn't answer Aaron's question?

Aaron's own answer, however, was, "We could help them."

Felix's incredulous laugh didn't have time to make it to his mouth. It burst out his nose, a snort. "Help them do what? Finish the job of annihilating us?"

Aaron said, "I walked to Birobidzhan from Ukraine. It took me weeks, maybe months. I lost track, I was so exhausted, starving. If kind people along the way hadn't shared what meager foodstuffs they had with me, I wouldn't have made it."

"Share?" Felix was no longer incredulous. Felix was flabbergasted into near incoherence. "You want to share… Our food… We don't… We barely have enough to feed ourselves!" On any other occasion, the admission would have been treasonous.

"I thought this year's yield was fifty percent greater?" Aaron asked innocently.

"That wasn't for us! Nothing we harvest belongs to us. That was for the people! We can't give away food earmarked for the people to… to…"

"The people?"

Regina knew she shouldn't giggle. The stakes were too huge, the tension too high, the possibility of disaster too imminent. And yet, the only way she could stop herself from laughing was to clamp both hands over her mouth and turn away, hoping her actions would be interpreted as horror at Aaron's impertinence, and not amusement. She couldn't remember the last time she'd laughed. She couldn't remember the last time there'd been anything to laugh about.

"They're enemies of the state," Felix corrected, cheek twitching from the Herculean effort of regaining control—over himself and those listening.

"I'm going to go help them," Aaron repeated, his tone unchanging, turning towards the door.

Regina wondered if Felix would try to stop him. Regina wondered if anyone would try to stop him. The same crowd which, seconds earlier had been screaming for blood, remained motionless. They were waiting for Felix to model the correct choice to make. No, they were waiting for Felix to model the safe choice to make. The same way Regina had been.

She, too, took a step towards the door. Then another, and another. She politely nudged several Comrades out of the way, telling herself it was alright, she hadn't done anything wrong yet, she could still stop, she could still turn back, still come up with an innocent explanation for her actions. Regina paused at the exit. She paused long enough to give Felix the chance to ask, "Where are you going?"

She paused long enough to give herself the chance to come up with a suitable answer.

"I'm going to help them," Regina said.

Chapter Thirteen

———

Regina hurried towards where Aaron stood in conversation with the Cossack men. He was right. Regina couldn't identify one younger than sixty, though it was hard to feel certain, considering their bedraggled state. Their clothes were shredded, some missing shirt sleeves, others with pant legs split in two, held up with scraps of rope or twine that left red welts dotting their emaciated stomachs. Dirt and cracked burrs dotted the matted hair on their heads and beards, once presumably gleaming gold, now filthy. How long had they been on the run? How long had they been in hiding?

These were her enemies. These were the soldiers who'd fought the coming of The Great Socialist Revolution. These were the men who would not have hesitated to kill her, either as a loyal Communist or a Jew. And yet, in some ways, Regina felt more kinship with them than she did with the Comrades she'd left behind. None of them had a place to belong, either.

One of the men wrenched into a hacking cough. Aaron pulled the threadbare sweater he was wearing up over his head and handed it to him.

Aaron wasn't wearing anything beneath his sweater. Regina had struggled to differentiate between their trespassers in the moonlight. She realized it was because what meager glow the quarter moon did possess, it was prioritizing to illuminate Aaron. She didn't blame the moon one bit for her choice. Regina would have done the same.

His skin appeared to glow, the kind of alluring sheen that made moths dive into flames and pirates steer towards a mirage. For a moment, Regina could do no more than stare at the peaks and valleys beneath Aaron's shoulders, at the ripple of the muscles of his back as they flexed and loosened against his spine. Each was a path of enticing mystery, a lure for her to follow, a siren song written not in sound but in flesh.

Aaron either heard her coming or he heard her skid to a stop. She primarily hoped he hadn't heard her intake of breath, or the gulp that came afterwards.

Aaron turned to face Regina. His chest was covered with a light, honey-brown down that she'd love to burrow her face in, to feel the softness against her cheeks, to brush her lips along the chilled, puckered flesh beneath.

Instead, she said the only conscious thought she'd entertained over the past few minutes appropriate for vocalizing. "How should I help you?"

She'd said "you," not "them."

Aaron expressed no surprise, her query the final detail he'd been awaiting. "Let's take them to the storehouse, give them as much grain as they can carry, so the lighter the better."

"Thank you," the man who stood steadiest on his feet and, as such, had become the de facto leader, managed to croak out. "God bless you."

His Russian was old fashioned, formal, cultured, with the elongated Moscow vowels and hard "sh" sound Regina had grown up with and hadn't realized she was aching to hear again. He reminded her of lost teachers and friends. Lost parents. Lost lives.

"Comrade Kramer!" Felix's American accented Russian ripped Regina out of her reverie and back to where she was, not to mention what she'd put on the line. He'd caught up to them, trailed by a combination of those excited to watch the drama play out, and those who figured literally following in Felix's footsteps was the safest bet. He looked to be leading a small parade, only lacking a flag to wave like a preteen Pioneer.

"Yes, Comrade Luria?"

Felix stood on a slight incline from Aaron, yet somehow still came out the smaller man.

"Explain yourself!" Felix put the authority he feared he'd lost when compelled to tag after Aaron from Felix's own meeting into his demand, intending to redistribute the balance of power that should never have been so much as waggled in the first place.

Regina heard Aaron's response before his tongue began forming the first syllable. She knew what he was going to say by observing the lazy grin that preceded it. He was going to point out that he already had explained himself back in the hall. Was Felix not listening? Did Aaron need to repeat himself? Was Felix inviting Aaron to humiliate him further?

Regina couldn't let that happen. Not for Felix's sake. For Aaron's. Felix could put up with a great deal. In their two years of chats, Regina had come to realize the reason Felix had yet to turn Aaron in for insubordination was not because he lacked evidence or because the women of Amerzut inevitably flew to Aaron's defense. It was because, like it or not—and Felix detested it—Aaron's hectare regularly produced more than any other in Birobidzhan. While Felix may have been a modern man, a progressive, a believer in science above all else, he was still enough of a Jewish boy whose grandmother tied a red string around his crib to keep evil spirits away, and who spit three times over her shoulder for good luck, to superstitiously fear banishing the man responsible for Felix's rank as JAR's best manager. Rationally, he knew Aaron was just lucky, and they had Felix's leadership to thank for their supremacy. But why risk it?

Felix could tolerate Aaron arguing with him over planting matters, especially when Felix still ultimately got his way. It was to his advantage. It demonstrated how Felix listened to all his comrades, then made the best decision. That was how Comrade Stalin governed, as well. He was known for being an exemplary listener. The thing Felix would never be able to stand was Aaron openly challenging his leadership. And getting away with it.

One sardonic answer from Aaron, and it would be the end. Aaron may not have cared what happened to him following this standoff. Regina certainly did. She cared more than she ever had about anything previously.

Which was why, before Aaron had the opportunity to emasculate Felix further, Regina burst in, "No, Comrade Luria, you explain yourself!" She positioned her body so she could pivot between Felix and their intruders—without catching Aaron's eye. If Regina caught Aaron's eye, she knew she wouldn't be able to go through with it. "Explain to these relics from a dead age the difference between Cossack cruelty and Soviet liberality. Twenty years ago, their Czar would have banished us to his Siberian prisons for a lesser crime than this." She indicated the garden they'd ravaged. "Instead, thanks to the example of Comrade Stalin, we offer a progressive response. No one goes hungry in the USSR. Not even enemies. You Cossacks claim to be Christians, but it took Communism to bring genuine mercy to every Soviet citizen. We are showing it to you now, though you never deigned show it to us. We will feed you, we will clothe you and we will send you freely on your way. Never forget the munificence of a state that believes all can be rehabilitated to see the error of their ways."

"Thank you," the leader of the group said, dropping to his knees, as if Felix were, in fact, the long ago Czar Regina had been invoking. The rest of his men followed suit. "Thank you, Your Excellency, thank you."

For the first time since he and Regina met, Felix's head seemed the one spinning. He knew his first order of business ought to be barking for the disgraced soldiers to stand up. No scraping and bowing in the USSR! They weren't honoring him by treating Felix like royalty, they were offending him and everything he stood for. On the other hand, the slight smile tickling the very edges of his lips did suggest Felix was enjoying their veneration.

Remembering he was being watched by all who'd spilled out of the hall in his wake, Felix snapped out of his reverie. He jerked his arm and the Cossacks instantly sprang to their feet, as wired to take orders from a superior as they'd ever been.

"There is no need to thank me." Felix switched smoothly from the singular to the plural, "We are doing the correct, Soviet thing." He looked around, spotted a group of young men, and snapped his fingers in their direction. "You. Help him," Felix indicated Aaron without looking his way, "get these men what they require."

"Bless you, Your Excellency, thank you." Instead of hitting their knees, the Cossacks held their hands together in prayer, bowing from the waist and murmuring their gratitude as they followed a still shirtless Aaron and the boys Felix had deputized towards the supply house.

As they walked away, Aaron did finally manage to catch Regina's eye. She'd been afraid that him looking at her while she improvised her smoke blowing would either make her laugh at the absurdity—or cost Regina her nerve. She feared glimpsing Aaron's censure. She'd debased herself, acted the sycophant, something Aaron, Regina felt certain, would never, ever do.

Yet, when he looked her way, Aaron offered a barely perceptible nod.

Felix was looking particularly pleased with himself. He stood, gazing proudly, as the ragtag group stumbled off into the distance, not quite a general sending troops off to war, more like a proud father on the first day of nursery school. When Felix caught sight of Regina, she thought he might give her a pat on the head, so paternalistic was his expression. "That was an excellent explanation you gave, Comrade."

Regina bowed her head in maiden-like modesty. It was a much safer bet than anything she could have said at the moment.

Felix belatedly remembered he still had a meeting to adjourn. Those who'd been patiently waiting for the dispensation began to drift off. He bid Regina farewell, heading towards his car. She searched those remaining for Marta and the rest, wondering if they were still angry with her or whether Regina had managed to win back at least a fraction of their goodwill. Despite all that had gone on afterward, Regina still recalled the way she'd gagged on the thought that she'd been the one to inadvertently betray them.

Regina caught sight of her roommates headed for the barracks, and hurried to join them. Before she could catch up, Comrade Klara stepped in Regina's way. She'd been silent through her presentation, and during Felix's embrace of it. Now, she looked at Regina as if meeting her for the first time, despite all the dinners and talks they'd shared. "You are a very clever girl. I'm going to remember that."

"YOU ARE A very clever girl," Felix echoed his comrade's words the next day. The group of Cossacks left at daybreak, wearing fresh clothes and tying burlap sacks stuffed with bread and potatoes on their backs. Aaron had supervised the distribution, but Felix came down personally to see them off. The men, once again, thanked him profusely.

"Don't thank me," Felix deferred. And stuck a copy of Karl Marx's *Das Kapital* into every makeshift rucksack. When one had trouble fitting in, Felix removed two potatoes, and slapped the man heartily on the back, sending him on his way.

Felix had ignored Aaron throughout the entire exchange. Afterwards, he said, "I am pulling Comrade Regina from this morning's work detail."

Lousy worker though she was, Regina knew losing a single pair of hands for even a few hours still put them behind. With what they'd given away, it wouldn't be enough to meet quotas this week, they'd have to exceed them. Which meant Aaron would need to fill in for her, on top of the other extra work he did daily.

"I don't believe Comrade Kramer can spare me," Regina told Felix.

"He'll manage," Felix assured, taking her by the elbow and guiding Regina away from the field, toward an open grassy area. One Felix planned to develop next, no matter how many times Aaron told him that would be to the detriment of both hectares.

"Clever, clever, clever," Felix repeated. "What better way to prove the superiority of the Soviet system to those Czarist heathens than by demonstrating true Communism in action. Of course," Felix added, "it will do them little good."

"Oh, I think it will. Once they realize the benefits of cooperation, I'm sure they'll become productive citizens, like the rest of us."

Alina Adams

Felix shrugged. "I've alerted the authorities. They'll be apprehended before they reach the next settlement."

Regina's sense struggled to catch up with his words. "Why would you—"

"We can't let criminals roam free. Their mere existence poses a danger to our survival. We can't let them remind people of what the world was like before the revolution. Next thing you know, they'll have whipped their supporters into a frenzy with nostalgia, raised an army and are once again storming our gates, slaughtering us in the streets."

"Then why did you agree to let them go? Give them our food, our clothes?"

"Because you were right. We'd been handed a golden opportunity to demonstrate the virtues of progressivism in action for those simpletons who still refuse to concede that we are offering them the best possible world here. They saw how Communists feed the hungry, clothe the naked, shelter even our worst enemies. That should give them something to think about the next time they dare consider sneaking off in the middle of the night, imagining a better life to be found outside Birobidzhan, outside the Soviet Union. You think Zionists would have shown such charity? Certainly not capitalists! You should see how hobos are treated in America. Those poor men pass through towns with signs telling them to keep walking, there'll be no food, clothes, or shelter offered them here!"

"What will happen to them? The Cossacks?"

Felix shrugged, unconcerned to the point of having not given it a moment's deliberation. He had more important issues to discuss. "I was impressed with your quick thinking."

"It was no more than what you'd taught me," Regina demurred. And also deflected, in case a reprimand was coming, either from Felix or anyone else.

"You have a fine mind," Felix said, as if Regina had suggested otherwise. "A mind too fine to be wasted in the fields."

"There is no calling more noble than working with one's hands in honest labor." Regina had no idea whom she was quoting at this point.

"Yes, yes," Felix agreed. "Marx?"

"Engels," Regina said. That sounded right.

Felix didn't let it sway him from the topic at hand. "A mind like yours should be serving the people on our village Soviet."

Regina's chin jerked in surprise. "I—is there," in lieu of asking a dangerous question, she went with the safer and more obvious, "the village Soviet is full."

"It's important we have women there. To demonstrate the equality of sexes Communism brought. However, if a woman doesn't subscribe to the proper ideology, if she has unacceptable ideas of her own, what's the point? Better appoint a man with the right attitude towards women's issues, than a woman with the wrong one. Don't you agree?"

Again, Felix was putting together words that made perfect sense on their own, yet looked like a funhouse mirror when pressed one against the other.

Luckily, Regina had no need to parse them for meaning. She knew the correct answer to this one. "Yes, of course, I agree."

"Which is precisely why you belong on the village Soviet. It will take some doing," Felix mused, taking Regina's assent for granted. "But it should be possible once we are married."

"Once we are..." Regina repeated slowly, unable to utter the final, most important, word.

"What better example of consensus could there be?" Felix asked, reasonably.

"You wish to marry... me?"

"Absolutely!" Felix made it sound like the compliment he believed it to be. "I can think of no one who deserves it more."

"You think I deserve to marry you?" Regina realized she sounded like an imbecile, parroting Felix's words. But it was all she could think of to make them sink in.

"No one has worked harder or been more dedicated to Birobidzhan. Why, I couldn't have carried out my duties nearly as well without your input."

She'd helped him carry out his duties. She'd helped him call out Agneska, which helped to attack Marta and Leon. She'd helped him implement Comrade Lysenko's modern, scientific policies, which helped to nearly destroy their entire harvest. Regina had helped him.

So that he would not change his mind about helping her.

She wanted to cry.

Felix saw tears of joy.

"Once we're married," he began, "I can make the case for placing you onto the village Soviet and removing Comrade Klara—"

"No," Regina interrupted, shaking her head lest he was too busy looking into the future to take note of the present.

"Don't worry, I've accumulated enough evidence of her ongoing dissent from appropriate opinion to make it a simple procedure."

"No," Regina repeated, more patiently this time, more quietly, as a way to make Felix slow down and listen. "I don't want this."

Felix stopped short, going so far as to turn and finally look at her. "Turning down a seat on the village Soviet can be interpreted as a great affront to the Party."

"I don't want to marry you," Regina clarified, wondering how great of an affront that would turn out to be.

Now Felix appeared to be the one having trouble making the words he was hearing gel.

"Ridiculous," he sputtered. "Who else could you possibly want to marry?"

Regina didn't answer. Regina simply turned on her heels. And ran.

WHEN REGINA RAN from Moscow, she'd been running away. Now, as she ran from Felix, she was running toward. Regina ran, tripping, nearly falling out of her shoes, landing painfully on the side of her foot, feeling a pull and twinge in her ankle. She kept running.

Regina kept running until she was back on her own hectare, in front of Aaron, gasping for breath, bending over, arms wrapped around her rib cage, nearly retching. She could imagine what she looked like, face the color of watermelon, hair either pasted to her scalp with sweat or sticking out in every direction, skin a perennial maze of insect bites connected by the red lines of furious scratching. No wonder Felix felt generous offering to marry her. He'd made a point of complimenting her mind—and nothing else.

She'd created enough of a scene arriving, huffing and puffing and late, to boot. Half the workers turned in Regina's direction. Aaron crossed from where he'd been standing until he was right above Regina. He tapped her gently on the shoulder. "Are you alright?"

It was the lightest touch possible, and yet Regina felt it absolutely everywhere. She looked up at Aaron and, no longer capable of feeling humiliated, no longer capable of feeling chastened or belittled or self-conscious, shook her head.

AARON SENT REGINA to work without another word. Yet she felt confident this wasn't the end of it, that he'd understood. Which was good. Because she still wasn't sure that she did.

Aaron hung back at the end of the day. So Regina did too. They were the only ones left outdoors at sundown, which Regina appreciated. Seeing him in the full light didn't seem right. Not with everything she had to tell him. Not with everything she wanted to tell him.

So, naturally, for the first few moments, Regina didn't tell him anything.

Aaron didn't appear to mind. He simply walked companionably between the rye stalks, Regina silently by his side. He gave every indication of being willing to do so forever. It was a tempting fantasy, the two of them strolling and strolling—right up till the edge of the Earth. The idea of plunging into nothingness, no sensation, no feeling, no worries, loomed as welcoming as a clear, cool lake on a blistering summer day.

Finally, Regina said, "Felix asked me to marry him." Phrasing it that way made it sound like she had a smidge of agency in the matter. It also made it more real. The revulsion that had initially been overruled by shock, struck Regina like an undulating wave from head to toe.

Aaron nodded, indicating that either he knew or he'd suspected.

"I don't want to marry him," she said. So far, Regina wasn't telling Aaron anything she hadn't told Felix. "I want to marry you," she said. That part was new.

Another nod from Aaron. Did he know or suspect, too?

Part Two: 1917-1945

Chapter Fourteen

———

Regina's parents never celebrated her birthday. She'd been born on November 7, 1917. The day the Bolshevik Red Guard occupied the government buildings of Petrograd and formally established the Russian Soviet Republic. Every year, on Regina's birthday, Moscow observed the anniversary of the Great October Socialist Revolution. There were mandatory spontaneous demonstrations, parades of citizens carrying placards trumpeting images of their great leaders, speeches in tribute to all the USSR had already accomplished and what it still would accomplish courtesy of the latest five-year plan, followed by fireworks over the Kremlin.

Every year, on Regina's birthday, her parents stayed inside, blew out the kerosene lights and pinned shut the drapes lest anyone see they were staying inside and report their lack of patriotism. Then Regina's parents mourned all they'd lost. Which included the apartment that had once been theirs, but now was a *communalka*, where they didn't even get a say in who was moved in or out. That was up to the district authority.

The day after Old Woman, Daughter, Son, and Son's Wife unexpectedly decamped and Cecilia arrived, Mama instructed Regina, "You are not to go near her."

"Why not?" Regina stared longingly down the hall. "She has so many books!"

"One type of woman is the kind of important," Mama snorted the word, "to warrant a whole room to herself."

"What type?" If everyone knew the secret, Regina wondered why everyone didn't become that type of woman. Especially if it also came with books.

"Keep your distance," Mama advised.

IT WAS IMPOSSIBLE, considering all their doors opened into the same hallway.

"Hello! I'm Cecilia Melamed!" She stuck her hand out to Mama and Papa as they stood in line for the water closet. Cecilia had to switch her toilet seat from her right to her left hand.

A rule of communal living was that you didn't make eye contact with neighbors while on the way to do your personal business. You especially didn't do it in the morning, while it was still dark, eyes were at half-mast, and bodies stood shivering in withdrawal from the warmth of their blankets.

"How do you do?" Mama replied in her most cultured voice, surprising Regina. Was it only she who was supposed to keep her distance?

"Welcome," Papa boomed more heartily than Regina had ever heard him, especially so early in the morning.

"Why…" Regina began. Mama pinched her arm to keep quiet.

It wasn't until they were back in their room, dressing for the day, that Mama instructed, "If she is important enough to deserve space to herself, she must have powerful protectors. We do not want to risk her reporting us for being subversive. We must be friendly, friendly, friendly!"

"While keeping our distance?" Regina clarified.

"Exactly," Mama said.

THE MEN BEGAN arriving that evening.

"You see?" Mama jerked her head in the direction of Cecilia's room. "As I said."

"So many at the same time?" Papa wondered.

"Many powerful protectors," Mama repeated.

Peeking through a crack in the door after her parents had gone to bed, Regina counted at least a dozen men, some dressed in the finest tailored suits, others in coarse fabric ripped at the knees. Expensive shaving lotion mingled with day old sweat to configure a dizzying fragrance. There were women, too. Some wore floor-length skirts even Mama would have been obliged to pronounce proper, while others slipped on dresses with hems ending scandalously above the calf. A handful, including Cecilia on some nights, were daring enough to wear slacks!

As far as Regina could tell, all they did was talk. They began the evening with dignified murmurs which, as Regina observed various bottles and flasks make the rounds of the room, grew to agitated raised voices. By midnight, they'd become bellows and challenges, turning to unassailable dictums and pronouncements at sunrise. Whoever remained standing while others collapsed into inebriated sleep around them, presumably won.

They shouted about the future of socialism, the inevitable death of capitalism, the rise of internationalism, the subjugation of that opiate, religion, to peoplehood. It was a world Regina had never imagined. One where there wasn't a single correct answer. One where comrades could hold conflicting opinions and neither were banished. One where speech, passion and dissent were celebrated, not shushed. It was a world Regina hadn't realized she was starved for until she was made aware of its existence. And, in the middle of it all, was also a word Regina had never heard before: Birobidzhan.

"WHAT'S BIROBIDZHAN?" REGINA needed to be strategic with her timing, sneaking a slot when Mama and Papa were at work and no communal neighbors were about to report Regina's disobedience, but Cecilia was awake—she rarely rose before noon, having adjourned to sleep as others were rising—and not locked in her room with her books. Reasoning Cecilia would have to exit to eat *obed* at midday, Regina stationed herself outside her door during the dinner hour, so they might bump into each other by accident.

When they did, Cecilia laughed and asked in that tone adults believe is ingratiating to children, "Well, if it isn't the little queen!"

Regina had heard it before. When your name was Latin for Queen in a country which had executed their royal family, the association was bound to come up. Never favorably.

"Your parents must have some fancy aspirations for your future!"

Regina shrugged. Her parents never talked about the future. Only mourned the past.

That's when she blurted out, cognizant they didn't have much time, "Please, what is Birobidzhan?"

Cecilia raised an eyebrow. "Someone has been listening at keyholes!"

Was that supposed to be a bad thing? Mama made it seem like somebody was always listening at keyholes. It was how people made "powerful friends." Was Cecilia complimenting Regina or chastising her?

"You are all very loud."

Cecilia laughed. "My friends are passionate people. They have big ideas and bigger dreams." She leaned to eye level with Regina. "Are you someone with big ideas and big dreams, my little queen?"

Regina knew what Mama would want her to say. Mama would want Regina to say no, she had no ideas of her own, only the right ideas, the ones they taught her at school, the ones written on great, flapping, red banners all over Moscow: "Glory to the Communist Party of the USSR," and "Lenin Points the Way To Our Shining Future!" Yet, Cecilia's ideas had to be the right ideas. Mama said she was an important woman. She had a room of her own! Mama wanted Regina to keep her distance. What if Regina could turn Cecilia into a powerful friend of theirs? Besides, if Cecilia promised answers to Regina's questions, what harm could answering one of her questions first do?

Regina gathered her courage and, swallowing hard, nodded her head. Once. Easier to deny that way, if she had to. Regina could claim Cecilia had misunderstood.

Cecilia held out a hand. "Then come with me."

"BIROBIDZHAN." CECILIA'S ROOM was a maze of books. Books on shelves, books on tables, books on chairs, and scattered along the floor. She led Regina towards a desk in the far corner, under the window, where a typewriter stood, surrounded by more books, on which drooped stacks of loose paper splattered with ink and brown tea rings, beneath a kerosene lamp. "Is the first Jewish homeland, founded less than a year ago, right here, in the Union of Soviet Socialist Republics, between the Bira and the Bidzhan rivers of the Russian-Chinese border."

Regina recoiled. She'd made a terrible mistake. Cecilia had said that word. The word Mama warned Regina never to admit to. Cecilia had said *Jewish*. Like Regina was. Like Mama and Papa were. Like Cecilia obviously was, you could see it in her dark hair, the epithelial folds of her eyes, that nose which dared you to avoid looking at it, that accent Mama pinpointed instantly. They were all Jews. But they were supposed to feign ignorance. There were no more Jews in the USSR. Everyone was Soviet now, nothing else. To suggest otherwise was to be a nationalist, a cosmopolitan, a traitor.

"Don't be scared!" Cecilia recognized and dismissed Regina's panic in the time it took her to reach over the piles on her desk and rifle out a black and white printed sheet which she thrust into Regina's hands. "It's perfectly official! This is our newspaper, *Evreyskoya Izvestia*. Can you read Yiddish?"

"Mama says Yiddish is for uneducated peasants," Regina replied, then instantly wished she could suck every word down like a spoon of cod liver oil, slick, disgusting and out of sight.

"Of course she does!" Cecilia laughed, unoffended. "Bourgeoisie like your Mama believe they're too good for their native tongue. Yiddish literature and poetry is the most lyrical, the most trenchant, the greatest in the world. But for philistines like your Mama," Cecilia flipped the sheet of paper in Regina's hands, "we print our text in Russian, as well."

"This is... allowed?" Regina couldn't process what she was hearing.

"Of course! *Evreyskoye Izvestia* is authorized by the Committee for the Settlement of Toiling Jews on Land—KOMZET, we call it. The complete name is a mouthful, don't you think?"

Regina had never been asked what she thought before. Not by somebody who sounded like they wanted to hear it. Still, she was too much of a Soviet child—too much Mama's child—to reply honestly. Instead, Regina did as she'd been taught and remained silent, waiting for the person who'd asked the question to tell her what the correct answer should be.

Cecilia went on, "KOMZET is under the oversight of Lazar Kaganovitch, Secretary of the Central Committee, Commissar of Communications, the most powerful Jew in the USSR!"

There she went again. Saying that word as if it were any other. As if it weren't something to be ashamed of.

"Not every Jew lives in Moscow luxury like you," Cecilia said, confusing Regina further. Moscow luxury? Mama cursed their living conditions—sotto voce—on a daily basis. She waxed poetic about the lost years, when there'd been satin sheets and porcelain plates, fur muffs and leather boots with silver buckles, a girl to do the washing, another for the cooking, and bowls of veal *pelmeni* swimming in vinegar, black caviar on triangles of buttered black bread with freshly brewed *kvas* to wash it down. Now, their sheets were made of flax, holes darned with whatever color thread was available. Their plates and mugs were rusty tin, their gloves knit from undone, unmatched woolen socks, their food whatever they could scrape together using ration cards for flour, eggs, shortening and bread. There were ration cards for meat, fish, and sugar, too, but they—even those for the top category of manual workers, followed by white collar workers, then their dependents, then children under age twelve—did little good if there were no such foodstuffs available for purchase. So what Moscow luxury was Cecilia talking about?

"Your parents were capitalist exploiters," Cecilia happily explained. "While the majority of Jews in the USSR are either tradesmen in the cities, or farmers in the country. Following the October Revolution, refugees flooded the cities. There was hardly enough work for the tailors, shoemakers and blacksmiths already there, much less for the displaced thousands, especially those with no transferable skills. Jewish citizens were, of course, accorded their share of communal farmland on ground that previously belonged to Russian or

Ukrainian kulaks. It—it was not a… congenial arrangement." For the first time since she began proselytizing, Cecilia's confident tone faltered as she struggled to explain how, if all Soviets lived in brotherhood, it had been decided that, in the interest of keeping antisemitic violence down to acceptable levels, the best thing to do was convince the Jews of the USSR and its surrounding territories to relocate to the furthest eastern point on the Trans-Siberian railroad, where they would be safely out of the way and no longer annoying their Gentile neighbors with daily reminders of their existence.

"Hundreds of families and workers have settled there since April last year." Cecilia regained her equilibrium to continue. "They've been sent cattle to milk and raise, steel for putting up factories, wood to build homes, farm equipment to till the soil and plant crops. Birobidzhan will be the salvation of our poor, displaced Jews, first in the USSR, then the entire world!"

"What about America?" Regina asked. "Mama said some have left for America."

"Jews in America," Cecilia snorted, "sell their souls to become just like everyone else. In Birobidzhan, we'll be able to speak and write in our own language, teach our children in our own schools. Once the fields are flowering and the factories are at full production, we'll be self-reliant. We will be in control of our own destinies for the first time in five thousand years. And we'll do it in a socialist framework, to benefit the many, rather than the few." Cecilia glanced in the direction of Regina's parents' room, making it clear who the few had once been, and why they deserved to be supplanted by the many. "Forget America. Forget the stupid, futile Zionist dream, too."

If Jewish was a forbidden word, then Zionist was an irremissible one. To say it within another person's hearing was to ask for the death penalty. You might as well put your head into the guillotine and wait patiently. The closest Papa ever came to uttering it was when he railed against those "imprudent hooligans who want to make matters worse for the rest of us."

"Look at this." Cecilia used a finger to draw Regina's attention to a headline at the bottom of her newspaper. "This is what their Zionist dream has gotten them."

Regina read quickly. In August, in the city of Jerusalem, there had been riots, triggered by Jews raising their flag over the Western Wall, which led to an Arab attack on the Jewish quarter of the Old City that spread to Hebron, Safad and other smaller towns. By the time the uprising was contained, one hundred and thirty-three Jews were dead. A British commission had determined the cause of the violence "without which disturbances either would not have occurred or have been little more than a local riot, is the Arab feeling of animosity and hostility towards the Jews consequent upon the disappointment of their political and national aspirations and fear for their economic future, as well as Arab fears of Jewish immigrants as a menace to their livelihood." Cecilia wrote that *Evreyskoya Izvestia* stood in solidarity with the Palestinian Communist Party in supporting calls for a mobilization of a Jews Defense Force, especially as the British had not allowed the Jews arms with which to defend themselves, forbidding Jewish soldiers in their own ranks from taking part in holding back rampaging mobs.

"Do you see?" Cecilia stressed. "Zionism leads to the death of the Jewish body, America to the death of the Jewish soul. Birobidzhan is our people's only chance."

"Then why is everybody always yelling about it?"

Cecilia laughed, "Well, we haven't exactly agreed on every detail yet. It's a Jewish state, my little queen. What else would you expect?"

CECILIA INVITED REGINA to come back and listen to the arguments about what this new Jewish state could be—and what it should be. "And not through the keyhole, this time. Young people like you are our future. You must be a part of whatever we build."

Whatever we build. The phrase stuck with Regina during her walk down the corridor from Cecilia's room to theirs, and through the remainder of the afternoon. Cecilia had used the future tense. No one at home used the future tense—only the past. At school, they constantly used the future tense. They talked about Five-Year Plans and Great Leaps Forward. Those were things their Great Leaders were magnanimously giving them. The people would be a part of it, of course; the people were the fuel that kept the engines of Socialism running. But they had no say in where those engines went, no influence, no agency. Mama, Papa and Regina's teachers agreed that the future—good or bad—was something that happened to you. Cecilia made it sound like something you could have a hand in creating.

Regina had to wait until her parents were asleep before sneaking out. That was alright. Cecilia's guests were merely warming up. Regina stuck her head tentatively through the door to Cecilia's room. Adults, she knew, did not appreciate children eavesdropping. Mama was always shooing Regina away, especially when friends came over to whisper furtively about how things used to be. "None of your business," Mama would say. "Adults are talking."

Cecilia was in the middle of what looked like a most serious discussion with a bald man smoking a pipe. When she caught sight of Regina trying to be unobtrusive, Cecilia shouted, "My little queen!" across the room, and waved her over. A dozen faces turned in Regina's direction. A few smiled, amused. The rest paid her no mind. Nobody shooed her away.

"This is Comrade Berger," Cecilia introduced. "He comes to us all the way from Berlin!"

"*Willkommen in Moskau, Genosse Berger.*" Regina used her best German. Mama would disapprove of her being so impudent, not to mention showing off. But Regina felt giddy from the thrill of feeling welcomed into adult conversation.

"Typical," Cecilia sniffed. "Pretentious parents teach the child German, not Yiddish."

The child. Cecilia had called Regina *the child*. There went her confidence and giddiness. Regina curled her shoulders, shrinking into herself, feeling foolish. She clamped her lips, vowing not to utter another word until she could think of something impressive—and mature—to say. It wouldn't be easy in such illustrious company. Everywhere Regina turned, a furious debate was unfolding. It was here, among Cecilia's compatriots, that Regina heard Comrade Kaminsky insist factories were Birobidzhan's path to financial independence, while Comrade Berger accused him of being a modern day Pharaoh. Arguments she would repurpose to impress Felix nearly a decade later.

That wasn't the only aporia Regina encountered that night. She was on her way out, yawning and rubbing her eyes, embarrassed by how much like a child this made her look; she was clutching the latest issue of *Evreyskoya Izvestia*, when a headline at the bottom of the back page caught her eye. It asserted that this publication, in complete agreement with Communist International, condemned calls from the Palestinian Communist Party to arm the Jewish interlopers of Jerusalem. They stood, instead, in solidarity with their Arab brethren as they mourned the deaths of their comrades during the unprovoked attacks of August.

Regina paused, turning to Cecilia, "Didn't you write last week you supported—"

Cecilia maneuvered Regina towards the exit in a way that suddenly seemed rushed. "No. Supporting Arab Commitern over the Palestinian Communist Party has been *Evreyskoya Izvestia's* stance from the start. We'd never go against Communist International."

Regina protested, "I still have the previous issue in my room. Let me go get it. I'll show you where you—"

"No," Cecilia shrieked. It was the closest Regina had ever seen her come to losing her composure. She lowered her voice to repeat, "No. The position of Communist International is that the Arabs are in the right, and the Palestinians are in the wrong."

"Palestinians are Jews. You publish a Jewish newspaper. Shouldn't you be on their side?"

"The Jews of Palestine are Zionists. *Evreyskoya Izvestia* is a Communist publication. We don't look to separate Jews from other proletarians. We're not blood-thirsty nationalists like those Zionist thugs. We don't think we're better than any other race. We look to bring everyone together. That's always been our policy. Go to your room, find that issue you were talking about, Regina." It was the first time she'd used her real name. That, more than anything, drove home how serious Cecilia was. "Then burn it."

THE INCONGRUITY OVER what was truly happening in the East failed to dampen Regina's enthusiasm for Cecilia's salons. If anything, it made her more curious. The notion that there could be more than one side to any happening was so fundamentally anti-Soviet, and thus so simultaneously seductive and terrifying, Regina couldn't help finding it irresistible. She kept dropping in, night after night, week after week, year after year. Regina went from merely listening to tentatively dropping in a tidbit of thought. Eventually, she progressed from whispering a fact to shouting an opinion. It was clear to Regina why Cecilia had warranted a room all to herself. How else could you possibly accommodate all the diversity of people and their viewpoints! From night to night, you couldn't predict which way the crowd would swing. Regina had never known such excitement! The guest list was forever changing. Thanks to Cecilia, Regina met everyone from the Yiddish actor Solomon Mikhoels, to Canadian Arctic explorer Vilhjalmur Stefansson, to Baron Dudley Aman of England. The latter brought Regina books so she could study English, assuring her it would come in handy when all Canadian, British, and American Jews relocated to Birobidzhan. Not only did philosophers and artists show up to Cecilia's, but also high-ranking party members. There was at least one at every gathering, laughing, talking and drinking along with the rest.

"Of course they are keeping tabs on us." Cecilia dismissed Regina's concerns when she relayed Mama's fears that their neighbor's guests were monitoring them. "So what? We have nothing to hide. Birobidzhan and *Evreyskaya Izvestia* are under the protection of the Central Committee. Kaganovitch himself recently visited Comrade Kaminsky in Amurzet. Comrade Berger staged an original play to honor him. They hosted a banquet in Kaganovitch's honor. He praised the gefilte fish they served as the best he'd ever tasted! Let them file their reports on us. They will read what loyal citizens we are!"

By the time she turned eighteen, Regina could distinguish the artists from the statesmen from the foreigners from the hangers-on. But, in February of 1936, into Cecilia's room walked a man who didn't fit any previously identified category. His clothes were neither those of a dandy, nor of a worker. Instead, they seemed a collection of odd pieces thrown together, with no care for effect. Those who traditionally visited Cecilia's room tended to care very much about the effect they presented. This man's boots were scuffed, his overcoat patched at the elbows. He had a boy with him, maybe ten or eleven years old.

Though Regina had long stopped thinking of herself as a child, she was, nevertheless, accustomed to being the youngest participant. It was a point of pride for her to be accepted by such distinguished adults. The sight of the boy unsettled her. Would he be Regina's competition? But not nearly as much as it unsettled Cecilia. Cecilia cut off a conversation midstream to float across the room, skulking along the edges, keeping out of sight. She placed herself between the man and the boy, nudging them into the hallway. She closed the door behind them. Cecilia's door was always at least part way open. Because Cecilia had nothing to hide.

She returned no more than ten minutes later. The man and the boy weren't with her. Cecilia went back to the conversation she'd abandoned, as if nothing had happened. No one inquired if anything had.

Except for Regina.

Chapter Fifteen

━━━━━━

She didn't ask right away. She spent days avoiding the subject. She told herself it was none of her business. She told herself Cecilia didn't owe Regina any explanations. She told herself Comrade Stalin's credo: *The less you know, the sounder you sleep.*

She couldn't sleep, for wanting to know.

She told herself she was being as brave as Cecilia by opting to ask her. She told herself it would be good practice for the bravery she'd need once she relocated to Birobidzhan. She told herself Cecilia might be aching for someone to talk to.

Cecilia was not.

Cecilia claimed not to remember who Regina was talking about—she met so many new people on a daily basis, you couldn't expect her to… Regina had her chance to back down. She couldn't. Because she couldn't shake the feeling that Cecilia's answer to this particular question would answer other questions Regina had nurtured through the years. Cecilia rarely talked about herself. When she did, it was primarily about the future, rarely about the present, never about the past. Cecilia never shared how she'd come to her path. How had she gotten permission to settle in Moscow? People filed request after request and still waited years for a *propiska*. How had she been made editor of *Evreyskoye Izvestia*? Every other editor of similar papers from around the country Regina had met was a man. She'd been too timid to ask Cecilia about that. So she dug her heels in about this. Maybe because it seemed safest. Maybe because it seemed the most dangerous. Maybe because it seemed the most connected to herself, and her own life options.

Cecilia shrugged. Cecilia sighed. Cecilia confessed, "The man is my husband. The boy is my son."

At some level, Regina had been expecting as much. It was the obvious answer. Yet she couldn't help feeling shocked. "Why—where— why don't they live with you?"

Cecilia swept her arm the length of the room, the crumpled papers, the floor covered in books, the leftover glasses, the half empty bottles, the smoldering cigars that didn't make it to an ashtray and, most of all, herself. "Do they look like they belong among... this?"

"Where do they live?"

"Back home." She still refused to name the exact location. "Where my parents have sat *shiva* for their wayward daughter, and my in-laws curse my name at every opportunity."

The question burst from Regina's chest like a butcher's cleaver through a cow's ribcage. "Why don't they belong here? What's wrong with them?"

"Nothing is wrong with them! They're exactly who they should be," Cecilia snorted. "Ask what is wrong with me."

Regina didn't think she was serious. Yet Cecilia kept looking at her expectantly, daringly. Eventually, Regina felt compelled to obey and stammer, "What—what's wrong with you?"

"I want," Cecilia said simply. "That is what's wrong with me. I want to think, I want to speak, I want to do. I want more than I am allowed to want."

The words coming from Cecilia's mouth were like labels being affixed to the unformed thoughts swirling through Regina's head. They were all Regina dreamed of. Cecilia made them sound like curses.

"And your husband, your son..." Regina prompted, wondering what one had to do with the other.

"They want only what they are allowed to want." Cecilia smiled wryly. "Lucky them."

"My Mama and Papa don't even want that much," Regina said, trying to convey that she understood what Cecilia was saying. They were the same.

"Women," Cecilia said. Had she heard Regina's reply, or was Cecilia responding to the thoughts swirling through her own head? "Women are forced to make choices men are never confronted with. For women, it is always 'this or that.' Women are not allowed 'this and… anything.'"

THE DOOR TO Cecilia's room stood open. Her belongings scattered in the hall, with more being flung out. Coming home, Regina had seen the two Chaika limousines parked outside, but their building housed multiple families; there was no reason to believe they'd come for anyone she knew. In fact, in the past, similar raids had deliberately avoided Cecilia's room. The most the soldiers did was flirt with her, before they moved on to arresting someone else.

"Cec—!" Regina tried calling out her friend's name. She'd barely gotten a syllable out before a hand clamped over her mouth and Regina was jerked off her feet, into her family's room. Papa had been the one to grab her. It was Mama who hissed, "Sha! They know about you!"

Regina didn't have to ask who. For months, NKVD officers had been arresting those accused of being untrustworthy, counter-revolutionary bourgeois-nationalists plotting against the state. Regina was not an untrustworthy, counterrevolutionary bourgeois-nationalist plotting against the state, so: "What could they know about me?"

"That you're associated with… her." Mama might have spat if it wouldn't have soiled her own floor.

"Where is Cecilia?"

"They took her," Papa said. "Hours ago, in the morning, right after you left for school. We stayed in here and hid, scared to come out and go to work, scared they would notice us."

"We heard them," Mama added, "asking the neighbors about her associates." Another word that might have earned spittle.

"Why? What for? What was the charge?"

"What does it matter?" Mama snorted.

"If someone lied about Cecilia, all she has to do is tell the truth, and this will be quickly straightened out."

Mama and Papa exchanged looks. They might have laughed… if they weren't so close to tears.

A loud banging on the door. All three of them jumped from the noise.

"Don't open it," Mama urged.

"They know we're here," Papa said. "We don't want to make them angry."

He opened the door partway. An NKVD officer, dressed in a summer uniform for the heat of September—a lightweight brown tunic, belted at the waist, over loose azure slacks tucked into black knee-high boots—scanned the room, ignoring Mama and Papa to settle on Regina.

"Your name," he demanded.

She told him.

He looked her over from head to toe, taking a bit more time with Regina's bustline than necessary for a simple confirmation of identity. And smirked.

MAMA WAITED UNTIL the officers left the flat, taking with them whichever of Cecilia's things they wanted—her typewriter, a gilt-edged mirror, two rugs, and all the bottles of alcohol she kept for guests, leaving the rest for her neighbors to scavenge—before she let out a keening shriek that somehow managed to be glass-breakingly loud and whisper-soft.

"They're coming," she whimpered. "They are coming for us!"

"No," Regina insisted, "Cecilia won't let that happen. She'll straighten everything out, for her and for us."

"Cecilia isn't coming to rescue you," Mama hissed. "Do you not understand, you foolish girl? Your friend was in favor for the last few years, now she is out of favor. It is always like this. Yesterday, you send others to the firing squad, tomorrow you are in front of it. You think we keep our mouths shut because we're cowards? We keep our mouths shut because what is approved to say one time is treasonous the next. Your Cecilia sits in a rat-infested cell where bright lights shine around the clock. Interrogators keep changing, but she gets asked the same questions over and over. It doesn't matter what she did or didn't do. It matters what confession they will force her to sign. And she will sign one, sooner or later. Everyone does. And then they will come for you. For us."

"Then we have to go."

Cecilia had been arrested on false charges. And though Regina still believed those interrogating Cecilia would eventually realize their error and set her free, she also believed they would be coming for Regina and her parents next, either as witnesses against Cecilia, or as co-conspirators. It would be best if they weren't there when that happened.

"For a little while," Regina clarified, "until this… misunderstanding is cleared up." She dropped to all fours, crawling under the bed for the single suitcase they kept there.

"Go where?" Papa looked helplessly about, lost in his own room.

"Birobidzhan."

Mama laughed bitterly. "A fairy story! You want to escape into a fairy story!"

Regina opened the suitcase, proceeding to empty her bureau drawer into it. Underthings, wool stockings, a shawl for when it grew cold, the other dress she owned besides the one she was wearing. "We can buy train tickets without authorization, receive official permission for residency once we arrive. Comrade Kaminsky is Village Soviet Chairman—he knows me."

"Pick up and leave?" Saying the words seemed more than Mama could manage.

"Before they come back. We'll return. Someday. Soon."

"No," Mama said. "We can't. We have always lived in Moscow. Your Birobidzhan, you think I don't know about it. It's on the edge of the world. No running water, searing heat, floods, flies, murderous Chinese—it's all the twelve plagues in one! We could not possibly go there!"

"You'd rather stay here and take your chances with NKVD?" Regina asked, incredulous.

"Maybe they will not come," Papa offered feebly. "We hardly knew the woman. There are many more important people they must have to round up before they get down to us."

"Are you just going to sit and wait then? Mama, you know they'll come, you just said so. Please, you and Papa, come with me."

Her mother looked from her daughter to her husband. Papa was shaking head to toe. He'd covered his mouth with his hands and was breathing in short, desperate gasps. His eyes blinked frantically, like a cornered animal.

"There is nowhere to run," Mama spoke for both of them. "Wherever we go, they will find us. And if we run, they will be even more angry."

"Mama." Regina played the last card she had available, especially since it also happened to be true. Her parents weren't the only ones who'd never lived outside Moscow. "I don't want to go alone. Please. I need you."

"We will stay here," her father repeated. "We have done nothing wrong." The shaking in his legs got the better of him. He reached behind himself, grasping blindly for something to hold onto. His hand found a chair, then accidentally knocked it over. Papa stared at the fallen object, as if he didn't know what could possibly be done to set it upright again. What could possibly be done to set the world as he knew it upright again.

Mama took a long look at Regina. This was her child. Her child was begging Mama not to abandon her. Sure, Regina had made mistakes. But she was young. Foolish. Idealistic. She understood how wrong she'd been, wrong to believe that anyone could ever keep them safe in this place. She was willing to admit it, to beg forgiveness. She needed clemency. She deserved it. How could Mama refuse her own child's pleas for help?

"I must stay with my husband."

"Why?" Regina realized how selfish and unreasonable she sounded, but she couldn't help herself. She felt abandoned. Betrayed. This wasn't how a mother was supposed to act.

"He needs me."

"I need you," Regina pleaded.

Mama looked at the items Regina had haphazardly thrown into their suitcase and shook her head. "This is not enough." She scurried to her chifforobe drawer and frantically dug through it. "It is warm now, but it will be cold soon." She yanked out a moth-ridden hat made of rabbit fur, leather gloves lined with wool, a pair of Papa's thickest socks, and stuffed them next to Regina's other things. She pulled up a chair, climbed on it, and felt the top of the closet until she managed to reach a dusty envelope. She blew on it, then lifted the flap, removing a stack of colored rubles dated from the third denomination launched by Comrade Stalin in 1924. A gold one was worth fifty thousand of the previous issue, as a means of ending inflation. The one-ruble note featured a miner, the three ruble, soldiers, the five ruble, a pilot. Mama shoved the bundle into Regina's hands. "You will need this."

Regina gaped at the offering. She'd learned at school that the cause of inflation was self-serving hoarders and exchange speculators. They were what led to the silver shortage, and the revaluation of paper money. She had no idea her parents were among the wrongdoers.

"You can't give her all of it!" Papa piped up. "It's everything we have!"

Mama whipped her head, glaring at him. Stunned by her ferocity, Papa sighed and shrunk back, not daring to say another word.

"Go," Mama urged Regina. "Quickly."

"I'm scared," Regina confessed as she was closing her suitcase, snapping locks shut, reaching for her coat, despite the afternoon heat outside. She'd told her parents this trip was for a short while, to lie low until Cecilia's and, by extension, her name was cleared. Yet she pleaded, "I might never see you again." Regina wanted to be brave. Nonetheless, she heard herself repeating, "Come with me, Mama. Please."

Regina's mother looked at her father, sitting immobile, save the shaking wracking his body. "Papa is too frightened."

"Then leave him," Regina trilled, hating herself, unable to stop herself.

"He will never survive without me," Mama said, pushing Regina out the door. "You go. You survive." The last thing her mother said to Regina was, "Never write us. That's how they will find you."

Chapter Sixteen

"I made terrible decisions," Regina told Aaron. "I trusted the wrong people. I don't know if my parents are dead or alive. I don't know what happened to Cecilia. I don't know if she and Kaminsky were innocent or guilty. I don't know if I was innocent or guilty for listening to them. I don't know anything. Except I was a selfish coward who ran to protect myself."

"Wise choice," Aaron observed. He'd listened to Regina employing the same inscrutable expression with which he listened to Felix's directives. She had no idea how he felt about what she'd confessed. Either about her past in Moscow. Or her turning down Felix's proposal. Or her desire to marry him, instead.

"You wouldn't have done it. You wouldn't have let anyone cower you. You didn't vote to freeze the seeds no matter how hard Felix intimidated you. You left to help the Cossacks when no one was on your side."

"You were."

Regina gulped and shook her head. "I was a coward then, too. I used to think I knew everything. I thought I was smarter than my parents. They clung to the past. I was forging a brave path into the future." She raised her arm and pointed her finger, echoing Lenin. She'd done it before. With Felix. She'd meant it then. She had no idea what she meant now.

"You defended Marta," Aaron said. Raising Regina's chin with his hand, forcing her to look at him in a way she hadn't since that day when he'd smeared her face with balm, triggering previously unknown sensations in Regina, Aaron reminded, "You defended me."

"Because you were right. How do you always know the right thing to do?"

In lieu of an answer, Aaron dipped his head and kissed Regina. He went about it slowly, first merely brushing his mouth against hers, then bringing it back for another pass. His upper lip slipped inside, catching her lower one between his, followed by a flick of his tongue. He pressed himself against her and Regina felt the ground shifting beneath her feet, like she was falling. She instinctively reached out behind her. But there was nothing to steady herself on, forcing Regina to lurch forward and clamp onto Aaron's elbow, holding on tight as the world around her spun, the only stability coming from the spot where they'd inexorably connected.

"Was that the right thing to do?" he asked innocently upon pulling back and surveying Regina at arm's length.

"Y-Yes…" It was impressive Regina was able to get the single word out, considering the utter lack of breath left in her body.

"How do you know?" Aaron teased.

She kissed him back. Not slowly, not patiently, but like Regina was making up for all the times she'd wanted to, all the times she hadn't realized she'd wanted to, and all the times she hadn't done it due to reasons Regina was now having trouble recalling.

"I want to marry you," Regina said. "But I don't want to put you at risk. They could still come for me. And if you're associated with me… That's why I had to tell you everything."

"You're not afraid to be associated with me? I didn't vote to freeze the seeds no matter how hard Felix intimidated. I left to help the Cossacks." Aaron repeated Regina's words not to tease, but to warn.

She assured him, "You know the right thing to do. I know the right time to run. We're a perfect match."

MARTA, AGNESKA, AND Georgetta were delighted to learn of Regina and Aaron's engagement, as were several others Regina had previously only known well enough to nod hello to in the fields or dining hall. She'd expected more outward jealousy, considering what Felix told Regina about Aaron's popularity among the female population. And there was a bit of that. Definite snubbing, though from those who'd never given Regina the time of day previously; it hardly cut deep. Among the rest was a sense of glee that Regina, in allying herself with Aaron, had cut her ties with Felix. Maybe they were happy Regina had declared her loyalty to the workers, not their overlords. Maybe they were happy Regina was no longer under Felix's protection and would now experience the brunt of life in Birobidzhan. Regina didn't care. She had Aaron. She had friends. She could weather anything life threw her way.

She could certainly face any retribution from Felix.

She'd gone to tell him in person, before scuttlebutt from the fields reached his house. Regina thought it the right thing to do, and Aaron backed her up. It was amazing how having him in her corner gave Regina confidence. True, it was confidence in Aaron. But at least she was no longer paralyzed by indecision over the simplest of things. Having him believe in her went a long way towards helping Regina believe in herself.

"You've changed your mind," Felix predicted upon spying Regina on his doorstep.

Regina shook her head. And then she blurted out, "I'm marrying Aaron."

She expected Felix to rage. She expected Felix to try and dissuade her. She expected him to harangue and belittle her.

She didn't expect him to burst out laughing.

AS FAR AS Regina was concerned, there was no reason for her and Aaron not to marry immediately. She agreed to postpone the wedding for a few months—a year at most—because Aaron wanted to write his brother in Palestine and invite him. Aaron wasn't certain where he was living at the moment, which meant composing a series of letters and posting them to a series of organizations, then giving his brother

time to write back and, if possible, travel to Birobidzhan. He'd asked
Regina if she wanted to contact her parents. Maybe enough time had
passed that the kerfuffle with Cecilia had been cleared up, and the
three of them could be reunited. Regina asked Aaron if he truly believed that. He admitted he didn't. He was willing to take the risk, for
her sake. At least they would know something about what happened
to them. Wouldn't that help Regina's peace of mind, not to mention
her guilt? Regina remembered what Mama made her promise. And
refused.

Just because they couldn't yet sign a piece of paper which would
officially bind them in the eyes of the state, was no reason, as far
as Regina was concerned, for her and Aaron not to have sex immediately. What were they waiting for? This wasn't the Czar's time!
They weren't provincial, reactionary, capitalist Victorians. They were
modern, progressive, liberal Socialists!

"This one time," Aaron held Regina at bay, "let's be traditionalists."

"For whose benefit?" Regina demanded.

"Ours."

Regina pouted. Regina cajoled. Regina did her best to change
Aaron's mind. But though he continued to kiss her to make the
world tilt and fracture, though he allowed Regina to peel off his shirt
and finally run her hands over every centimeter of glowing skin, the
peaks and valleys beneath Aaron's shoulders, the ripple of muscles
along his back which had first mesmerized her under the moonlight,
and though he buried his face in Regina's neck, locating the precise,
tender spot at the tip of her spine which made her moan with pleasure and all but collapse into him, there was a firm line which Aaron
refused to cross.

Regina turned to her friends for help. Everyone had deeply
specific advice. Suck on his nipple, men can't resist that. Run your
hand down his stomach, he won't have the strength to stop you.
Remove your blouse and lean over him until your breasts are cradling his face, he'll have no choice but to react. Regina's friends were
modern, progressive, liberal Socialists, as were all their boyfriends.
How had Regina ended up with the sole old fashioned gentleman in
Birobidzhan?

"Rotten luck," Aaron advised, proving he did, in fact, possess the strength to stop Regina's palm from running down his stomach. Even if it did come with a groan and gritted teeth, not to mention a shaking hand at visible war with its owner.

Regina was getting somewhere.

HER MOTHER HAD described Birobidzhan as on the edge of the world. Ideal for fleeing. But with downsides. When, despite Felix's creative math, they ended up with half, not twice as much food for the winter, they were too far from Moscow to receive reinforcements. Anything sent was looted before it got to them. Felix explained that capitalist agents wanted to make it look as if the USSR wasn't growing enough food to feed its population, so they were stealing rations along the train routes. The USSR, in truth, was growing so much they were selling surplus to truly hungry countries, like America. Every collective was producing double their quota, like Amerzut.

There were also upsides to living on the edge of the world. It took weeks for them to hear about doings in Poland, where Germany had reclaimed land that belonged to them, and the rest of the citizens voted for the Soviet Union to administer their remaining territory. As it didn't affect Birobidzhan, nobody gave the political machinations much thought. Later, when they heard how Germans had attacked the Soviet Union without warning or provocation, they were shocked, of course. But they knew the fighting would be thousands of kilometers away from them. The Soviets didn't merely outnumber the Germans, they were also decades ahead in technology. This latest war would be settled in months, the citizens of Birobidzhan assured those who fretted over fates of friends and family now living in Nazi occupied zones. To believe otherwise was unpatriotic!

The sole way the conflict affected Regina's life was Aaron admitting he'd never be able to get in touch with his brother now. If he did receive any of the invitations to their wedding, he'd be stopped from crossing the border.

Did that mean they could get married immediately?

It did!

They only had one more obstacle to overcome, and that was yet another *samokritika*, this one called as an emergency session by Felix.

He got right to the point, not bothering to ask if anyone had something to confess before looking straight at Aaron and accusing him of subversive activity.

Since the engagement, Aaron had ceased lurking by the door. He'd joined Regina in the main gallery, next to Marta and Leon, as well as Agneska, Georgetta, and their beaus. James and Barbara Cohen used to assume spots not far from their group. Once Regina fell out of favor with Felix, they made a point of moving across the aisle. When Felix called out Aaron, Regina didn't flinch. She'd been expecting it. She understood he'd take his revenge on them one way or another. Frankly, it was a relief to no longer live in suspense.

Aaron rose languidly, of his own free will, not Felix's injunction.

Felix waited for Aaron to defend himself. Aaron said nothing. He looked to his right. He looked to his left. He looked behind him and he looked ahead at the five person village Soviet. Was he looking for support? Was he looking to see who would betray him? The one person he didn't look at was Regina. He didn't accept her hand when she offered it. He was going to face this alone. He would take no one else down with him.

Though Aaron declined to contest Felix's charges, Felix proceeded as if he had. "I have proof!" He raised a stack of papers in his hand, waving them around, not unlike they'd recently watched a newsreel of the British Prime Minister declaring he had secured "peace for our time." "Aaron Kramer has been corresponding with Zionist agents! He's been giving away our scientific agricultural secrets, and plotting to sabotage our output in order to discredit Comrades Lysenko and Stalin!"

Regina recognized the letters. Aaron must have too. They were all the ones he'd sent his brother. The ones he'd put off their wedding for.

"Would you read one out loud?" Aaron asked politely.

"You'd like that! You'd love for me to read your filthy propaganda out loud, so you might attract more converts to your anti-Soviet cause. Do you see what a malefactor this is?" Felix raged, "Rather than confess to his crime, he tries to trick me into spreading his poison further? Do you see what kind of conspiracy we are up against?"

She'd believed him once. That's what was killing Regina, pressing down like a nail driven into her skull. Not long ago, she'd believed Felix. About the villains in their midst, the conspiracy. Like she'd believed Comrade Berger about the utopia of Birobidzhan. Like she'd believed Cecilia when she said they had the Party's support. None of it was true. Would Regina ever learn?

When Aaron took his look around the hall, he'd appeared resigned that no one would step up to defend him. But Regina couldn't give up. Not when she knew the room was filled with people Aaron had helped. Nobody knew he'd rearranged the seed bags to keep them from losing their entire harvest. But everybody knew how hard Aaron worked to get them the meager rations they did have. They knew how frequently he stepped in for an exhausted worker, how diligent he was about distributing the insect repelling salve, how he turned a blind eye to the black market dealings he saw going on in his hectare, not asking for a cut like the other directors had. Aaron looked out for everyone. Was there no one now who would look out for him?

Regina shot a pleading glance to Marta, to Leon… Agneska… Georgetta. No one would meet her eye. No one would help. The irony was, Regina knew Aaron wouldn't want them to. He would never want anyone to put themselves on the line for his sake.

The way Felix kept peeking nervously about the room suggested he, too, knew of Aaron's heroics, and, despite it being in everybody's worst interests, harbored a tiny fear of rebellion breaking out. The longer it remained silent, the more relaxed Felix grew, allowing the hint of a smile, before remembering himself and suppressing it. This was serious business.

He used his most serious tone to declare, "Comrade Kramer demonstrates no loyalty to our Motherland. Surely, we remember how he forced us to cooperate in his furtive scheme to steal our food reserves for winter and sell them under cover of night to our enemies."

A furtive scheme, Regina thought, carried out under electric lights before every member of their cooperative; the contraband goods changing hands being Aaron's sweater. They'd all been there. They'd all seen what happened. But daring to contradict Felix was asking for a charge equal to Aaron's.

Instantly, the hall filled with cries of, "Yes, yes, we remember."

"He forced us!"

"We had no choice!"

"He threatened us!"

"At gunpoint!" That last came from James Cohen.

Leave it to Americans, Regina thought, to believe we might have access to guns here!

"The penalty for collaborating with our Fascist enemy," Regina noted Felix skipped the trial and conviction portion of the proceedings—they were a given—as easily as he skipped from the Cossack enemy to Fascist, "is prompt deportation to a work camp in Siberia, where our comrade will be rehabilitated into a productive Soviet citizen." Felix's smirk betrayed what he thought the odds of that happening were. It wasn't clear whether that was because he expected Aaron to resist—or die. "All in favor?" Felix's arm was halfway up. Soon, everyone else's would be, too.

Regina sprang from her chair. The shock prompted Felix's hand to waver and plop to the table, as she'd hoped. As long as his arm remained down, so would everyone else's. Felix may have looked shocked by Regina's actions. Aaron looked furious. She couldn't brood about that. She was too focused on getting her words out. Before Felix caught on.

"Comrade Luria is right."

If Felix had appeared shocked before, that was nothing compared to what his expression conveyed now. If the stakes weren't so high, Regina would have taken pleasure in finally getting one over on him. As the saying went, it wasn't evening yet...

"Our motherland is under attack from the Fascist threat. We must all band together to fight them off our territory, set aside our petty differences and unite in Socialist brotherhood. Comrade Luria is right. Comrade Kramer is obliged to be rehabilitated into a productive Soviet citizen. He is obliged to prove his loyalty to the state. Thank you, Comrade Luria, for your leadership. Thank you for submitting that Comrade Kramer's rehabilitation and loyalty can be demonstrated by his taking up arms to fight the Germans as a member of the Red Army!"

They'd all been there. They'd all heard what Felix actually said. But daring to contradict Regina meant taking the risk that what Regina said wasn't, in fact, what Felix had meant. And no one was willing to do that until Felix, himself, contradicted Regina.

He certainly appeared headed in that direction. His initial shock morphed to confusion as Regina spoke, to be quickly replaced with rage. He opened his mouth. His fingers twitched. His palm was on its way up from the table.

When Comrade Klara cut him off.

"All in favor?" she cried, beating Felix to the punch, raising her own arm high in the air.

In an instant, every hand in the hall followed suit. In an instant, every face swiveled her way. In an instant, Klara had wrenched control and authority from Felix, putting herself in charge. Clever girl...

Chapter Seventeen

"Operation Typhoon. You've heard of it?" Felix stood outside the Birobidzhan telegraph office, proudly handing Aaron the scrap of paper he'd managed to procure after hours of intense back and forth communication. "I've wrangled you the most prestigious posting. Defending our beloved Moscow from the Fascist invasion. No honor could be greater!"

As far east as they were, it could take weeks for news to arrive. Nevertheless, they'd heard of Operation Typhoon, the Nazi push to the capital. Hitler promised his followers Moscow would be captured within four months of invasion. Once Smolensk fell in July 1941, every Soviet feared he'd be successful. But then the Nazis opted to eliminate opposition forces in Leningrad to the north and Kiev to the south, which delayed their approach until September, giving Soviets time to raise fresh forces, including bringing in units from Siberia. As two million German troops, including three infantry units, three panzer tank divisions, and air cover by the Luftwaffe, surged deep into Soviet territory, they were met with a defense line stretching over three separate fronts from the towns of Vyazma and Bryanzk. Nazis smashed through it by mid-October, surrounding Moscow and its defending armies, leaving the scattered units to battle attacks coming from all sides while they waited for reinforcements from the East. They hoped the snowfall that turned accessible roads into muddy quagmires—the Russian word for it was *rasputitsa*—would slow down the German's advance more than it was hampering the Soviet's defense.

It was into this standoff that Felix had arranged to send Aaron. A great honor, indeed.

He'd been unable to prevent Comrade Klara from holding the vote that allowed Aaron to avoid deportation to Siberia for his crimes. But, once the clapping stopped, Felix had wrestled back a fraction of authority for himself by announcing he would take care of Aaron's enlistment and field assignment—tonight! He stormed down to the telegraph office, forcing the woman who ran it to send an immediate telegram to Moscow. When the one he received in return proved not what Felix had hoped for, he continued firing off missives until achieving his desired result.

Aaron and Regina waited outside, shivering in the fall mist. Aaron waited to learn his fate. Regina waited for him to say something about her having doomed him to it.

After what felt like an eternity, but was merely the half hour it took them to walk from the meeting hall to the town square—Aaron was hardly going to say anything while Felix was within hearing distance—Aaron finally spoke. "Thank you."

Regina startled. She hadn't been expecting it. She was so used to presuming any choice she made would inevitably backfire that she'd been waiting for Aaron to explain to her why her latest decision had also been a mistake. Instead, he followed up with, "You saved my life."

"He's sending you to Moscow." Regina employed the argument she'd anticipated Aaron making after Felix announced Aaron would be leaving on the first morning train. As Felix headed home, looking satisfied, Regina lamented, "We've already lost tens of thousands of men there!" That number had come unofficially. *Pravda* was only reporting victories. Which made Regina believe the true casualties had to be higher than what was rumored.

"I'll have a fighting chance," Aaron said. "Wars end. Siberia is a one way trip."

"I'll come with you." In Regina's mind, she was already moving as swiftly as she had when she made her decision to flee Moscow.

"It's not a dinner party." Aaron held up the telegram Felix had smugly shoved into his hand. "I'm not invited to bring a guest."

"I'll take care of you," Regina insisted.

"But I won't be able to take care of you." Aaron reasoned, "Supplies and food are rationed per soldier. If we try to survive on my allotment, we'll starve. You're safer here. The Nazis will never get this far east. They don't have the men or the supply lines."

"What about Japan?" Regina dug in her heels, grabbing for the latest piece of news she could think of to make her point. "They're already holding most of China. What's to stop them from crossing the border into Birobidzhan and opening a second front?"

"I am not debating this!" For the first time since she'd known him, Aaron raised his voice. He hadn't gotten angry all the times she'd challenged him in the fields. He hadn't gotten angry when Felix passed resolutions that would starve them and send Aaron into exile. But when Regina expressed her wish to be with Aaron, no matter what, he raised his voice. It was all she could do not to jump back. "For the next who knows how long, my focus must be on survival. I can't focus on my safety if I'm worrying about yours. You want to take care of me? Let me take care of myself, without distraction."

"Then we should get married before you go." Regina clung to something she could still control, something she could still hold onto in the face of risking never seeing Aaron again.

"No." Aaron was no longer yelling. He sounded exhausted, and about as close to defeat as Regina had ever heard him. He held up Felix's telegram. "This could be a trick. I could still be arrested the moment I get off the train." Regina thought of the Cossacks, who believed they, too, had been granted amnesty. "You don't want to be legally tied to me."

As quickly as Regina could conjure up ploys to keep them together, Aaron was equally as swift at knocking them down.

"At least swear you'll come back for me." Regina realized she was acting like a child. But none of her attempts at behaving like an adult had done any good. The least Aaron could do was join her in the realm of magical thinking.

She should have known better. Aaron would always be Aaron. Which meant practical, and honest, and true to himself. "You know I can't."

"I could," she insisted. "I could promise to always come back for you, no matter what."

Aaron kissed her then, in that way he had of making Regina forget everything, including promises. She vowed she would remember this one. No matter what.

IT WASN'T A trick. True to his word, Felix had arranged for Aaron to enlist in the Red Army, and be sent directly to the front. He arrived after the painfully undermanned Mozhaisk defense line had been disemboweled by the Wehrmacht. A quarter million women and children dug trenches and anti-tank moats day and night under air-raid attacks to surround Moscow, breaking up three million cubic meters of frozen earth using shovels, spades, and their bare hands, as all mechanical tools had been requisitioned for the military.

By November, the snowfall that had softened the ground, making it difficult for German tanks to advance, turned into a deep freeze, the result of the coldest recorded winter to that point of the twentieth century. This solidified the formerly swampy roads and allowed the Nazi 3rd and 4th Panzer group to entrench their position north of Moscow, getting close enough to the capitol where both sides could see each other through field glasses.

Aaron understood which way was north because that was the direction his unit had been ordered to fire. Otherwise, he'd long lost all sense of meaningful bearing. Everywhere he looked, he saw snow, ice, corpses left to stiffen where they fell. His ears vibrated with the pummeling of artillery even during lulls in fighting. He blinked obsessively to keep crystals from forming on his eyes, and smacked his lips to prevent them freezing together. The tips of his fingers and toes had long turned a grey-yellow, layers of skin swelling into translucent blisters. He heard that the Nazis were in worse shape, having failed to receive provisions for winter. They were still fighting in summer uniforms. But knowing it didn't make Soviet appendages warmer. The one hundred grams of vodka prescribed per soldier, per day went a bit further, but it wasn't enough to make you forget where you were, even if it grew harder and harder to remember why.

Some days they were told they were on the defensive, some days on the offensive, and, other times, the objective was to crawl onto the battlefield, ducking bullets to strip fallen bodies of uniforms and bring them back to outfit the next wave of soldiers. They blew up reservoirs and dams, flooding their own villages, driving citizens from their homes in the dead of winter, in order to melt ice that might otherwise prove solid enough to transport German artillery over the Volga River. By spring, their movement was labeled a counteroffensive, though it felt no different than any other. Officially, their position was decreed a stalemate. Unofficially, they called it "the Rzhev meat grinder," as a conveyor of bodies was fed into the maw of a forest swamp between Rzhev and Bely. Officers began admitting their goal was no longer to seize territory held by Germans, but rather to keep them distracted so they wouldn't be redeployed to battles near Stalingrad. The men were kept motivated via repetition of Comrade Stalin's mantra, "The Red Army and Navy and the whole Soviet people must fight for every square of Soviet soil, fight to the last drop of blood for our towns and villages. Onward, to victory!" And by Order #227, also known as Not One Step Backward, which decreed any troops who retreated from battle were to be mowed down by blocking detachment units stationed behind their own lines to shoot men acting in a cowardly fashion.

As soon as the snows stopped and the skies cleared, the Luftwaffe began flying again. The Soviets were outgunned. Each artillery battery had two rounds per day, and no more than three bullets per rifle, while the Germans seemed to be manufacturing their ammunition on the spot. Soviet tanks were failing, and communication between various units was nearly nonexistent, making coordinated attacks impossible, especially when, without warning, Comrade Stalin redeployed divisions into alternative battle positions. What they did have was men. They came in wave after wave, dropped off from boats, from trucks, on foot, outfitted against the cold, handed a rifle and shoved forward, most likely not to return. In the winter, you never got to see their faces, so tightly were they wrapped in scarves against the snow. It was worse in the spring and summer, when you could. They grew younger and younger with each delivery. Or maybe it was Aaron who felt older and older. Acne dotted chins and foreheads. Voices cracked. Some were actively crying, wiping their eyes on their sleeves or with the back of a fist.

Aaron dreaded the sight of a convoy approaching, though he knew, if not them, then him. He'd been shot twice. Both times lucky the bullet merely tore flesh, but didn't embed in bone or organ. He was missing a chunk of calf, which prompted a limp, and the lower part of his left ear. He hadn't bled to death, and he'd fought off the subsequent infections. He didn't expect his good fortune to last much longer. In August of 1942, Aaron realized his luck had run out.

When he spied Regina disembarking from the trucks bringing their latest cannon fodder.

THAT WASN'T WHAT they were officially called. Officially, this group consisted of desperately needed doctors and nurses. But bullets rarely discriminated between those assigned to combat and those relegated to support positions. The reason they so desperately needed more medical staff was because the majority of their predecessors were dead, felled sometimes by bullets, but as frequently by hunger and disease.

When Aaron saw Regina getting off the trucks bringing their latest cannon fodder, his first thought was he was hallucinating. His second was he was dreaming. His third was he was dead. And so was she.

He found the latter option most attractive.

At heart, he knew it was none of those things. At heart, he knew Regina had disregarded his plea she stay away, and managed to insert herself into a war zone thousands of others were desperate to escape. And she had done it for him.

She approached him slowly, tentatively, almost shyly. The most beguiling combination of culpability and defiance. She knew he would be angry. She knew he had every right to be angry. She was prepared to accept his anger. She was equally as prepared to push back against it.

Aaron read all that in Regina's face. He saw it in the way she strode towards him… while managing to look absolutely everywhere but directly at him. She couldn't decide whether to keep her hands at her sides or crossed against her chest, and so tried both. Regina was so much herself in that moment, the ultimate contradiction, that in spite of everything, the furor around them, the new recruits being processed, the tents and other supplies being distributed, and, as always, the never-ending echo of gunfire growing closer and withdrawing like waves, Aaron nearly laughed with delight at seeing what he never again expected to see.

Regina stopped in front of him. She finally looked up and met his eyes.

In yet another reply to a question Aaron hadn't asked, she explained, "Comrade Klara arranged for me to train as a medic and be assigned to your unit. She wanted me out of the way to consolidate her power." When Aaron didn't respond, Regina blathered on, "Klara got Felix demoted, sent to a new posting and that made the Cohens angry and now they're gunning for Klara, and I took advantage while there was still time, and I came here to you because I promised before it was too late."

She waited for Aaron to say something. Anything. She expected a redux of his anger, the same as when she'd first suggested joining him. She expected him to order her back onto the truck, she expected him to denounce her, to claim he wanted nothing to do with her, to turn his back on her once and for all.

Instead, almost as much to Aaron's shock as to her own, he lurched forward, wrapping his arms around her, pulling Regina to him, burying his face in her hair, and murmuring, "Thank you."

NO ONE BLINKED when, instead of reporting to her assigned quarters, Regina moved into Aaron's tent. By this point, nobody blinked at anything. Base camp was constantly shifting, soldiers were constantly packing up the tatters of their tents, flinging them over their shoulders, and marching, dead eyed, to the next location, where they set up again until the following move. The meat grinder assured never-ending turnover of tents to loot once you were vaguely certain the original owner wasn't coming back. Boots—didn't matter what size—were the most stolen items, followed by coats, caps, gloves, cigarettes, food and vodka rations. But there was a surprisingly thriving black market in photos of wives, sweethearts and sisters, too, not to mention letters from home. It didn't matter whose home. Remembering that somewhere, in some way, life was going on somewhat close to normal was enough. Because there was certainly no semblance of it at the front.

It wasn't just the death and the mutilation and the screams coming from the medical tent. It wasn't the two meals a day of canned goods where you couldn't tell meat from vegetable, or the stench from the overflowing latrines or the weather that took turns freezing and broiling you. It was the acceptance. The way boys who'd never gotten the chance to finish school dutifully picked up their rifles and headed where they were told, some not bothering to lift it defensively, simply waiting for the inevitable. It was the way surgeons moved from stretcher to stretcher, taking a look at a gaping stomach wound or a blown off leg, and continuing onto the next patient, not even pretending there was anything to be done. The way officers gave orders they didn't expect to be followed, and the way enlisted men charged blindly ahead, even if they weren't familiar with a nineteenth century general's observation, "No plan of operations extends with certainty beyond the first encounter with the enemy's main strength," long since shortened to, "No battle plan survives first contact with the enemy."

Aaron had been one of those men. Until Regina's arrival.

That first day, when no one blinked at her following him back to his tent, Aaron woke up not just from his battle fatigue stupor, but from the antediluvian notion of chivalry that had been drilled into him by his father and brother. Regina had been right. What was the point of waiting—for anything—when their lives were as good as over? Earlier, he'd been convinced he and Regina were already dead. On top of the relief, came frustration that he'd once believed in the luxury of a future including marriage enough to resist Regina's passionate entreaties to seize any opportunity for happiness, no matter how short lived.

Aaron knew better now.

Regina had barely set down her travel bag next to the rolled up mattress Aaron used for a bed before he was yanking her into his embrace, his mouth crushing hers. She responded equally as frantically, no time for formalities, hesitation, or shyness. They'd both waited too long. They'd both lived through too much.

They tried to be gentle, even when desire overwhelmed common sense. They tried to be careful. After the first time, they attempted to keep track of the dates when Regina was most likely to get pregnant, the way they heard the Catholics did. But when one day blended into the next with no change beyond which frozen stretch of land you were calling home that week, a calendar became just another remnant of a world that no longer mattered. Actions no longer had consequences. It wasn't throwing caution to the wind, it was not resisting where the wind took you.

They made it through fall and winter, surviving the Velikiye Luki offensive in November, the Rzhev-Vyazma in March. Soviet troops pushed German ones into retreat and reclaimed villages Nazi forces had occupied. They found hospitals looted for equipment, library books turned into firewood, family homes burned to the ground and surrounded by charred corpses. Stripped children's bodies had been piled into barns or laid out in lines on the streets, while adults swung from ropes attached to lampposts.

At every village they reoccupied, Aaron helped Regina track down survivors. Some ran out to greet the arriving army, waving crimson flags and bursting into sobs at the sight of their liberators. Others needed to be coaxed out of hiding places under floorboards and in the forest, unconvinced these soldiers were here to help and not launch another assault. Within minutes, posters of Comrade Stalin were being nailed onto the few walls still standing, while loudspeakers broadcast his greetings, and copies of *Pravda* were distributed into eager hands.

"Get all your latest news now!"

Regina figured she would never get a better segue. She turned to Aaron. He was in the process of sharpening the knife he'd be using to cut down the bodies hanging macabrely over their heads. She told him, "I'm pregnant."

Chapter Eighteen

———

"You should go back to Amerzut. No matter what Klara and the Cohens are plotting, it'll still be safer there for you and the baby."

The baby was currently nothing beyond a lump below her stomach and a stopper of phlegm in her throat that refused to move no matter how much Regina swallowed or coughed. And yet its fate had become the most important thing in the world.

"No." Regina had already anticipated and gone through all of Aaron's arguments in her head. She'd won no matter what she imagined he might say.

"You could be shot. You could freeze. You could starve."

"So could you." Regina reminded.

"Don't do this, please." Like once she'd never heard him yell, Regina now realized she'd never heard him beg. He hadn't begged Felix for his life. But he was begging her for their child's.

"We've taken care of each other so far," Regina pleaded to match. "We can take care of our baby. We'll certainly do a better job of it together than alone."

"What happened to the girl who didn't trust herself to make decisions?" Aaron's voice quavered between teasing and tears.

"I met you."

"Please don't make me regret it."

THEY WERE LOSING. Despite what *Pravda* insisted on printing. By the middle of 1943, every Soviet military position was a defensive one. They'd stopped advancing and were endeavoring anything they could to hold on. Germany occupied half of European Russia and oppressed forty percent of their population. The majority of the five million soldiers who'd enlisted in the Soviet Army in 1941 were dead. The eleven million currently mobilized had primarily been conscripted afterwards.

Aaron and Regina weren't dead. Aaron had no idea why. Regina had a theory. "Because we're taking care of each other."

He was able to trade Regina's daily ration of vodka, along with his, for more food to keep her on her feet. They were all so thin, basically walking cadavers, her pregnancy was barely noticeable. She told him not to worry. Women had given birth in more adverse conditions than hers throughout history. Besides, help was coming. Comrade Stalin was meeting with America's Franklin Roosevelt and Great Britain's Winston Churchill in Tehran. He would convince them to open a second front against the Germans. Once that happened, the Nazis would have to pull their forces from Soviet land to beat back the fresh onslaught from the west, and the Red Army would overwhelm them once and for all. Regina couldn't be prouder or more confident of the plan if she'd come up with it herself.

Aaron felt less positive. Regina spent her days at base camp, frantically dealing with the repercussions of their botched battles, the mangled limbs, the fractured faces, the incessant bleeding where you could apply direct pressure to one spot only to spy three more opening up, standing by helplessly as you watched the life drain out of a man, a boy, really, as he begged you to please, help, please, do something, you must be able to do something, you don't understand, his wife… his mother… his children… he promised them… they needed him…

Regina wasn't out in the actual battles themselves. She didn't see the disorganization, the blind panic, the running to and fro with no sense of direction. North, east, west, south, none of it meant anything when bullets were coming at you from every quadrant. It felt like they were pouring from the ground and sky, too. Where the shouted orders of one commander sounded the same as the bellowed directives of another, no matter the language, no matter the formally assigned unit. Aaron feared, no matter how many fronts were open, no matter how many men America poured into France, Italy or Germany, nothing would change. The theater of war would simply grow larger, swallow up more bodies into its meat grinder, but it would never, ever end.

"Do you know how to pray?" Regina asked Aaron. It was the last week of November. By Regina's calculations, the baby was due any day now. She joked it was biding its time, waiting for Mr. Roosevelt to acquiesce before doing the same.

With the Red Army dug in on the outskirts of Moscow, they'd been able to upgrade from tents to hastily thrown together wooden lean-tos. They weren't much bigger, but did do a slightly better job fending off the freezing winds blowing in across the Moskva River. If this winter proved to be as punishing as the last, every centigrade would make a difference. They'd stuffed burlap sacks with grass and straw to makeshift a mattress barely big enough for two people. At night, they pressed against each other, Aaron's chin on Regina's shoulder, his arms wrapped around what was left of her waist as she clutched his hands for warmth. And for the reminder that he was still there. In daytime, though, if either had so much as a few moments free, Aaron urged Regina to stretch out on her own, get as much rest as possible before the next onslaught. He crouched on the ground nearby, watching her now in advance of all those times when she'd be out of his sight, and he'd have to rely on nothing but faith of ever seeing her again.

"Pray?" Aaron repeated slowly, the word feeling as unfamiliar in his mouth as the texture of food that didn't come from a can or smell on the wrong side of rotting.

"My parents never did it," Regina said. "They were sophisticated Moscovites. They said savages from the provinces prayed."

"Like me?" Aaron asked with a half-smile.

"Did you?"

"My parents believed. Fasting on Yom Kippur, no bread on Passover, candles lit every Sabbath."

Regina shook her head in bafflement. None of it meant anything to her.

"My brother and I looked down on them," he said. "Imagine, believing some unseen force you were required to placate controlled your life. We were so much smarter. We were modern men. Our lives weren't controlled from above. We had free will. Our choices in life determined our fates."

Regina and Aaron looked side to side, taking in their slapdash surroundings. It didn't take long. They burst out laughing.

"Will you show me how to do it?" Regina asked. "Pray?"

"It's not… There isn't… I don't remember…" Was this the first time Regina saw Aaron lost for words? Was this the first time he ever had been lost for words?

"How did your mother do it," she prompted, "on the Sabbath? You said she prayed every week. You must remember something."

"She lit candles. And it was Friday." Aaron noted, "We have no candles. And it's Monday. I think."

"What did she say?" Regina pressed. The external details didn't matter. She wanted the words.

Now Aaron actually did appear flummoxed. It was adorable. He raised both hands in the air, palms up. He opened his mouth, then abruptly closed it, shoulders slumping. Aaron looked off into the distance, as if peering back through time, straining to make out the sounds, squinting to read the lips of his mother through the haze of distant memory. "It was in Jewish," he recalled slowly, "thanking God for making the light… maybe. No," he said, pivoting abruptly. "It was thanking God for commanding us to light the candles. That used to make me so angry when I was a boy. Why were we thanking someone for giving us orders?"

Regina laughed. "At least God didn't force you to vote unanimously on them!"

Aaron's grin matched Regina's. "Felix would appreciate the comparison."

"Would God, though?"

The question sobered Aaron. "Do you believe this," he gestured broadly with his arm, taking in not just their tent, but the world outside which necessitated them living this way, "could be anyone's plan?"

"I don't know. It couldn't hurt, could it? Praying? It can't make matters any worse."

"Things could always be worse."

"Show me how to do it. Show me how to pray."

She saw the denial bubbling in Aaron's throat. He swallowed it. For her sake. Regina had thought she couldn't love Aaron any more than she already did. He proved her wrong. It wasn't solely this. It was all the things he'd done against his better instincts. For her. Aaron yielding to her desires wasn't a path of least resistance. It wasn't merely a means for making her happy. It was evidence of his belief in her. Where Regina had no faith, Aaron did. It was the greatest gift anyone had ever given her.

"I think it went something like this," Aaron began. "She would wave her hands. To gather the light. There were candles. And she would cover her head. I don't know why. She'd say," he tapped his tongue against his upper lip, "she'd say, Baruch atta, Adonai." The words came out slurred. Regina had no idea what they meant. She doubted Aaron did, either. She repeated them as closely as possible, as, in her mind, the face of God was the face of Franklin Roosevelt, and, instead of thanking him for commanding her to light candles that weren't there, she entreated him to help them, to open a second front, to end this madness.

Did she believe, like Aaron asked. Regina didn't know. But, just in case God Franklin Roosevelt needed more evidence of her devotion, when their daughter was born on the last day of the Tehran Conference, Regina insisted they name her Eleanora, in honor of their potential savior's wife.

It was the only offering she had to give.

THE BABY WAS small but, as far as Regina could tell, healthy. She also quickly became the darling of the medical staff. It was a pleasure to deal with someone who wasn't sick, who wasn't maimed, who you could believe might live long enough to see a future without war.

Regina returned to work within days of giving birth, feeding little Lena in between shifts, leaving her in a cradle jerry-rigged from a sack and some scraps of wood, in the corner of the hospital tent. Not only was it warmer there, but, whenever Lena cried, there was always a pair of competent hands to pick her up, or rock her back to sleep if Regina was unavailable.

Their commanding officer, Colonel Zagorodnik, withdrew Aaron from the battlefield in honor of his new father status for the first few months of Lena's life. However, by March of 1944, they were running too low on men to extend his unofficial dispensation any longer. Three years of ceaseless fighting had driven so many soldiers to desperation that they were seeing a huge uptick in self-inflicted wounds as men took drastic measures to earn a discharge. In response, NKVD officers descended without warning onto field hospitals, hunting down traitors to the motherland, dispatching them directly to death by firing squad. The first time her supervisor ordered Regina to scrub in, they'd be amputating a boy's hand, she couldn't understand it. His injury was minor, there was no reason to...

"A shot through the left hand is the most common type of self-inflicted injury," the doctor explained, sotto voce. "If the NKVD suspects him, he'll be executed or, at best, transferred to a penal battalion. If we remove the evidence, he'll have some chance of survival."

Under such circumstances, able-bodied men like Aaron had no choice but to return to the battlefield. Regina got used to his being gone for days, sometimes weeks. She never asked him where he'd been or what he'd seen. The only conversation they ever had about any specific battle action was when the Americans finally made their move, sending hundreds of thousands of US, Canadian, and British troops to land along five separate beaches on the Normandy Coast in the first week of June 1944.

"Maybe prayer does work," Regina exulted.

Instead of arguing, Aaron picked the baby up from her crib and gently spun her around, cooing, "Thank you, Eleanora. You did it!"

HIS LONGEST ABSENCE came soon after, when Aaron was sent, along with thousands of others from their unit, towards the Polish-Soviet border, where an attack on the German Army Group Centre, code-named Operation: Bagration, had been planned at the Tehran Conference. A swift victory was predicted. The USSR was pitting over two million troops against a defense line held by less than a million Germans, now that, as prayed for, their attention was split between two fronts. The city of Minsk in Belarus was quickly liberated, and the Red Army continued their march west.

With good news outnumbering bad, they received regular updates from their head officer. Lvov retaken by Soviet troops! A coup in Rumania led to an armistice! Finns were withdrawing! An uprising in Warsaw!

Regina was starting to believe the war might be over and Aaron would be home in time for Lena to never remember his being gone, when Colonel Zagorodnik called her into his tent.

When Regina got there, the grim look on his face knocked the air out of her lungs at the same time she felt a ghostly blow to the backs of her knees. It was all she could do to remain standing.

"We regret to inform you," he said, "Comrade Kramer has been taken prisoner."

Chapter Nineteen

Colonel Zagorodnik thought he was being kind as he told Regina, "Prisoners of war are deemed a liability. All break under torture eventually and reveal secrets. Their rescue is not a priority. It's best for you and your girl to consider Comrade Kramer killed in action. He will be accorded full military honors, an orphan's pension for the child—"

"No." Regina shook her head, slowly at first, then picking up more speed. "Aaron may not be your priority, but he is mine. Where is he?"

Startled, Zagorodnik didn't have the opportunity to make up a lie before blurting out, "His unit was sent to Stalag 3-K, on the border between Poland and Germany."

"Thank you." Regina turned to leave, looking as if she intended to immediately head in that direction.

"Wait," the Colonel called. He was used to the freshly bereaved breaking down. He was used to them denying, arguing, raging, casting blame. He was not used to them poised to launch a one woman rescue mission.

Regina paused, half pivoting back his way. Her face suggested he best make it snappy.

Unaccustomed to feeling compelled to defend himself, he stammered, "You see, I—we—the USSR, we are not signatories to the Geneva Convention. Not how Germans, Americans, or British are. When our boys are taken prisoner, their captors are not obliged to treat them... well." It was the gentlest word he could think of. Lest she miss what he was trying to tell her, he added, "They're stripped of their uniforms, starved, beaten. The Red Cross can't deliver them supplies."

Was she going to make him continue? Was she going to make him articulate the most unpleasant fact of all? With any other woman, Zagorodnik would have deferred to her delicate, ladylike sensibilities. Except this woman was glaring at him with an expression so feral he feared any attempt at sensitivity would prompt her to turn all that barely restrained fury his way. So he went with the truth. Against everything that had allowed him to move up the ladder of Soviet command—and life, up to this point. "The Germans, they are particularly brutal with the prisoners of your nationality. Most of them are shot on sight, they never make it to the POW camps. Which is why, you see, as I said earlier, it's better of you to think of him as—"

"Aaron isn't dead." He expected her to shout the denial. It came wrapped in cold, quiet steel, instead. "I promised I would take care of him. I promised I would come for him."

"You're making an irrational decision." Now that Regina was acting more in the manner he expected, acting like all women when faced with a reality they didn't wish to face, Zagorodnik felt back in control of the situation. His earlier disquiet forgotten, he assumed a tone befitting a commander speaking to his subordinate.

"Those are my best ones," Regina said.

"WHAT ARE YOU doing?" Comrade Sania, the doctor in charge of the medial ward overnight caught sight of Regina, Lena strapped to her chest with a pair of worn, woolen scarves, stuffing a rucksack full of canned food, a canteen of water, and a bottle of rubbing alcohol.

"You didn't see me." Regina kept her voice down to give Sania the chance to deny she'd heard her, too. This woman had been nothing but courteous to Regina during the almost two years they'd worked side by side. Regina had no interest in making Sania's life difficult. Same as she had no intention of letting her keep Regina from getting to Aaron.

"He's already dead." Sania didn't read Regina's mind, she read the situation. The entire unit had been captured. Everyone had lost someone. Everyone felt the desperate urge to go charging to the rescue. Except everyone knew it was futile.

Regina continued packing while swaying side to side to soothe Lena from fussing.

Sania tried another tack. "How will you find him?"

"This map." She slid a folded piece of paper from her blouse's front pocket to show Sania she wasn't going off half-cocked. "Railroad tracks lead to a few hours walk from the camp. I can follow them."

"You're going to walk to Poland?" Sania wasn't sure whether to laugh at or sedate her.

"All trains have been requisitioned for military use. Only troops are being shipped east."

"There's a reason." Sania grabbed Regina's wrist, stopping her methodical, yet frantic packing. "This is suicide. Not just you, for Lena." Realizing there was nothing she could do to dissuade Regina from the self-destructive path she was catapulting down, Sania tried to save one life. "Leave the baby with me," she suggested, stroking Lena's cheek, smiling as she rooted towards her finger. "I'll take good care of her. I still remember how, though my boys are... gone." Sania made a vague gesture with her arm, indicating they could be anywhere from safe at home in a faraway village, at the front, or... gone for good. Regina had lived in a war zone long enough that she understood it was intrusive to clarify. "You've no idea what risks await you. Exposure, hunger, violent deserters roaming the woods, preying on anybody they can. If you refuse to save yourself, save your daughter. Aaron's daughter," Sania added for emphasis.

Her words struck a chord with Regina. She had no qualms about putting her own life on the line to save Aaron. But did she have the right to put Lena in peril? Regina knew what Aaron would want her to do. He'd want her and Lena to stay put. Traveling with a military unit offered them protection she'd forfeit by striking out on her own. She was taking an unnecessary risk for a man who, cooler prevailing heads kept telling her, was already dead. Or, based on what they knew happened to Soviet prisoners in German POW camps, Regina should be praying he was already dead, the quicker and least painfully, the better.

She gazed down at her baby, who replied with an uninterested glance. Lena focused on Regina's eyes before moving onto something she found more interesting, like the overhead light, or the glistening medical bottles. Lena proved as interested in Sania as she was in her mother, plopping the thought in Regina's head that if she were to leave Lena behind, the child wouldn't remember her. She'd be safe and, to judge by the longing look Sania gave her when invoking her lost sons, loved. Regina could move quicker without Lena. She wouldn't need to stop to nurse or wash out her diapers. She'd be lighter on her feet without the extra weight or needing to tread carefully so as not to jounce and wake her. She could scale fences, plunge through thorny thickets, climb trees to stay out of sight. She'd have no one to look out for save herself. She'd be able to get to Aaron faster. There were no two ways about it. Regina's surest path to rescuing the man she loved was to leave their child behind. And it would be best for Lena, too.

Regina had complete confidence in Sania's ability to take care of Lena. What she lacked was confidence in her own ability to make this mammoth of a decision. Despite the confident demeanor Regina was doing her damndest to project—primarily to persuade herself rather than anyone who might attempt to stop her, like Sania or Colonel Zagorodnik—her thoughts refused to quit zig-zagging like a rabid dog tied to a peg in the ground. One moment, she was brimming with confidence, convinced her course of action was the right one, the solitary means to ensure Aaron's survival. Then, in the middle of the euphoria propelling her forward, came the crushing self-doubt, memories of the times she'd thought she was right before getting everything foolishly, tragically wrong. Was Regina, once again, barreling into a situation she incorrectly thought she understood? Would she be making Aaron's fate grimmer, risking Lena in the process?

Sensing Regina's resolve weakening, Sania pushed, "The war won't last forever. The Germans are on the run, Comrade Stalin assures us. After it's over, you and Aaron can return together for Lena. I'll register where we're living with the central authorities so you'll have no trouble finding her, I swear it, trust me, please."

Regina trusted her. That was the problem. In trying to reassure her, Sania made it clear why the plan was untenable. Regina shook her head, almost regretfully. She'd been so close to convincing herself that leaving Lena behind would be best for everyone. She still believed it, too. Except... "I can't. I'm going AWOL right now. And Aaron... Colonel Zagordnik said prisoners are assumed to have betrayed the motherland. If we have to go through official channels to find you and Lena once the fighting ends, we might... they might..." Regina didn't dare finish her thought. To finish her thought would be to articulate the fear that she and Aaron might be branded outlaws at war's end. That they might be arrested, tried, deported, executed. To articulate such a thought would be to suggest it wasn't solely the guilty who were prosecuted in the Soviet Union. And be deemed guilty of heresy, instead. "We might never see her again."

"Yes," Sania replied reluctantly. Regina couldn't be certain if she were agreeing with her, or saying it would be best if Regina and Aaron didn't. Regina didn't care what Sania thought of Regina choosing to keep Lena with her. Regina only cared what Aaron would think. He'd always assured Regina he thought her capable of making the correct decision, no matter if anyone else differed.

Regina barely remembered the lesson in praying Aaron had given her months ago. But, she prayed Aaron was right.

REGINA WALKED. SHE thanked God—again, probably incorrectly—the railroad tracks she'd counted on to lead her way were still there. Even where stretches had been bombed out, Regina was able to trail, by following scorch marks, where they picked up again. She started her trek at first light, and refused to stop again until she was forced to determine where the tracks were by dragging her foot along the edge, unable to see its outline any longer. On nights with a full moon, she told herself she could keep on walking indefinitely. Reality, however, usually in the form of a squalling Lena, got in her way. The child was young enough she could still be entertained by either her mother's face or the passing of scenery. Also young enough to require feeding every few hours. Regina attempted to breastfeed while continuing to trudge forward. The strain on her back combined with the nipple bobbing out of Lena's mouth should Regina stumble quickly put an end to that experiment. Regina also attempted to keep moving if she smelled that Lena had soiled herself, but found it was more efficient to pause and swap out her swaddling immediately than to wait for Lena to get fussy and for the oozing liquids to stain Regina's clothes, as well.

She'd left her army uniform behind, opting, instead, to don the civilian blouse and skirt she'd arrived in. She didn't want to broadcast her affiliation, frightened of Nazi stragglers lurking in the countryside, not to mention Russian and Polish ones who might still harbor twenty-five year old resentments from the revolution. Most importantly, a Red Army uniform was the last thing that would get her through the gates of a German prisoner of war camp.

Regina felt fortunate the summer days and nights were warm enough that she never required more than a shawl to cuddle underneath with Lena for the few hours of sleep she allowed herself between treks, and she could wash out their clothes in nearby streams and put them on again wet without fear of catching a chill. She scrubbed the pair of Lena's diapers that Regina alternated between, and the worst of the sweat from her clothes. The blood was a bit harder to rinse out. It started with Regina's stockings. Her feet blistered and tore within days, no matter how much cloth Regina attempted to stuff between her flesh and the sturdy leather boots she'd selected for durability, not comfort. By the time those managed to scab over and turn into calluses, Regina's back had ripped right across the middle from the pressure of lugging a sling, followed by her shoulders where the straps of her rucksack dug in, and finally the skin below her breasts, where Lena's constant wriggling managed to chafe through. Regina assured herself it was only a matter of time before each wound grew numb. For now, however, all the separate pains had joined together, in the spirit of socialism, to form a constant throb. Regina didn't mind.

She counted along, like the ticking of a clock, reminding herself that each pulse brought her closer to Aaron. It was when Regina couldn't feel its pound that she grew anxious, frustrated she wasn't making adequate progress.

Regina had lost track of how long it took her to make it to the Polish border. She had no inkling of what she must look or smell like. All she knew was, once she saw the signs switching languages, she realized she now had a further problem. She had no papers permitting her to enter. She could attempt to sneak across through an unguarded area of forest, but that would not only take her away from the railroad tracks which had, up to this point, been her primary guide, it also put her at risk of arrest—by both nations.

She needed a safer plan.

She found it at the sight of a lone Soviet tank rumbling down the road.

Up to this point, Regina had avoided being spotted. At the first sound of train, tank, truck, or even a horse and cart, she'd ducked into the woods. If that wasn't available, then behind a tree, a rock, into high grass. She couldn't risk being seen and questioned. Now, she couldn't risk being overlooked.

Taking a moment to run her fingers through greasy and dust covered hair, pinch her cheeks and bite down on her lips to make them plumper and rosier—as if that could undo the damage from weeks of hungry, thirsty, exhaustive travel—Regina stepped onto the road, directly in front of the tank, where they couldn't miss her. She was counting on chivalry, patriotism, and, if that didn't work, on men who hadn't seen a woman in weeks.

She planted herself in front of their churning wheels, arms on hips, chin up, eyes locked into the driver's visor. The behemoth didn't so much as slow down. It barreled straight towards Regina. She briefly reconsidered her approach, before digging in and refusing to budge. When it hit an arm's length away, the tank screeched to a halt. Regina let out a sigh of relief, tensing up anew at the sight of the access hatch opening, a head peeking out.

She'd been expecting a boy. The recruits rotating through her field hospital were growing younger and younger. This was a man twice Regina's age, his nose a bulbous topography of vodka induced bulging veins, his lips chapped and nicotine stained, his eyes slits of suspicion.

"*Shto hochesh?*" he demanded. "What do you want?"

"Help." Regina aimed for that perfect combination of need and come hither. She couldn't guess which he'd prefer.

He sighed, looking around at the empty countryside. He sighed again, deeper this time, held out his hand and, in one heave, tugged Regina inside, dropping her through the hatch and onto the tank floor. She landed on her knees, using her hands not to break her fall, but to cradle Lena from the worst of the impact. Regina blinked, startled by the sudden shift from daylight to dimly lit hutch. The air reeked of unwashed men, stale food, grease, and… something else.

Desire. That was it. Regina had no other word for it, except the smell of frustrated males who, she now realized, might have been deprived of women not weeks as she's assumed, but maybe months. Maybe years. She started to shiver despite the stifling, stale air. How badly had she miscalculated this time?

Five men clustered around Regina. She heard them breathe. She felt their eyes break her down, disassembling a machine based on what use each part could bring them. Regina's instinct was to curl around Lena, to protect her daughter and herself by shrinking as small as possible. So, naturally, she did the opposite. Regina rose to her full height, the top of her head brushing the ceiling, making it clear why the men needed to hunch. Instead of cowering, she glanced from soldier to soldier, daring them to continue seeing her as an object, a toy provided for their enjoyment. She'd been aiming to cower them, to force them into seeing her as a fellow human being. She'd been aiming to shame them, to remind them they were all fellow Soviet citizens united for the same glorious cause. She failed miserably.

It was the sight of Lena peeking from beneath Regina's chin, her eyes wide with wonder at the first new people she'd spotted since Regina hit the road, that prompted the men to cease hungrily assessing Regina, and break into completely different grins from the ones they'd been directing Lena's way.

"How old?" asked the gunner.

"Boy or girl?" from their leader.

"I have a little one at home. Haven't seen him since he was this size."

"What are you two doing out here alone?"

"Eight months," Regina answered. "Girl." And, finally, "We are going to find her father."

That stopped the men short. They cleared Regina a space to sit. They offered to rock Lena. Regina acquiesced with gratitude, stifling a groan of pain as she straightened up without the sling, without the rucksack, her arms and back spasming from the freedom.

"Stalag 3-K," the driver repeated slowly when Regina divulged where she was headed. "One of the worst."

She nodded to indicate she'd heard him but refused to listen. Words were meaningless. Regina resolved to feel nothing, to fear nothing, until she located Aaron and saw for herself.

"We can't take you there," his co-driver confirmed, "it's out of our way."

"And it would be suicide," their commander spat. "Area is still German controlled."

"I'll be grateful for you driving me as far as you can. I'll find the rest of the way myself."

The more she spoke, the angrier their leader grew. "What kind of man would want his woman taking a risk like this?"

"I promised him." Regina didn't expect anyone to understand.

She only hoped Aaron would.

THEY DROPPED HER off a day's walk from the camp. They couldn't risk coming any closer. And they had orders to report for battle at the border. Regina thanked each man profusely. She'd learned their names. She'd learned the names of their wives, their children. The last thing the commander said to her was, "Remember us. If no one else does." She promised she would.

And then he called her a fool.

New pains from sitting crouched and sleeping upright for several days joined the familiar ones as Regina resumed her odyssey.

She spied the camp a good hour before she reached it. It was a

sprawling, makeshift complex of wooden one-story buildings surrounded by dirt roads, half-plowed fields, and barbed wire. If it
weren't for the barbed wire—and the Nazi flag flapping above it—
Regina was forced to admit it looked similar to Amerzut as she'd first
seen it.

As Regina drew closer, she spotted more differences. Watchtow-
ers on the outskirts, men with machine guns stationed above as well
as on the ground. She spied dog patrols, a gate with a lock the size of
Lena's head.

Regina had to get past that lock. She had to get past that gate.

She approached cautiously. In the time Regina had been making
her way to Stalag 3-K, she'd refused to imagine what Aaron could be
going through. She'd told herself there was no advantage to letting
fear get the best of her. *What if's* would be a waste of time. Instead of
driving her anxiety through the roof conjuring up solutions to what
might be, a better use of Regina's energy would be to determine what
was, and go from there. As a result, she'd made no plans. Not for how
she would rescue Aaron, not for how she'd get past the first obstacle;
entering the camp, itself.

A guard had spotted her. It was too late for Regina to format a
plan of action instead of charging in headfirst. The only option left
was to turn back… or to keep going.

She approached the gate. In the two dozen steps it took her to
arrive face to face with the guard through the barbed wire, she made
up her mind.

Regina raised her arm in the air, like she'd done before. Regina
flattened her palm and pointed her fingers to the sky. Regina proclaimed, "Heil Hitler."

Chapter Twenty

She used her knowledge of the German Cecilia had sniffed at Regina's parents teaching her, to explain. Regina was an ethnic German, trapped behind Polish boundary lines in Danzig, living among disgusting Slav peasants whom Herr Hitler had so aptly called "rabble not worth a penny more than the inhabitants of the Sudan or India." She'd been overjoyed in 1939 when the Fatherland reclaimed what was rightfully theirs and she could breathe the clear air of home again. Her husband had been among the first to enlist to defend their Reich against Polish aggression. She hadn't heard from him in a year. (At the last minute, Regina altered her plan to claim widowhood. Saying her husband was dead might suggest she thought Germany was on a path to defeat.) Her racist Polish neighbors had driven Regina from her home. Now she and her child had no place to lay their heads. She'd been walking for days, searching for sanctuary, and her prayers had been answered! Christian prayers, of course. Regina was a trained nurse. She could be of help. She required no payment in return, merely a place to sleep and food for her and her daughter. Surely, in a camp this large, they could use an extra pair of hands at the infirmary.

Regina held her breath while she waited for her fanciful tale to sink in. Her German was a bit rusty—expected of a poor soul raised under Polish occupation. Her story was a bit short on details, but, truly, a woman couldn't be expected to keep track of dates and battles. That was men's domain. Regina's biggest obstacle, she knew, were her looks. Dark hair, dark eyes, and a full figure that traditionally served her well in situations ranging from distracting ticket takers to flagging down a tank. It also put her first in line to star in a German propaganda film with a name like "Eternal Jew." Regina hoped she was emaciated enough, her hair faded enough, her eyes sagged enough for all that to be overlooked. Luckily, Lena, with her mix of Regina's dark coloring and Aaron's light, had ended up with hair of indeterminate brown and eyes a nondescript shade of blue to make passing easier.

It had been simple to get past the boy at the gate. She didn't try flirting with him. Though she was only a few years older, she must have appeared closer to his mother's age, the baby strapped across her chest confirming the impression. All Regina had to do was bark a demand, and he dutifully escorted her inside, passing Regina off to yet another boy to walk her toward the kommandant's office. She'd expected a Prussian officer from a history book, polished uniform, knee-high boots, rigid posture, maybe a monocle. What she got was a country grandfather, his epaulets faded, a pair of spectacles perched on his nose, and a bad knee—"From the last war"—that made him wince apologetically when he took a seat behind his desk, across from Regina. He appeared absolutely harmless, avuncular. And, yet, during her walk to his office, Regina had spied the gallows with their dangling nooses, seen the splashes of blood on the concrete, caught sight of skeletons in ragged uniforms shuffling from place to place, dragging buckets and tools weighing more than they did. This kindly old man was in charge of it all.

He spoke kindly to Regina. Made cooing noises at Lena. Showed her a photograph of his grown son and daughter, told her about his grandchildren. He clucked his tongue in sympathy at Regina's made up tales of Polish harassment for being a German daring to live on her ancestral land. It was easy. She simply took her own and others' stories of Russians harassing Jews and changed the designation. She threw herself on the gentleman's mercy. She told him she knew of a poultice she could make that would help with his knee pain. She cursed Josef Stalin. That one was easy, too. By the end of their delightful afternoon together, during which tea was brought in lest Regina go thirsty, she'd secured a nursing position for herself, and a room for her and Lena.

The kommandant called the boy who'd brought in their refreshment to escort Regina to her quarters, and to show her around the camp, though he did caution her against wandering too far from the infirmary. The men being held here were absolute animals. Who knew what sort of atrocities they might inflict on a beautiful young woman?

"There are two sides," the soldier shepherding her explained. "Americans, they signed the Geneva Convention so we're allowed to work their enlisted men, but nothing that benefits our war effort. We keep them busy farming, earning their own daily bread. Funny, right?" Regina smiled to indicate he was, indeed, hilarious. "Their non-commissioned officers are allowed to supervise, no labor. And we're not allowed to make commissioned officers work at all. Lazy bastards. Their half is over there." He pointed to the right quadrant, where the stretched wooden barracks Regina first saw from outside the wire stood side by side. "We're required to give them light, heat, same as our lodgings, another rule." He grinned and pointed to his left. "That's the Soviet side." There, the buildings were less barracks than they were shacks. The only light or heat Regina could see came from tiny fires sputtering on the doorsteps. The men weren't carrying buckets or farming equipment. They were dragging rocks. To no purpose Regina could identify. Her comedian friend grinned when he told her, "Soviets didn't sign nothing."

THE INFIRMARY, AT least, wasn't segregated. Not by rank, not by nationality. It looked, in fact, a great deal like Regina's former field hospital. Row upon row of beds, the mattresses stripped of sheets and dotted with indifferently scrubbed blotches of yellow, brown, and crimson. A strong scent of lye and rubbing alcohol barely covering the stench of blood, vomit, and feces underneath. A lack of windows made it perennial night and, due to the constant surgical lamps, perennial day. Without their uniforms, Regina could barely tell the Soviet men from the American ones. It was more productive to keep track of them by injury: broken bones, infected wounds, pneumonia, tuberculosis, general malnutrition. Regina spoke genuinely halting English to the Americans, and pretended to have trouble with Russian for the Soviets, lest her cover be blown. She spoke German to the other nurses, the doctors, and, especially, to the head of the infirmary.

His name was Viktor Schafer and, Regina gathered, this was his first posting. He was fresh out of medical school. With friends in high places. Viktor strode up and down the ward, randomly sticking his face in to observe that a splint could have been wrapped tighter, a stitch threaded more efficiently, or a chest cold didn't require hospitalization, the fresh air of getting back to work would do the patient good! He double-checked every diagnosis, questioned each prescription, and was repeatedly reminding his staff that resources were limited and should be rationed accordingly. First priority went to German personnel, then American officers, then their enlisted men, and, finally, the Soviets, officers and enlisted alike. It was bad enough the bastards were killing so many good men at Stalingrad and the beaches of France, it was unconscionable that they were obliged to keep them alive to do more of it. If anyone dared contradict him, either by continuing to perform a procedure the way they saw fit, or referring to their own professional experience, he would loudly belittle them in front of the other employees; patients, too, followed by a write-up to the kommandant's office for insubordination, and a coerced apology, complete with a pledge to do it Viktor's way from now on. His confidence in his infallibility, as well as his insistence that those who didn't agree were simply ignorant if not downright subversive, Regina was afraid to admit, reminded her of herself back in Moscow. How, as the youngest in the room, she felt the need to assert her superiority to be taken seriously. How the less she knew, the louder she felt compelled to claim she did. How any disagreement with her position felt like a personal attack that required a full scale escalation, complete with an offense is the best defense policy.

She understood Viktor better than she wanted to. Which is why she understood her best opportunity for finding Aaron lay in staying on Viktor's good side. It was Felix and Klara and the Cohens all over again. Smile, nod, agree, and keep any doubts to yourself. It wasn't merely her safest choice, it was Regina's—and Aaron's—only choice.

SHE'D BEEN AT Stalag 3-K for a month, and she was no closer to tracking down Aaron than she'd been while on the road. Regina was prohibited from venturing into the Soviet side of the camp, and the American one. She couldn't tip her hand by asking about a particular prisoner. Regina could also not stop thinking about how Colonel Zagorodnik said that Jewish prisoners of war were sometimes immediately executed or sent to camps deeper in Poland. Aaron didn't look Jewish, but his name was a giveaway. Regina couldn't risk drawing attention to it.

She also couldn't help seeing Aaron in every patient who passed through the infirmary. They were all so skeletal, their skin mottled with rashes, wracked with sores, pummeled with bruises; their cheeks sunken in, eyes bulging, teeth cracked and crumbling from their mouths. No matter their nationality, no matter what color their hair had once been, no matter the shade of their skin, they looked more alike than they did different. It terrified Regina to consider Aaron might be right under her nose, too desiccated and deformed for her to recognize him.

She asked every Soviet soldier what unit they'd been with, pretending it was necessary for their case file. She was looking for anyone from Aaron's squad, his battalion, the same basic geographic area. She was desperate for clues, but no joy to be found. By the time a Soviet soldier made it to a cot, he was so near death from dehydration, starvation, or exhaustion, there was little Regina could do but trickle water over a swollen tongue, or cluck sympathetically at a hysterically shouted plea. Some hallucinated she was their mama, their wife, their sweetheart. They begged her—in Russian—to help them, to answer them. It broke Regina's heart that, to protect herself, she couldn't offer them last minute comfort in their native language. But the risk of being found out was too great.

"*Gavorish po Russki?*" A soldier with an infection in both lungs, grabbed Regina's hand as she passed by his bed, taking advantage of Viktor having stepped out for his dinner break. "You speak Russian?"

Regina yanked her wrist from his grip. She was about to deny, but he was looking at her so beseechingly, and his prognosis of recovery without antibiotics, which Viktor kept under lock and key and distributed at his discretion so slim—and dead men tell no tales, that she conceded, "*Chooch-chooch.*" Little bit.

He jerked his head in the direction of the boy one bed over. The soldier could barely speak, but forced himself to rasp out, "He's dead."

A cursory look confirmed the diagnosis. No one had checked on him for hours, and the youth had politely expired without causing anyone extra trouble. Regina couldn't remember what malady he'd come in for. She moved to make the appropriate notation so the body could be evacuated and a bed freed up, when the soldier pleaded, "Don't tell anyone."

She stared at him, confused but relieved that a bewildered facial expression crossed all language barriers, and she didn't need to utter a word in her fake, accented Russian.

The soldier continued to squeeze out, in between desperate gasps for air as he slowly drowned in the liquid filling his diseased lungs, "Please. That orderly." He indicated an old man who'd been given permission to work in the hospital rather than laboring in the fields, endlessly mopping up bodily fluids which smeared the floor. "He can smuggle the body into our barracks. You need to mark that he recovered and was discharged. Quickly, while no one sees."

"Why?" Regina demanded, stunned, almost forgetting her accent.

A good thing the soldier was too frantic to notice. Or maybe too far gone to care. "Roll call," he explained. "We prop him up between two living soldiers, he gets counted. We get an extra food ration for the day. Please, Fraulein." He used the German address. It made Regina gag in revulsion. Something else she was required to hide. "We get one fifth the food rations the Americans get. No Red Cross packages for us. Please, in the name of God, I am begging you."

Regina knew what it cost a Russian soldier to invoke God. It went against everything he'd been taught, against everything he'd been commanded to believe. Even if he came from one of those felonious homes where ancient religions were secretly practiced in the dead of night in deliberate opposition to Soviet policy, merely uttering the sentiment was enough for a fellow soldier to report him as soon as they returned to the USSR. He was taking a massive risk. And not merely for himself.

He was asking Regina to take it along with him.

It would be so easy for her to just walk away. To pretend she hadn't heard his request. No, better, to pretend she hadn't understood it. After all, she'd only copped to speaking a little Russian. Why would a good German girl know enough to comprehend, much less acquiesce to his treacherous entreaty?

Regina thought of Aaron. He was one of the Soviet soldiers getting one fifth of the rations prescribed by the Geneva Convention. If she went along with this deception, Aaron might be one of the soldiers who received an extra morsel of food. The extra morsel might be the thing that kept him alive until Regina could find him.

She hadn't said a word yet to the soldier enjoining her. It was safer that way. But she did step over to the deceased patient's cot, scribbling the mark on the chart that had been asked of her. She looked across the infirmary and gave the slightest of nods in the orderly's direction.

He offered her the slightest of nods in return.

THAT WASN'T THE end of it. As Regina feared, word got around. It was limited to the Soviet camp for now, but, like a virus, it could hop sides at any moment. Which meant Regina could be exposed at any moment. Which meant she was living on borrowed time. Regina understood how fragile her position was. Yet, the next time she was asked to mark a dead body as healthy and discharged, she did it. And the next time. And the next.

It got so Regina realized she was keeping an eye out for it. When she suspected a Soviet patient was close to death—either due to withholding of medical care or because he was too far gone to benefit—she'd alert the orderly, and they'd plan for extraction as soon as Viktor's back was turned. It wasn't always a simple matter, anticipating death. Regina had witnessed men who barely managed to take a breath every minute linger for days. And she'd seen ones with injuries guaranteeing they'd be walking out good as new, unexpectedly expire. The common denominator she'd been able to narrow down was that those who already appeared lifeless and those deceptively resilient would, a few hours before the end, start plucking at their skin, trying to escape their bodies. That was Regina's cue to leap into action.

She'd tried, several times, to use her service to their cause as a way to sneak into the Soviet sector. The men in charge of spiriting bodies away refused to accommodate her. They said it was too great of a risk. Regina was too useful to them where she was. If she was caught, there went their operation. And, one of the boys reminded her sternly, Regina's life. What would happen to her little girl then, he asked, personally offended by Regina's irresponsible mothering.

She hadn't forgotten Lena. Lena was fine. The Polish women from the village who came to cook, clean and provide other duties the German soldiers believed were beneath them had formed a cooperative to watch their own offspring in shifts. They were happy to add Lena to the brood—once the kommandant ordered them to. Regina's daughter was perfectly well taken care of. To buttress Regina's lie, Lena understood Polish better than any other language. German was in second place. At least Mama would be happy it wasn't Yiddish. Regina knew there was nothing funny about this joke she told herself. She laughed anyway. What else was there to do?

"WELCOME BACK, HERR Doctor." Viktor greeted the new arrival and, instantly, Regina knew two things about the man. One: He was American. It wasn't the uniform. She hadn't noticed the uniform initially. It was the innocence and openness of his face. Even here, even as prisoners of war, there was still something unsullied about them. They acted like—though they should know better by now—they still thought anyone they met could turn out to be a friend. They entered life with their big, American smiles first.

The second thing Regina knew was he was Jewish. With his close cropped, dark curly hair, nearly black eyes and the prominent nose above that big, American smile in a moon face framed by jug ears, he certainly looked more Jewish than Aaron did. And he was still alive. That gave Regina hope. Though, of course, he lived on the right side of the stalag.

"Our dentist is here!" Viktor announced to the infirmary in German, switching to English to direct, "Get to work, Dr. Burns," adding, "Staff first, then patients. If there's time."

Still smiling, Dr. Burns nodded hello to everyone he passed on his way to the back of the room, where a chair had been set up in advance of his arrival. Regina must have been the only new face, because he paused, stretched out his hand and attempted to introduce himself, in halting German. "My name is Tommy Burns. I am a dentist. Do you need any help with your teeth, today?"

"It is a pleasure to meet you, Tommy Burns," Regina replied in her equally as mangled English. "Yes, there is something you can help me with."

REGINA VOLUNTEERED TO help Tommy with his work. She claimed to have experience as a dental as well as a nursing assistant. It took him a whole minute to realize she was lying. Regina didn't know the name of a single tool. She pretended it was because she didn't know the correct word in English. He pretended to believe her.

Still, he let her stay. He taught her the name for each tool and demonstrated what he did with them, in case she ever needed to perform a tooth extraction or pry a crushed one from a split gum with no dentist available. It was actually interesting and potentially helpful. But Regina had bigger plans for their interaction.

By the end of the day, she'd gotten Tommy's life story. He was from San Francisco in California. He'd been drafted straight out of dental school, endured six weeks of basic training, shipped out immediately, and was captured with his unit almost as soon as he landed on D-Day. Because Tommy was the sole dentist in the entire camp, he'd been ordered to work on the Nazi soldiers. As an officer, they couldn't force him to do any labor against his will. So Tommy

struck a bargain. He would examine and perform whatever procedure was necessary on each German—volunteering was allowed by
the Geneva Convention, as long as he was also supplied with the
appropriate tools and permitted to work on his fellow Americans—
and the Soviets, too. As such, Tommy was one of the few prisoners
allowed to move between the two camps.

By the end of the day, Dr. Tommy Burns had himself a new
assistant.

HE CALLED FOR her the next morning. It was Regina's one free day of
the week, so she couldn't be accused of shirking her assigned duties.
Tommy traveled alongside Regina as she dropped Lena off with the
Polish women. She felt a spike of guilt because she wasn't spending
the day with her daughter. Regina told herself what she was doing
was critical to the welfare of their family, as she followed Tommy
through the gate that led to the Soviet portion of camp.

They'd only walked a few minutes, but the differences were palatable. The stench struck Regina first. The American side may have
smelled of too many sweaty, unwashed men living in too close quarters, but the Soviet one reeked of bodies decaying from disease, of
pus, of human waste no one removed because there was nowhere to
remove it to. They were thinner than the Americans, their uniforms
tattered, their boots worn through until every step carried the echo
of a loose, flapping sole. They seemed drained, not just of food and
water, but of spirit, of life.

Aaron. Where was Aaron among these pathetic men? It was all
Regina could do to follow Tommy from one tottering barracks to
the next as he poked his head in and inquired if there was anything
he could do for them. Each barrack featured bunks with crumpled
prisoners facing the wall. Regina wanted to scream Aaron's name. She
wanted to shake Tommy off and rush toward each, roll them over
and see for herself if he wasn't the one she sought.

She did no such thing. She kept her mouth closed—though her
eyes open—as they set up makeshift dental chairs and Tommy did
the best he could in dimly lit corners while Regina attempted to
hold a flashlight and pass him the instruments he requested. They

worked through the morning and afternoon on those patients too weak to leave their bunks. As the sun began to set, she heard the shuffle of hundreds of footsteps as the able-bodied laborers returned from where they'd been breaking rocks and lugging cement bags to lay roads that would make it easier to drop off even more prisoners.

Hearing Dr. Burns was about, they gravitated towards his work area, not so much interested in teeth as in news from the other side of the camp, especially the war's progress. Newly arrived American prisoners often possessed information unavailable even to those who might have access to radio broadcasts. The Germans listened to news that assured them they were winning. The same went for Soviet radio sources. Only Americans might have picked up flashes which could be counted on.

Murmurs went up about needing someone who could translate Tommy's English into Russian for the rest of them. Regina almost spoke up that she could do it, before remembering she was supposed to be Polish not Russian, and firmly clamped her lips shut. Even here, there could be people willing to sell her out for their own advantage. Especially here.

"Here he is, we found him!" somebody shouted, shoving a body to the front of the crowd gathering around Tommy.

And bringing Regina at long last, finally and miraculously, face to face with Aaron.

Chapter Twenty-One

He was alive. First and most importantly, Aaron was alive. He looked well. As well as could be expected. He wasn't nearly as emaciated as some of the men she'd treated. Some of the men whose deaths she'd covered up. He was standing of his own accord, walking of his own accord. Regina's standards had sunk so low that her heart leaped with glee at both those things. His hair had been cropped short, likely to stave off lice, which made the outlines of his face look more skeletal. His eyes, however, were still the same shade of blue. And they were staring at Regina.

With a complete lack of recognition.

Regina understood. She was also looking back at him as if he were a stranger. This was no time to let down her guard and risk revealing the connection between them.

Regina stepped aside and let Aaron talk to Tommy. He asked about the latest news from the front. Tommy relayed that the US Army had taken Rome, trapped the German garrison at Cherbourg, and liberated Paris, while Soviet troops had freed Lvov in Ukraine, and arrived at the border with Bulgaria. At the latter updates, his men cheered silently, afraid a clamor would attract Nazi attention. It was quite a sight, over a hundred prisoners, opening their mouths, pumping their arms and stomping their feet—all without making a sound.

Regina barely noticed. She was too busy looking at Aaron. While making it seem like she wasn't looking at Aaron. Regina focused on the top of Tommy's head while looking at Aaron from the corner of her eye. It was a painful contortion not just for her pupils but for her neck. She didn't give a damn. She was finally looking at Aaron again. Noting how much he'd changed. How much he was still the same.

He still spoke in short, terse sentences, trying to cram as much information as possible into as few words as possible. Yet he remained patient, answering the same question multiple times, even when the answer remained, "I don't know. He doesn't know." He and Tommy had clearly done this before. They'd developed a shorthand, where minimal words spoke volumes. Nonetheless, the formerly indefatigable Aaron appeared exhausted, his nerves frayed to the point where it took visibly more effort to keep his composure. He'd been pushed to his limit, there was no telling how much more he could take. Regina had no intention of letting him find out. She was going to get him out of here. Her first task, though, was to speak to him. She had to figure out how to do that. Except Aaron beat her to it.

As Regina and Tommy were leaving, in the bustle of asking when they'd be back, Aaron sidled up to Regina and, in English so the least number understood, hissed, "North gate. Dark. Tonight."

"THE HELL?" AARON was so enraged he didn't bother finishing his sentence. The remainder was implied.

Regina had obeyed his directive and met Aaron after sunset along the compound's north perimeter. It was the sole area the towering searchlights couldn't reach. To keep prisoners from taking advantage of the blind spot for escaping, it was reinforced with barbed wire and landmines on the other side. She'd brought along Lena, certain Aaron would want to see his daughter. The baby's presence only infuriated him further.

He refused to look at her. He could barely stand to look at Regina. Even if, somehow, at the same time, he seemed unable to take his eyes off them.

"Why would you do this?" Aaron both whispered and shouted.

"I promised you." She hid behind stubbornness so as not to break into tears at his attack. She'd expected a loving reunion, not a cross-examination.

"If they find out who you are, you and Lena will be deported to a concentration camp so quickly, you'll be on the goddamn cattle car before you've realized what's happened. How long have you been here?"

"About a month," Regina stammered.

"Have you seen the Gestapo storm through the Soviet sector? Looking for undesirables? Do you know which ones those are?" Aaron counted off on his fingers, "Slavs, communists, and Jews! Once it became obvious we were about to be captured, I tore my identity papers and swallowed them. Gave a fake name. No one has squealed on me yet, but how long do you think a *zhid* like Aaron Kramer will survive if the truth comes out? How long do you think until they come after you and my daughter?"

"That's why we have to get out," Regina pleaded, "all three of us."

Aaron pointed at the wire, and mimed being stabbed if you tried climbing it. He pointed at the dirt patch on the other side, and mimed being blown up upon landing.

"I'll think of something," she swore, "give me a little time. Now I know where you are—"

"Go away." Aaron's injunction was also a plea. "Walk out the front gate like you need milk from the village for Lena, then don't come back. Our Army has pushed into Poland, Tommy says. Find them. They'll take care of you."

"And who will take care of you?"

"I'm fine." He crossed his arms for emphasis, elbows poking through the holes in the sleeves. His defiant gesture couldn't disguise their trembling.

"Aaron…" Regina's voice cracked. She took a step forward, wanting to brush her fingers against his face in a pale imitation of how he'd first done it all those years ago.

Aaron deliberately ducked his head, leaning backwards. "No," he said, colder than she'd ever heard him. "No, Regina."

"You said you trusted me with our lives."

"I was wrong."

HE MAY AS well have struck her. Except Regina knew Aaron didn't mean it. He didn't know what he was saying. How could he, after everything he'd been through? He was in shock. Battle fatigue, they called it. He wasn't thinking rationally. That was alright. Regina could do the thinking for them both. She needed to. Aaron was counting on her. Even if he couldn't admit it.

She continued tagging along on Tommy's appointments. She visited the American side and, though the men there could, under no circumstances, be described as thriving, they were undoubtedly healthier than the Soviets. Unlike the Russians, who were fed a single serving of soup a day, Allied prisoners were allocated nine pounds of potatoes per week, five pounds of bread, and two and a half pounds of cabbage, as well as a coffee-like substance brewed from acorns. This was periodically supplemented by Red Cross packages of dried meats like SPAM or pork liver paste, cheese, prune spread, powdered milk, and chocolate bars. They combined the latter with their potatoes into a concoction nicknamed "goon soup." On Sundays and special occasions, they fried up the SPAM in gravy made of mixed milk and liver paste, using spatulas and strainers twisted from bits of found tin, cooked in stoves fed with wood torn from the sides of outhouses and asphalt ripped from roofs. Regina assured herself the reason the Americans were more optimistic about being rescued was because they were better fed and thus had more cause for optimism. Not because they feared what their government might do to them once they'd been liberated.

Matters were a great deal more dire on the Soviet side. Six weeks was about the most a prisoner could hope for, between the grueling work detail and the single serving of soup before they collapsed. Those who could be counted remained prostrate in their bunks, only dragged out for roll call. The infirmary was exclusively for those suspected of carrying contagious diseases. The corpses which Regina allowed to be smuggled in lasted a day or two before smell betrayed them, and were eventually reported as having mysteriously died overnight.

It didn't take Regina long to observe that on days she and Tommy made their visits, Aaron made a point of being elsewhere. It wasn't her imagination. She heard other prisoners asking, "Where's Ivanovitch when we need him?" using the very Russian pseudonym Aaron had adopted for himself. The men were getting antsy without their translator.

Regina, on the other hand, was getting used to Aaron's disappearances. She told herself it was alright. She didn't have anything new to tell him. She hadn't yet formulated a foolproof plan. She did miss him. That was the worst part. On top of everything, Regina simply missed him. She missed seeing his face at the end of a hard day. She missed lamenting to him about her hard day. She missed him making her feel like her hard day hadn't been that hard. It seemed selfish, in the middle of a world war, that the primary reason Regina wanted to free the man she loved was because she missed seeing his face, missed curling up against him in bed, missed the feel of his lips on the back of her neck, missed having him to talk to. It sounded so trivial. Yet so true. She was taking mammoth global risks for tiny domestic reasons. Aaron was right. She was acting irrationally. Except she couldn't conceive of any other way to act.

So many visits had passed without her seeing Aaron that, when she finally did, Regina had to blink to make sure it wasn't a case where she could no longer tell one half-starved man from another. No, it was Aaron. Regina would recognize Aaron anywhere, in any condition. He hung towards the back of the throng who'd come to see Tommy, head down as if he wanted to avoid being recognized. Yet Tommy must have recognized him. As he and Regina were leaving, Tommy made a point of separating from her, which he rarely did. Tommy usually played the gentleman, escorting her through the crowd by the elbow, making sure Regina wasn't jostled or otherwise inappropriately touched, surrounded as they were by prisoners who hadn't been near a woman in years. Now, Tommy zig-zagged Aaron's way. He barely stopped before him. Tommy said something quickly, which Regina arrived too late to hear. Aaron nodded in agreement. When he spied Regina heading towards them, he made himself scarce.

"What was that about?" she asked Tommy once they were in the neutral zone of the infirmary.

"What was what?" he blinked so frantically he was either a terrible liar or communicating via Morse code.

"What were you talking to…" Regina almost stumbled, recovering just in time, "talking to Ivanovitch about?"

"I wasn't talking to Ivanovitch," Tommy said, which was blatantly untrue. And blatantly unlike Tommy. He'd always been open with her. How else would she have gotten his entire life story within hours of meeting?

Regina could have pressed him. But then he might wonder why she was interested. She couldn't afford to have him be the one asking questions of her.

Regina recalled what Felix once drummed into her: Americans were always looking for opportunities to discredit and betray Soviets. What if Tommy had something nefarious planned for Ivanovitch? Or, worse, for Aaron Kramer? She'd pegged him as a wide eyed, good natured GI Joe cliché. What Comrade Lenin had called "a useful innocent," but which she'd heard cynics translate as "useful idiot." Regina had certainly been mistaken in her assessment of peoples' characters before. It wasn't outside the realm of possibility she'd done it again. Hadn't Aaron said he might have erred in trusting her judgement?

Aaron, of course, was wrong. But that didn't mean Regina was right in this case.

She resolved to keep a closer eye on Tommy. After he left the infirmary, having dropped off his dental tools until next time—Viktor double-checking each item was accounted for, lest it be traded or used for nefarious purposes—Regina followed the American. She expected him to head back to his barracks. Instead, Tommy paused to exchange words with the Nazi guard who patrolled the no man's land strip between their East and West sides. It took less than a second. Tommy barely broke his stride. But something was definitely said, similar to his earlier, cryptic exchange with Aaron.

Regina's heart sped up with panic, then slowed down at the subsequent shock. Sweet, friendly, open-hearted Tommy was unquestionably up to something. He was colluding with the Germans. And Aaron was trapped in the middle. Regina felt terrified for Aaron. And furious at Tommy. Also disappointed with herself for having been duped again. And at Tommy, too. She'd genuinely liked him. It had been nice, amongst all the blood, carnage and death to believe there were still good, unsullied people left in the world.

But Regina had no time to mourn her hope. She had Aaron to protect.

"HERR DOCTOR," REGINA called to Viktor, leaning over a dozing patient whose chart said he was suffering from influenza, but his basic symptoms of sore throat, fever, and vomiting were enough cover for Regina to proclaim, "I fear we have a case of poliomyelitis on our hands."

While a mere handful of soldiers had been stricken in Europe, they'd received reports of an epidemic rolling through China-Burma-India, the Middle East, and Africa, and were instructed to be on the lookout.

Viktor recoiled at Regina's words. "Disgusting savages." It was well established that polio spread due to filthy personal hygiene. Regina knew the Nazis considered Americans and Slavs subhuman. She wondered how the spic-and-span Germans expected anyone to stay unsullied in a camp with minimal water, no changes of clothes, and outdoor toilet facilities.

"It won't stay confined to prisoners, we'll be infected, too," Regina said. Viktor nodded. He was aiming for thoughtful. It came off as terrified. "Someone should be sent into the Soviet sector to scout for potential cases." Regina looked at her chief expectantly, waiting for him to show the bold leadership key to his position.

"You do it," he snapped. "You diagnosed this. You know what to look for."

"Yes, Herr Doctor," Regina lowered her head meekly. He'd certainly shown her!

"Go in the evening," Viktor added. "We don't want you coming back, carrying the plague." What he meant was, we don't want you coming back, carrying the plague, while he was still on duty.

"Yes, Herr Doctor," Regina answered, still peering down at her shoes lest he catch her smiling.

She hurried towards Aaron's barracks. He didn't know she was coming, so he wouldn't know to avoid her. Before Regina could make what she hoped wasn't too unpleasant of a surprise appearance, she caught sight of Aaron stealthily slipping out the ramshackle door, headed towards the dark patch where they'd met earlier, where the distance between Soviet and American areas was narrowest, barely a prone body's length distance to separate them. Aaron wasn't the only one. As Regina followed, she spied other figures creeping in the same direction. In the parallel shadows, she made out Tommy, as well as six other men. And, in between, the German soldier Tommy had spoken to earlier.

Aaron was headed for a trap. Regina opened her mouth to cry out, to warn him, beg him to turn back. Before any sound could squeak from her throat, Aaron turned Regina's way, his translucent eyes shining in the darkness. There was no warmth in them. He raised a finger to his lips. Regina froze. How could he do this to her? How could he force her to watch him walk into danger and not let her do anything to help? He'd rescued her so many times. Why wouldn't he allow Regina to return the favor? Wasn't that love? Not merely saving, but allowing yourself to be saved?

The Americans huddled on their side. Aaron stood on his. The Nazi guard approached, looking almost casual. Another moment and he might start whistling. Tommy raised his arm and a tiny, paper object went sailing over the wire into the dirt of no-man's land. Regina strained to make out what it was.

Lucky Strike, read the package. Cigarettes. The five-pack was distributed to American soldiers by the Red Cross on humanitarian grounds; they were vital for health.

The guard swooped down to pick up his booty, then walked away, never having looked at the prisoners on either side. But the exchange wasn't over. Once their guard pointedly turned his back, Tommy and the others pulled their arms behind their heads like hefting those US footballs which never made sense to Regina—what was the point of a ball that wasn't round and couldn't bounce? They let fly a barrage of items to crash on Aaron's side of the wire. Regina recognized cans of powdered milk, packages of prunes, bars of soap, blocks of cheese and K-ration biscuits. Many of the throws overshot and sailed behind Aaron. Regina expected the men were putting all their strength into the effort since anything that failed to reach their destination and landed short wouldn't exactly be picked up, dusted off, and handed over. It would be lost forever, ending up in the guard's pocket. And the Soviets couldn't afford to sacrifice a single calorie.

Tommy wasn't betraying Aaron and the rest. He was trying to save their lives.

Regina's eyes filled with tears. He was the man she'd thought him to be, after all. And braver than she'd known. He was also more foolish. The risk he'd taken was enormous. Though perhaps she wasn't one to pass judgment.

Aaron scrambled along the ground, stuffing his booty into a rag that had been a shirt. A uniform worn proudly by a young man marching off to defend his motherland. Aaron wrapped up the goods, pressed them to his chest, and scurried off more stealthily than he'd arrived. After warning her to keep quiet, he'd never looked Regina's way again. The Americans also melted into the darkness. Within seconds there was no evidence anyone, Aaron, Tommy and his squadron, or the guard had been there.

Regina felt like she'd been shoved into a tornado, then just as unceremoniously ousted. She knew what she'd seen, but was uncertain how she should react. Americans could be severely disciplined for what they'd done, assigned dangerous work, sentenced to solitary confinement, deprived of the very rations they'd so generously shared. Aaron could simply be shot. She had to persuade him to stop; order him to stop, if it came to that. He had no right to endanger his life like this. Not when he had Regina and Lena waiting for him. Not when he was the only thing they had left.

Regina was almost back at the infirmary, ready to leave a note for Viktor telling him it had been a false alarm, she'd found no polio cases—the last thing she wanted was for him to ban her and Tommy from ever visiting there again—when she heard running footsteps behind her.

Regina half-turned to see who it was. She wasn't fast enough.

A pair of arms grabbed her roughly from behind, a grime en-crusted hand clamped over her mouth, as they dragged Regina away.

Chapter Twenty-Two

━━━━━━━

"Stay quiet," Tommy hissed in Regina's ear as her elbow made contact with his rib-cage. He grunted in surprise and released her, letting Regina slide to the ground. She scrambled to her feet and pivoted to confront him. Tommy straightened up and lunged forward, this time managing to grab Regina by the wrist, his grip hard enough to keep her from running off. When it appeared like she might scream, he menacingly raised his palm and glared. "I said shut up. And listen up. You tell anyone about what you saw, you'll regret it. Think about that little girl of yours. I'll put my hands, one on each side of her head, and I'll smash her skull like a walnut."

Regina hesitated. Tommy's open palm hovered above her head. She'd seen how far he could throw, even in a weakened state. She had no doubt he possessed the power to knock her unconscious or worse. And Lena wouldn't stand a chance.

Regina said, "Mr. Clark Gable."

Tommy's arm wavered. "W-what?"

"Mr. Clark Gable. In the movie, *Gone With the Wind*. He says this. We were shown this movie. To explain American racism."

For a moment Tommy looked like he might laugh. Then he looked like he might cry. He let his hand drop, slapping himself on the side of the face. "My one attempt at acting the tough guy, and I blew it." The menacing Tommy that had never quite been there completely gone. "You can't tell anybody what we're doing. Please. I beg you. You've seen them. They're starving. They're dying. I know Soviets did terrible things to your people in Poland. I don't defend them. But we're stuck here together now, and if there's something one person can do to help another person, shouldn't we do it? No matter what side anyone is supposed to be on?"

Regina thought of Aaron shoving lumps of bread into the desperate clutches of Korean enemies of the people. She thought of him striding out of the meeting hall to help Cossacks. And she thought of Tommy, useful innocent Tommy, currently espousing the Communist ideal better than she'd ever seen anyone—save Aaron—live it.

Regina didn't trust her voice to speak. She did trust Tommy enough to tell him, "I'm not German. I'm from Moscow." She'd let him draw his own conclusion that this meant Russian.

"Thank you." Whether Tommy was thanking her for agreeing to keep quiet or for sharing her secret with him remained unsaid.

"Let me help you," she said. "The sling I use to carry Lena. Everyone is used to seeing me wear it. We could use it to smuggle more food to the Soviet side."

It was a race to see which expanded quicker, Tommy's eyes or his mouth. Overwhelmed by the idea, moved by Regina's generosity, thrilled this traumatic evening had turned out better than he could have dreamed of, the only way Tommy could think to accept her offer and express all of his churning feelings was to grab Regina and spontaneously kiss her.

The second Tommy realized the inappropriateness of what he'd done, he let Regina go and ricocheted away, hands folded in supplication. "I'm sorry. I shouldn't have done that. Forgive me. It's just—you—thank you—I'm sorry. Thank you."

Fearful he might continue in such a loop forever, Regina rushed to reassure, "It's fine. No, please, stop apologizing. I'm fine. You're fine. We'll work together. Everything will be fine."

TO PROVE TO a still nervous Viktor how confident she was there was no polio lurking on the Soviet side of the camp, Regina volunteered to take Lena along on her next incursion. No mother would put her child at deadly risk for a plague to alibi a lie she had no logical reason to tell. Regina and Tommy slipped the flat, smoother items like boxes of raisins and packets of Vitamin C loaded orange concentrate beneath Lena. The little girl squirmed. They then piled cans of tuna and corned beef on her lap. She first whelped from the cold metal, then became intrigued by the light reflecting off the lids. The weight on Regina's neck was now twice what it would have been merely carrying Lena. She winced as her skin chafed under the knot, and needed Tommy's help to rise from a sitting position so she could begin walking. He rested a hand at the small of her back as support. He looked embarrassed to be doing so.

"It's fine," Regina reminded. "If there's something one person can do to help another person, shouldn't we do it?"

"You're wonderful," Tommy told her. She didn't dare speculate what he'd think if he knew the whole story.

They'd been afraid to tip the men off about their arrival in advance, lest they be caught with their smuggled goods and implicate more soldiers in the scheme. As a result, Aaron had no opportunity to make himself scarce. He was forced to be there when Regina arrived. He stood up to leave the moment he caught sight of her. Then he saw Lena. It was now November. Aaron hadn't laid eyes on his daughter since June. She'd been barely sitting up and cooing nonsense syllables then. Now she was a week short of her first birthday. She was pulling herself up to stand, which Lena demonstrated when Regina set her down on the floor while unloading what she'd brought. Lena was also making more pointed sounds, babbling, "Ma, ma, ma," and "Da, da, da," and "Pa, pa, pa," which almost froze Aaron into immobility.

She didn't mean him, of course. Lena had no idea who Aaron was. She didn't know the title could be applied to a person. Her life featured no such figure. Yet, for a moment, Aaron had thought she was talking to him. The saddest part was, so did multiple others. The instant a child cried out, "Papa!" at least a dozen men whipped their heads in her direction.

"*Yeahhalee, me yeahhalee, po gladenkay doroszhke.*" A prisoner Regina had never seen smile, much less sing, scooped Lena up on his lap, and began bouncing her on his knee. "*Prig, skok, ee v'yamko oopahly!*" He held onto her hands while opening his legs and letting her drop, catching her before she hit the ground much to Lena's giggling delight. "We rode, we rode, on a smooth road, then, oopsie, we fell in a ditch!" He told Regina, "My little ones love this game."

Other men lined up for the chance to make Lena laugh. One took her tiny palm, and drew circles with his finger, chanting, "The crow made some porridge, she fed her children." He tugged gently on her pinkie, "She gave some to this one," he tugged on her index finger, "She gave some to this one," he tugged on her middle finger, "She gave some to this one," he tapped the pointer and then the thumb, "But none to this one!"

"Crow must not have signed the Geneva Convention," a voice called from the back, triggering a mountain of guffaws.

Lena's next suitor danced around the room while reciting a nursery rhyme about a rabbit who went out for a walk, then "piff, paff, oy, oy, oy," the farmer shot him. Now the rabbit is dead.

"Rabbit definitely didn't sign," the same voice said. To considerably less merriment.

Regina took advantage of the festive commotion to sidle closer to Aaron. He was so busy gazing longingly at Lena he didn't notice until Regina had backed him into a corner. Any sudden move now would draw attention to them. Which was the last thing Aaron wanted. Regina understood she wasn't playing fair. Neither was the rest of the world. She took the greatest chance of all, moving her hand ever so slightly, so she might brush the back of Aaron's palm with her fingers. It had been so long since she'd touched him. So long since he'd touched her. She was shaking, her heart beating frantically, every muscle clenched. Regina was skittish, but the minute her skin made contact with his, her middle finger tracing the path of the vein that throbbed below Aaron's knuckle, her body relaxed from the familiarity. No matter where she was, when that spark of electricity leapt from his flesh to hers, Regina was home.

Aaron allowed Regina's touch to linger for a fraction of a second. He didn't possess the willpower to deny it completely. Then, as briefly as he'd succumbed, he pulled away. Not abruptly. That could attract scrutiny. He did it so nonchalantly their connection might never have happened.

"You're killing me," Aaron whispered, teeth clenched. "It requires all my energy solely to stay alive. Thinking about you and Lena being here takes away from that. You are killing me."

Regina must have looked so pale and shaken on their walk back to the infirmary that Tommy felt moved to ask her twice if she were feeling alright. The question sounded as foreign to Regina as if he'd asked it in another language. What did her physical or mental state have to do with anything? That issue had long become moot.

Instead, she turned to Tommy with such fervor that he took a step back in surprise. She demanded he reassure her, "We're doing some good here, aren't we? Some small good? It may look like we're doing nothing, because there's so much wrong, but it's not all going to waste?"

Tommy understood what she was asking, "There's a story. A man and his friend are walking along the beach. It's always a man in the story. For this version, let's make it a woman. A woman and her friend are walking along the beach. She sees a struggling starfish in the sand, picks it up, and tosses it back into the ocean. Her friend says, *There must be thousands of starfish on this beach. You won't be able to make much of a difference.* The woman says, *I've made a difference to this one.*"

He was looking at her so expectantly, so hopefully, so happily— all sentiments in short supply behind the barbed wire… and on the other side of it—that Regina didn't have the heart to ask Tommy the follow up that instantly surfaced. "What if the starfish didn't want her to?"

"NURSE!" VIKTOR SNAPPED his fingers in Regina's direction and pointed towards a guard who'd stumbled in, cap pressed to a gash in his forearm, blood seeping through his fingers where he hadn't applied enough pressure. "Take care of him!"

Regina beckoned the soldier to a table set with rubbing alcohol and gauze. He plopped into the chair and presented his arm, smirking, expecting Regina to either be impressed or disgusted. She wasn't in the mood for either. Regina had moved perfunctorily from patient to patient all day, barely hearing anything through the echo in her head. Aaron wanted her gone, Aaron wanted her gone, Aaron wanted her gone. Because he said she was killing him…

The wound was neither impressive nor disgusting. Regina had treated worse, and she wasn't interested in hearing stories about whatever manly way he might have acquired it. She took a cursory look. "Needs stitches."

Regina reached for the spirit to clean it out. It wasn't a good sign when the once puffed up guard winced and tried to jerk his arm away, snarling, "Be careful, *hundin*, that hurt!" If he was calling her a bitch already, wait till they got to the stitching part.

"Where's the anesthesia?" he demanded as soon as Regina got the needle out.

"We save it for the neediest cases."

"I need it," he insisted.

"No, you don't." Regina wasn't in the mood for this, either. "Stop whining and act like a man. There are patients much worse off than you." Not to mention prisoners, Regina thought.

She didn't try to be harsher with him than she would have with any other case. Though she didn't aim for excessive gentleness, like she might have with a child or a man on his deathbed, either. Regina treated this guard the same way she'd have treated any healthy soldier who needed a few stitches in a non-delicate extremity. He acted like she'd placed him on a torture rack, groaning, writhing, calling her more names.

Regina wondered if, like his wound, he thought those names were anything she hadn't heard before? She sent him on his way with orders to come back if the area grew hot, tender, or filled with pus, that would indicate it was infected. Otherwise, she'd likely take the stitches out in a week or so. "And I hope you're a little braver about it then." Regina recalled the men whose burnt skin she was forced to peel off in chunks, the ones whose broken bones she'd set while they remained conscious, the bullet wounds that bled out in minutes. It was difficult to summon up sympathy for a cut that, to Regina's experienced eye, looked like it had come from a slash with a broken bottle in the middle of a drunken fistfight. She could still smell the alcohol on him.

"You've got a sadist working here." The guard had barely gotten up, cradling his arm like an infant, before he was headed for Viktor, bellowing at the top of his lungs. He thrust the wound forward, as evidence. "Look what she did to me!"

To Viktor's credit, he remained unimpressed. A benefit to having friends in high places was not only did they get you assigned to the most cushy jobs while your contemporaries were freezing to death at the Russian front, you didn't have to pay attention to every piddling complaint that came your way from a nobody.

Grasping this sortie wasn't gaining the traction he craved, the guard changed course and, glancing slyly over his shoulder to ensure Regina appreciated his maneuver, added, "And she's a traitor, too!"

That one got Viktor's attention. It was one thing to dismiss a soldier's complaint about his medical care. He could defend against that by claiming civilians had no idea what was and what wasn't appropriate. It would be quite another to ignore claims of malfeasance taking place under his nose. That one could actually get him in trouble, no matter who his family was.

Seeing he was finally being listened to, the guard went on triumphantly, "Your nurse refused to give me anesthesia while stitching my wound. She claimed there wasn't enough to go around. I ask you, would the Fatherland allow for such shortages? The only way we could not have enough anesthesia for our brave fighting men would be if she were stealing it right out from under your nose!"

He'd stumbled on the key turn of phrase to make Viktor nervous. Not to mention that, to disagree with him, Viktor would have to claim that yes, as a matter of fact, the Fatherland did allow shortages. So many shortages. Not just medicine, but food, uniforms, and pretty much every other necessity. Viktor was not about to claim that. Especially not to defend Regina.

"She's conspiring with the Americans." Now that he knew he was on the right track, he ran with the rest. "We've suspected they operated a black market, we've just never been able to figure out how the contraband goods were getting to them. Now we know! It's this woman!"

Through her fog, Regina had to fight the urge to laugh. The guards didn't know where the Americans were getting contraband for their black market? The guards were the black market! Soldiers bribed them with cigarettes and chocolates from their Red Cross packages, and the guards would buy them whatever they asked for from the village. Guards also carried the goods from one part of the camp to the next. Especially this one since, now that she actually looked at his face rather than his arm, Regina realized was the same one who'd been paid to look away while Tommy threw whatever he could to Aaron.

"He's the traitor," Regina shot back, years of instinct honed by *samokritika* coming out before she had a chance to think through the prudence of it. You defended yourself by accusing someone else. Good or bad no longer entered into it. It was the only choice.

"Liar!" he screamed with the furor of a man who knew she knew she was telling the truth.

"Search him," Regina suggested, "I know he has American cigarettes on him right now."

She knew no such thing. She was taking a hell of a chance. Not just for herself but for Lena. Aaron would be furious. Aaron wasn't here.

"Please empty your pockets, Private." Viktor requested in a tone that made clear the please would be employed but once.

"Of course." The guard tried to smile nonchalantly. He made a show of fumbling with his sore arm as he laid out the contents of first his right, then his left pants pocket. The results failed to turn up anything improper. "There, you see?"

"All of your pockets," Regina insisted, fully aware she was usurping Viktor's authority. The deeper in she got, the worse the consequences of failure would be.

The guard kept smiling as the front pocket of his shirt proved equally innocuous.

Regina had one shot left. She was determined to take it, no matter how risky.

"And your boots."

His smile faltered. A paleness that couldn't be attributed to his recent blood loss seized the boy's face. "You're being ridiculous."

Viktor has seen the change in disposition too. "Your boots," he mimicked Regina.

That's where the cigarettes were hidden. Two packs. No way to claim it was anything but conspiring with the Americans.

"He made me do it! That dentist, Tommy Whateverhisnameis. He threatened to kill me if I didn't help him set up a meeting with a Soviet prisoner, so he could pass on supplies. He said he'd cut my throat. He had a knife. That's how I got hurt!" That final lie a burst of inspiration. "He shoved the cigarettes in my boots and told me there'd be more. I couldn't stop him! He forced me! I had no choice!"

UNDERSTANDING THE SEVERITY of the situation, Viktor promptly punted the issue up the chain of command, eager to keep as broad a distance between himself and something this potentially incendiary as possible. It was the camp's kommander who personally led the team of men who dragged Tommy out of his barracks, flung him to the ground, beat him with the butts of their rifles, and kicked him in the back, stomach, head, and face.

It was Regina who watched, hands covering her mouth to keep from screaming, to keep from saying anything that could make this already grim interrogation worse. This was her fault. She'd started it. She'd leapt in without thinking. Aaron had accused her of killing him. Now she would be responsible for Tommy's death. Regina knew that should be her overriding horror.

Yet, in her selfishness, no matter how blameworthy Regina was for Tommy, her primary fear was that Tommy would break and finally answer the question his torturers kept asking as they beat him to a bloody pulp. "Give us the name of your Soviet contact."

Chapter Twenty-Three

Regina didn't want Tommy to die. She wept at the thought. More though, Regina didn't want Tommy to give up Aaron's name. There was only so far the Nazis could go punishing Tommy—they were already in violation of the Geneva Convention. Aaron, however, could be executed without penalty. It didn't need to be officially recorded. He was nothing. If he ceased to exist, it wouldn't matter to anyone. Except Regina. She didn't want Tommy to die. But if the way to protect Aaron was for that to happen, then Regina knew which side she was on.

Tommy lay on the ground. He'd tried to avoid the worst of the beating by curling into a ball. Kicks to his back snapped him open, the opposite of a pill bug. He rolled onto his stomach, pressing his face to the ground and covering his head with his hands. A stomp on the conjoined fingers atop his skull drove Tommy's nose deeper into the dirt. When he stopped flinching at every blow, Regina wondered if he'd lost consciousness or was suffocated. The soldiers must have thought the same thing, because a boot tip under Tommy's chest flipped him over. Blood ran from a hairline wound into his eyes, his nose was squashed to one side, the edge of his lip flapped loose.

Regina squared her shoulders and pushed her way through the circle around Tommy. Using authority she knew she didn't have but hoped the soldiers didn't realize, Regina barked, "You're done here. This man can be of no more use to you. Take him to the infirmary!"

A nod from the kommandant confirmed they should do as she said.

Regina was supervising Tommy getting properly loaded onto a stretcher, making sure his spine remained as immobile as possible, when she realized that while the soldiers were done with Tommy, they were not done with their interrogation.

All two thousand Americans were summoned for an immediate roll call. They staggered out of their barracks, some of their own volition, others with an arm swung over the shoulder of two comrades on either side of them. Some used a stick as a crutch, others were covered in sores. The sound of so many men gathering was enough to attract attention from the Soviet side of the camp. An almost equal number pressed along the perimeter of barbed wire, trying to catch a glimpse of what was happening. Regina wondered if Aaron was among them.

The kommandant inquired of the Americans, in the same avuncular tone that disoriented Regina on her first day, wondering who the Soviet soldier was that had been Tommy's contact. He needed a name. Once he had it, they could all go back to what they were doing.

Regina nearly tripped over the stretcher. Had Tommy's suffering been for nothing? Would Aaron be exposed in any case?

Over two thousand men heard the politely phrased request.

Over two thousand men stayed mum.

They looked side to side. They looked down at the ground. They looked up at the sky. They scratched behind their ears, they crossed their arms against their chests, they shuffled from foot to foot. But over two thousand men failed to answer the question.

As a result, over two thousand men were ordered to line up in the square in between sectors. The kommandant informed them they'd remain that way until one of them was able to produce a name. Collective punishment was against the Geneva Convention. The kommandant appeared unconcerned. He returned to his office. He told the guards to let him know when there was something to discuss.

Regina followed Tommy's stretcher to the infirmary. She kept sneaking peeks over her shoulder. At any moment, one of the Americans might burst forward with a finger pointed Aaron's way. No one had. Yet.

Once settled into a bed, Regina tended Tommy's wounds. She cleaned off the blood and stitched the gashes, unable to stop thinking how it was her lack of sympathy for a similar injury that put Tommy and Aaron's lives at risk. When would Regina ever learn? When would she stop acting so impulsively?

She wrapped Tommy's broken ribs. She gently tucked the loose scrap of his lip back in place and bandaged it, hoping the scab would heal it naturally. The entire time, Regina also kept looking out the infirmary window. She had a view of at least half the square. Where, so far, no one had yet to budge.

It was getting darker. It was getting colder. The relatively mild November afternoon, sun shining brightly, was drifting towards dusk. A frigid wind roared up. Many of the men weren't wearing jackets or hats, they'd filed out so quickly, assuming they'd return within minutes. Some of them, Regina knew, were recovering from chest colds, pneumonia, scarlet fever.

A flash of movement, and Regina feared it was all over. Someone had decided to hell with protecting a damn Commie, stepped up, and offered Aaron's name for the chance to warm up. But it proved merely one who'd fainted from exertion. He was dragged as far as the infirmary steps, then dumped outside the door. Regina asked an orderly to help bring him inside.

She'd thought midnight would be the most fraught hour, but it was early morning, when temperatures plunged and shivering men began dropping from exposure, that Regina feared the end was near. They wouldn't be able to take much more. It was, frankly, illogical to put their lives on the line for somebody they likely didn't know. Someone who, less than a half decade earlier, was considered a mortal enemy.

And still, among those who avoided collapse, nobody said a word.

The kommandant arrived at nine, surprised to see the majority of his prisoners where he'd left them. Most of the Soviets were still on their side, too, radiating a combination of support, gratitude, fear, and, most importantly, understanding to those who couldn't keep going.

"Stubborn American sons of bitches," the kommandant mumbled before, with the wave of a hand, dismissing them from his illegal damnation.

As some of the men sank to their knees, needing help to make it back to the barracks, Regina nearly did, too. Was it over? Was Aaron safe?

Leaving Moscow, she'd thought it was over. She'd thought she was safe. Only to realize it was just the beginning of something far worse.

TWO DAYS AND nights passed before Tommy opened his eyes. Regina never left his side. She changed his bandages, propped up his head and trickled water down his throat so he wouldn't dehydrate. When he spiked a fever, she requisitioned an aspirin, claiming it was for herself—"Female trouble," no squeamish man ever questioned that— and snuck it to Tommy. But Regina's mind was with Aaron. Where was he? How was he? Was he still in danger? Would an American soldier who hadn't wanted to squeal publicly sneak off and betray him in private? Regina wouldn't blame them. They'd be protecting their own against further collective torture. They owed Aaron nothing. They were the ones doing the Soviets a kindness. And what about the Soviets? Aaron's comrades? Would one of them out him for a chance to curry favor? If they were back in the USSR, Regina would have no doubt about it. But the rules were different here. Until they weren't.

Tommy's first word, torn lips sluggish, tongue gnawed, larynx bruised, were, "Caught?"

Regina shook her head. In a whisper, she filled him in on everything he'd missed. "Not a single man broke. Not one."

Tears spilled from Tommy's eyes. Regina quickly wiped them away. Most men would be embarrassed. Tommy had more important matters on his mind. "Wanted to protect..."

"I know," Regina reassured.

"... You." That she hadn't known. "You and Lena."

Oh. Through the entire ordeal, Regina hadn't given herself or her daughter a moment's thought.

"If they found out you were involved, too, who knows what they'd do to the two of you?"

Guilt sliced Regina like a scalpel to the chest. *She hadn't given her daughter a moment's thought.* What kind of mother did that make her? Aaron had accused Regina of killing him. Was she risking the same with Lena?

Tommy struggled to sit up, gagging from the pain. Regina eased him onto the mattress. In case he harbored any ideas of leaping back into contraband delivery, Regina advised, "They'll be watching you. You can't."

"Then what are we going to do?" Tommy panicked.

"I'll think of something," she promised. Again, thinking only of Aaron.

ONCE TOMMY WAS no longer in immediate danger, Regina strove to make sure it didn't look like she was spending any more time with him than she did with any other patient. Tommy was right, she couldn't afford to be connected to his smuggling operation. Even as she was desperately trying to figure out a way to take it over for him. The only opportunity Regina and Tommy had for anything outside of perfunctory conversation about his health was when she shaved him. He'd shyly asked if she would mind, since he was currently incapacitated, and "I don't like looking unkempt." A new word to add to Regina's English vocabulary.

It was a strangely intimate experience, between feeding a child and a kiss. She was making contact with his skin, stripping it bare, straight razor poised above the most vulnerable vein beneath his chin. He had absolute faith in her to do the right thing. Same as he had from the start. Same as Aaron. In some ways, Tommy reminded Regina so much of Aaron. But not in the ways which mattered most.

Tommy kept his eyes closed while she went about the business of grooming him. But, on one occasion, he'd opened them unexpectedly, just as Regina's fingers circled the edge of his mouth. Their gaze locked, and she couldn't shake the suspicion he might turn and kiss her hand impulsively, the way he'd kissed her lips the night she'd vowed to help him. He had been so apologetic then, she'd felt no need to summon a response. Regina suspected he wouldn't be nearly as apologetic now. Which meant some kind of response would be required on her part. Did she dare tell Tommy the truth?

As it turned out, she didn't need to. Not yet. Regina's hunch had been in error. Despite the intensity of his gaze, Tommy did not kiss her hand. He didn't do anything inappropriate. He simply closed his eyes again and leaned back, enjoying the sensation.

"I HAVE AN idea," Regina whispered. She passed by Tommy's cot, pretending to drop the metal bowl she was holding so she'd have an excuse to bend over, pick it up, and place her head near Tommy's ear. Before Regina could get more words out, she noticed the side of his face was covered in sweat, his teeth chattering. Bowl forgotten, she leapt to her feet, grabbing a thermometer. A fever of forty-one degrees Celsius confirmed that Tommy was burning up. After she'd prodded, he did admit to feeling cold. He assured her it was nothing. It was wintertime, after all, who didn't feel cold?

It had to be an infection. Regina did her best to clean out his wounds, but the infirmary, despite all their collective efforts, was hardly the most sterile place. Needles, bandages, cups, and all of the heavier equipment was supposed to be sterilized between each use. But when a group of patients came in, either due to a measles out-break, or a mass injury at a work site, like a collapsed wall or a truck going off-road and striking a tree, it was difficult to keep track of what was clean enough. When doing triage, the choice came down to grabbing a tool that would save a patient's life immediately and hope to stave off infection down the road, or hesitating long enough to ensure spotlessness, and losing the patient in the interim.

Tommy needed antibiotics. Regina knew better than to ask for them. Prisoners, even the Americans, were far down the priority list. If Regina dared put up a fuss, she'd be reminded of what she'd told the guard who'd started all this trouble. And she'd be the first one they suspected if medication went missing.

Regina excused herself for a few minutes, telling Viktor she needed to check on Lena. The baby had been fussy as she dropped her off with the collective this morning. When Regina got there, the woman assigned to watch all the children assured the girl was fine, no problems. Regina said she wanted to make certain. On their walk back to the infirmary, Regina pinched Lena hard on the leg. Startled, the child yelped, peered at her mother suspiciously, but settled back down quickly. She'd always been docile. She didn't get it from Regina. No good. Regina pinched Lena again, this time twisting the soft, tender skin for good measure. Lena burst into tears, which got worse when Regina set her down on the ground and forced Lena to walk the rest of the way, stumbling through the cold mud that seeped through her shoes and stockings. By the time they got back to the infirmary, Lena was red-faced, hysterical, and hot to the touch.

"I'm afraid it could be scarlet fever," Regina told Viktor. "We can't let it spread to the other children, their mothers won't be able to work in the kitchen if they have infected ones at home."

She got the antibiotics she asked for.

Regina took Lena into a corner where she rocked her and soothed her, and whispered, "I'm sorry, I'm so sorry, Lenachka, forgive Mama, please." Lena sniffled and eyed Regina warily.

The next time Regina brought Tommy water, Lena's antibiotic was mixed in.

REGINA CONTINUED HER charade for the next week, but Tommy's fever refused to go down. He grew paler, then weaker. His skin felt so tender he told Regina not to bother with shaving. "I have no one to look good for." Sick as he was, Tommy managed to make clear it was a joke, not self-pity.

"You will recover." Regina had gotten into the habit of making promises she had no way of keeping. It comforted the patient, even when both knew she was lying.

"It's not that I'm afraid of dying." Tommy mused as reasonably as another man might say he didn't necessarily object to neckties or fried beef tongue. "It's that I'm afraid of dying alone." Once again,

Tommy didn't seem embarrassed by the confession. "It's sad. Like you never existed. Like you never mattered."

"You won't die alone." This time, Regina resolved to see the promise through, no matter what. She picked up his hand, linking their fingers. "I am here with you. You are not alone."

"A BODY DISAPPEARED last night," Regina informed Viktor. "The Russian." She made a dismissive gesture towards the far end of the infirmary, the beds housing the hopeless cases. Tommy had never made it that far. Thanks to the redirected antibiotics, he was on his way to making a miraculous, unassisted recovery. He was an exception. For most, once the downward slide began, there was no coming back, especially if the use of medication would be considered a waste. "Fluid in his lungs. He died around midnight." A time Viktor never appeared. "I waited until morning to alert the burial unit. No sense waking them up. Or you to sign the paperwork." Viktor was about to object. He didn't care what time gravediggers were dragged out of bed. She did have a point about him. "Except the body disappeared between then and now. I checked with the cemetery, they don't have him."

Viktor's disgust fought with his confusion. "You must have made a mistake."

Regina let the suggestion fly by without acknowledgement. "I heard a rumor," she said. Viktor loved rumors. "Slav bastards have been sneaking in at night, stealing dead bodies and propping them up to inflate the headcount at roll call."

Disgust was definitely winning. "Do they eat and fuck corpses, too?"

Regina's shrug suggested she would put nothing past such subhuman *untermenschen*.

"We should catch them in the act," Regina suggested. "I know who I'm looking for. I'll go in and see what I can find out."

REGINA ENTERED THE Soviet sector allegedly looking for a corpse. She found thousands of men who could fit the bill. In the weeks since her last visit, conditions had deteriorated. Bunks quavered, loaded with soldiers too weak to moan. Those who could still move dragged shriveled limbs from place to place. The notion that Aaron might have died and Regina not know of it flitted through her brain. She ground it out with the intensity of a caterpillar beneath her boot. Regina needed to visit several barracks before she tracked down Aaron. He crouched in a semicircle of a half-dozen other skeletons, trying to keep warm around a sputtering fire from what appeared to be boards ripped right off the side of their building. They huddled shoulder to shoulder, palms and feet pointed at the flames.

"Ivanovitch!" Regina barked, remembering to give the name a German twist. "You are wanted for questioning!"

He painstakingly stood up, allowing Regina to see that Aaron hadn't managed to escape the scourge ravaging the rest of his camp. His legs were as scrawny as the others. What made Regina's breath truly catch in her throat were his shoulders. Those shoulders which drove her to lose the power of speech multiple times... the first night, rain-drenched while steering his wagon... striding through the rye fields, yanking stalks with his bare hands which took others multiple tries... peeling the shirt off his back to cover the wretched Cossacks... lying on his stomach, eyes closed, while Regina ran her fingers along the impossibly smooth skin, marveling at the coiled muscles underneath as he tried not to laugh... Aaron's shoulders were hunched now, scarred, covered in open lesions. They folded inward like broken wings, looking barely capable of holding up a neck where an Adam's apple encompassed the entire width.

He shuffled towards Regina, face neutral, while his eyes blazed. The moment they got outside, Regina expected another tirade, another admonition, another plea. Instead, the moment they stepped behind the barracks and could trust no one was watching, Aaron seized Regina's face with his hands, kissing her more deeply, more hungrily and with more relief than when he'd seen her climb off the truck delivering her to the front. Stunned, she could do nothing more than kiss him back. Because there was nothing more she wanted to do.

Aaron pulled away first, gasping for air, propping a hand against the wall to stay upright. Despite everything Regina had already been through and seen, she couldn't help thinking this was the most cruel thing of all. Aaron was so weak that kissing her winded him.

"I'm sorry," she pleaded. Sorry for this, sorry for that, sorry for everything. "I had to see you. I had to know if…"

"Still alive," he confirmed grimly. She wondered if he wished it were otherwise.

"I'm fine," she assured him, knowing it's what worried him most. "Lena is fine."

He indicated the main complex. "They still have food there?"

"Some."

"Good. None left here. You made the right decision. Who knows if supplies are still getting through to our military units. Or if they're even still fighting. You could have ended up trapped, like in Leningrad."

His change of tune stunned Regina to some level beyond tears. Beyond rational thought. "I… did the right thing?"

"You always do." Which reminded him. "Tommy?"

"Still alive," Regina echoed. "It'll be a while before he can get back here. I had an idea—"

"He's in love with you," Aaron said with the same confidence he'd earlier used to tell her she'd done the right thing.

"I know," Regina cringed. "I hate leading him on. He's such a good man. I don't want to do anything to hurt him. Maybe if I told him you and I—"

"No." The denial gave Aaron his second wind.

"He'll see it's nothing personal. If he knows you and I…"

"No," Aaron repeated. "Tommy is a good man. The best. He didn't break this time. Who knows what might happen the next? If he knows about you and me, he might tell. We have no right to put him in the position of keeping our secret."

Chapter Twenty-Four

First, Stalag 3-K lost their power lines and the electricity that came with it. Next, the water supply became erratic, creating a shortage for drinking and cooking, much less washing. The good part was it meant the Nazis had to be losing. The bad part was it meant there would be no heat, no light and no fresh water for anyone. The worst part came when Germany forbade the Red Cross from entering any of their POW camps. Which meant no more extra rations for the Americans. Which meant nothing for the Soviets.

The Poles who used to come in for work stopped doing so once the food ran out. Guards deserted in droves. Regina no longer needed a plan for smuggling to the Soviet side, as nobody cared anymore about the two sides mixing. And there was nothing to smuggle. Even Viktor and the kommandant were reduced to watery soup with a blob of stale meat or fish chunk floating in it—though theirs came without maggots, and the "blutwurst" they used to serve the prisoners, a sausage made of congealed animal blood that had to be eaten cold. Warming it up made it melt into a clotty blob.

Before supplies ran out, the Germans used to smash holes into the Americans' canned goods to keep them from hoarding food to escape with. Smearing margarine into the punctures preserved it a while longer, but once no more Red Cross packages were arriving, they had to break into the emergency stash. By April, they were reduced to digging up whatever scraps were left in the gardens they'd planted, scraping up sawdust, euphemistically called "tree flour" and grass, then attempting to bake the concoction into bread via a camp stove featuring a fire pot, air shaft, and blower all jerry-rigged out of used tin cans. Fights over portion size broke out among those who had the strength to throw a punch. Aaron and Tommy stayed out of it. They passed most of their rations to Regina, who was still attempting to breastfeed Lena. Though over a year old, the child barely had any teeth and, in size, looked closer to six months. Regina tried to protest Aaron and Tommy giving up their food to the two of them, pointing out they were in worse physical shape than she was. She was merely starving. They were starving, and nearly worked to death.

"I hate to see anyone go hungry," Aaron reminded. "Not if I can help it."

"For Lena," Tommy urged.

With no more work details—the Germans had given up trying to make the prisoners do anything; they patrolled with rifles now to quell any potential revolts, they barely cared about escapes—Regina, Aaron and Tommy spent most of their days staggering from barracks to barracks, looking for men who'd died, organizing shifts to get them buried quickly to prevent disease outbreaks.

In early May, the kommandant made his first public appearance in weeks. His uniform was freshly washed and ironed. It also appeared two sizes too big. He looked like a snowman, the uniform suggesting a much larger body with a tiny head perched on top. The bags under his eyes puffed purple. His jowls sagged until his face looked square. He had to lick his lips and swallow between words to keep from hacking dryly as he ordered all prisoners—American and Soviet—to rip up what was left of their clothes and fashion them into sacks to carry provisions. They'd be abandoning the camp, leaving Poland, heading deeper into Germany.

"They've lost," Tommy cheered under his breath. "They're retreating."

"Then why take us with them?"

The four of them—Regina, Aaron, Tommy, Lena—had taken over a corner of the recently abandoned infirmary, dragging three cots over to where the primus stove could still be cajoled into belching some heat if fed with sticks, pea sized coal remnants and diligent, though cautious, blowing. All medication, gauze, needles, and rubbing alcohol—which some were now drinking straight—had long run out or was ransacked. The pillows and mattresses had been sliced open, their straw stuffing repurposed for food or warmth. They'd laid wood planks atop the rusty metallic springs. Better than sleeping on the linoleum floor, where rats scurried, hunting for food, unaware they were being hunted for food, themselves. Aaron, Tommy and Regina—Lena dozing against her chest—sat in a semicircle, their backs propped against the bed frames, feet and hands stretched towards the stove, whispering. Not because they expected anyone to overhear them, but because speaking up required an energy no one possessed any longer. It was all they could do to take turns, once a day, to teeter out, looking for scraps of food.

Tommy answered Regina's question. "Slave labor? Hostages? Cannon fodder? They'll need every body they can commandeer to defend Berlin."

"They're hiding the evidence of what they've done," Aaron added. "How they treated us."

"I won't last long in Germany." Tommy looked from Aaron to Regina, hesitating. She saw the calculations taking place in his head, as Tommy wavered on the front steps of a confession. Finally, he must have decided in the affirmative. Tommy sighed and looked to either side of him, in case the walls still had ears. "Burns," he said. "That's just what my old man changed it to so I'd have the chance of getting into college." He stretched out his hand to Aaron and announced, "Thomas Samuel Bernstein. Pleased to meet you." Then, to explain the sudden divulgence, meekly added, "I didn't want to die without someone hearing my real name." Like he'd never existed. Like he'd never mattered. Like he'd died alone.

Aaron and Regina weren't sure how to respond. They understood the implication—and danger—of his confession. Regina was still trying to fashion an adequate response when Aaron also stuck his hand out, grasping Tommy's. "Aaron Kramer. A privilege serving with you."

Tommy gasped. It was his turn to understand the implication of Ivanovitch actually being Kramer.

Which left Regina with nothing to do but place her hand atop theirs. "Regina Shraiman." Not Schmidt.

After which there was nothing left to do but laugh.

TOMMY HAD FALLEN asleep. They all periodically did at odd times, without warning, whether due to exhaustion, or the mind's inability to deal with the situation for another minute, and craving the brief, temporary release of oblivion.

This allowed Regina to whisper to Aaron, "Is Tommy right? Are they taking us to use as cannon fodder?"

"Doesn't matter. You and Lena won't survive a forced march."

Regina was about to tell him what she'd survived on her march to him, then recalled Lena had been lighter. And Regina stronger.

"We'll run then," she said. "Into the woods. The guards don't care anymore. Half of them did it first. Summer is coming. We can take our chances with the elements over anything the Germans have planned for us."

Aaron nodded thoughtfully, seemingly in agreement with her. Then he said, "I won't let you two starve to death. Or die of thirst."

"You'll kill us before you let that happen." Regina finished the thought he couldn't. "Me, Lena, yourself. We'll die together, as a family. On our own terms. We won't let them get us."

After which there was nothing left to do but cry.

"It's nice to have so many choices," Regina quoted Marta, hurriedly wiping her eyes as she spied Tommy beginning to stir awake. "Shame none of them are good."

"LOOK! LOOK!" REGINA tugged on Aaron's sleeve, then on Tommy's, needing confirmation she wasn't hallucinating. She'd been awakened by a chorus of shouts, followed by gunfire. That wasn't unusual. Aaron and Tommy slept right through it. Lena had startled awake, crying more in surprise than anger. Regina and Aaron's daughter learned early there was no point in getting angry. Nothing was going to change. She cried so little, in fact, it was the novelty which woke Regina. She stood and picked Lena up, intending to take her aside so the men could continue resting, when Regina's eyes fell on the cracked southern window, and through it the flagpole she'd seen every day since arriving in Stalag 3-K, with its red, white and black Swastika proudly flapping in the wind.

"Is that…" For the first time, Regina relied more on Tommy's expertise than Aaron's. He'd know best. "Is that the…"

"Stars and stripes," Tommy breathed slowly, as if saying the words in a foreign language, unsure whether he was pronouncing them correctly. "That's the stars and stripes. It's the stars and stripes," he fumbled to his feet, long past a second wind, but newly energized, first crawling, then forcing himself to rise and run for the door, Aaron, Regina and Lena right behind him.

"The Americans are here, the Americans are here." It was a buzz, it was a roar, it was in English, it was in Russian, Polish, German even. The camp hummed with it, the camp vibrated with it. "The Americans are here!"

Healthy, beaming non-emaciated soldiers were climbing out of tanks, they were rushing the gates, knocking down and tearing up the barbed wire like it was nothing. They were handing out blankets and food and being grabbed and hugged and people were crying and people were screaming and Regina felt herself grabbed by the shoulders and spun around and kissed and she gave herself to the kiss because it was over and they were free and they were alive and they had persevered. They had persevered and they had won.

And it was Tommy.

Tommy was the one kissing Regina. Tommy was the one holding her by the shoulders, and minding he didn't crush Lena. He was grinning at her, and he was laughing, and he was the one who had kissed her. Because it was over and they were free and they were alive.

While Aaron stood off to the side and watched.

Tommy didn't apologize this time. He didn't look chagrined. He looked thrilled. Thrilled with himself, with Regina, with everything between them and outside them and beyond them.

She couldn't blame him. She couldn't chastise him. She did need to be honest with him. She owed him that much. And it was safe. Aaron couldn't have any objection now. She looked over at him quickly and reached out her hand so they could tell Tommy together. So they could thank him together for everything he had done for them. They would never be able to thank him enough.

But Aaron was no longer looking at Tommy and Regina. Aaron's eyes were fixed on the horizon, where another tank convoy could be seen making their way up the road to the camp.

"The Soviets are here," Aaron said. His tone nothing at all like how Tommy had sounded when he'd spied his own men.

THE RED ARMY arrived barely a half day behind the Americans. They announced that since they were in Poland, the USSR was in charge. They quickly split the camp back into its original two sectors. And ordered all citizens of the Union of Soviet Socialist Republics to step forward.

"No," Aaron hissed as Regina attempted to follow orders. They stood in a crowd where, except for those still wearing their uniform, it was impossible to tell who belonged on which side. Everyone looked hungry, everyone looked battered, everyone looked relieved and skittish about what came next. "You're a Polish citizen working for the Germans as a nurse in order to provide for your child. A thousand men will confirm."

Regina understood what he was saying, and why he was saying it. "Stay with us. You speak English. Tommy will vouch for you."

"My entire unit knows who I am. I can't hide."

"What happened with Felix was so long ago." Was it barely four years? It felt like more than that in decades. "No one will hold it against you."

"We don't know what's going to happen. We don't know what will be held against who. We've been here so long. We have no idea which way the wind is blowing in Moscow today."

He was right. Regina had seen for herself how fast the right thing to do could turn into the wrong thing to have done. Better they suss out what the latest correct thinking was, before they inadvertently suggested they might be against it.

"You and Lena stay with Tommy. He'll look out for you."

"I'll come back for you, no matter what," Regina swore.

Aaron was already moving away.

"HE'S RIGHT," TOMMY insisted, leading her back to the US sector, as Regina couldn't stop gazing left, towards the newly segregated Soviet block. "Did you see how scared some of those boys looked? You don't know what they might do to you and Lena if they think you collaborated with the Germans."

She had. She'd collaborated with the Germans. For over a year, Regina had kept herself from dwelling on the reality by rationalizing she was only pretending to collaborate. She may bandage Nazi wounds and treat their fevers. She was also undermining them by spiriting out dead bodies and smuggling food and slipping medicine to dying men. She wasn't collaborating in her heart. At least, that's how she would explain it. That's how Tommy would see it. But, also in her heart, Regina knew the deeper truth. If she'd conceived of a plan where collaborating with the Germans allowed her to release Aaron, she'd have done it without a second thought. Tommy didn't see it. Tommy wasn't capable of seeing it. He was too American.

"I'll explain everything you did to help us," Tommy went on, losing her in the pronouns.

"I did help the Soviets." Regina feebly counted her blessings. "Maybe they will take that into account." Even as a Polish citizen, collaborating with the Germans could earn her a stint in a Warsaw jail, rather than a Moscow one. Especially if, as they proclaimed on arrival, the USSR was in charge of Polish territory now.

"I meant the Americans," Tommy said.

"What?" From the moment she'd woken up to see a red, white and blue flag flying in the place of a Nazi one, Regina felt time passing upside down. She wasn't the German's employee anymore, she was a Soviet prisoner. She wasn't Jewish, and she wasn't Russian. She was Polish. Maybe.

"I'll tell them everything. How you got me medicine when I was sick, how you helped me bring food to the Soviet side, all the American patients you insisted on treating when the Krauts would have been happy to let us die. They'll take it into account, I know they will."

Regina had no idea what Tommy was talking about. "It's not the Americans I'm afraid of. They can't do anything to me. It's the Soviets."

"I won't let them hurt you," Tommy swore, as if a reasonable explanation had ever gotten anyone out of trouble once their fate was decided. As if innocence were a defense. Innocence hadn't protected Regina when she actually was innocent. What good would it do now that she was guilty? "Aaron is right. You shouldn't go back to the USSR."

"I have no proof I am Polish. They'll ask for documents."

"You shouldn't stay in Poland, either. I heard some of them were worse than Nazis when it came to Jews. You and Lena would be no safer here. And you'd still be under Soviet control."

Regina wished she could tell Tommy how little she cared. Yes, she was worried. Not for herself, for Aaron. He was the one with the precarious future. Regina wished she could tell Tommy how nothing mattered as long as she and Aaron were together. She needed to find out what would happen to him, where he would be sent next, so she could keep her promise.

"The US consulate is bound to take into account what you did for us. That should help."

"Help with what?" Could the US consulate help Regina with Aaron? She didn't see how. The USSR was not known for their love of foreign interference in their affairs.

"Help with getting you and Lena papers to come to America."

He finally had her complete attention. "You think we should go to America?"

No. Out of the question. Not without Aaron.

"It's where you'd be safest."

So what? Not without Aaron.

"Of course, the process could take months, years."

Good. If that was the case, Tommy would be long gone and she wouldn't have to hurt his feelings, turning down an offer thousands of others would leap at. He'd return home and forget all about her, leaving Regina free to focus on Aaron. No harm done.

"We could speed it up, though," Tommy said. "There are ways to cut through the red tape. If we're married."

Chapter Twenty-Five

━━━━━━━

She must have misheard him. She had to have misheard him. Because what Tommy was proposing was... Tommy was proposing!

He tugged at the front of his shirttail. A comical gesture for a uniform top ripped and scuffed beyond repair, but also painfully endearing. He looked down at the ground, he looked up at Regina. He looked back down again. He tapped the sole of his boot, heel flapping, against the ground like a pony performing arithmetic tricks. When he glanced up for the final time, it was to look her in the eye and pronounce, "I love you, Regina. You are brave and strong and virtuous. I know I'm not nearly good enough for you, but I would like it—lots—if you'd agree to be my wife."

She wanted to laugh. Not at his proposal, which was, like everything Tommy did, genuine and heartfelt. At his perception of her. She wasn't brave, she wasn't strong, and she certainly wasn't virtuous. Every action she'd undertaken to make him believe those things had been done for selfish reasons. She helped feed Soviet prisoners because that meant helping feed Aaron. She'd taken care of all patients because that meant being allowed to take care of Aaron. It was bad enough Tommy thought he was in love with her. It was worse that he was in love with a Regina who didn't exist!

"I know I have no right to ask you," he continued, still addressing a phantom woman. "I never would've gotten up the nerve, I would've kept my feelings to myself, gone home probably without confessing, but then Aaron said…"

Regina's head jerked up. "Aaron?"

Tommy nodded sheepishly. "Aaron convinced me. He's been convincing me for months. He's the one who gave me the guts to propose to you. He's the one who convinced me I was good enough for you and Lena."

"ALL THIS TIME," Regina raged, having snuck over to the Soviet side, now without any food—or excuses. She balanced Lena on her hip as she raged at Aaron, "All this time, I've been so worried about leading Tommy on, when it was you doing it!"

Unlike Tommy, Aaron did not appear the least bit sheepish at the accusation. He didn't raise his voice to match Regina's. "I was dying. I needed you and Lena taken care of."

"Not anymore," Regina said. "It's over. The war is over. We're alive. We made it."

"The NKVD is here." Aaron jerked his chin in the direction of the familiar uniforms, the olive green jackets, the navy pants with red piping stuffed into calf high black boots, the cap with the red, five point star in the center. "They've started interrogating."

"Nobody is going to care about Felix's stupid accusation. Not now."

"They're asking about collaboration with the Americans."

"Collaboration? We're on the same side!"

"Anyone who had any sort of contact with foreign elements is being detained for further questioning. They'll get to me eventually." Aaron reminded, "I was almost deported to Siberia for sending a wedding invitation to my brother in Palestine. What do you think the penalty will be for how closely Tommy and I worked together?"

"To save our boys!" Regina exclaimed as she flashed back to her earlier thought: *As if a reasonable explanation had ever gotten anyone out of trouble once their fate was decided. As if innocence were a defense.* She changed tactics on the fly. "We'll run away. The three of us. Hide in the woods. We were planning to do it a few days ago. We can still do it."

Aaron sighed, "Prior to our troops entering Poland, they sent out radio messages, urging the local resistance to rise up ahead of their arrival. They did. They cleared the way for the Red Army to obliterate the Nazi forces. The Red Army then turned around and obliterated the resistance. They're going through the woods, hunting down any stragglers."

Regina shook her head, unwilling to believe it, unwilling to accept it. "We'll go somewhere else then. We'll go back to Birobidzhan. The edge of the earth, my mother called it. We'll be safe there. Felix is gone. Likely even Comrade Klara is gone. No one will remember us."

"Marry Tommy," Aaron said. "Take Lena and go to America."

"No!" Regina continued shouting, despite how ineffective her vehemence had been up to this point. "You don't know there will be trouble for fraternizing with the Americans. This isn't like before. We're allies now."

"How many allies did Comrade Stalin purge? Before?" Aaron held up his hand and began counting down per finger, "Kaminsky, his wife, your friend, Cecilia."

"Stop it!" Regina willed herself to calm down, taking deep breaths, trying to think, trying not to sound as hysterical as she felt, realizing it wouldn't help her cause. "Just don't tell them anything about working with Tommy."

"If I don't, someone else will. Which will make it worse for me."

"What you and Tommy did saved so many lives. Why would they betray you?"

"Why did Agneska turn on Marta?"

"This is nothing like that!"

"This is exactly like that. To save themselves, sooner or later, someone will turn me in. My single defense is to beat them to it, make a full confession. *Samokritika*," Aaron smirked.

"Please," she begged, but the fight drained out of her, replaced solely with despair. "Don't do this." Regina thrust his daughter forward. "Think of Lena."

"I am thinking of Lena." Aaron took a step back, looking everywhere except at his child. "And I'm thinking of you. If I'm branded an enemy of the people, you'll have no future, no life, no chance. Tommy is offering you all of those things, and more."

At Tommy's name, Regina grasped at a final straw. "Tommy will help us! He'll help all of us! If we go to him and explain. He's a good man. He won't hold this against us. He'll understand why we had to lie to him. He'll help all three of us get to America."

"Tommy is a good man," Aaron agreed. "But who do you think he'll fight harder for, some soldier he was forced to team up with under brutal circumstances, or his wife and daughter?"

"Lena is your daughter!"

"I've been thinking about that." Aaron looked at the little girl for the first time since Regina had cornered him. He stroked her cheek with one finger. He tickled her under the chin and made Lena giggle. He was still looking at her, not Regina, when he suggested, "She's so small, she could easily pass for younger. Less than a year old, don't you think? If you roll back her birthday, six months, maybe seven or eight, the timing works. She could be yours and Tommy's. She has an American name, Eleanora, like the First Lady!" Aaron swallowed hard when he added, "We're lucky. We were never married. We never recorded Lena's birth at the front. There's nothing tying the two of you to me."

"There's everything," Regina countered.

Lena was tugging on Aaron's finger. He gently worked it out of her grasp and took a step back to his original position.

"If you won't do this for me, do it for Lena. Think of her first—for once."

He knew. Of course, he knew. Aaron had always been able to figure out what was going through Regina's mind, even when she wasn't certain of it herself. He knew how guilty Regina felt about constantly putting him ahead of Lena.

Aaron drove the point home when he said, "You followed me to the front after I begged you not to. You wouldn't go back when you were pregnant, you wouldn't go back when she was born. You followed me here, putting her life at risk, and now you want to follow me to Siberia? It's been one horrible decision after another, Regina. It's a miracle our daughter is still alive!"

"She's alive because I took care of her. The same way I'll take care of you!"

"She's alive because of Tommy Burns' generosity, and she'll stay alive thanks to him." Aaron drove the knife in deeper. "No thanks to you. You made another rotten call, Regina, in a self-absorbed life full of them. Have you gotten a single thing right?"

"You." Regina blinked back tears. "Being with you was the right call. Being with you will always be the right call."

He didn't mean it. He couldn't mean it. He was manipulating her. Using the one thing he knew Regina feared above all else, her inability to make the correct choice, against her. That was alright, Regina told herself. She understood. She could forgive him. Aaron using Regina's insecurity against her was still preferable to his actually believing what he was saying.

"You don't love me. If you loved me, you would do what I asked. I asked you to let me be. I told you I needed every bit of energy I possessed to focus on my survival. I couldn't waste a drop on worrying about you and Lena. You didn't care. You did what you wanted. Well, now I am asking you again. I am telling you: Let me concentrate on saving my own hide without being distracted by what my actions might mean to you and Lena. If you love me, be realistic for once. Stop dreaming. Open your eyes and see what's happening instead of what you want to happen. Listen to what I want. Listen to what I need. More importantly, listen to what our daughter needs. Let me be, Regina. Take care of Lena. Put her first. Put her ahead of me. Put her ahead of *us*. Or else you never loved me at all."

"YES," REGINA TOLD Tommy. She tried to sound enthusiastic. She tried not to sound gutted and drained and shell-shocked and done. He deserved that. He deserved every blessed thing life could possibly give him. What a shame he'd be getting Regina, instead. "I'll marry you," Regina told Tommy. Then added, "I love you." Because it was true. It simply wasn't the way she loved Aaron. And always would.

The way Tommy leapt off the bench he was sitting on, the way his face lit up, the way he, at first, didn't know what to do, so he merely waved his arms in the air, not quite a clap, since his palms didn't touch, before pulling Regina to him, kissing not only her lips, but her cheeks, her brow, her chin, her ears; his obvious and contagious joy almost made everything worth it. And it made Regina pity him more.

Tommy immediately began making plans for the future. He told Regina he had a thought—it would be simpler to fill out Lena's paperwork claiming she was his. They could roll back her birthday, six months, maybe seven or eight, she was so small, the timing worked. She had an American name, Eleanora, like the First Lady!

Regina smiled and nodded, agreeing it was a terrific idea, understanding more and more how deep of a foundation Aaron had laid. How long he'd been planning to get rid of her.

She knew that wasn't true. She stuck by her initial thought; Aaron was manipulating her, using the one thing he knew Regina feared above all else against her, in order to force her into prioritizing Lena over him. Over them. She still thought that was alright. She still understood. She just could no longer forgive him.

Because, while she understood everything, Regina also felt everything. And what she felt was fury. And betrayal. Worse than Cecilia. Worse than Felix. Worse than Marta. Aaron had turned on her in the worst way possible. By stealing the main thing he'd given her. Her belief in herself. She'd lost it after what happened in Moscow. He'd helped her regain it. Which was why he was the one capable of wrenching it away again. For good.

She questioned her decision to marry Tommy, though his glee did assuage her concerns somewhat. She questioned her decision to alter Lena's age, though she told herself any woman would embrace the opportunity to be younger. She questioned moving to America and, most of all, she questioned leaving Aaron behind. She'd made a promise. She was breaking it.

At his request.

To her sorrow.

The last time Regina saw Aaron was the day the Americans evacuated their personnel out of the camp. Tommy had arranged for Regina and Lena to come with them. He'd arranged for him and

Regina to be married by an Army rabbi as soon as they arrived at their new location.

They were being loaded onto the backs of US military trucks, Tommy holding Lena with one arm while he used his other to help Regina climb in. Four NKVD officers marched past, leading a line of soldiers stretching from one side of the camp to the next.

"Where are they taking them?" Regina instinctively searched for Aaron. She'd determine whether or not she was hoping to spot him once she found out what this assembly was for.

Tommy sighed, "Further questioning. These are the men accused of fraternization."

Aaron was there, marching along with the rest, eyes straight ahead. They trooped past the Americans without so much as a glance in their direction. Admitting they'd ever known them would make their situation worse.

The Americans, being Americans and unable to understand what their former comrades were facing—not because they were stupid, because they were, well, Americans, they expected happy endings—responded by smartly pivoting the Soviet soldiers' way and saluting them for the duration of their trek. They had no way of knowing the damage they were doing. No way of knowing that over five percent of those liberated from German POW camps would end up being deported to Siberia or executed for collaboration.

Regina refused to take her eyes off Aaron. If he broke for a second, if he snuck so much as a single peek her way, Regina would forget everything. She would throw away her chance to escape to America, she would throw away Lena's chance for a life as the daughter of a war hero, not an enemy of the people. She would give up security, safety, food, shelter, a man who adored her—though he shouldn't—for uncertainty, peril, hunger, cold, and a man who would hate her for doing it. If Aaron snuck so much as a single peek Regina's way.

Aaron knew it, too.

Which was why he kept on marching.

Chapter Twenty-Six

At some point during Mama's story, they'd moved from Dad's office in the basement upstairs to the kitchen. At some point during Mama's story, Lena must have gone to the stove, picked up the kettle, filled it with water, put it on a burner, turned the burner on, waited for it to boil, gotten a tea-bag from the cabinet, put it in one cup, drenched it with hot water, put it in another cup, drenched it with hot water, brought a cup to Mama and one to herself. Because there those cups stood. Tepid now, filled to the brim, untouched. Lena had no memory of doing any of those things. She'd gone from a numb shock at Mama's words, "Aaron Kramer is your father," to a stomach churning, throat clenching horror as Mama described the conditions at both Birobidzhan and Stalag 3-K, to mute, worn out exhaustion as Lena failed to think of a single appropriate thing to say in response.

Did Mama want Lena to say anything? The entire time she'd been speaking, Lena never got the sense Mama was asking for her sympathy, her understanding, or her forgiveness. Mama was simply giving her the facts. "Aaron Kramer is your father."

"Did Dad know?" Despite hearing of desperate flights from the KGB, deported Koreans, hungry field workers, starving and beaten soldiers, her own malnutrition to the point where it was possible to pass her off as a baby half her age, Lena's heart went out the most to the upstanding American soldier who'd innocently fallen in love, with no idea he was being used.

"No." Regina stirred her tea, without bothering to taste it. "He never asked me who your father was. He loved you like his own. That's what he was trying to say with his last words. You never knew the difference. He treated you the same way all other fathers treat their children."

"He treated me better." Lena didn't know why she felt compelled to defend Dad. It's not like Mama was criticizing him. "My friends were always so jealous."

"Tommy was a wonderful, wonderful man."

"So wonderful that you lied to him for over forty years?"

Other mothers, when their daughters mouthed off, snapped back a retort, ordered them to behave, issued a punishment. Mama withdrew. No matter how much Lena misbehaved, no matter how much she deliberately baited her, especially during Lena's teen years, Mama would walk away, rather than engage. Lena always ended up apologizing. Because Dad asked her to. "It's tough for her," he'd explain. "She comes from a place where saying the wrong thing could get you killed. She's frightened of disagreement." Mama didn't look frightened to Lena. Mama looked indifferent. Leave it to Dad to always choose the best possible interpretation.

When her question failed to stir Regina, Lena pressed on, "If Dad didn't know about you and Aaron, why did he spend all this time looking for him?"

"Because he was a loyal man. Because he and Aaron were friends. Because he worried about him."

So few words. Such simple words. Dad in a nutshell.

"What about you?" Lena demanded. "Weren't you worried about him? Where was your loyalty?"

Lena felt nothing for this man. No matter what Regina said about him being her father, he was just Aaron Kramer, some Soviet soldier her dad met during the war. Lena wasn't incensed on Aaron's behalf, but on Tommy's.

Regina was angry, too. At whom was debatable. "Whatever happened to Aaron when he returned to the USSR, inquiries from America would have made it worse."

That brought Lena up short. "Dad wouldn't have wanted to make things worse for him."

Regina smiled. It was a wistful smile, one that belonged to a past Lena never dreamed existed. "Tommy couldn't imagine his good intentions going wrong. Even after everything he'd lived through. They beat him half to death for feeding starving men, and still, Tommy believed in happy endings. He was so American. It's why we loved him, isn't it?"

The pronoun use startled Lena. She tried to recall the last time her mother had employed the word "we" to bind herself and Lena. Regina spoke exclusively in "I," as in "I need to go to the store," or "I'm going to be late," leaving it up to the listener as to whether they wished to join her. Lena wondered if Dad would've attributed that tendency to Mama's traumatic past, as well; not wishing to incriminate others in her actions. As far as Lena was concerned, at a certain point, trauma warranted being dumped as a crutch, and you had to admit this was the fundamental personality peeking through.

"It's why we loved him," Lena agreed, moved, in spite of herself. "Do you think Dad looking for Aaron hurt him?"

The idea would have broken Tommy's heart. It broke Lena's. Once again not for Aaron's sake, but for Dad's.

Regina shrugged. She didn't appear optimistic. "If he'd told me, I'd have asked him to…"

"Stop? Didn't you want to know?"

Another shrug. If this was how Regina reacted to news about the supposed love of her life, no wonder Lena hadn't been able to squeeze much emotion out of her growing up.

The files with Dad's letters lay between them on the kitchen table. Lena had carried them upstairs, gingerly pushing them as far away as possible while they spoke. Now, she reached for the most recent one, thumbing through the paperwork. Like Mama and her refusal to say "we," Lena gave her the option of joining in, but didn't request it. Regina merely sat, watching Lena. She sipped her tea, which, in addition to having grown cold, also had no sugar or lemon, the way Regina liked it. She drank it mechanically, making no move toward the files. Not taking her eyes off of them, either. If Lena hadn't spent her childhood stared at silently by her mother, she might have found the experience disconcerting.

Lena's hands began to shake. While her spoken Russian was decent, especially after Vadik insisted they speak it with Angela, her reading and writing stagnated at the level of a first grader. Regina had read Lena some Russian books as a child, because it was easier for her than reading English ones, so Lena knew the alphabet, especially if it was printed and not in script. She could put together simple words, but it took effort and time. She wasn't in the mood to waste either. As soon as Lena caught a glimpse of what she thought was an official answer, she thrust the nearly translucent sheet of paper Mama's way. "What does it say?"

The print was so small, Regina needed to hold the document at arm's length and cock her head, squinting her eyes as she made out, "In response to your inquiry… Citizen Kramer… Disloyalty to the Union Of Soviet Socialist Republics… Convicted…"

"So he was arrested," Lena said, "like he feared."

Her face impassive, Regina kept reading, "Hard labor… twenty years…. Siberia."

Her mother's arm began to tremble until Regina was forced to set down the paper. She closed her eyes and pinched her lips, muffling either a scream or a curse. When she opened them again, she told Lena, without needing to continue reading, as if she'd instantly memorized the part that mattered. "He was pardoned in 1955. When Khrushev came to power, he pardoned thousands. Part of his plan to acknowledge Stalin's crimes. Aaron left Siberia alive. They sent him to Odessa, in the Ukraine. The village he came from, it no longer existed. Decimated in a famine some still say never happened." Mama's ire took Lena by surprise. "So they sent him to the next closest destination. Thirty-three years ago, he was still alive. Alive and in Odessa."

Lena continued leafing through correspondence. "It looks like Dad wrote to the address they gave him. He got no response, kept trying for years."

She wasn't sure if Mama was listening. She also wasn't sure who Mama was talking to as Regina's pinched lips turned to the hint of a smile. "They didn't break him." For the first time in her life, Lena heard what she recognized as pride. "The *mamzers* didn't break him."

"MOM? WHERE ARE you?" Lena was in her childhood bedroom, paging through an album of family photos, unsure what she was looking for as she scrutinized every shot of her and Dad, Dad and Mama, the three of them, when she heard her daughter calling from downstairs. She'd forgotten she told Vadik he could pick her up in the afternoon. Obviously afraid that Lena might opt, once again, not to return home, Vadik had collected Angela from school and brought her along as reinforcement.

Lena rushed to the living room, finger to her lips, "Shh, Baba Regina is sleeping."

"Are you done here?" Vadik asked, sneaking what he thought was a surreptitious peek at his watch.

"Not even close. There's so much to do."

"Angela's missed you," Vadik accused.

Lena asked her daughter, "Did you have a good time with Baba Olga and Ded Artur?"

As soon as Dad entered the hospital and Lena took up vigil there, Vadik's folks swooped in to take care of Angela. They picked her up from school, fed her dinner (and a before bedtime snack), and insisted she spend the night. Poor Vadik had too much on his mind to be bothered with taking care of a child all alone, they fretted.

"Baba Olga took me shopping at TJ Maxx and we got a bubble skirt, it's white and pink. It's not a real LaCroix, but it looks it, and we got it for eighty percent off, too!"

From the day Angela was born, Lena's in-laws had stepped up to help. Vadik's mother moved in with them for the first two months, taking on nighttime feedings while the new parents rested. As soon as Lena went back to work, they assumed childcare, watching Angela until she started Nursery, when they continued picking her up from school, taking her to museums, to her music lesson, to the park, gathering pine cones to bring home and shellac, then displaying them on glass cabinet shelves like precious works of art. Once Angela outgrew needing babysitting, Olga and Artur still had her over to their house several times a week, whether it was to watch their VHS collection of Russian movies, go shopping, or, as Olga teased, "For a good meal." Lena was too busy and important—a lawyer!—to cook every night. Let them help!

According to TV, women's magazines, and the few friends she'd dared tell about it, Lena should be deeply offended. She should assume this meant her in-laws didn't think she was a fit wife, a fit mother, and they were insulting her with every act. To be fair, it was only her American friends who felt that way. Her Russian friends took it as a given their or their husbands' parents would be available at any hour of the day or night for childcare and other household duties. But they admitted to rolling their eyes or stuffing down their resentment when a Soviet grandparent chucked the carefully balanced meal they'd prepared for their child in favor of something fried and smothered in sour cream. Or when they'd dismiss the antibiotic their pediatrician prescribed in favor of treating an ear infection by heating up olive oil, dripping it in the sick child's ear, then stuffing it with cotton balls to keep warm. Lena nodded sympathetically, pretending she agreed with the grievance. Personally, she was grateful for every bit of care and advice Vadik's parents offered her. She listened to them when they advised her to put cereal in Angela's bottle starting at three months so she'd sleep through the night. She listened to them about mustard plasters on her chest and alcohol soaked compresses around her throat to treat a cold. She obeyed their directive to, whenever somebody complimented the girl, stick her thumb through her next two fingers, in order to keep the Evil Eye away. Lena listened to any advice her in-laws had to give. Because, goodness knows, her mother offered none.

Lena wondered whether she'd fallen in love with Vadik—or with his family? Sure, she'd loved the way Vadik took charge. The way he saved her from having to make decisions, the way his confidence let her sleep soundly, knowing her life was under control. She'd also loved the way his family took an interest in her. From the first day, they'd made it clear they wanted to know everything about her, peppering

Lena with questions about her parents, her education, her plans for
the future, her dreams, her opinions. They didn't always agree with
them. In fact, they were the ones who'd convinced Lena it was more
practical for her to go into real estate law, so she could help Vadik in
his practice, then stick with criminal law—so time consuming and
the cases could be so unpleasant. At least they asked. They listened.
They cared.

Now, Lena couldn't be more thrilled they were lavishing the same
attention on Angela. Her daughter would never grow up believing
she wasn't worth bothering with.

Sometimes, Lena wondered whether she stayed with Vadik because she was loath to lose his parents—for herself, and for Angela.
Though, to be fair, Vadik was a caring, attentive father. Lena had no
complaints on that score.

Just on a whole host of others.

The minute Lena filled Vadik in on what she and Mama had discovered about Dad—and Aaron Kramer—Vadik's response was not
one of concern or incredulity, but of practicality.

"Your mother committed immigration fraud. She lied about
your parentage and your birth date. I wonder if that might affect
your citizenship? And if it does, what will that mean for mine?"

Lena once loved how Vadik would leap in to take stock of a situation, analyze what could go wrong, and quickly move to circumvent
it. Now it seemed crass. And rather heartless.

"You will be fine, Vadik." Mama's voice floated down the staircase
before she appeared, clutching the bannister to creep her way down.
"Hello, Angela."

"Hello, Baba Regina," Lena's daughter said politely. When Angela
greeted her Baba Olga, however, she flew into her arms and promptly
picked up whichever conversation they'd been having the last time
they saw each other. Lena did the same thing.

"Do not worry, Vadik. There is no way to prove immigration
fraud. Lena's birth was never registered prior to our immigration ap-
plication. There is no paper trail to contradict it."

"You listed the wrong father!"

"I made a mistake," Regina shrugged. "Mistakes happen."

Vadik sniffed to indicate they didn't happen to him.

"It's such a romantic story," Angela said. "Do you think he's still alive?"

"Of course not," Vadik dismissed. "Let's be realistic. He would be how old now? In his seventies, right? He should've died of natural causes."

"I'm in my seventies," Mama reminded.

Vadik ignored her implication—and her taunting. "That's assuming an uneventful life. Throw in starvation during the Holodomor, working the fields in Birobidzhan, a stint as a Great Patriotic War soldier, then a German prisoner of war, followed by almost ten years of hard labor in Siberia? No one could survive all that."

"Aaron could," Mama said. "Aaron did. Now I must travel to Odessa to find him. Lena, will you come with me?"

Chapter Twenty-Seven

"Don't be ridiculous, Regina Solomonova." When Vadik pulled out the patronymic, it was to remind himself to sound particularly respectful. "You know we can never go back there."

Lena thought of her Mexican friends, her Irish, Iranian, Chinese, Filipino, and Caribbean friends. They were constantly talking about visits "home," even if they'd been born in the United States. There was nothing stopping those who'd been born in the USSR from buying a ticket to Moscow. Except the certain knowledge they'd never be allowed to leave.

Gorbachev now claimed to have altered that. He claimed all who once left were welcome to return. And they would be equally welcome to depart again.

Vadik wasn't buying it. Vadik never bought anything the Soviets had to say. He loved to remind Lena that while she'd immigrated as an infant, and thus had no memories of the USSR, he'd been a teenager. Vadik remembered being told he lived in the most prosperous and best run country in the world as he stood in line for hours, hoping there would still be a scrap of meat or bucket of potatoes left by the time he reached the counter. He remembered his father drawing a cardboard outline of Vadik and his sister's feet so, on a trip to Leningrad, he'd be able to buy them shoes if he saw any available. Vadik remembered newspapers reporting that there was no crime in the USSR as he was chased from school and beaten by delinquents calling him a dirty Zhid. When they heard about the Chernobyl disaster, Vadik's parents had desperately tried to call friends in the Kiev Oblast. They were told by the operator the people they were trying to reach were out. They gave the operator another name. She said they were out, too. Finally, Vadik's mother demanded to be put through to absolutely anyone in the area. "They are all out," she was informed.

Vadik told Mama, though he was truly speaking to Lena, "They've just made it possible for former citizens to visit. We have absolutely no information about how you'll be treated, or if they'll let you out again. What if you get trapped there? It's too big of a risk."

Vadik was right. The wise choice was to stay in the US and continue Dad's efforts to track down Aaron. If he was even still alive after everything he'd been through, like Vadik said. Lena had absolutely no logical argument to make.

But neither had Regina when she'd stood up for Marta and Aaron against Felix. When she'd followed Aaron to the front, then to Stalag 3-K. If she hadn't, Aaron likely would have died. Maybe Tommy, too. Lena certainly would never have existed.

She had absolutely no logical argument to make, or words to explain why, in response to Vadik's perfectly reasonable objection, Lena blurted out, "Yes, I'll go with you, Mama."

"YOU CANNOT BE serious, Lenachka!"

Vadik had gotten nowhere haranguing Lena on their way home in the car. Failing to adequately frighten her with the big issues, he'd switched to the smaller. "Your spoken Russian is subpar. How will you make it even from the airport to your hotel? The taxi drivers will see an easy mark. They'll overcharge you. So will the shopkeepers, once they realize you don't understand the exchange rate. You'll get lost going from street to street, you read Russian so badly. Odessa still has wandering gypsies, you know. You'll be robbed. Your mother is old, fragile. If she gets ill, God forbid, what will you do? Do you know what a Soviet hospital is like? Do you think they'll give a damn about the insurance we slave so hard to pay for? Do you think you'll get a private room? More like a prison ward, beds lined up side by side, deathly contagious patients a breath away from drunks detoxing. They reuse bandages. And needles. No pain medication, no anesthesia unless you pay a bribe. You need to know how to navigate the system. How will you manage, Lena? What will you do?"

And when all that still failed to persuade her, Vadik called in a higher authority. He drove Lena and Angela to his parents' apartment, letting them have a crack at her.

"It's too dangerous," his father protested. "They could arrest you, lock you up, throw away the key. We could do nothing for you from here. We are immigrants. Your father was a citizen, a war hero, a true American, and he could not help this Kramer man. What do you think you and your mama could do? And then you will be stuck forever!"

"Think of Angela!" Olga pleaded. "You cannot do this to her! Leave her motherless!"

When Regina first proposed going to Odessa, Angela had appeared intrigued. Such a romantic gesture, like something out of the movies she and Baba Olga were always watching. But, the more worst-case scenarios Vadik and his parents spun, the more terrified Angela grew.

She asked, "Could they really make you and Baba Regina stay?"

"Of course, they could," Vadik blustered. "Did you not listen to your own story, Lena? How they drove your mother from Moscow? How they all almost ended up in Siberia? They can do whatever they want to anyone they want. Who do you think you are? Sharansky? Sakharov? Begun? You think they're going to have thousand people parades for you in New York, chanting *Let My People Go*? You think President Reagan is going to bring up your name next time he and Gorbachev shake hands for the cameras? Of course not, don't be foolish. You'll disappear into a Soviet prison, and it will be like you and your mother never existed!"

"Stop it," Lena snapped, "you're scaring Angela."

The child had gone from nervously biting her lower lip and

wrinkling her nose to blinking furiously in an attempt to hold back tears. She swiveled her head anxiously from Vadik to Lena, not only unused to her parents fighting, but to them disagreeing on something so important.

"Good," Vadik said. "She should be scared of the USSR. Everybody should be scared of the USSR. Angela should know what garbage that *Don't the Russians Love Their Children, Too* is. You were a Russian child, Lena. How loved were you? So loved your father was sensible enough to do whatever he had to, to get you and your mother out of that loving country. He was the smart one. Angela must take after him. She's showing more sense than you are."

If Vadik meant to hurt her with that remark, he'd miscalculated. Lena no longer cared what he thought of her. Every synonym for foolish he could conceivably toss her way, she'd beaten him to it. She knew what she was proposing was irresponsible and brainless. As irresponsible and brainless as anything Regina had ever done. Not to Aaron, but to Lena. Aaron had been furious with Regina for putting Lena in danger. He'd wanted Regina to prioritize Lena. Something Regina had never done. Something Lena had always resented her for. Did she dare risk Angela feeling the same way about her? Worse, did Lena dare risk making the same choices as Regina? Had a single one of them ever turned out well?

AS LENA APPROACHED her mother's house, she rehearsed what she'd say. She would tell her she'd spoken rashly. She'd still been under the spell of the story Regina wove about herself and Aaron when she'd impulsively agreed to accompany her to Odessa. She would then bring up Vadik's point about this being a wild goose chase. No matter how much Regina would like to believe differently, the odds of Aaron still being alive, much less living at the same place where he'd been sent to in 1955, were extremely slim. Vadik was also right that it was senseless to take a risk as massive as returning to the USSR with no guarantee of a safe journey back on a mission more likely to fail than succeed.

Finally, Lena would invoke Angela. Vadik and her grandparents had whipped the child up nearly into hysterics with their dire predictions of doom.

Angela had cried, "Please, Mama, don't leave. Don't leave me."

Personally, Lena suspected the dramatics had been for Vadik's benefit, their daughter wanting to prove she was on his side. That, if Lena hadn't listened to his cautions, Angela had. Lena didn't begrudge Angela for favoring her father over her mother. Lena had been the same way. Nevertheless, Lena believed Vadik and his parents had genuinely frightened Angela. Lena would never forgive herself if traveling to Odessa caused Angela suffering. A good mother placed her child's comfort and happiness over anyone else's.

Even her own mother's.

Even her own.

Surely, Regina would be able to understand.

Lena let herself into Mama's house with the key she'd had since high school. She didn't know what state she expected to find Mama in. Would she be in the bedroom, still packing up Dad's things? Would she be in the basement, combing through files, looking for more clues to Aaron's location? Would she have surrendered, the way Mama said some prisoners did at the camp. One day, they'd be relatively fine, still moving, still eating, still going through the motions of life. The next, they'd sit down, some didn't even close their eyes, and, within a few hours, they'd be dead.

That didn't sound like Mama. But, as Lena had learned over the past few days, she'd never known her mother at all.

Mama was neither in a flurry of activity, nor had she capitulated to despair. She was sharing a cup of tea—actually drinking this time, rather than listlessly allowing it to grow cold—with... was that Sergei? Dad's nurse? The pair of them sat across from each other in the dining room, the massive oak table making both look smaller. Mama was using the good tea set, the one for guests, a small plate of strawberry preserves, another of sugar cubes, a third of lemon slices, between them. Sergei had poured his tea onto a saucer to cool, sipping from it using two hands to bring the delicate china to his mouth. Out of his scrubs, he looked younger than Lena recalled. She'd pegged him as closer to Mama's age. Now she realized he was likely only a few years older than Vadik. Of course, you couldn't compare the thick head of sable hair Vadik brushed so diligently every morning to the grey wisps that circled the crown of Sergei's skull, which he patted down when they stood on end, or Vadik's gym-crunched stomach to the jiggly paunch peeking from beneath Sergei's brown and white checkered button down shirt. Vadik's idea of casual Friday was khaki slacks with a crease down the front and a striped Ralph Lauren polo in at least three colors. Sergei, Lena suspected, wore his frayed at the knees Wrangler jeans and decade-behind dress shirt every day of the week.

"Hello, hello!" Sergei called, as if there was nothing odd about him sharing a weekday cup of tea with his former patient's widow. "I come to check on Mama, see she is well!"

"That was nice of you," Lena said. *Nice* sounded better than *odd*.

"Mama says you are traveling to Odessa. Beautiful city. My city," Sergei said proudly. Like New Yorkers, *Odessits* took great pride in their hometown being not as boring as Moscow, not as stuck up as Leningrad, but as the art, music, literature, and joke capital of the USSR.

"Yes, well," Lena hedged, "I'm not sure that's the best idea…" She trailed off, hoping that, after a night sleeping on it, Mama would agree and that would be the end of their common delusion. Instead, Regina's head jerked up and her eyes narrowed Lena's way.

Lena explained, "I talked to Vadik. And to his parents. They were *v'Souyze* much more recently. They brought up some issues we hadn't thought of. Like, how will we get around? We don't know the city, or the financial conversion rate. What if we're cheated? Or robbed?"

Sergei scratched his head, musing, "You will get in taxi? You will tell driver where to go? He will to take you. If he ask too much money, you will say, no, this is too much, and you will give him what is correct amount? You can do mathematics, yes?" Sergei's eyes twinkled to show he knew the answer to his question. He was reminding Lena she did, too. He made it sound so simple. He made Lena feel stupid to invoke the Gypsies Vadik mentioned. He made Vadik sound foolish to have mentioned it.

So, instead, Lena brought up the more serious topic. "They might not let us out again. They might keep us prisoner."

Sergei had no pithy response. It was Mama who said, "They are keeping Aaron prisoner now." Clearly all that mattered to her.

Stymied, Lena reached for the single rationale that might resonate. "What if you get sick, Mama? A Soviet hospital, Vadik told me, they don't have medicine or sterilized equipment, and you have to pay bribes and bring your own sheets and food and—"

They were supposed to be horrified. Mama and Sergei exchanged looks and chuckled.

"Hospitals, they are necessary, yes," Sergei agreed amiably. "But even in America, you must to look out for your patient. It is like Russian expression: *Trust in God, but don't stop doing for yourself.* With your Papa, Mama and me, we let hospital do what hospital do, then we add the little bit more."

"You did what?"

"I bring little calendula with me to work. Is made from flowers, marigolds, Americans call them. Safe. Good for skin when patient has been lying still a long time."

Lena turned to Regina. "You knew about this?"

"I ask Mama for permission," Sergei reassured. "She knows, she understands. She remembers. Medicine is good, but often, we have none in USSR. So we, what is this word? Improvise! We use what we have. Mama did this when she is nurse, I do this when I am doctor."

"I thought you were a nurse." Lena remembered Vadik making fun of Sergei, asking what kind of a profession nursing was for a man.

"In America, I am nurse, yes. In Soviet Union, I am doctor. I come to America, they say my diploma no good here. Must go back to school, start again at the beginning. Test, residency, everything. I have no time for this. I have no money. So I study for different exam and I become Registered Nurse. I do not," he smiled to show no hard feelings, "buy this degree on Geary Street."

Lena marveled at Vadik's ability to make her blush in mortification when he wasn't even in the room.

"It doesn't bother you?" she blurted. All the doctors Lena knew— she'd married into San Francisco's Russian Jewish community, she knew an obscene amount of doctors—would have been humiliated if demoted to nursing. The loss of respect and prestige alone...

"I like to help people," he shrugged. Then, unexpectedly added, "I can to help you." He turned to Mama and said, "Lena is worried what will happen if you become sick in Odessa. I go with you, yes? Take care if anything happens?" To Lena, Sergei added, "And I will help you find where you are going? Make sure you are not cheated by drivers or shopkeepers?" Sergei was smiling. But he didn't appear to be making fun of her.

Lena had no doubt his offer was sincere. She also had no doubt about the proper, Russian-Jewish way to respond to such a generous proposal. "Absolutely not. I cannot let you put yourself out like this."

"It would be my pleasure," he insisted.

"It is too much."

"It is no trouble."

"It would be too great of an imposition."

"Please do me the honor of allowing me to do this for you."

They might have gone on in such a vein indefinitely, each playing their assigned role to prove each had been raised with good manners, if Sergei hadn't cut Lena off. He was still smiling, still amiable, but hit an undertone of steel as he said, "Please permit me to accompany you. I have my own business in Odessa to take care of."

"ARE YOU HAPPY now?" Vadik jammed his finger in the direction of Angela, sitting on their couch, arms crossed, head dropped, quietly sobbing in response to Lena telling them she and Mama would be flying to Odessa Saturday morning. "Look what you have done!"

Lena saw. And Lena's heart broke. The last thing she wanted was to make her daughter unhappy. But there was something else which concerned her equally.

Lena squatted so she and Angela could be face to face. She raised the girl's chin in her hand and looked her in the eye when she told her, "I am doing this for Baba Regina. I am also doing this for me. And for you."

Vadik snorted behind her. Lena ignored him.

"Baba Regina was so brave when she was younger. I had no idea. I wonder if I could be as brave. I'm afraid I can't. I'm afraid of so many things." Lena heard Vadik fuming. He believed parents should never show weakness in front of a child. It diminished their authority and made the child doubt their parent would be able to protect them. Lena understood. She knew what she risked taking away from Angela. Lena had grown up confident Dad would always look out for her. She wanted Angela to feel that kind of security. She also wanted her to know, "I'm so tired of being afraid. Of always wondering if I'm saying the right thing, or doing the right thing, or what people think of me. I need to be more like Baba Regina. I need to make a decision, and then I need to follow through with it. She never taught me to do that. After what happened to her, Baba Regina also became afraid. I thought, when she never gave me advice or told me what to do, it meant she didn't care. It was the opposite. She was scared of being wrong. She was scared of leading me down a dangerous path. She had confidence once. Then she lost it. That's the saddest thing, to lose faith in yourself. I'm hoping going back to Odessa, Baba Regina can be brave again. And I'm hoping she can teach me to be brave. And, most important, I want to set an example for you. So you can be brave. So you'll listen to your own judgment. So you'll trust it, instead of ceding it to somebody else." No matter how many noises Vadik was making, Lena didn't dare turn in his direction. She didn't need to make it obvious.

Angela wiped her damp cheeks with both palms. She used her fingers to pull down the corners of her eyes and get rid of the excess moisture remaining there.

When she looked at Lena, she'd never looked more like her father. "You don't care about Papa or me. You only care about yourself."

Chapter Twenty-Eight

━━━━━━

Sergei slept on the plane. Lena tried. Mama didn't bother. She sat upright the entire time, staring ahead, willing the 747 to arrive at its destination faster. They disembarked at Moscow Airport and boarded a connection to Odessa. Most flights anywhere in the USSR went through Moscow. Even if it wasn't on the way.

They were greeted by teenage soldiers wearing red-starred caps who grimaced when they spied Mama, Lena, and Sergei's blue, American passports. Lena wasn't sure if they were grimaces of condemnation for absconding the Motherland—or envy. The walls were plastered with colorful signs exhorting, "Glory to the Communist Party" and pointing the way towards "Our glorious Soviet future!" Lena seemed to be the only one pausing to read them. Mama hurried her along to their next flight. Sergei picked up their suitcases, and followed.

Lena wondered what it was like for him, being back. Was he recalling his youth, spent under similar inspirational posters? Did he feel more comfortable with them than he did in San Francisco, where the walls, layered with advertisements, exhorted you to glory in a new brand of cereal, or pointed the way towards less static cling?

Lena supposed she was focusing on Sergei's feelings about his return because it was less dangerous than wondering what Mama might be feeling. She'd barreled through the airport. As their plane ascended, Regina didn't bother looking out the window at the city where she'd spent her entire childhood, the city where her parents had presumably died and been buried, the city that had driven her to Birobidzhan—and Aaron Kramer.

Lena supposed she was focusing on Mama's feelings about the cataclysm that led her to Aaron Kramer, because it was less dangerous than wondering about her own. She'd gone out of her way to give the mysterious figure minimal thought, seeing him solely through the lens of what his being found would mean to Mama. Not what his being found would mean to her. Aaron Kramer is your father, Mama had said. But what did that mean? Lena had a father. Lena had the World's Best Dad, even without the holiday mug. She didn't need another. So what was she supposed to do if she got one?

AS SERGEI PROMISED, they made it from the Odessa airport to their hotel with a minimum of fuss. Sergei took care of hiring them a cab, Sergei took care of him taking the fastest route, and Sergei took care of paying him. After chatting for half an hour about the schools each had attended, the football teams they rooted for, and the best places to sneak a decent glass of beer, Sergei and the driver parted as friends.

It wasn't quite as trouble-free at the actual hotel, where the white-haired matron planted by the elevator doors on each floor eyed their group warily as she counted the dingy coins slid across a well-worn table to get her to be selective about whose comings and goings she chose to report. Lena tried smiling to make a good impression. Mama grabbed her arm and shook her head, "This isn't America."

Sergei carried Mama and Lena's suitcases into their room, then picked up his and turned to leave for the one across the hall.

Mama said, "I have Aaron's address. We will go now."

"Don't you want to rest?" Lena suggested. "It's been such a long flight."

"We will go now," Regina repeated.

THE ADDRESS DAD had managed to pry out of some Soviet government flunky over thirty years earlier led Lena, Mama, and Sergei to a blanched, four-story building, yellow paint peeling in strips, and a cellar dugout whose windows peeked out over a gravel courtyard where even the cats and the rats had lost interest in taunting each other.

"No Aaron Kramer here." The young woman who answered the door might have been pretty if she also didn't look completely exhausted. Laundry hung from a rope across her ceiling, brown-stained cloth diapers, and grey, sweat stained undershirts. "I've lived here my whole life. My parents moved in before I was born. Three other families have come and gone since. No Kramer."

So Vadik had been right. They were on a wild goose chase. Lena thought of the lecture she'd given Angela about bravely trusting your own judgment. Look where it got them!

"Is not time to give up hope yet," Sergei said, reading Lena's mind; it would have been difficult not to. "When your Papa moves, he must to register with local neighborhood office. I will visit old friends, ask questions. They will to look through records, see what they can find."

It was strange to hear Sergei refer to Aaron as Lena's papa when, a week earlier, that's what he'd been calling Dad.

THEY TOOK MAMA back to the hotel. She collapsed into her bed, the determination that had been keeping her upright through two flights and the rushed journey to Aaron's last known address seeping out of Regina like the last spurt of water from a hose. Lena had expected she'd want to collapse, too. But, for her, the nervousness and fear she'd been tramping down—not to mention the relief of not needing to come face to face with Aaron, forced to address how she felt about the situation—converted into manic energy. She couldn't lie down. She couldn't sleep. She couldn't sit still.

Sergei picked up on her restlessness. "Come," he said. "I will to show you something interesting."

"YOU KNOW GEARY-BASOVSKAYA, yes?" Sergei casually slipped his arm through Lena's as he escorted her down a cobble-stone promenade with a patch of green grass running down the middle, trees swaying to provide a cooling breeze along either side. "This is Derybasivskaya, the one they name it after."

It was a real place! She'd always known it on an intellectual level. But that meant nothing to Lena emotionally. As far as she recalled, she had not a single memory of her pre-American life. Which, now that she knew her first six months had been spent on the Eastern Front and the next year in a German prisoner of war camp, seemed like a blessing. It did, however, make her feel out of place. But that was nothing new. She'd never fit in. Not with American Jews, the ones for whom Russian Jews meant *Fiddler on the Roof*, and the immigrant experience was *All Of a Kind Family*. Lena's mama was neither of those things, and neither was Lena. Then again, Lena didn't fit in among Vadik's friends, either. They'd immigrated to America in the 1970s, whether as elementary school kids clutching raggedy teddy bears on their half year long journeys through the refugee centers of Vienna and Rome, or as surly teens, furious at being ripped from the life they knew and determined to make their already overwhelmed parents pay. These were the kids who'd been pressed into service to translate for their elders with the landlord, the welfare office. The ones who'd learned about how things worked here and how to be cool from TV, not from those who were supposed to be their guides into adult life. That wasn't Lena either. She never felt forsaken like that. Because Lena always had Dad.

She'd worried Angela would find herself equally as stuck between two existences. Lena remembered her own embarrassment at Mama's accented English, how she'd begged her not to talk around her friends. But Angela went in the opposite direction. She was embarrassed Lena was basically a native. One of those Americans Vadik's parents and the parents of Angela's friends made fun of for being ignorant, not knowing anything about arts and culture, thinking history began in 1776, having no clue how to raise children. Imagine, asking a child's opinion on what they wanted to eat or do or wear? Imagine letting them talk to you like you were equals! Angela also wanted Mom to refrain from speaking around Angela's friends. So they wouldn't find out Lena *didn't* have an accent.

"Thank you for bringing me," Lena told Sergei as they strolled Derybasvskaya alongside dozens of couples, families, old people and groups of children. "Mama never talks about her life in the USSR. It's strange. In America, we're always hearing about Vietnam veterans. How they were traumatized by what happened to them in the war and how the way to deal with trauma is to talk about it, tell your story, get it out, it's therapeutic. Every adult I know lived through World War II. Either as American soldiers, or Soviet soldiers, on the Russian home front, even some who were in concentration camps. They hardly ever talk about it. Maybe a reference once in a while, but not the way we're told you're supposed to. I had no idea what Mama and Dad went through." A thought struck Lena. If Sergei was older than her, "Where were you during the war?"

"Here," he said, like it was the most uninteresting answer imaginable.

"In Odessa? While it was occupied by Germans?" Lena wasn't an ignorant American. She knew her World War II history outside of D-Day and Pearl Harbor.

"Rumanians," Sergei corrected. "They occupied Odessa for Germans. My father was fighting at the front. My mother—she was arrested after the bomb went off in headquarters."

Lena wasn't an ignorant American. She knew some of the Jews arrested after an attack which killed sixty-seven people, including the Rumanian military kommandant, were shot in the public square. She knew others had been doused with gasoline and burned alive. Anyone left was deported to a ghetto outside the city, then to concentration camps in Transnistria.

"You spent the war in Odessa?" Lena repeated, confused about how that could happen.

"Little boys are slippery. They can crawl on their hands and knees, through adult legs, out of crowds. Little boys can live in bombed out, abandoned buildings. Wallpaper in the rooms, the paste to put it up is made from flour and water, like what children play with. You can dig your teeth in, bite off chunks. Go from room to room for months, years. If little boy can survive war eating wallpaper paste, strong, clever man like your Papa can find a way to live until your Mama comes for him." Then, expecting it would make her laugh, Sergei, not humming this time, but booming across all of Deryb-asvskaya, sang, "Hope, my earthly compass/ It's luck, it's a trophy for bravery…" Despite heads turning to stare, he proceeded to the next verse, "We only need learn how to wait/ We must be calm and be stubborn."

"You can be calm," Lena agreed. "And Mama can be stubborn."

She wondered what role that left for Lena to play.

SHE SOON FIGURED it out. Lena's role was to keep Mama from running through the streets of Odessa, knocking on every door, flinging it open if not answered fast enough, and demanding to know if the stunned inhabitants knew of Aaron's whereabouts, or of any information that could lead Mama to him. Lena doubted such a house to house search would endear them to the KGB agents assigned to monitor all recently returned former Soviet citizens, though Mama seemed determined to go through with it, regardless.

"We can't draw attention to ourselves," Lena lectured in a tone she otherwise reserved for a misbehaving Angela. "We can't tip our hand and let them know we're looking for Aaron. Especially if they don't want him found." When Mama appeared unconvinced—she'd woken at dawn, dressed, filled her purse with granola bars and dried fruit they'd brought from the States, not knowing what food would be available, and had one foot in the hall—Lena went for an argument she suspected her mother couldn't refuse. "Didn't Aaron chastise you for rushing in without thinking through the consequences? Do you want a repeat of your past bad decisions?"

Mama recoiled at Lena's words, shrinking into herself, shoulders curling, back sagging, knees buckling. She meekly stepped back into the hotel room, closing the door behind her. She set down her purse, removed her cardigan, and sank onto the bed, head down, hands clenched in front of her. Lena might as well have hit her with a stick. Instead, she'd hit her where it hurt. She'd taken what she knew was Mama's greatest vulnerability, her weakest point, and she'd exploited it. She'd wounded her under the guise of protecting her to get her to capitulate. No wonder Lena heard a familiar echo in her words.

She'd sounded like Vadik.

TO DISTRACT THEM from the interminable waiting, Sergei offered to give Mama and Lena a tour of Odessa. There was so much to see, after all, not just Derebasovskaya. There were the famous steps featured in the classic film, *The Battleship Potemkin*. There was the statue of the Duc de Richelieu. There was a monument to the 1928 Soviet satirical novel, *The Twelve Chairs*. Granted, it was a life-size metal chair atop a marble platform. Not much to look at. Still beat sitting around.

They'd almost convinced Mama to step outside—post Lena's tongue-lashing, she was terrified to venture from her room, lest that somehow cause Aaron to disappear permanently—when there came the knock they'd been waiting for: A representative of the Soviet Government wished to "chat" with their prodigal citizens.

A polite young woman, hair pulled into a bun, holding a slim folder, escorted Sergei into one room. A soft-spoken, older man invited Regina and her daughter to step into another. Lena had been expecting someone more foreboding. Her knowledge of KGB operatives came from American movies, where they were squinty-eyed and straight-backed, every word squeezing from their barely parted lips a threat. This fellow reminded Lena of the cherubic *Ded Moroz*, who brought New Year's gifts to lay under Russian children's *yolkas*. (Not to be confused with the cherubic Santa Claus who brought Christmas gifts to lay under Western children's trees. Any resemblance was purely coincidental.) Lena felt herself relaxing in his presence. Mama, on the other hand, tensed. Which prompted Lena to do the same. Here she was, lecturing her mother on making ill-advised decisions when, apparently, Lena couldn't recognize a threat even when it stood in front of her.

Their interviewer introduced himself as Stanislav Ivanovitch. Again, Mama twitched, as if the name itself were an implied threat. Lena was clearly out of her depth, unable to understand what was upsetting Mama so, suspecting she herself wasn't nearly upset enough.

He opened a folder and spread it on the table in front of them. He skimmed one side, then the other. Both had a sheet paperclipped to the top. He confirmed Mama's address in San Francisco. He confirmed Lena's. He observed, "Nice neighborhoods. You have done well for yourselves in America."

When Mama declined to respond, Lena followed her lead. She figured Regina Shraiman knew better how to deal with a KGB interrogation than Eleanora Burns did.

"My condolences on the loss of your husband. It must be frightening, left alone in a strange country without him to protect you." Was that the threat Lena had been expecting? Mama didn't take it as such. She continued staring at a region beyond Comrade Stanislav's right ear. "Would you not be more comfortable back home? We could make arrangements for you to return. To Moscow. You'd live in the same area where you grew up, among like-minded people. Surely preferable to spending your golden years among uncouth strangers." Lena wondered if Stanislav included her among the latter. He generously added, "Your family could visit whenever they liked. There are no travel restrictions in the new USSR."

Lena snuck a look at Mama. Her facial expression didn't flicker. But Lena could see her practically vibrating with fury. She was obviously dying to say something. Dying to lash out, to tell him what he could do with his very generous offer. The Regina of fifty years ago definitely would have. The Lena who grew up in America wanted her to. The Lena who recalled her husband's warnings was relieved when the Regina of today merely pushed back her chair, stood up, and calmly advised, "My husband is buried in San Francisco. I must stay with him."

"DID THEY INVITE you to come back, too?" Lena questioned Sergei after Mama, worn out from her encounter, begged off from his tour of Odessa. They left her to rest in the hotel while Sergei steered Lena to Primorsky Boulevard, between the statue of the Duc and the Potemkin steps. They rode a funicular down to the Black Sea harbor, standing off to the side and speaking English, to prevent eavesdropping. He nodded. Lena wondered, "What did they offer you?"

Sergei stuck his hands into his pockets, gazing out at the churning water. The wind was blowing the few tufts of hair he still had around his scalp. He rocked on his heels, wondering how to answer Lena's question. Finally, he confessed, "They offered to reunite me with my son."

"You have a son?" Lena wondered why she felt so surprised and, if she were honest, offended not to have been informed earlier. Which made no sense. Why should Sergei have told her anything about himself? Just because she was regularly stunned by how well he understood her didn't mean the intimacy went both ways.

Another nod. "His name is Gregori—Grisha. He is twenty-six. He was seventeen when I immigrated. His mother did not wish to go with me. She said I was fool. We had good life. I was doctor. Anesthesiologist. Do you know what gifts people brought me, to make sure I took care of them during surgery? That I did not forget to give right dose? My wife, she also doctor. Health inspector. Every restaurant in city bribed her with food. We eat delicacies most *Odessits* dream of, some never seen. We were in position to give Grisha best life possible. University, good job when he graduate, apartment when he marry. She said I'm not thinking of him. I'm jeopardizing his future. I'm being selfish."

Lena wasn't sure how to phrase it tactfully, except she wanted to know, "If you had such a good life *v'Soyze*, why did you want to leave?"

Based on what she heard from Vadik, those who emigrated weren't those with political connections, access to commercial goods or means to push their children up the social ladder. They were the ones who lived three, four, five families to a communal apartment. Who stood in line for hours to walk away with a few canned goods, nothing fresh, no meat, not even entrails. Jews who were kept out of top universities by ethnic quotas, who were harassed at work and denied promotions, who were called names in the streets, beaten.

"I wanted to take chance," Sergei said. "*V'Soyze*, my fate was written. I do this, this, this, so I get this, this, this. Is not living. Is, how they say in America, connecting dots. I want to see what I can build in freedom. I am tired of looking over my shoulder, watching my words, afraid if I say wrong one, I lose everything."

"So you risked… losing everything to accomplish that?"

Sergei laughed, tickled that Lena recognized his absurdity. "Yes! You understand why my wife calls me fool! This is exactly what I do! I risk losing everything because I am tired of being afraid of losing everything! She says is ridiculous to give up being doctor. She will not to do this. She says, here, we know how system works. We know how to twist system to our advantage. In America, we start from nothing. We have no advantage. Here, we are not top, we are not bottom. In America, we very bottom. She will not live this. She will not allow Grisha to live this. She is mother. I cannot take son without her permission. And Grisha does not want to go. He agrees with her. Risk is too big. So I file papers to leave alone. And my wife and my son, they take me to public meeting at work. They say I am traitor. They say they are not connected with me. It is necessary. So they are not punished when I am gone."

"Does your son still live in Odessa? Have you contacted him yet?"

Sergei finally turned his head to look Lena's way and confessed, "No. I am coward."

"Then you need to do it right away!" Lena understood her instantaneous enthusiasm for reuniting Sergei's family was a way to keep from thinking about her own. That didn't make her wrong. It made her… self-aware. "Do you know his phone number?"

"I look it up, yes," Sergei admitted.

"Let's call him now!" The minute they stepped off the funicular, Lena looked around for a public phone, spotting one and dragging Sergei to it.

He hesitated, resting his hand on the receiver, making no move to pick up. He looked from it to Lena, his face a combination of bravado, terror, and sheepishness.

"Grisha isn't a teenage boy anymore. All teenagers disapprove of their parents." Lena understood that her instantaneous enthusiasm for paying no mind to teenage negative opinions was a way to keep from thinking about how she'd left things with Angela. That didn't make her wrong. It made her… more self-aware. "He's a grown man now. He's much more capable of understanding why you made the choices you did."

Sergei nodded thoughtfully. He smiled at Lena, still tentative. She smiled back. She said, "Learning about the decisions my mother once made helped me understand her better. It helped me empathize with where she was coming from." Lena hoped that would be true. Someday. It was one of the primary reasons she'd embarked on this trip. Sergei didn't need to know she was still waiting for the comprehensive understanding to kick in. It was irrelevant to his situation.

Sergei dialed the number he'd memorized. He said, "Grishka? It's Papa. I am in Odessa and—" that was as far as he got. Grishka did the rest of the talking. And then Grishka hung up.

Sergei stood frozen, clutching the phone. Unlike what US television led you to believe, a hang up didn't result in a dial-tone. A hang up resulted in silence. Desolation. Rejection.

Lena tentatively reached out, resting her palm in the crook of his elbow. She wouldn't have held it against him if Sergei jerked away. Instead, he hung up the receiver, slowly. Turning first his head, then his entire body away from the offending device. He tried to keep the 'I told you so' out of his voice—obviously for Lena's benefit, since he wasn't striving to protect his own feelings—when he relayed, "Well, he still disapproves of my choices." Sergei tried to chuckle, but only succeeded in clearing his throat. Lena could hear the lump embedded there when he elaborated. "He says, I have made my decision. Now I must to live with the consequences."

"Unacceptable," Lena snapped, hoping she was responding exclusively to Sergei's situation, and not to the dozens of others swirling through her head to which the answer should have been the same—if Lena were brave enough to admit it. "You can't let him treat you this way. You must go to him and explain your position. It's much harder to ignore someone in person. He'll have to listen to you."

"Is," again Sergei was grasping for tact, "a very… American way to look at things."

Lena was aware the designation wasn't a compliment in their circles. "You're American now. Let's go show your son what that means."

Chapter Twenty-Nine

———

Sergei's son was taller than Sergei, but considerably thinner, as if he were Play-Doh, rolled out and stretched. Grisha's hair was the chestnut Sergei's must have been before the grey colonized it. His eyes were the same shade of murky blue. Sergei had marched to his son's door, knocking without hesitation. Once the young man appeared, however, Lena's friend seemed lost for what to do. Should they embrace? Shake hands? Should Sergei introduce himself in case it had been so long Grisha had forgotten him, despite the resemblance?

His son wasn't as flummoxed. After the initial moment of shock, he made it clear he'd been expecting him. And he'd prepared what to say, "Get lost, Papa."

And Vadik claimed American children were ill-mannered! Lena may have mouthed off to her parents in a manner her in-laws would have found unacceptable, but she'd never been this brutal. She turned to gauge Sergei's reaction. If it were her, Lena would be fuming... or sobbing. Sergei was neither. His face suggested he'd expected nothing less. Which was when Lena was forced to admit she'd been the one to coerce him into this. For her own selfish reasons. She'd wanted to compel this reconciliation between Sergei and Grisha, so Lena could cling to the hope that a similar miracle would happen for her and Angela.

"Grishenka, I wish to explain." Sergei's tone was passionate, but also woebegone. Like his son had prepared a response for when Papa showed up at his door, Sergei had already had the conversation with his son in his head. He knew there was only one way it could end.

"Go away," Grisha repeated. "Do you want to get me into more trouble? After you left us, Mama and I lost our apartment. She was demoted at work. I was kicked out of the Komsomol. I couldn't go to University in Odessa. I had to travel all the way to Perm to find a place that would accept me. I thought I might never be allowed to return. Do you know how many favors Mama had to call in to get me a job? No one wanted to hire the son of a traitor. Now we are almost back to where we were when you abandoned us. And now the whole country is changing. We don't know what's right, what's wrong, who is in charge, who we're supposed to kiss up to. We don't know what might happen if anybody finds out I talked to you. So leave me alone, Papa. You say you love me. So listen to me and do what I ask. Do what I need you to."

Lena was listening to Grisha. But she was hearing Aaron telling Regina, "If you love me, be realistic for once. Stop dreaming. Open your eyes and see what's happening instead of what you want to happen. Listen to what I want. Listen to what I need. More importantly, listen to what our daughter needs. Let me be, Regina. Take care of Lena. Put her first. Put her ahead of me. Put her ahead of *us*. Or else you never loved me at all."

GRISHA SLAMMED THE door in Sergei's face. Lena felt it reverberate all the way back to a prisoner of war camp in 1945. Yet, she still couldn't quit. It was the opposite of everything she'd been taught, everything she'd been raised to believe about sticking to your guns. If at first you don't succeed, try, try again. The little engine that could.

"Don't give up," Lena urged Sergei. "Fight. Make him listen to your side of the story."

"I can't," he said.

"Why not?"

Sergei shrugged, spreading his hands from side to side. "I am not American."

LENA EXPECTED SERGEI to be devastated by the encounter, but his Soviet fatalism proved a bulwark. If you anticipate the worst, you can't be disappointed when it happens. He remained as upbeat when they settled at an outdoor cafe after the confrontation with his son as Sergei had been the entire morning beforehand.

Lena glanced down at the menu and, unwilling to take a risk with an unidentifiable food combination, asked for a salad.

The waitress, a young woman whose face suggested the late teens, but whose *can't be bothered* attitude suggested Regina's aforementioned golden years, smirked at Lena's naivete. "No cucumbers today. No tomatoes."

Lena did another cursory survey of the menu offerings and asked for the chicken cutlet.

"No chicken today," the waitress said.

"What do you have today?" Sergei asked pleasantly. For a moment, the waitress almost dropped her look of dissatisfaction with life—before remembering that one cordial customer wasn't enough of a reason to.

"Pelmeni."

"Meat?"

"No meat today. Potato."

"We'll have two orders," Sergei said.

"And may I have a glass of water?" Lena asked.

The waitress pointed toward a faucet along the cafe's back wall. "Sink's over there."

Once she'd gone, Lena felt compelled to ask Sergei, "No tomatoes, cucumber, chicken or meat today. Does that mean they have it on other days?"

"Only days when we are not here."

Lena smiled, then felt guilty. "Are you OK," she pressed Sergei. "Your son—"

"My son is right. We do not know how all this," Sergei gestured his hand around the cafe, but he meant more. "How all this perestroika will end. Think of your parents. Your papa, he work with Americans because they are allies. Then war ends, and he is put in jail because he collaborates with enemy. Your mama, she is friends with important woman, who is protected by important person in KGB. Then important person is called traitor, so important woman is now traitor, and Mama is now traitor. This happens in circles. Khrushchev, he is First Secretary, but he is not safe. You know this, yes? First, Stalin calls Lenin allies enemies, then Khrushchev calls Stalin allies criminals, then Khrushchev is removed and his allies are criminals. Grisha is right, he must to be careful. I am risk to him."

"Maybe things actually will get better," Lena proposed tentatively.

"Yes. We always to hope for this." Sergei grinned. "Do not worry. I will not sing again."

Lena laughed. "How do you do it? How do you always see the bright side of things?"

"Is choice. I make choice when I am little boy. I think nobody, not Nazis, not Rumanians, not Soviets, they will not make me hate my one life. There is no other. Why spend it unhappy? It is why I leave USSR. I believe somewhere there is more happy for me to find."

"That doesn't sound very Russian."

"I am not Russian. You have seen Mama's passport? Under nationality, it does not say Russian. It says Jew. Same with me. I am born here in Ukraine. My passport does not say Ukrainian. Jewish. The fifth line."

"Jews I know aren't exactly brimming with optimism either. You're something special."

"You are special, too, Lenachka." Sergei reached across the table and rested his hand atop Lena's. He'd touched her multiple times since they embarked on this journey. Their fingers met hefting their suitcases off the airport carousel, when helping Mama out of a taxi, when he directed Lena's attention to a particular monument or while guiding where they should go next. This was different. Lena was an avid reader of what Vadik deemed "nonsense literature." Sidney Sheldon, Judith Krantz, Jacqueline Susann. She knew about the sparks of electricity that were described in great detail by each author as a prelude to wanton debauchery. This wasn't that either. This was a person attempting to make a connection, a person who, Lena couldn't articulate why she felt convinced of it, appeared to see her as who she truly was, not as who they'd like to see her as. Sergei was reaching out to the real her, not to the idealized Lena in his mind. Oh, and there were sparks, too. But, under the circumstances, they were secondary.

She looked down at where their hands met. Sergei's thumb gently stroked across the top of Lena's knuckles. His were Communist-approved hands. The skin weatherworn, calloused and rough. A worker's hands. Lena's, in comparison, were the hands of the enemy. White, soft, and coddled, making it obvious she'd never performed a moment of physical labor in her life. All thanks to Mama and Dad, and to Aaron Kramer. The three of them had conspired to safeguard Lena from a childhood of forced labor and mandatory volunteering *subbotniks* picking up scrap metal, of not enough to eat, and too much surveillance. If not for them, she might have lived an adulthood like Sergei's, where she'd have to decide whether to turn her back on everything she knew, everything she understood, everything she could pretend to have under control, to leap off a cliff into the black chasm of the unknown, leaving behind everyone who sensibly feared joining her. She liked to think she'd have been as brave as Sergei, as brave as Mama, as brave as Aaron and the American Tommy Burns. Lena felt pretty confident she wouldn't have been. A coward was a coward no matter what the choice before them.

Look at Lena now. A brave woman would have allowed her eyes to travel from where her hand met Sergei's, up his freckled arm, the tufts of hair as tangled as those upon his head, to his sturdy shoulder, to his kind face. She'd have smiled, an open, unguarded expression to mirror his. She'd have made clear she was interested in seeing where this might go. She was open to where this might go. She liked where this might go.

Lena slid her palm out from under Sergei's. She didn't meet his eyes. She addressed his left cheekbone and ear instead. "How did you do it? How did you know the decision you made was the right one? How does anyone ever know?"

Because she deliberately avoided it, Lena didn't see Sergei's reaction to her ignoring his compliment… and his hand. She took solace in the fact that he didn't sound offended—at least by her—when he observed, "My son does not believe I made the right decision."

"You do." Emboldened, Lena allowed herself a sneak peek at his expression.

"I do," he conceded. "But I always believe last decision I made was correct. How else can I find courage to make next one?"

"My husband, Vadik, also believes every decision he makes is not just the right one, but the best one." Lena, perhaps, put more emphasis on the word husband than it warranted.

"Vadik is man who knows what he wants," Sergei agreed, as neutral and pleasant as he'd been back in Dad's hospital room.

"And he's usually right." Lena was justifying something to somebody, she simply wasn't sure what and to whom.

"You are fortunate woman then."

"Yes. I am."

Wasn't it nice they got that settled?

"I knew what I was doing when I married Vadik," Lena said, before qualifying, "I thought I knew what I was doing when I married Vadik. And he's been exactly the husband I expected."

Sergei did not repeat his previous statement. Sergei didn't say anything at all.

Feeling put on the spot, Lena babbled on, beginning her sentences with no idea of where they might end. "I knew he would take care of me. And he has. I never need to worry about the household bills or if the car needs to be brought in for an oil change, or the taxes getting paid. He looks out for us. If I have a problem at work, like somebody's being unfair, Vadik always knows what to do. You know how the cliché goes that when women come to you with a problem, they don't want you to fix it, they want you to listen? Well, that never made any sense to me. If I could fix my problem myself, why would I come to you with it? If I'm coming to you and telling you my problem, obviously I want you to fix it!"

"You would like me to fix your problem?" Sergei asked innocently.

Yes, Lena thought. "No," Lena insisted. "I don't think I have a problem. I mean, what kind of a problem is saying the man I thought

I married is exactly the man who my husband turned out to be? That's not a problem. That's a success!"

"Wonderful!" Sergei slapped the table with both hands.

Lena wished she could be equally as enthusiastic. "It's not Vadik's fault I'm ungrateful. He's doing exactly what he promised me he'd do. I'm the one who's, all of a sudden, feeling smothered. Like he's trying to control what I do or what I think. As soon as I suggest making a change—any kind of change—something stupid, like do we need to go to his parents' for dinner every Sunday night? Can't we rotate the days of the week? Or, what if I leave my firm and go into business for myself? Dad did it. I could do it, too. Sure, it's more risky. It would also give me more flexibility. Vadik says that's not how life works. You can't do what you want, you have to think of the consequences. Next thing I know, he's listing all the things that could go wrong, and I'm too terrified to make a move."

"You are here," Sergei reminded. "You are fine. All the things Vadik predicts. They do not come true. We arrive on plane alright, we check into hotel alright. You manage meeting with KGB fine, no problems."

"Thanks to you."

"Vadik predicts problem. You need solution. I am solution. Solver is still you."

"You're very sweet, Sergei."

"Yes, this is so." He nodded thoughtfully until Lena laughed and Sergei joined her.

"I've been thinking of leaving him for a while now," she confessed, more comfortable in hiding behind a pronoun. Speaking Vadik's proper name would make it too real. "I have so much to lose if I do, though. Not just going out into the world without Vadik to watch over me. I don't need him to tell me, I know all the risks. It's his family. They're so different from mine. I never have to wonder if they care, not like Mama. They care about everything. What I eat, how I sleep, where we vacation, who we're friends with, why I enrolled Angela in this afterschool activity and not that one." Lena paused. Then she repeated, "Angela."

"Yes," Sergei said. "Children. They to make decisions more complicated."

Lena thought of Grisha ordering Sergei out of his life. "I can't let what happened with you and Grisha happen with me and Angela."

It was a terrible, wounding thing to say. Lena couldn't help it. She'd been unable to think of anything but that possibility since the door was shut in Sergei's face. "Angela loves Vadik so much. She loves his parents and his sister. They've been there for her since the day she was born. She feels secure with them. They're her home. They're her—her grounding."

"Very necessary in San Francisco," Sergei agreed, making Lena smile in spite of herself.

"I could never take her away from them." That wasn't the issue, and they both knew it. She wasn't Regina or Sergei. She wasn't proposing moving to the other side of the world. She was, at most, proposing moving into an apartment across town. The issue wasn't Lena taking Angela away from the father and the family which nurtured her better than Lena ever had. The issue was, "If I leave Vadik, Angela will want to stay with him."

"I understand," Sergei said. Based on what had happened, Lena didn't doubt him.

"I tell myself I'm putting my daughter first by staying with her father. Truth is, I'm the one who's afraid of losing her. I'm acting like it's some kind of Sophie's choice, me deciding between my own happiness and hers. But it's actually me being selfish."

"When I leave USSR, I am selfish. And now I to pay price."

"My mother had to choose. Staying and taking care of Aaron, or leaving and taking care of me. I wonder if she regrets her decision." Lena asked Sergei, "Do you regret yours?"

She didn't think he was capable of looking uncomfortable. He took everything in such stride. She'd made him uncomfortable. Sergei fidgeted in his chair, tapping his fingers on the table, scratching the back of his ear, eyes darting. Lena was about to apologize and change the subject, it was the least she could do, when he spoke up. "There is always regret. One move, it cuts off many others. You always wonder if maybe different is better. What is it Voltaire says?"

This was one of the things that never failed to stupefy Lena's American friends. That a Russian immigrant who didn't look, sound, dress, or speak the way they believed an intellectual should look, sound, dress, or speak, could recite, from memory, pages of poetry, or make a literary allusion to a text not in his native language. It's what Vadik and his family meant when they said all Americans were uneducated peasants.

"I disapprove of what you say but I will defend to the death your right to say it?" Lena guessed, looking around nervously as she uttered the most non-Soviet sentiment ever?

"No," Sergei said. "The one about the best of all possible worlds."

"You think that's what we're living in?" Lena asked incredulously.

"Hope," he repeated. "I hope that is what we are living in."

"What if I make the wrong choice? What if I leave Vadik, and it turns out terrible for him, for Angela, for me?"

"Yes, this could happen."

She'd been fishing for more of Sergei's unending positivity, not agreement. Was he patronizing her? That didn't sound like him. Then again, she barely knew the man. What if Lena had simply been projecting a personality onto him? Seeing what she wanted to see. Yet another misguided call.

"If this to happen, you will figure out how to solve this problem, same way you solve Mama's problem, bring her to Odessa, take care of her."

"By having you do it?"

"I am at your service," Sergei offered a mock bow from his seat. "I am yours."

Chapter Thirty

By the time their food finally arrived—"No potato today, cabbage,"—
Sergei was deep in explaining to Lena that she was more competent
than she presumed. Not by articulating those words precisely, but by
swatting down any calamitous examples she came up with.

"What if Vadik won't agree to a separation?" It was an easier word
than the next step.

"You are attorney, you will fix."

"I'm a real estate attorney, not a matrimonial one."

"You have friends, yes?"

"Yes."

"They will help."

"What if Angela won't come with me?"

"You will see her in morning before school, you will see her in
evening after school. You will see her more than when she live with
you, because you will make more effort."

"What if Vadik's parents hate me?"

"You will be polite to them, until they to feel bad."

"What if Angela hates me?"

That was a tougher one.

"You will to change her mind," Sergei said, at last.

"You didn't change Grisha's." Lena felt guilty pointing that out, but also obliged to.

"You are smarter than me," Sergei assured.

Lena tried to recall the last time anyone had said anything close to all the encouragement Sergei just offered her. There was Dad. Dad was always encouraging, supportive, loving. But he was her dad. It was his job. Lena had never taken him seriously. Partially because of the whole Dad's job thing. And partially, she now realized, because Mama made it clear he was American. They saw the bright side of everything. They were fools. You were a fool if you believed them.

"What if I make the biggest mistake of my life?"

"This is the beauty of hope. Belief there is always opportunity to make bigger one."

EMBOLDENED BY SERGEI's belief in her—at least his belief that she was capable of making a bigger mistake than the one currently under discussion—Lena returned to their hotel, thanked him profusely, nodded to the elderly woman whose job was to monitor the floor on this shift, let herself into the room she was sharing with Mama, and asked, "Do you regret giving up Aaron for my sake?"

Lena's voice shook as she posed her query. She was terrified of hearing Mama's honest answer. Did she regret choosing her child over the love of her life? In other words, did she regret Lena?

"Yes, I regret," Regina said.

Lena felt as if the window had blown open, a frigid wind slamming her across the room, into the opposing wall. She started to shake, first her hands, then her knees, as her stomach plummeted. Lena was grabbing for the back of a chair to remain upright, when Mama clarified. "I regret for Tommy."

"You regret... Dad?" Lena's self-pity morphed to indignation. How could anyone dare regret spending their life with a wonderful man like Dad?

"Good man deserves good woman. A man who can love like Tommy, deserves woman who can love him back in same way. Not woman who loves somebody else."

Oh. Lena's righteous indignation drained as quickly as it had swelled, replaced by pity—for all of them.

"I could not even give him children," Regina said. "Doctors think it's because I'm hungry for so long during the war. Or maybe because of the long walking. I make stupid decisions, and I fail Tommy on every front."

"No." This wasn't Lena disagreeing with Regina. She'd certainly agreed while growing up, even without knowing the details of her parents' unconventional courtship. This disagreement flowed from a different time, from a man who'd been wiser than either of them. Lena said, "When I was in high-school, I was picking my classes for Senior Year. Should I do AP or Honors? What would look better for college? Which might hurt my GPA? Everyone I knew, American, Russian, Jewish, Chinese, it didn't matter, their parents were sitting down with them, giving their opinions, telling them what the right choice to make was. If they fought, they knew their parents cared. I asked you. You looked at me like you couldn't imagine a more stupid question. You said, 'What do I know about this nonsense?' and walked away. I lost it. I was so furious. When Dad asked what was wrong, I unloaded on him. Told him you didn't care, you never cared, I meant nothing to you, you didn't love me at all. Then, when Dad tried to defend you, I said it was obvious you didn't love him, either."

The frigid air—despite the outside June temperatures—was back. It wasn't pinning Lena to the wall. It was emanating directly from Mama. Lena knew she'd taken a huge chance with her disclosure. They still had multiple days to spend together on this trip. She might have poisoned their time for good. But Lena had her reasons for picking at this particular scab. "Do you know what Dad said to me, Mama? I thought he'd be furious. I thought he might hit me, which he'd never done before. He didn't. He didn't even raise his voice. He told me: *I know your Mama loves me. Not from what she says, from what she does. How she stays up, waiting for me, so I don't walk into a dark, lonely house. The way she learned to cook my favorite foods. She still doesn't understand the appeal of tuna casserole or meatloaf, but she cooks them, just the same. How she looks out for when my favorite movies will be on TV and reminds me so I won't miss them. Your mother would give her life for me. She would give it for you. I know this. I've seen this. She loves us. In the ways she can. Learn to look for love, Lena, in what people do, and in places where you expect least to find it. You won't regret it. I haven't. Not from the first time I laid eyes on Regina Solomonovna.*"

The memory was still burned onto Lena's heart. It was her most precious possession. And now she wanted nothing more than to help Mama feel the way Lena had then. "Don't you see, Mama? He never regretted being with you. He knew you loved him. You didn't fail him."

"He did not to tell me this," Regina said slowly. "He did not tell me what you say, he did not tell me what he say back."

Lena watched her mother's face. Ever since dad's death, Mama seemed to be aging at an accelerated pace. The bags under her eyes deepened, the corners of her mouth drooped. There was a slight tremor to her chin, which made the skin of her neck quaver, and permanent furrows between her eyebrows, above her nose. Now, however, Mama sat up straighter. She raised her chin, smoothing out the skin below and above. Her eyes widened, her brows lifted, her lips curled not precisely into a smile, but, at least, into an anti-frown. At Lena's words, her mother didn't merely cheer up. She aged down. She became the Regina Solomonovna that Tommy Burns first met—and fell in love with.

"Thank you, Lenachka," Mama said. "Thank you for telling me this."

Lena knew she should leave this alone. This detente was the closest she and her mother had ever come to a cease-fire, and they needed it now more than ever. It was one thing to be furious and give Mama the silent treatment when they lived at opposite ends of the city and had the time and distance to cool off, move on by never discussing the issue again. It was another to exist in a state of cold—or worse— hot war while sharing a hotel room and passing through a country where they needed to work together to keep from getting shipped off to Siberia.

Yet Lena couldn't leave it alone. She had to know. "Do you still think you did the right thing, Mama? Giving up Aaron for my sake?"

Regina's shrug was identical to the one she'd given a frazzled Lena looking for guidance in what classes to take. Only now, Lena saw not indifference, but immobility. Mama was telling the truth. She knew nothing about making the correct decision.

"Life gives us so many choices," Regina said, her voice coming from another time, another person. "Shame none of them are good."

"What do you mean?"

"All choices can end bad. When you try to imagine everything, you cannot."

Lena knew Vadik would take offense at Mama's assertion. He'd claim that he could.

"I have never made a single correct decision in my life. How could I dare give you—or anybody—advice about anything? Aaron ask me to do this. Aaron order me to do this. So I do this. And I spend every day, second-guessing. I am second-guessing now. Aaron says, leave and never come back. It will be too dangerous for me. I have come back. What if I am again doing wrong thing?"

"I have good news!" Sergei announced after knocking on the door and waiting for Lena to let him in. He'd barely stepped over the threshold before announcing, "I have found him!"

Lena had hoped she and Mama would spend the afternoon talking. She wanted to hear more about Aaron, about Birobidzhan, about Cecilia and Felix and Marta, as well as the choices Regina thought she'd bungled, all of which lead to Lena's birth, not to mention the two of them in Odessa now. After their initial connection, Regina grew close-mouthed. She insisted the past wasn't worth digging up, there was nothing to gain from dissecting situations long passed, people long dead. She didn't say whether she now believed Aaron was among them.

"You have an address?" Lena gasped, afraid to look at Mama and gauge her reaction.

"I have an address," Sergei confirmed. "Aaron Kramer, seventy-three years old, moved there in 1975. It is housing for Great Patriotic War veterans. They build it outside of city proper."

"Is there a phone number?" Lena asked, too polite and too

American to drop in. Their other option was to make like the locals, and stand outside the window, pitching pebbles.

"Only address."

Lena stared at the piece of paper in Sergei's hand, her birth father's name written in the formal, flowery script that made every ex-Soviet's cursive in English, look identical.

"We can go." She turned to Mama. "We can go right now. It's still light out."

She expected Mama to leap at the chance. She'd been leaping since the first, when she'd been ready to race to the SF airport, no luggage, no ticket, no escort, no plans. Only Aaron. As always, only Aaron.

She wasn't budging now. She perched on the bed, palms folded primly in her lap, eyes anywhere but on the address which had mesmerized Lena. Her voice barely above a whisper, Mama said, "Maybe not today."

Lena's head spun off her shoulders. "What do you mean? What's going on?"

"Tomorrow, maybe," Mama said.

"Are you not feeling well?"

"She is frightened." Sergei sat down next to Mama and clasped her hand between his.

"You've been waiting for this for over forty years, Mama. Aaron is here. He's alive."

"What if he is angry with me?" Mama challenged. "He asked me to leave, never contact him again. I do this, yes, because he tells me to. What if I am wrong? What if Aaron needed me, and I was not there? What if he is disappointed in me? What if he hates me? Hates me for what I did then to him, hates me for what I do now to him? What if he is gone, died blaming me? I have no opportunity to apologize. What if he is alive and will not accept my apology? What if I see him now, and he says things to me which destroy all happy memories I cherish. What if this—what if this is the biggest mistake I ever make?"

Chapter Thirty-One

Lena looked at Sergei. She looked at her mother. Lena said, "This is the beauty of hope. Belief there is always opportunity to make bigger one."

She regretted her words the moment they emerged from her mouth. Her mother was in crisis; not the first she'd experienced, but the first she'd allowed Lena to witness. The moment should be meaningful, cathartic; an occasion for them to rebuild their fractured relationship. And Lena had responded with a thoughtless platitude. Her excuse was, she'd felt better when Sergei employed it on her. She was merely paying it forward.

Regina laughed. As Lena was gearing up to beg her mother's forgiveness, Regina's cheeks trembled not with tears or fear, but with unmistakable mirth. The giggle that emerged next, once again, might have come from the eighteen year old girl leaping on a Moscow train to escape danger—and search for adventure.

"This is a good point." She addressed Lena, but a slide of her eyes Sergei's way made it clear she knew where her daughter had picked up this wisdom. "Worst part of living through most terrible moment of your life is fear it might not yet be worst moment. This is comforting, thank you, my dears."

And with that quintessentially Soviet observation, they were off to visit Aaron.

THEY TOOK A taxi to the outskirts of the city, into a neighborhood made up primarily of Khrushchyovkas. Sergei explained that hundreds of these three to five story concrete-paneled apartment buildings went up in the 1960s, named after then Party head Nikita Khrushchev. The goal was to make them cheap and efficient to put up. Prefabricated pieces were constructed in Moscow and trucked in on an as-needed basis. Bathrooms were assembled separately. Every unit looked the same. Every building looked the same. Every complex looked the same. For a city like Odessa, and a country like the USSR, which saw canyon swaths of housing wiped out in bombing raids and combat, it was a quick-fix solution that persisted for decades afterward.

Lena thought Mama might be interested in seeing and hearing what had happened to her country since she'd left, but it was obvious she was only pretending to listen to Sergei out of politeness. She nodded her head at the end of each sentence, and she looked where he pointed, but her eyes failed to focus.

The taxi dropped them off at the address Sergei provided. He peered up at the imposing grey structure and told Mama apologetically, "Khrushchyovkas have no elevators. His room is on the 5th floor."

Lena said, "We can go up and see if he's home." If he's alive, if he's him, was implied. "Then maybe he can come down and—"

"I will walk up," Mama said.

"It's five floors!"

"I've walked farther." For Aaron, was also implied.

Lena took one of Mama's elbows, and Sergei the other. They did their best to prop her up so she didn't need to lift her knees too high or land on the balls of her feet too hard. They made it up the first flight, then paused so Mama could catch her breath. The remaining stairs required a break every few steps. Lena didn't mind. Despite regular visits to the gym, she wasn't prepared to charge up five flights, either. The air smelled of cigarettes and human sweat, with a touch of perfume. No one spoke. They pretended it was so they could concentrate on helping Mama. They knew it was because there was nothing to say.

This was it. This was what they'd come for. They would either find Aaron or hit a dead end. Nobody wanted to discuss the possibility of finding Aaron... and hitting a dead end.

They hesitated outside of his door, #5A. Again, they pretended it was to give Mama the opportunity to pull herself together. She lifted her head, pointing her chin to the sky. She took a deep breath. She swallowed. She let her hands fall to her sides and she lowered her head until her chin touched her chest. Another inhale. Another exhale.

Just when Lena thought Mama might stall forever—an option growing more attractive by the second—Regina raised her arm and rapped firmly on the door. Twice. So there'd be no mistake she meant it.

The man who appeared was grey haired. Stooped. Skin hung loosely from the sides of his face, making his jaw appear squarer. His lips were pale, almost colorless. He leaned on a cane, his left knee locked in place so he dragged his foot behind him. He was missing a portion of his left ear. His shoulders, however, were still as broad as advertised. His eyes still the same dazzling blue.

When nobody said anything, when everyone simply took head to toe inventory, Lena felt compelled to ask, in a Russian she'd never been confident of, "Are you Aaron Kramer?"

"That is me."

"I'm Lena Mirap—" she cut herself off. "I am Elenora... Burns."

His expression didn't change. Had he known it the moment he opened the door? Had he known it as soon as he saw her through the peephole? Lena didn't look much like Mama. She was, at best, a washed out version, her hair brown to Mama's one-time black, her eyes dusk to Mama's caramel. She was the predictable result of a dark mother and a blond, blue-eyed father.

"You look like me," he said, drawing his index finger from Lena's forehead down her face. "Your nose. Your mouth. Beautiful. But different from your mother."

At that, Aaron reluctantly turned away from Lena to fully drink in Regina. She'd watched him acknowledge his daughter without saying a word. She kept quiet as he studied her. Another woman might have fidgeted self-consciously, smoothed down her hair, attempted to stand up straighter. Regina simply appraised him back. Meeting his eyes, all but daring Aaron to find fault with what he saw. It was difficult to ascertain which one of them began smiling first, who echoed whom. One was tall, one was short, one was dark, one was light. Yet they were mirror images.

Aaron stepped aside and welcomed Regina, Lena, and Sergei into his home.

The front room was sparsely furnished, a polished wood table in the middle, four chairs on either side. A maroon carpet on the floor, another hung on the wall, both an attempt to keep warm. A bookshelf featured titles standing upright and lying on their sides. A couch faced a television. A clock ticked on the windowsill.

"Sit, please," Aaron urged. As he reached for a chair with one hand, he reached out to Sergei with the other. "I am Aaron."

"I'm Sergei. A friend of Regina Solomonova's and Lena's."

"Sergei found you for us," Lena interjected. "Friend" didn't come close to covering what he was.

Mama had yet to say a word. Now, she reached into her purse, withdrawing a stack of papers Lena recognized instantly but hadn't realized Mama had brought along. She wondered where she'd hidden them when their things were searched at the airport. She wondered what might have happened if they'd been discovered. She wondered why Mama had taken such a risk. And then Lena remembered. For Aaron.

"Tommy found you." Mama slid the letters he'd spent forty years writing across the table to Aaron.

He pulled a pair of glasses out of his pocket, opened them gingerly, perched them on his nose, and quickly scanned the documents. "Yes. I have my own."

"He didn't know if you received them," Regina said.

"Received and burned. Except for one." Aaron stood, shuffling to a carved wooden box perched on a shelf in front of his books. He opened it, removed a black and white photograph and brought it back to the table to show Regina, Lena, and Sergei.

"That's me!" Lena exclaimed. "Right, Mama? I was, what, ten? That's the bike Dad got me for my birthday!"

"Yes." Aaron checked the date written on the back. "1953. You are ten." He passed the picture over so Lena could read the rest of what Tommy wrote.

"Our Eleonora is clever, loyal and brave." Lena hesitated, unable to believe the words that came next. "She does you proud."

She heard the air which escaped Mama's lungs, not so much a gasp as an eruption. She'd been prepared for everything that had happened up to now. She hadn't been prepared for this.

"He knew?" She challenged Aaron, accusing. "You told him?"

"He knew. I did not tell him. He just knew."

Mama buried her head in her hands, shaking it side to side, the self-control she'd reigned in so tightly for the last few days, for the last forty years, draining out as she moaned. "One thing I wanted to do for him. One thing, and I could not even do that."

Lena moved to comfort her mother, but, somehow Aaron, cane, glasses and all, got there faster. He scooched his chair closer to Regina's, peeled her hands away from her face and forced her to look at him. "He knew and he loved you. He knew and he wanted you. He knew and he forgave you. He forgave me, too. It is Tommy."

"It is Tommy," Mama repeated, head bobbing up and down now, instead of side to side.

"He was a wonderful dad." Lena needed to say it, unsure if Aaron needed to hear it.

"I expected no less," Aaron praised.

"Did you expect this?" Regina pointed to herself, to Lena, sitting in Aaron's home. "You told me to go and never come back," her bitterness, fury and resentment as obvious today as it must have been the first time he brought it up.

"And yet you came back," Aaron sighed.

"Do you hate me?"

"Hate you?" Aaron paused between the words, unable to reconcile one with the other.

"For leaving you. For coming back to you."

Lena had spent her life trying to interpret Mama's cryptic, fragmented pronouncements. She hoped Aaron would prove better at it.

"Are you married?" Mama unexpectedly demanded.

Lena shot Sergei a panicked look. She felt embarrassed that the possibility never occurred to her. The way Mama told her and Aaron's story, it sounded like a romantic saga out of one of Lena's Vadik-mocked books. Romantic sagas always had happy endings. The star-crossed couple always ended up together. It had never crossed her mind that Aaron might be—

Sergei caught Lena's eye and offered a quick shake of the head as Aaron answered Regina's question. "No."

Mama looked around the room suspiciously. "A woman lives here?"

"No."

Lena let out a sigh of relief and flashed Sergei a grateful look. Of course, he would have checked out the information beforehand. Even if Lena hadn't thought to ask.

"You are alone?" Mama was a big believer in asking the same question over and over in different ways, fishing for a contradictory response. Thank you, KGB.

"No."

Mama should have been devastated. Instead, she looked triumphant. Unlike Lena, she'd come prepared for bad news. Finally hearing it was a perverse validation that she'd been right to expect the worst. Thank you, KGB.

"I have you," Aaron said. He didn't let go of Regina's hand as he reached for Lena's. "And our daughter."

Mama surveyed his clasped chain with a neutral expression, still unwilling to crack, to hope, to believe. "You don't hate me for coming back? You said never come back."

"No."

"You don't hate me for leaving?" Talking about herself, Mama could be stoic. With Aaron, her warring emotions trampled each other in the haste to stampede out. "Why didn't you answer Tommy's letters? We could have helped you!"

"If I answered Tommy's letters," Aaron said, "you would have known I was alive. If you knew I was alive, could anything have stopped you from coming back and rescuing me?"

"No." Regina echoed Aaron's earlier denials, half-mocking, half-defiant.

"One time, Regina, one time, you did what I asked. Knowing you and Lena were safe in America, kept me safe. As long as I knew you were out of the KGB's reach, there was nothing they could do to me. You took away their leverage. That is how you already rescued me."

Lena watched Mama process Aaron's declaration. She leaned back in her chair and studied him critically. She didn't let go of his hand.

Finally, Mama said, "I must rescue you again."

Lena looked confused, Sergei looked amused. Aaron looked resigned. And impressed. And familiar.

"You must come to America. Soon. Quickly. Before they change their minds."

"Mama!" Lena felt compelled to interrupt. "You can't— He's a grown man. He has a life here. You can't order him to—"

"We're betrothed." Regina turned to Aaron. "Correct? We never broke our engagement."

Aaron cocked his head to the side, mulling.

"No," he agreed.

In her mother's world, being married to another man for forty-three years apparently did not constitute grounds for a broken engagement. Merely a postponed one.

"We should get married as soon as possible," Regina said. "To speed up the paperwork."

"Yes," Aaron agreed. While also acting like he was trying his hardest not to laugh. Or to let go of her mother's hand. Ever again.

The look on his face… Lena had never seen anything like it. Was it pride? It was more than pride. Was it tolerance? It wasn't exactly tolerance. Affinity, intimacy, memory, nostalgia, love, like, passion, past, future, regret, hope… Lena spun through each of the possibilities and came up with all of the above. And none of the above.

It was something deeper. It was connection, understanding, compatibility. It was fate, it was destiny, it was kismet and providence. It was mutually assured destruction and mutually assured survival. It was a look that said he believed Regina could do anything, handle anything, survive anything. It was a look that said he still believed in her, long after he'd stopped believing in anything else.

It was a look Lena had never seen in her own husband's eyes. Or in hers, when she looked at him.

Lena turned to Sergei, wondering if he could see it, too. Any of it? All of it?

He nodded. And then he winked.

Epilogue: 1989

"Think you've got enough flowers?" Angela asked, demonstrating that promotion from age twelve to thirteen came with an increase in teenage attitude.

She, Lena, and Sergei were speed-walking through San Francisco International Airport, weaving in and out of kiosks selling miniature Golden Gate Bridges and Ghirardelli chocolates, and ducking the rushed traffic in both directions as they raced for their gate. Sergei carried a bouquet of roses covering the length of his arm and half his face.

"Is tradition," he informed Angela, avoiding her baiting tone the same way he had every other time since Lena introduced the two of them six months earlier.

Lena had forced Regina to return with her to America. Mama made it clear she never intended to leave Aaron's side again. It was Sergei who convinced Regina she'd be better off launching the immigration process from the US. So Mama came back with them, dug through Dad's papers for the names of politicians he'd been in touch with, and launched her campaign to get Aaron out of the USSR. After a month, she'd journeyed back to the Soviet Union in order to finish up the process from there.

Vadik and his parents had been just as against this second trip. They were happy Lena learned her lesson and wouldn't be tagging along, but they harangued her to condemn Mama's actions, too. When Lena refused, insisting her mother was capable of making her own choices, Vadik looked at her with such disgusted disappointment, that whatever choices Lena hesitated to make, at long last became clear. Unlike Aaron, Vadik's was a look that said he believed Lena couldn't do anything, handle anything, survive anything. It was a look that said he never believed in her.

Lena told Vadik she was leaving him a week after Mama departed for Odessa. She didn't want him blaming Mama for Lena's decision. Though, of course, he did. Vadik advised Lena she was making a grave mistake. How would she manage without him? Did she think she could do better than him? Had she thought through the financial implications? What was the point of them paying for two homes? She was being impractical. And what about Angela? Had Lena thought through what this would mean to Angela? Children of divorce were scarred for life. Everybody knew that. Angela would be devastated, her grades would drop. She'd be unable to secure a spot in a decent high-school, and forget about college! Her life would be ruined! Why was Lena doing this to her? Why was she acting like a spoiled, stupid American? Did she want Angela to become a spoiled, stupid American? Did she want her taking drugs and voting for socialists?

Angela didn't threaten to begin taking drugs or voting for socialists when Lena told her she was moving out. She simply informed her mother she knew Lena never loved her, and this latest betrayal was no surprise. She said Mom could do whatever she wanted, what did Angela care—but Angela would stay with Vadik.

Lena told Angela she respected her choice. But she would still come and see her every evening. In that, Angela had no choice.

It took weeks before her daughter would concede to speak to her. Weeks before she agreed to spend the night with Lena at Mama's house, where Lena was staying while Regina remained in Odessa. Lena tried to tell Angela snippets of her grandparents' story, stressing the importance of living with the consequences of your choices. Angela listened to tales of Regina and Aaron in Birobidzhan, Regina and Aaron in Stalag 3-K, Regina and Tommy in America. What she didn't want to hear was anything about why Lena had left her father—and her.

She eyed Sergei suspiciously at their first meeting.

"Is he your boyfriend?" Angela demanded, making it sound like a school-yard taunt.

"I am her oldmanfriend," Sergei corrected jovially, sticking his hand out and stubbornly leaving it there until Angela felt compelled to shake it distastefully.

She continued to make distasteful faces in Sergei's direction on every occasion Lena forced them to interact. Sergei said it didn't bother him, and Lena opted to believe it. "Reminds me of Grisha," he joked, only a little bit disconsolate.

They'd agreed to approach their relationship cautiously. Not everyone was destined to be Aaron and Regina, love at first sight, then forty years in between.

Mama did specifically ask if Sergei would be at the airport to greet her and Aaron.

The three of them stood outside the Arrivals area, Sergei's massive bouquet ensuring he'd be the first one spotted by Mama and Aaron. (Lena hadn't settled on what to call him yet. Dad would always be Dad. Aaron agreed wholeheartedly. He did wonder if Lena might one day consider calling him Papa. That day wasn't today.)

As all around them reunited families flung themselves into each other's arms, Lena accepted that today wasn't the day for her reconstructed household to become an all-American, happy family, either. She introduced Angela to Aaron. Both seemed quietly intrigued with each other. She called him, "Deda," which was more than Lena could bring herself to do. Mama gave her granddaughter a kiss, which Angela accepted perfunctorily. Like her father, Angela wasn't convinced Baba Regina wasn't behind this whole broken home thing.

Mama sent Aaron and Sergei to fetch their luggage from the carousel. She told Angela to tag along in case they needed help translating. Angela rolled her eyes, but obeyed.

"Nu?" Mama asked. "How is everything?"

It was the first time Lena could recall Mama expressing an interest in her life. After years of yearning for Regina to act like other mothers, Lena didn't know where to begin.

"Not great. Vadik is still angry with me. Angela is still angry with me."

"You are surviving?"

Lena took a moment to think. "Yeah. I guess I am."

"Sergei is helping?"

Lena blushed. "Yeah. I guess he is."

"You are doing right thing," Mama said.

It was the first time Lena could recall Mama expressing an opinion on her life. She liked it. She did wonder how she'd have felt if Mama had disapproved. Maybe she'd get the chance to find out one day soon. Anything was possible now.

"Angela wants to throw a wedding for you and Aaron. Those Polaroids you sent from the registrar's office didn't do it for her."

"It was enough for us," Regina said softly. Lena believed her.

"Well, think about it, at least. It would make Angela happy."

"I will think about it," Mama promised, then changed the subject. "What about you and Sergei? What is next for you?"

"We're discussing it," Lena admitted. "Maybe we'll get a place of our own. Somewhere big enough for Angela to spend the night, hopefully stay longer, eventually."

"Use my house. Is too big for pair. Aaron and I, we will find elsewhere."

"Maybe," Lena echoed her mother. "I'll think about it."

Regina smiled. It was the biggest, broadest, happiest, most optimistic expression Lena had ever seen from her mother.

"It is nice to have choices. Especially when, finally, many of them are good."

"What are you talking about?" Angela popped up between Lena and Regina. Ever since her mother and grandmother returned from the USSR with a warmer relationship than Angela could remember previously, Lena's daughter had been eyeing both suspiciously, trying to figure out what was going on and why she felt she'd been left out of the loop.

Lena winked at Mama, answering, "My mother's secret."

"And what's that?" Angela demanded.

"Choosing wisely," Regina said.

THE END

Fact From Fiction

———

Growing up Jewish in the Soviet Union, I'd always been vaguely aware that there'd once been a Jewish Autonomous Region in the USSR, the place where all the Jews of the world were supposed to go to live in blissful socialism under benevolent Soviet rule.

I remember my mother mentioning a friend who'd wanted to get her hands on some books in Yiddish, writing to a school in Birobidzhan, and being told they had no copies to send her—there was not enough demand to justify the printing.

As my parents neither found socialism blissful nor Soviet rule benevolent, we immigrated to the United States in 1977.

And it was in America, in English, that my curiosity about Birobidzhan was truly peaked, via a book by Masha Gessen entitled, *Where the Jews Aren't: The Sad and Absurd Story of Birobidzhan, Russia's Jewish Autonomous Region.*

Eager to learn more after listening to them discussing the story on NPR's *Fresh Air*[1], I went down the rabbit hole known as YouTube,

———

1 NPR: Fresh Air, "'Sad And Absurd': The U.S.S.R.'s Disastrous Effort To Create A Jewish Homeland," Radio Interview, Posted September 7, 2016, https://www.npr.org/2016/09/07/492962278/ sad-and-absurd-the-u-s-s-r-s-disastrous-effort-to-create-a-jewish-homeland.

a place from which few return unscathed.

There, I found a documentary that combined footage from a film made in 1928 to entice Jewish immigration to Birobidzhan with new film shot in 2009.[2]

I found random clips of what the train station looked like in the 1930s[3] and yet another modern documentary titled *The Jewish Autonomous Oblast of Russia* from 2019.[4]

From the archives of Swarthmore College came a treasure trove of propaganda posters, books, photographs, and political slogans specifically created to encourage immigration to Birobidzhan and to acclimatize new citizens to life there.[5]

I cross-referenced what I learned from Gessen with entries in *YIVO Institute for Jewish Research*[6] and the *Jewish Virtual Library*.[7]

But my most thrilling discovery was *Seekers of Happiness*, a 1936 Soviet film produced to convince the Jews of the USSR to move to Birobidzhan immediately.[8] It was the perfect example of what

2   Broken -Britain, "Birobidzhan Jewish autonomous region," YouTube video, 25:05, Posted August 9, 2014, https://www.youtube.com/watch?v=DbGKhY8iQbA.

3   Seventeen Moments in Soviet History, "Arrival in Birobidzhan (1936)," YouTube video, 01:09, Posted March 31, 2014, https://www.youtube.com/watch?v=j6Qs1KgQhrs.

4   Sebastian ioan, "The Jewish Autonomous Oblast of Russia," YouTube video, 07:27, Posted November 1, 2019, https://www.youtube.com/watch?v=1VNIRuxjAjw.

5   "Stalin's Forgotten Zion: An Illustrated History, 1928–1996: Birobidzhan and the Making of a Soviet Jewish Homeland," Swarthmore College, https://www.swarthmore.edu/Home/News/biro/.

6   David Shneer, "Birobidzhan," The Yivo Encyclopedia of Jews in Eastern Europe, 2010, https://yivoencyclopedia.org/article.aspx/birobidzhan.

7   "Birobidzhan, Russia," Encyclopaedia Judaica in Jewish Virtual Library, 2008, https://www.jewishvirtuallibrary.org/birobidzhan.

8   History Club, "Seekers of Happiness (A Greater Promise)," YouTube video, 1:20:59, Posted April 19, 2017, https://www.youtube.com/watch?v=PZrnFpcc7Fc.

the government wanted people to think the Jewish Autonomous Region was, versus the reality painstakingly researched and written by Gessen.

The second half of my novel was inspired by a segment I caught on the television series, *Through the Decades* (the perfect show for the history obsessive). I was so moved by Charles Kuralt's story of a Soviet dentist, who, forty years after the fact, wanted to get in touch with the American soldiers who'd kept him and his comrades alive in a World War II Prisoner of War camp by sharing their supplies, that I dove back into research.[9]

This led me to numerous articles such as, "The Treatment of Soviet POWS" published by *The United States Holocaust Memorial Museum*,[10] "The Liberation of Stalag Luft 1" published by *The National World War II Museum*,[11] "World War II prisoner-of-war diary recorded daily life, quest for food in Stalag Luft 13" published by *The Baltimore Sun*,[12] "8 Things You Should Know About WWII's Eastern Front" published by *History*,[13] and finally "Moscow Strikes Back," a documentary originally produced in 1942 and narrated by Edward

---

9   "Through the Decades: Russian Dentist," Decades TV Network, Facebook Watch video, Posted March 6, 2019, https://www.facebook.com/watch/?v=264253324466051.

10   "The Treatment of Soviet POWS: Starvation, Disease, and Shootings, June 1941–January 1942," United States Holocaust Memorial Museum, https://encyclopedia.ushmm.org/content/en/article/the-treatment-of-soviet-pows-starvation-disease-and-shootings-june-1941january-1942.

11   Kim Guise, "The Liberation of Stalag Luft I," The National World War II Museum, Published April 30, 2020, https://www.nationalww2museum.org/liberation-stalag-luft.

12   Frederick N. Rasmussen, World War II prisoner-of-war diary recorded daily life, quest for food in Stalag Luft 13," The Baltimore Sun, Published April 2, 2011, https://www.baltimoresun.com/maryland/bs-xpm-2011-04-02-bs-md-backstory-pow-20110401-story.html.

13   Evan Andrews, "8 Things You Should Know About WWII's Eastern Front," History, Published May 27, 2014, https://www.history.com/news/8-things-you-should-know-about-wwiis-eastern-front.

G. Robinson.[14] And then I did what every historical fiction novelist ultimately does—I kept the authentic parts I liked... and finessed the rest.

The characters in the Birobidzhan section are based on real historical figures. There truly was an ongoing conflict between those who wanted the area to remain agricultural, and those who advocated for factories and industrialization, just like there were those who lived on site and had a realistic view of the JAR's challenges, and those who only periodically visited and wrote prose poems of praise from a distance.

The Stalinist purges of the 1930s are tragically true, and they did hit Birobidzhan, down to the accusation of attempted murder via gefilte fish. American Jewish Communists really did travel to the region and some did assume positions of power over immigrants they judged less worthy. Evidence of this can be found in an academic article by Henry Felix Srebrnik titled, "Dreams of Nationhood."[15] Also, many of the American Jews were later arrested and found that giving up their American passports meant they couldn't go back. However, for the purposes of this novel, I changed the names of those involved in order to better make them serve my narrative.

The same goes for details of the Soviet-American POW camps. Rather than try to make my timeline fit precisely into actual history, I borrowed a plethora of details from a cross-section of German camps to create Stalag 3-K. The detail about a percentage of Soviet prisoners of war being accused of collaborating with the enemy and being sent to gulags at the conflict's end is a recently confirmed fact.[16]

As for those who question whether a woman could flag down a tank in the middle of war-time, I don't have a link for that. You're

14   Nuclear Vault, "Moscow Strikes Back (1942)," YouTube video, 55:30, Posted March 6, 2016, https://www.youtube.com/watch?v=NDZqK4dBQvI.

15   Henry Felix Srebrni, "Dreams of Nationhood: American Jewish Communists and the Soviet Birobidzhan Project, 1924-1951," Academic Studies Press, 2010. https://doi.org/10.2307/j.ctt1zxsj1m.

16   "Soviet repressions against former prisoners of war," Military Wiki, https://military-history.fandom.com/wiki/Soviet_repressions_against_former_prisoners_of_war.

just going to have to take my grandmother's word for it that she did.

Finally, when my family left the USSR in 1976, we ended up in San Francisco, CA, where I grew up in the 1980s, often frequenting the street nicknamed Geary-basovskaya. In 1988, my mother and I returned to Odessa, USSR for a visit, where we stayed in a hotel with monitors to watch us on each floor, and where my mother did have a chat with a KGB officer who read a file about what a nice life she was leading in America... and offered her the chance to come home. She, like Regina, declined.

Unlike my periodically ambivalent characters, we always knew we'd made the right choice.

About the Author

―――――
―――――

Alina Adams is the NYT-bestselling author of soap-opera tie-ins, figure-skating mysteries, and romance novels. Born in Odessa, USSR, Adams immigrated to the United States at age seven and learned to speak English by watching American Soap Operas. After receiving her B.A. and M.A. in broadcast communications at San Francisco State University, Adams worked in television as a writer and researcher. Years later she penned the *As The World Turns* book tie-in, *Oakdale Confidential*, which became a New York Times bestseller. Adams continued writing and is now a prolific and innovative writer who has authored more than a dozen books, both fiction and nonfiction. *My Mother's Secret: A Novel of the Jewish Autonomous Region* is a follow-up to her previous release, *The Nesting Dolls*, a Soviet-Jewish historical novel published by HarperCollins in July 2020. Adams lives in New York City with her husband and their three children.

Other Books by History Through Fiction

Resisting Removal: The Sandy Lake Tragedy of 1850
by Colin Mustful

The Education of Delhomme: Chopin, Sand, & La France
by Nancy Burkhalter

The Sky Worshipers: A Novel of Mongol Conquests
by F.M. Deemyad

The King's Anatomist: The Journey of Andreas Vesalius
by Ron Blumenfeld

If you enjoyed this novel please consider leaving a review. You'll be supporting a small, independent press, and you'll be helping other readers discover this great story.
Thank you!

www.HistoryThroughFiction.com

CPSIA information can be obtained
at www.ICGtesting.com
Printed in the USA
BVHW040947151122
651995BV00011B/42

9 781736 499030